Kate Beaufoy has an MA in Fre  from Trinity College Dublin. professional actor before becoi Kate Thompson she has had a dozen novels published, including the Number One bestseller THE BLUE HOUR which was shortlisted for the RNA award. LIBERTY SILK is her first historical novel. It was inspired by real letters written from Europe by her grandmother, Jessie Beaufoy, in the aftermath of the Great War. Kate scuba dives to an advanced level and is in thrall to her Burmese cat. Her website is www.katebeaufoy.com and you can find more about Kate at www.facebook.com/kate.beaufoy. There are a collection of images from LIBERTY SILK which you can find at www.pinterest.com/libertysilk

LIBERTY SILK

Kate Beaufoy

TRANSWORLD IRELAND

TRANSWORLD IRELAND
An imprint of The Random House Group Limited
20 Vauxhall Bridge Road, London SW1V 2SA
www.transworldbooks.co.uk

LIBERTY SILK
A TRANSWORLD IRELAND BOOK: 9781848271890

First published in Great Britain
in 2014 by Transworld Ireland
a division of Transworld Publishers
Transworld Ireland paperback edition published 2014

Addresses for Random House Group Ltd companies outside the UK
can be found at: www.randomhouse.co.uk
The Random House Group Ltd Reg. No. 954009

The Random House Group Limited supports the Forest Stewardship
Council® (FSC®), the leading international forest-certification organisation.
Our books carrying the FSC label are printed on FSC®-certified paper.
FSC is the only forest-certification scheme supported by the leading
environmental organisations, including Greenpeace. Our paper
procurement policy can be found at www.randomhouse.co.uk/environment

Typeset in 10.5/14pt Giovanni Book by Falcon Oast Graphic Art Ltd.
Printed and bound by CPI Group (UK) Ltd, Croydon, CR0 4YY.

2 4 6 8 10 9 7 5 3 1

This book is dedicated to three generations
of strong women:

My grandmother, Winifred Jessie Beaufoy

My mother, Hilary

My daughter, Clara

ACKNOWLEDGEMENTS

The idea for *Liberty Silk* was first mooted by my beautiful mother, Hilary, who sadly did not live to see this book published. The lion's share of my gratitude must go to her, and of course, to my grandmother Winifred Jessie, whose original letters were my inspiration. To her, thanks are also due for the cabochon sapphire ring and the Egyptian charm (both of which I wear), the leather-bound sketchbook she gave my grandfather, and the Liberty silk evening dress. These heirlooms – assembled nearly a hundred years ago – inform the narrative of *Liberty Silk*. Thanks also go to my sisters, Deborah and Pat, and to Morag Engel and Roy Storie for nuggets of Beaufoy family history.

While researching the novel, hundreds of books – from gossipy autobiographies to more scholarly publications – were consulted. Since to list them all would require an extensive bibliography, I'll mention just the three I turned to again and again. They were: *The World of Coco Chanel* by Edmonde Charles-Roux, *David O. Selznick's Hollywood* by Ronald Haver and Don McCullin's gripping and insightful memoir, *Unreasonable Behaviour*.

I have been blessed with a dream team: my agent and champion, Charlotte Robertson and my editors Harriet Bourton and Georgie Bouz. If I were to laud them as they deserve I would be gently advised to red-pen the adjectives, so I'll make do with three restrained ones: passionate, insightful, meticulous. *Liberty Silk* reunites me with copy editor Beth Humphries, eagle-eyed as ever, and with old friends at Transworld: copious thanks to you all, and to Steve Mulcahey and Claire Ward, who were responsible for the delicious cover.

Thanks also to those friends and fellow writers Cathy Kelly, Douglas Kennedy, Sue Leonard, Fiona O'Brien, Sheila O'Flanagan and Abby Opperman, who read early drafts and proffered encouragement and sorority. Tony Baines and Mark Long listened to me while hill-walking; Ciarán Hinds listened over Skype. Marian Keyes and Hilary Reynolds, friends of the heart, listened all the way up *and* all the way down the steepest hills.

Liberty Silk would not be in your hands today were it not for the unconditional love and support of my very best beloveds, my husband Malcolm and my daughter Clara. Simply put: I owe them everything. Final thanks must go to the little cat who sat on my chest and purred encouragement when I was unwell, never daring to dream that I would write: 'The End'.

Worn Out
by
Lizzie Siddal

Keep thine arms around me, love,
Until I fall to sleep;
Then leave me, saying no goodbye
Lest I may wake, and weep.

The senior mistress of Bournemouth High School for
Girls spoke these words to her sixth form in 1917:
'I have come to tell you a terrible fact. Only one out
of every ten of you can ever hope to marry. This is
not a guess. It is a statistical fact. Nearly all the men
who might have married you have been killed. You
will have to make your way in the world as best
you can.'

PROLOGUE
ARMISTICE DAY
11 NOVEMBER, 1918

ROUEN, FRANCE.

Y.M.C.A.
B.A.P.0.2
B.E.F.
France.
On Active Service.

Dearest Mother and All,
 Crowds and crowds of things have happened! At 12 o'clock a terrific hooting and bell-ringing and cheering set up. By the evening the streets were full of rowdiness and excitement. People let off fireworks under your nose, and dropped dud bombs from roofs of houses, and the anti-aircraft guns kept on firing from the neighbouring hills. Soldiers of all nationalities dancing and shouting and kissing girls and getting drunk. I have never seen such crowds in my life! We celebrated with champagne, and decorated ourselves with huge bows of Allies' ribbon, and we paraded the streets thoroughly intoxicated with excitement!

The dazzle, the gunfire, the clangour, the clamour, the ticker-tape festoons. The frenzy, the crush, the sweat, the huzzahing, the thrum of her hummingbird heart.

Water hastily splashed into a basin, cold flannel on warm skin, a spritz of Chypre, a hasty coiffure, a pirouette before a silvered pier-glass, the swish of silk as she descended the stairs.

Charades! Waltzes! The crackle of a log fire, the fizz of Dom Pérignon, a mandarin glow of lanterns, candied fruit in glazed dishes, a scattering of spilled almonds, a frisson, a glance as his hand brushed hers.

The woods at Canteleu: pine needles underfoot, ghosts soughing in bare branches, the gleam of holly berries in the undergrowth, a carillon wind-borne from the Cathédrale. His greatcoat around her shoulders, a graze of gabardine, his arms, his touch, his scent, his lips, his voice...

'You smell of moss,' he said. 'You taste of apricots.'

24 November 1918
I told you about the artist member of the staff, I think. He is thoroughly amusing and tremendously popular wherever he goes - you couldn't help liking him . . .

2 December 1918
You ask his Christian name - he, and I too, like to cover it up as much as possible, as we both hate it. His name is Albert Charles, but he is called Scotch. He is nice and straight and tall and is altogether adorable (but then, of course, I am prejudiced!).

21 December 1918

Don't worry about me, I'm quite flourishing and happy. I do know, we both know, that this has all happened rather suddenly, but that just can't be helped . . .

27 December 1918

I expect you can guess what Scotch's present was to me?!! A ring, of course, an awfully nice little one – plain gold and plain setting with a fascinating dark blue stone in the middle . . .

3 January 1919

Scotch found, tucked away in a dusty corner of an antique shop, a little Egyptian charm – most fascinating – a little figure of a devil or something . . .

12 January 1919

As the matter stands now we will get married in spring. I am waiting to hear what you think about the whole business. Isn't money a silly nuisance? What on earth do young married people usually start living on?

CHAPTER ONE

JESSIE

FINISTÈRE, AUGUST 1919

The aroma of coffee drifted under the door of the bedroom on the third floor of the hotel. Was that what had woken her? Or had it been the tinny sound of the church bell striking the hour? Or the squabbling of sparrows under the eaves? Or the plangent French accents floating up from the narrow street below? It was hot already outside – she could tell by the haze that shimmered beyond the open window. What a blissful way to wake up! Lying between crumpled linen sheets with her husband of two months beside her . . .

She turned to take him in her arms, but he was gone. Of course he was. Scotch was no slugabed. He was on the go from the moment his eyes opened in the morning until the moment they shut last thing at night, after making love to her.

She'd read about lovemaking of course, in romance novels, the ones she'd be ashamed to be seen borrowing from the library. In those books the heroines swooned and yielded and languished, and Jessie had deplored their inertia. In contrast, the feelings she had for Scotch were exuberant, galvanising; the way he looked at her charged her with an astonishing energy; his touch exhilarated her.

Her friend Tuppenny had quizzed her about 'the act' and the only comparison that Jessie could come up with in response – 'even better than being happy!' – was pitifully inadequate. Sex in all its wonder and absurdity thrilled her, and she was, as her new husband had learned to his amusement, quite shockingly unshockable.

Jessie felt that familiar cat-who-got-the-cream smile curve her lips – a smile she wore habitually when she thought of Scotch – and eased herself into a stretch. What was in store for them today? A lazy breakfast followed by a trip to the beach at Raguenez – a painters' paradise that lay a short train journey away, to the west. She would explore the coves and read and swim and write letters – she hadn't written home for weeks – and Scotch would take out his watercolours and brushes and work away until it was time for their picnic.

A knock came to the door, and Jessie reached for the broderie anglaise wrapper draped over the cast iron bedstead.

'Madame? I have brought your *café au lait*.'

'Come in, Suzette.'

The door opened, and a little girl of about ten years old came into the room, carrying a dish of coffee, and a pitcher. Water slopped over the rim as she lifted a foot and kicked the door shut behind her.

'Bonjour, Madame!'

'Bonjour, Suzette. Thank you, poppet – that coffee smells good. Is Scotch at breakfast downstairs?'

'Yes. If you don't get down there soon you'll find that he's guzzled all the croissants.' Suzette set the brimming cup down on the bedside locker, then crossed the floor to set the pitcher by the wash-stand. 'It's a beautiful day. Scotch says to hurry up and stop wasting it.'

'He's a big bossy boots.' Jessie cupped her hands around the coffee and took a sip.

'Are all husbands bossy?'

'I don't know – I've never had one before.'

'You're lucky to get one,' Suzette told her, perching on the edge of the bed. 'My cousin was in tears yesterday, and when I asked her what was wrong, she said that she'd never get a husband, ever, because all the young men she'd fancied were dead. She said that her *patronne* had told the girls they'd all be spinsters and they'd just have to get used to it, and never have children, only cats, and that they should be glad to have jobs. Will that happen to me?'

'Oh no, Suzette. There will be lots of boys who will want to marry you, when you're old enough.'

'Unless there's another war and they all get killed again.'

'There'll never be another war, ever. Humankind isn't that stupid.'

'Anyway, I don't want to get married and have snotty-nosed brats. I'd much rather keep cats. Just think – all over France soon there'll be hundreds and hundreds of cats roaming around. It'll be great. Will there be millions of cats in England too?'

'I expect so.'

With or without cats, there'd be millions of women living *solitaire* all over Europe, Jessie knew: spinsters, old maids, widows; women too mired in penury to be foot-loose or fancy free. At home in Blighty many of her friends were unmarried and would remain so: on her wedding day, decked out in satin and Carrickmacross lace, the guilt

17

Jessie had felt as she glided down the aisle observed by those envious eyes could have marred her happiness if she'd allowed it to. But Jessie's obdurate streak would allow nothing to impinge upon her bliss; not then, not now.

Bliss, for her, was sitting on a doorstep, safeguarding the paintbox while watching Scotch work. It was finding a creek where they could fling off their clothes and dive in; it was lounging in bed after love in the afternoon; it was dozing on a riverbank listening to him whistling; it was a *pichet* of wine shared on the terrace of some small café over omelettes and *fougasse*; it was looking up from a book and finding his eyes upon her.

'Drink up!' Suzette told her, moving to the threshold. 'Remember what I said about the vanishing croissants. I'm surprised your husband isn't as fat as Big Bertha.' The door shut behind her with a thud, and Jessie smiled.

She was glad to hear that Scotch was demolishing croissants: just a month ago, in Chambéry, he had been so ill that he hadn't been able to eat anything. He had caught a chill after they'd spent a night sleeping on the station platform at Turin, and had been diagnosed with congestion of the lungs and prescribed all kinds of concoctions: magnesia and quinine and a horrid plaster-poultice thing that Jessie had asked the *patronne* of the hotel they were staying in to apply and peel off, because she could not bear to see him in pain. She had been feeling so young and incapable that in a moment of weakness she'd written home in a panic, scared half to death and feeling frightfully alone; then regretted it as soon as she'd sent the letter, convinced that her mother might write back saying, 'I knew it would end in tears.'

Draining her coffee, Jessie moved to the window and

settled herself on the window seat to admire the view as she brushed her hair. The vista beyond the casement was of terracotta rooftops, with pigeons perched on chimney-pots and a church spire pointing to a cloudless sky above. Below her on the street a gaggle of women were gossiping, their voices ajangle, like Indian bells. They fell mute as a much younger woman sauntered past in a cloche hat and a flirty kick-pleated skirt, and sent poisonous looks in her direction before resuming their tittle-tattle.

What should Jessie wear on this last day of her honeymoon? Her bathing dress, of course, and over it something she wouldn't mind getting mucky. That frock she'd spilled ink over would fit the bill. A year or so ago she'd simply have chucked it out, but she couldn't afford to do that now. She was learning thrift.

Anyway, Scotch didn't seem to mind her looking – as she had written home –'dirty and disreputable and poor!' (She had been careful to add the exclamation mark, to show what a lark it was, honestly.) He loved her best, she knew, with nothing on at all, and mostly thought of clothes as a nuisance. The only time she had dressed up for him – *really* dressed up – had been at Christmas, at the dance in the little hotel in Rouen when they had announced their engagement. She had asked her mother to send over the flower-patterned silk gown from Liberty for the occasion, the one that reminded her of summer meadows. It was tiered like a Grecian tunic: a classic Doric column when one stood still; in motion, a swirl of colour – primrose and geranium and cornflower blue and moss green. And that night, as Scotch presented her with the ring, he had murmured into her ear a verse by Robert Herrick, substituting her name for that of the poet's mistress:

Whenas in silks my Jessie goes,
Then, then, methinks, how sweetly flows
That liquefaction of her clothes.

Setting down her hairbrush, Jessie poured water into the basin and set about washing, humming a little tune as she ran the flannel over her tummy, wondering when her baby would start to show. When should she tell Scotch? She knew she should leave it for a while, just in case something went wrong, but to hell with it! She'd tell him today. It would be a ripping way to cheer him up before they bade farewell to France and Finistère.

What serendipity, that they should have finished up here! Over the course of the past two months she and Scotch had travelled all over France and Italy, and now that they had reached '*Finis Terrae* – the end of the earth', they could journey no further. The honeymoon was finally over, and real life beckoned.

Real life. Cripes. Real life meant going back to Blighty, to where her mother would be waiting for her in that big house in Mayfair with her tight-lipped expression and her tragic eyes. Nothing had been able to convince Mrs Beaufoy that the marriage of her princess to the penniless painter was a good idea, but Jessie was determined to prove her wrong. Some day her husband would be so famous that he would sell every picture before it was touch-dry, like Picasso.

Still humming her silly song – '*Y'a une pie dans l'poirier, J'entends la mère qui chante*' – Jessie slid into her bathing dress, pulled her frock over her head, and ran downstairs.

Scotch was sitting in the sun-splashed breakfast room, spreading apricot conserve onto a croissant and chatting with Suzette. The little girl was leaning her elbows on the table, listening intently.

'Good morning!' Jessie dropped a kiss on her husband's forehead before sitting opposite and helping herself to the last croissant in the breadbasket.

'I was guarding that for you,' Suzette told her.

'Thank you, poppet.' She gave her husband a look of mock-rebuke. 'If it hadn't been for Suzette I suspect I'd have had no breakfast at all this morning.'

'It would serve you right for being such a lazybones,' Scotch told her. 'I've been up for hours.'

'He has been telling me the story about how his hand got hacked off,' announced Suzette. 'Did it hurt awful bad, Scotch?'

'Yep.'

'Did you cry?'

'Like a baby.'

'Was there masses of blood?'

'Bucket loads.'

'What did you *do* with the hand?'

'Suzette!' Her mother – who had been refilling cups at a nearby table – came bustling up, her face scarlet with embarrassment. 'What a shocking thing to ask! Now, leave the honeymooners alone and come and help me in the kitchen. I can't say how sorry I am for my daughter's rudeness, Monsieur.'

Madame was overcompensating, Jessie thought, for Suzette had not been unusually rude. *Where did you lose your arm, or your leg, or your eye?* was a perfectly legitimate question to ask of young men these days, since so many of them sported pinned-up sleeves, or crutches or eye-patches. The answer was usually 'at Verdun' (or Marne, or

21

Ypres), but Scotch's accident had happened before the war, when he was just fourteen. He'd been lucky, unlike millions of PBIs – poor bloody infantrymen – who had been horribly mutilated on the battlefields.

'No apology necessary, Madame Simonet. I'm quite happy to answer Suzette's questions.' Turning back to Suzette, whose eyes were agleam with interest, Scotch continued his story. 'After the scythe sliced through my arm – whoosh! shwoosh! vamoosh! – a farmer's dog seized the hand and took off with it—'

'No!'

'Oh, yes. The field workers chased the animal across the field with an almighty yelling and hullaballoo. They eventually cornered it by a well, but the bold thing wouldn't let go, and what with all the pulling and tugging the poor beastie tumbled backwards with the hand still between his jaws, and when they got him out of the well, there was no sign of it.' Scotch's tone was ominous. '*And no-one has ever dared to drink the water from that well again.* The end.'

Both Suzette and her mother were by now open mouthed. So, for that matter, was Jessie. But Madame Simonet snapped her mouth shut abruptly and cuffed her daughter sharply on her ear. 'The kitchen, Suzette. Now.'

Unchastened, Suzette got down from her chair. 'My uncle told me a horror story once about a severed hand that has a life of its own. It goes around terrorizing people and—'

'*Suzette!*'

Suzette made a face. '*Ouay ouay ouay,*' she intoned as she drifted off kitchenward.

With an apologetic smile, Madame backed away. 'I'll

have your picnic ready for you presently, Monsieur, Madame. Enjoy the rest of your day.'

'Thank you, Madame.' Scotch gave Madame Simonet the kind of smile that turned women to mush, before returning his attention to his croissant, tearing off a hunk and wolfing it down.

'Did a dog really run away with your hand?' asked an incredulous Jessie.

'Not at all. My hand was buried. But the truth wouldn't have made such a good story, would it?'

Jessie smiled at him, then leaned across the table and touched his face. 'No wonder children love you. No wonder *everyone* loves you. You're a complete charmer.'

Scotch wiped his mouth with his napkin, then set it aside. 'Talking of charms, where's the little Egyptian fellow I gave you?'

'He's here, in my pocket. I got him tangled in my hair when I was dressing.' She pulled the minuscule jade charm from her pocket, and held it up on the silk ribbon to which Scotch had attached it.

'Allow me.' Rising from his chair, Scotch moved behind her. Jessie held the ends of the ribbon together at the nape of her neck, and within seconds they were made fast. His adroitness never failed to amaze her.

'Eat up, youngster,' he said, dropping a kiss on her shoulder. 'We've a train to catch.'

CHAPTER TWO

BABA

LONDON 1939

'What do you think of Lisa as a stage name? Lisa La Touche?'

'Sounds like a Burlesque dancer, darling,'

'But "Baba" is so childish! And everyone pronounces my surname wrong.'

Baba MacLeod and her friend Dorothy Baxter were sitting in the Lyons Corner House on Oxford Street, having been to yet another screening of their favourite film – *A Star is Born*. They came here a lot because (a) they were fanatical film-goers, (b) the sticky buns were scrumptious, and (c) the manager of the joint was the spit of Errol Flynn.

They had visited a casting agency earlier, to make enquiries about Baba getting work as a movie extra, and Dorothy was sneaking looks at the application form her friend was filling in. Baba had cut out a square-inch head and shoulders photograph from a contact sheet and attached it to the form, which read like this:

```
Lisa La Touche.
Age: 19
Height: 5 ft 5½ ins.
```

```
Weight: 8 stone
Colouring: ~~Auburn~~. ~~Titian~~. Rousse.
Type: Smart crowd.
Experience: Phoebe in 'As You Like it',
Mayfair Players, 1938
Special accomplishments: Dancing,
fencing, swimming, singing, tennis.
```

'Where did "La Touche" come from?' asked Dorothy.

'One of my ancestors was a La Touche – some old baronet or something. It's in *Debrett's*.'

'You've put an awful lot of fibs on here. Are you really only eight stone?'

'I will be once I start that diet Paulette Goddard recommends.'

'And you've put "singing" and "tennis" as special accomplishments. You don't have a note in your head, Baba, and you can scarcely manage a return serve.'

'Pah! Do you honestly think I'll ever be asked to play tennis as an audition piece? As for singing – name me one aspiring actress who doesn't list it as a special accomplishment, and I'll name you a liar.' Baba returned her attention to the application form. 'Let's see. What else would look good? Hmm. I fancy I'd look rather fetching on a mount, sitting sidesaddle and wearing a riding habit and one of those elegant little veiled top hats. I'll put down riding too, even though I hate the brutes.'

Dorothy shot her a sceptical look. '*Can* you ride?'

'Of course not. But I can learn, if needs be.'

Baba wrote 'Riding' under 'Special accomplishments', then signed with a flourish. It was a shame, she thought, as she screwed the cap back on her pen, that she hadn't been able to add more to the 'Experience' section of the form. Playing Phoebe in the Mayfair Players' production of *As You Like It* had been terrific fun, and she'd had a reasonably good write-up in the parish circular, but she'd really much rather have played the gutsier role of Rosalind, who gets to dress up as a boy and run away from home. However, there was absolutely no question of Baba passing herself off as a boy. Baba had been a late developer, but the past two years had seen a remarkable transformation in the girl who had once been a skinny adolescent. It had taken her a very long time to get used to being perceived as quintessentially womanly, and she still found it confusing sometimes. But she was learning.

She held the form at arm's length and regarded her film-starrish new signature with satisfaction. 'I like it. It has style, and sparkle, and it suits my new persona better.'

Dorothy gave her an uncomprehending look.

'You know – like in a play. The characters are always called "dramatis personae". Lisa la Touche is mine.'

'Your persona?'

'Yes.'

'That sounds a little bonkers, darling, if you don't mind me saying so.'

Baba shrugged. She was used to Dorothy calling her bonkers.

'It works.'

'How?'

'Promise you won't laugh?'

'I'll try.'

'It's something about the way . . . No! I can't explain it. It's too weird. More tea?' Baba reached for the pot, and

26

poured, trying to ignore the curious expression on her friend's face.

'Oh, come on!' said Dorothy. 'You can't go all coy and abandon a subject once you've brought it up. That goes against all the girlfriend rules.'

Baba set the teapot down, gave Dorothy a thoughtful look, then said, a little hesitantly, 'It might be easier if I demonstrate. Watch this.'

Sliding a cigarette from the pack on the table, she rose from her chair and crossed the floor of the tea room, moving the way she'd seen Vivien Leigh move at a garden party once. The party had been held by the family of the film star's husband, Leigh Holman, but the normally intrepid Baba hadn't managed to pluck up the nerve to introduce herself. Miss Leigh had moved as gracefully as a trained dancer, with demurely lowered eyes and with a secret little smile playing around her lips; and the eyes of all the men attending the event had kept swivelling in her direction, as if their eyes were compasses and Vivien Leigh were North.

'Excuse me, sir?' Baba said in low, velvety tones to the young man sitting solo at a corner table, reading the *Evening Standard* and smoking a pipe. 'Do you have a match, by any chance?'

The man looked up from his paper, and his expression of indifference turned into one of complete confusion.

'Of course, Miss,' he said, getting to his feet and sliding a box of Swan Vestas from his pocket. 'Be my guest.' He struck the match a little clumsily, then held the flame to the tip of Baba's cigarette. She drew on it, raised her eyes to his, exhaled and smiled.

'Thank you so much. I'm sorry to have disturbed you.'

'My pleasure.'

Another smile, a sweet look, a switch of her hip as she turned away – and the unfortunate gent was her captive for ever.

Baba made her way back to the table where Dorothy sat observing her. 'Is he still looking?' she asked, sotto voce.

'Yes,' said a clearly amused Dorothy. 'With his eyes out on stalks. What did you *do* to him?'

'I'm not quite sure. I know it sounds crackpot, but if I want men to notice me, Dorothy, I just pull on this persona and they sit up and beg.'

Dorothy leaned forward, an interested gleam in her eye. 'Is it an "It" thing?'

'I – I guess so,' said Baba. 'I mean, usually I can walk down the street and no-one will look twice. But when I think "Lisa", people notice.'

It was true. Baba had discovered the secret of sex appeal, and it had come about quite by accident. She had been in the shoe department in Selfridges one afternoon, when she almost bumped into a girl who was approaching from the other direction. She had been about to say 'Excuse me,' when she realized that she was addressing her own reflection in a mirror. Oh, sweet Jehovah. How nondescript she looked! She could have been Miss A.N. Other, Josephine Bloggs or Joanne Public, and because Baba found the notion of being Joanne Public truly terrifying, she decided to do something about it.

Being a quick study, it didn't take her long to work out what made people look twice. She discovered that if she moved in that Vivien Leigh way, and adopted a certain expression, men looked; and once they looked, they quite evidently found it hard to *stop* looking. Some men looked in a knowing way, with narrowed eyes, some men looked in a slippery way, as if afraid to be caught, and some men just plain stared.

It had become a game for her. Some days she could walk the streets unnoticed, but when Baba 'thought Lisa', she became a magnet for the gaze of the entire populace – because women looked too. The women always glanced away quickly, of course, and made hapless efforts to distract their menfolk. Sometimes the expressions she saw were so comical that she found it hard not to laugh out loud – especially when she remembered the invisible sixteen-year-old she'd been – the girl with the knock knees, and the stupid name.

She wasn't Baba any more! She didn't *feel* like a Baba. But it was proving difficult to persuade those nearest and dearest to her that she was poised to become a woman of the world.

Baba had spent the past ten years of her life at a boarding school run by Benedictine nuns in a castle in the west of Ireland, where she had numbered among her friends the niece of the Japanese ambassador, the daughter of a Bajan millionaire, and an Indian princess named Rajkumari Rajendra Kumari of Jamnagar. Of course there were Irish students there as well, but most of them went home at weekends, leaving a handful of boarders to amuse themselves in the purlieus of the school: the walled garden, the woodland, the mountain paths and the lake, which was rumoured to harbour a monster and which was perfect for illicit swimming.

The school's promotional literature described it as being 'high-class', but it boasted none of the facilities tradition-ally associated with posh boarding schools (apart from an overgrown tennis court upon which sheep grazed), and bore little resemblance to the *Chalet School* books so beloved of pubescent girls. Ponies were of the half-wild Connemara variety which either bucked their riders or refused to budge; theatricals were infrequent, consisting of playlets such as *Episodes of the Turkish Conquest of the Ionian Isles* or *The Fisher Girls, Danced by Pupils of the Fourth Form*, and the only men the girls ever saw were moth-eaten priests in frocks, gnarled gardeners, and a goatherd-type boy who spied on them when they did PE al fresco.

Baba was glad of the occasional invitation to spend half-terms and holidays with a family of distant cousins in the nearby town of Clifden. But Clifden was small and parochial, and she yearned to escape to the city for a taste of what they called the 'high life'. Now that she was back in London and had discovered 'Lisa', she was ready to move on.

She took a long pull on her cigarette, as a thought struck her. 'If I can't get into the movie business through the front door, Dorothy, maybe I should try going in through the back.'

'What do you mean?'

'Like Alice White. She was a script girl before she was discovered.'

'You mean, you'd try to get a job behind the scenes?'

'Yes.' Baba picked up the form that she had so painstakingly filled in and proceeded to tear it into tiny little bits, which she then sprinkled into the ashtray.

'You'd need a contact in the business who could pull strings for you.'

'I have one. My grandfather had a friend to dinner last week—'

'Did you experiment on him?'

'With my persona?'

'No! With a new Countess Morphy recipe.'

'Yes. Beef Stroganoff.'

'Good choice. Go on.'

'He was a big shot from the Pru. He knows Alexander Korda—'

'He *knows* Alexander Korda? How?'

'The Pru's backing his latest extravaganza, apparently. It's a remake of *The Thief of Bagdad*. It's being shot in Denham Studios.'

'Wow. Who's playing the princess?'

'June Duprez. Anyway, the man from the Pru told Gramps that Mr Korda's having trouble recruiting staff now that everyone's going off to make propaganda films.' Baba was stubbing out her cigarette carefully, so that the torn-up pieces of her CV wouldn't catch fire. 'It may be a long shot, Dorothy, but there's no harm in asking Gramps's friend to have a word in Mr Korda's shell-like. Maybe he could find me a job.'

'You think Alexander Korda is going to take one look at his new script girl and say "My, but you're beautiful! I am going to make you a star overnight!"'

Baba shrugged. 'Mr Korda has a big reputation for discovering stars.'

It was true. Just four years earlier Alexander Korda had signed Vivien Leigh (the newspaper headlines had screamed £50,000 FILM CONTRACT FOR LAST WEEK'S UNKNOWN ACTRESS!), and before that he had signed Maureen O'Sullivan and Wendy Barrie, and now he was married to his latest discovery, the exotically beautiful Merle Oberon.

'Overnight stardom only happens in Busby Berkeley

musicals,' said Dorothy. 'And those musicals are about as far removed from real life as you can get.'

'Oh, come on! Allow me to dream a little. Your dream came true just last week.'

'I guess it did.' Dorothy smiled at the brand new cluster of diamonds on her ring finger, then tapped her Regimental Red fingernails on the tabletop. 'OK. Say you did wangle a job in Denham. What would your grandma have to say, since she's so set on a match with your oh-so-eligible neighbour?'

'He hasn't popped the question yet.'

'But you know it's on the cards, sugar. The Hon. Mrs. Richard Napier has an elegant ring to it, don't you think?'

'I'm just out of boarding school, Dorothy! Allow me to live a little. Anyway, Richard's too caught up in his political career to think about getting married, especially now that war's on the horizon.'

'Oh, Lord! War talk.' Dorothy gave an ostentatious yawn, then rose to her feet. 'Excuse me, dear "Lisa". I need to powder my nose.'

Off Dorothy went, snake-walking past the table where the pipe-smoker was still reading his *Evening Standard*. He didn't look up.

Baba leaned her chin on her hand and gazed through the steamed-up window of the café. A stranger waiting at a bus stop beyond was watching her, clearly mesmerized. He tipped his hat at her, but she was too absorbed in thought to see him, which was a pity, because the way he was looking at her might have made her realize that Baba didn't need to 'think Lisa' to attract attention from members of the opposite sex. The infrastructure was all there.

CHAPTER THREE

JESSIE

FINISTÈRE 1919

In the distance the sea was diamantine, its whisper seductive. The leather soles of Jessie's sandals made a satisfying slapping sound on the path, there was a pungent smell of wild thyme in the air, and fat clouds sculled lazily overhead. She felt sweat accumulating in the hair she'd piled haphazardly under her straw hat, felt the sun trace a burning finger along her collarbone. She longed to swim.

Her husband had been hellbent on getting to Raguenez, a Mecca for painters since Gauguin had discovered it. Jessie had been glad for sea air at last, for Scotch's sake especially. It would do him good after his recent illness. If only he would stop smoking: the doctor in Chambéry had insisted '*pas de tabac!*' but Scotch smoked like a chimney: there was a cigarette always between his lips, especially when he was concentrating on a canvas.

They tramped on, pausing occasionally to examine an unfamiliar plant, or to listen to birdsong, or to kiss and kiss, and kiss again. Jessie loved the weight of her husband's arm slung over her shoulders; loved the smell of him – sandalwood and sea salt and a hint of linseed oil; loved the sound of his voice: low, musical, with that lilting burr – Scotch ('but not too Scotch!') as she'd stressed in a letter to her parents, mindful of her mother's distaste for provincial accents.

They were nearing the beach. To judge by the crowd milling about outside a church, it was time for Mass. Some of the young women were sporting traditional peasant dress – full-skirted frocks plumped out by layers of starched petticoats and teamed with intricately embroidered aprons. Lace fichus were draped around shoulders, filigree earrings hung from earlobes, and tightly cinched waists showed off enviable figures. But the *pièces de résistance* were the beautiful headdresses: elaborate confections of felt and straw trimmed with ribbon. The gaudy colours gave the demoiselles the appearance of flirtatious butterflies as they preened ostentatiously for the youths loitering on the steps.

'They make me feel like a perfect frump,' remarked Jessie, casting covetous glances at them. 'Even the men are gorgeous! Look at the embroidery on that waistcoat.'

The most striking of the girls – who was wearing what resembled a lace-trimmed mitre atop her gleaming chignon – slid a rather too interested look in Scotch's direction, then tossed her head when she caught Jessie's eye. Jessie could have sworn there had been a curl of the lip too.

'Oh! Did you see the way she glared at me? Just because she's wearing the Leaning Tower of Pisa on her head doesn't entitle her to look down her nose, as if I'm some kind of a tramp.'

Jessie hadn't got used to the way girls looked at her, but she had got used to the way they looked at Scotch, and it made her swell with pride to be able to display her ring finger, with its wedding band and cabochon sapphire. He cut a Byronesque figure in his bohemian waistcoats, workman's trousers and wide-brimmed hats; his figure long and lean, his honey-dark hair worn a little long, falling over patrician features. She remembered the Italian girl they had encountered in the hotel in Chambéry, the one who had begged him to paint her. She was a sultry temptress of the Pre-Raphaelite kind – more beautiful by far than Jessie. Since Jessie had no Italian she could not follow the conversations she and Scotch shared, but their animated chatter and the girl's theatrical gestures made her laugh. Until one evening when she had seen her bite into a peach while regarding her husband from beneath her thick black lashes. That was when Jessie had decided that Scotch's health had improved enough for him to travel, and it was time for them to move on.

A gull shrieked above them. There was a heaviness in the atmosphere, suddenly, presaging a change in the weather.

'There's a storm on the way,' said Jessie, drawing in a lungful of air. 'They say that in this part of France the winds can blow up overnight. I hope it's an electric storm – it would be so exciting, wouldn't it, to have one on our last night? Maybe we could go out into the garden and watch the lightning show and get soaking wet. We could take a bar of soap with us, and then we wouldn't need to bother about washing tomorrow, and we could arrive in Folkestone smelling of rain and lavender. Tuppenny told me that rainwater's much better for the hair than tap water. When we set up home we should have a barrel to collect rainwater for me to rinse my hair in every day. I should be a real water nymph then. Maybe I could pose for you in a bath, the way Lizzie Siddal did, when Millais painted her as Ophelia? But with no clothes on. Then it would be just for us – we could hang it above our bed and no one else would ever get to see it, and—'

Beside her Scotch had fallen uncharacteristically silent. She gave him a look of enquiry.

'Scotch? Scotch, what's up? Have I bored you to death with my drivel?'

He said nothing – just shook his head.

'Come on. Out with it!'

'It's nothing, nothing.'

'Tell me!' she said, laying an encouraging hand on his arm. 'You can talk about it – talk away! We talk about everything!'

The honeymooners talked endlessly: they talked with their mouths full (Jessie's mother would be appalled!), they talked while cleaning their teeth, they spent hours every night after making love talking until the small hours, and then they would laugh and tell each other to shut up as the sun was rising.

The packed earth of the path had given way to softer sand. Emerging on to the beach, they found it deserted – apart from a couple of family groups and a handful of shrimpers who had staked their claim to the eastern stretch. Jessie glanced at Scotch, but he was gazing out to sea, refusing for some reason to meet her eye. She stooped to take off her sandals, noticing how the pale stripes left by the straps contrasted with the dark gold of her bare skin. She'd visit Dorothy Perkins on her return to London, to buy stockings. Lisle, not silk: she would have to learn economy now that she was a married woman.

Jamming her shoes into her satchel, Jessie turned to face

her husband. 'You're in rather a funk, aren't you? Tell me what's up, my love. We *have* to be happy today – it's the rule. We can't let anything spoil the last day of our honeymoon.'

Scotch abandoned his scrutiny of the horizon. 'You're right. It would be criminal.'

'Make me laugh, then. Tell me a joke.'

'You've heard all my jokes.'

'But I *love* your jokes!'

'I don't have the energy.'

'Oh, I'm sorry, Scotch. I forget sometimes that you're still recuperating.'

He took a pack of Gitanes from his pocket and extracted a half-smoked butt. Jessie wanted to say, '*Pas de tabac!*' but thought better of it.

'Hell, Jessie,' Scotch said, as he lit up. 'Forgive me. It's just that sometimes I feel so damnably inadequate.'

'Inadequate? Whatever for?'

'Don't think I didn't see the envy in your eyes when you spotted those girls back there. And I saw the way you ogled the displays in the Champs-Elysées last week, and I know you pretend not to mind when we travel third class. I know you still hanker after finery and fashion.'

'Finery and fashion mean nothing to me! I'm a socialist now, and perfectly happy to be one.' Pulling a lace-edged handkerchief from her pocket, Jessie dabbed her neck, wishing she'd brought some eau-de-cologne.

Scotch looked thoughtful, and flicked the ash from his cigarette. 'You know what Alexander Herzen said about your kind of socialism?'

Jessie didn't want to admit that she didn't know who Alexander Herzen was, so she gave a careless shrug. 'What did he say?'

'He said, and I paraphrase: "Some people talk about socialism over pastry and champagne while others die of cold and hunger."'

She looked at him uncertainly.

'You miss all that, don't you?' he said. 'Of course you must. The pastry and champagne, the boxes at the opera, the gala evenings, the Saturday-to-Mondays in grand country estates, the shopping, the cocktail parties . . .'

'On the contrary, I don't miss them at all.'

'Then why did you pack an evening dress? You knew we wouldn't be staying at the Ritz.'

'A girl has to think of every eventuality,' she said, with mock snootiness. 'We might have had an invitation to a high-class *vernissage*, or a salon. And we *did* get invitations. Count Demetrios suggested dinner, remember, should we happen to meet up with him in Paris.'

'And instead we end up carousing with low-life in spit and sawdust cafés, drinking cheap wine when you're used to vintage. What would your parents have to say about that?'

'Pawpey would just be glad that I'm having a lark.'

'A lark? With a penniless artist for a husband? A blasted amputee, at that?'

'Oh, come, my dear! You're more dexterous than some of the so-called able-bodied men I've known.' She slanted him a smile. 'I'll never forget that time in Chambéry when you challenged the Italian attaché to billiards and beat him so effortlessly. I thought his *amie* was going to swoon with ardour. No wonder she asked you to paint her.'

'She wasn't his *amie*.'

'She certainly behaved as if she was, driving out with him in his Isotta every day.'

Jessie had been furious that she had not been invited to accompany the attaché on his drives. She used to watch from the *pension* window as the signorina was handed into the car by a flunkey, then crane her neck to follow the progress of the car as it bowled off along the road: paint-work gleaming, engine purring, sleek and streamlined as the dusky beauty lounging in the passenger seat. She remembered how she had written home from Chambéry, affecting a blasé attitude as though she were quite indifferent to the allure the girl held for Scotch:

She was fearfully keen on him painting her portrait, so he did one, in water-colour, and tears his hair with rage to think that his oil-box is in Paris . . .

'She was an extremely intelligent woman,' Scotch remarked.

'She didn't look it.'

'You didn't spend as much time with her as I did. She was a student at Turin University—'

I studied at Cambridge! Jessie wanted to retort.

'—and had plans to become a professor of languages. She'd have made a top-class teacher, too. She even managed to interest me in Italian opera, and you know I've always found it a colossal bore.'

'What else did you learn from her? How to flirt in Italian? How very useful!' She had meant the words to sound light-hearted, jocular – but they came out as peevish, and she regretted them immediately.

Scotch gave her a perplexed look. Then he tossed aside his cigarette, turned away from her and strode off along the beach.

Flustered, Jessie had to quicken her step to keep up. They carried on walking without exchanging another word. Finding the perfect place for their picnic had become a kind of ritual for Scotch and Jessie, but this was the first time they had done it in silence. And it was a horrible silence, a rotten preamble to the news she wanted to tell him, about the baby, and about Pawpey's wonderful offer of help, and her plans for their future.

They finally found a spot to the west, to spread their rug. Further along the beach a group of children were playing what seemed to be a game of nurses and soldiers, the girls binding make-believe wounds with old broadcloth puttees, and telling the boys to keep quiet and be brave.

Jessie peeled off her dress and sat down, stretching out her legs and digging her toes into the sand. Lowering himself onto the rug beside her, Scotch picked up a stick and started hewing it with his penknife.

The silence stretched on and on until finally Jessie said, in a very small voice:

'Scotch?'

'Mm?'

'I have good news. Pawpey wants to give us a wedding present.'

'*Another* one? For Christ's sake, Jessie – I can't possibly accept anything else from him. He paid for your trousseau, he paid for that quite unnecessarily lavish wedding, he paid for our trip to Venice—'

'But he knew that our honeymoon would be incomplete without Venice! And this particular – gift – would solve all our financial headaches. We won't ever have to worry about money again if we take him up on this offer.'

40

'He wants to give us money?' Scotch sounded aghast.

'No, no. He wants to buy us a house.' She didn't dare look at his face. She busied herself unpacking her satchel, laying out her writing paper, her precious Onoto pen, Stevenson's *Songs of Travel and Other Verses* . . .

'No.'

'But, Scotch—'

'No. There's an end to it.'

Because Scotch's eyes were in shadow under the brim of his hat, Jessie could not read his expression, but suddenly she felt uneasy. Opening her volume of poetry she leafed through it randomly, and came across the following: *I will make you brooches and toys for your delight/Of bird-song at morning and star-shine at night./I will make a palace fit for you and me/Of green days in forests and blue days at sea.* Raising her eyes, Jessie contemplated the horizon, where turquoise met azure. This was a blue day, to be sure, one to be treasured. She must not do or say anything that might mar it.

Out of the corner of her eye she saw Scotch take from his rucksack the sketchbook she had bought for his birthday in Florence, in a specialist leather goods shop near the Boboli Gardens. It was a beauty, bound in hand-tooled calfskin with marbled endpapers, and inscribed in her most careful handwriting with a love poem by Sir Philip Sidney. Scotch had told her that she should keep it as a diary of their travels, that it was too special to besmirch with his scribbles, but she had insisted. 'Look!' she had told him, as they'd sat over birthday tea and cakes in the Piazza Repubblica. 'I've already dedicated it to you.'

And so she had; thus:

A present to my true-love!
This book is the record of an impromptu birthday. It came as
a ray of sun and illuminated with its glow a whole day. It is
a festive book, and is the child of a happy Love whose face
is always smiling and contented, but who has moments of
thoughtfulness and moments of wild unrestrained joy. It first
saw the light opposite the Strozzi Palace amid an aroma of
delicious tea and delectable cakes.

Aware that Scotch was sketching her, Jessie continued to
turn the pages of her poetry book, reading aloud a random
selection of verses, and chatting idly.

He was engrossed now, in his drawing. She could tell by
the frown that appeared between his eyebrows. What
went through his mind as he worked? What did he
see, that other people did not? Sometimes she felt
strangely vulnerable when Scotch painted her, as
though he were privy to the innermost working of her
mind.

By the time he finally put his sketchbook away, their
shadows had grown longer on the sand and Jessie thought
she might have fallen asleep because she was sure she had
dreamed something, something that for some reason she
did not care to remember. Her face was burning despite
the efforts she had taken to protect it from the glare of the
sun, and she had the kind of lump in her throat that she'd
often had when she was a little girl being scolded by her
mother, trying hard not to cry.

Scotch was looking at her with the oddest expression.
He turned away to rearrange the contents of his knapsack,
and there was something unfamiliar – something almost
hostile – about his demeanour. When he turned back to

her, Jessie was relieved to see that his smile was once more in place.

'Say something silly,' he said.

'I can't.'

'Go on. Say something that will make me laugh. You know how good you are at that.'

Jessie's mind cast around randomly. 'Um. I am your Dear Rib,' she said.

'What?'

'It was Doctor Livingstone's pet name for his wife. It comes from the Bible – you know, when God created Eve from one of Adam's ribs. She must have been frightfully skinny.'

Scotch laughed. 'Oh, just look at you!' he exulted, pushing her back onto the rug and rolling on top of her. 'How beautiful you are – how beautiful is my beloved! But look out – there's a fly on you, one of those nasty stinging ones.' He slapped her thigh robustly.

'I don't believe there was any fly on me!' she cried, rolling away from him. 'I believe you made it up just so's you could smack me.'

'And there's another one!' crowed Scotch, slapping her bottom. 'We can't have flies on you. There can be *no* flies on my Dear Rib!'

Jessie scrambled to her feet and made for the sea. He caught up with her and pulled her to him, holding her tight and kissing her over and over. Waist-high in water, they stood clinging to one another for many minutes. Then, releasing her from his embrace, he turned to face the horizon. His cheeks were wet: drops of water clung to his eyelashes.

'I love you,' he said, and suddenly everything was right in her world again. He *would* make a palace for her – this

43

beautiful, talented, creative man – of green days and blue days, and days in all kinds of other colours. She'd wait another week or two to tell him about the baby, and then he would reconsider Pawpey's proposal – of course he would. No newlywed in their right mind could turn down the offer of a house.

Plunging into the tide, Jessie swam three or four strokes, then turned over and floated on her back, gazing at the canopy of blue above her.

What colour would she paint the nursery? Pink, she hoped – palest pink with a stencilled frieze of daisies. She'd love a little girl to dress up and play doll's house with, and to delight with fairies' picnics at the bottom of the garden. But then, perhaps Scotch would prefer a boy.

He had swum out to join her. Taking his hand, she rubbed her cheek against his shoulder. He was gazing out to sea, his expression unreadable. 'What are you thinking, love?' she asked.

He looked down at her tenderly, and studied her, and she felt as though he were learning her face like a map; the contour of her cheekbones, the line of her jaw, the swell of her lips, the retroussé nose, every plane and curve . . .

'I'm thinking that I shall remember this day – this last, perfect, halcyon day – for as long as I live,' he said.

16 Aug. 1919

> The sands of Raguenez,
> Pont-Aven,
> Finistère.

We've had the most gorgeous day out here all day, bathing and running about in bathing dresses on deserted sands. This is the beautifullest stretch of coast, sands and lovely brown cliffs, and not overrun with trippers.

We are as fit as fiddles, and Scotch! – he's so brimming over with energy and good health that he can't leave me in peace for 2 seconds. He spends his time killing imaginary flies on me, and it's an awful job to keep him in order – quite hopeless.

We are getting faces the colour of nothing on earth. We are about to have a picnic now consisting of biscuits and jam, blackberry jam that we have made ourselves. We gathered the blackberries, sneaked the sugar from restaurants etc, and made it on the little stove in the tea basket – tray bon – this is the second lot we have made, so we're feeling very proud of ourselves.

Cheerio, dears. By jove! What a holiday we are having!

The aroma of coffee drifted under the door of the bedroom on the third floor of the hotel. Was that what had woken her? Or had it been the tinny sound of the church bell striking the hour? Or the squabbling of sparrows under the eaves? Or the plangent French accents floating up from the narrow street below? Or had it been the wind that was gusting fiercely in from the north through the open window and setting the curtains billowing?

She turned to take Scotch in her arms, but he was gone.

There came a knock at the door.

'Madame?'

'Come in, Suzette.' Reaching for her wrapper, Jessie shrugged it on.

It wasn't Suzette. It was Madame Simonet.

'Have you given your little girl the morning off?' asked Jessie, idly knotting her sash.

'No, Madame. I wanted to wake you myself. I have something to tell you.'

Jessie looked up. The woman's expression was anguished. She was twisting one of the strings of her apron and could barely bring herself to meet Jessie's eyes.

Jessie was instantly alert. 'You have bad news, Madame? What is it?'

'My – my husband was up early this morning, before cockcrow. He went to the milking parlour to fetch fresh cans for breakfast, and on the way there he saw Scotch get up on to a drover's cart.'

Jessie gave her a look of enquiry, then shrugged, trying to conceal her surprise. 'Maybe he wanted to make haste to paint today,' she hazarded, 'to catch the dawn light before we pack up.'

'He had his painting satchel with him, that is true. But he also had – other luggage.'

'What other luggage?'

'A suitcase. And a holdall. He left money to cover the bill. I'm sorry Madame, to have to bring you such news.' Madame Simonet bowed her head, then backed out of the room clumsily.

Feeling like a woman sculpted from ice, Jessie moved to the wardrobe and opened the door. All Scotch's clothes were gone, and all his effects. The only item that remained was a kerchief that had fallen to the floor, one that he habitually wore around his neck. She picked it up and pressed it to her face. He was gone. Of course he was. And she knew where.

Scotch had left her for the Italian girl.

CHAPTER FOUR

BABA

LONDON 1939

The big shot from the Pru pulled some strings, and Baba was put on the payroll at Denham Studios. Her job description – second assistant script girl on *The Thief of Bagdad* – turned out to be something of a misnomer, because (a) she was really just expected to run errands, and (b) there actually was *no* script. *The Thief of Bagdad* just sort of happened – with bits of it being made up as it went along.

Sometimes it seemed impossible that the movie would ever get finished, so gargantuan was the scale of the project. Baba got used to overhearing directives that went: 'Mr Korda wants a flying horse. Mr Korda wants a forty-foot genie. Mr Korda wants a six-armed goddess.' And everything Mr Korda wanted, he got.

Alexander Korda masterminded the operation, but Baba rarely saw him. Her dreams of being plucked from obscurity and groomed for stardom were dashed when she got stuck instead with a succession of different directors, one of whom was a lumpy-looking German with wispy hair and no sense of humour. Still, she managed to smile while she unfolded canvas chairs for him and Miss Duprez and the other leading lights, and she managed not to look too sick when the dancing girls wafted gaily past her in their diaphanous harem pants, and she even managed a joke when the dog star of the movie got loose one day and tried to savage her.

But she fell in love at first sight with Sabu, the boy who played the 'thief' of the title. *He* had been propelled to stardom three years ago when he'd been cast as the lead in *Elephant Boy*. Sabu Dastagir was only fifteen, but already he was the toast of London: he'd been sculpted by Lady Kennet, painted by Egerton Cooper, and he'd even appeared on television.

He might have been the toast of London, but Sabu was one of the easiest-going, most approachable people on the set, with a smile as broad as the Ganges and charm enough to lure the stripes off a tiger. It was only a matter of days before he and Baba became good friends, after he'd accidentally knocked off one of the goddess's six arms. Thereafter, Baba had nicknamed him 'Sabutage', and allowed him in return to call her by her pet name.

'How did your parents feel about you leaving India?' she asked him one lunchtime, when they were sitting together at the top table in the canteen. A gaggle of costume extras at the far end of the room were eyeing Sabu and giggling, clearly keen to pluck up the courage to ask for his autograph. Baba knew she was very privileged to be sitting at the top table, and she found it hard not to preen a little.

'I'm an orphan, Baba,' he said. 'My mother died when I was a baby, and my father died when I was six.'

'Oh. I *am* sorry.'

'My father was a mahout, like me.'

'A mahout?'

'An elephant handler. He looked after the elephants in the Maharajah of Mysore's stables.'

'What a swell job!'

Sabu gave her a cynical look. 'You don't get paid a pile of rupees for sweeping up dung. But he loved the elephants, and they loved him. He taught his favourite animal to rock my cradle when I was a baby, and even to pick me up in his trunk and rock me that way too. When my father died, that elephant went mad with grief. He broke his chains and ran off into the jungle.'

'Oh, how sad!' Out of the corner of her eye, Baba could see the extras nudging a slave girl in vermilion chiffon towards their table. 'Have you any family left in India, Sabu?'

'Yes. They are completely dependent on me now, since I was discovered by Robert O'Flaherty. The filmmaker,' he added, for her enlightenment.

'He made *Man of Aran*, didn't he?'

Sabu looked surprised. 'How do you know that? I wouldn't have thought that was your sort of film.'

'I went to the Aran Islands on a day trip once. I was at boarding school on the west coast of Ireland.'

'Ireland? Why didn't your folks send you to an English boarding school?'

'I have cousins over there.' Baba didn't want to tell Sabu that she had been shipped off to this remote outpost of Europe at her grandmother's behest. 'My best friend there was an Indian girl.'

'An Indian girl – at school in Ireland? How weird!'

'It's true. Girls came from all over the world to be educated at Kylemore Abbey. I had friends from Japan, Mexico and America, as well as India.'

'Was it a posh school?'

'I guess it was, but we ran a little wild. It was in the middle of the country, miles from anywhere, with lakes to swim in and mountains to climb.'

The extra was approaching, blinking in nervous supplication. 'May I have your autograph, Mr Dastagir?' she asked, her face nearly as purple as her pants.

'Sabu,' he corrected her, taking the pen and autograph book and signing with very good grace. And once he'd signed one autograph, a queue formed, and he was obliged to sign forty more.

'Do you know,' said Baba, when he'd finished, 'that until I met you, I assumed all child stars to be spoilt brats. You could give some of those Hollywood kids a run for their money. You're ten times more talented than most of them.'

Sabu frowned. 'I'll meet some of them soon. I'm off to Hollywood once this epic is in the can. I have hired an agent there.'

Baba looked at him, agape. 'A Hollywood agent? You lucky dog!'

Sabu shrugged. 'I don't mean to sound ungrateful, but I'm not too keen on the idea. Hollywood is my idea of hell. But Boss Man Korda advised me that America is the best place to be now that war is on the way.'

War really was on the way. Only the other day newspaper headlines had bellowed FRANCE MOBILIZES! and since July, air raid shelters were being built all over London. Sandbags and gas masks were being distributed, too. Baba dreaded the idea of donning a gas mask because they looked like pigs' snouts.

'That's my dream, you know,' Baba confessed. 'To escape from here and go to Hollywood.'

'No! Don't tell me you are hankering after stardom, Baba?'

'I'm hankering after excitement, really. I'm dreading this war. It's going to make life so bloody dreary. Everybody keeps droning on about the New Austerity.'

The 'New Austerity' was reflected in the fashions being showcased in *Vogue*. Fashion was no longer frivolous – it was borderline frumpy. Hair was pinned up and hidden away under scarves and duster hats, skirts were skimpily cut to save on fabric, and shoes were clumpy cork-wedged affairs. To Baba, it felt very strange to come to work in Denham Studios, where there was a profusion of riotous colours and opulent fabrics and exotic artefacts. While Churchill roared in Whitehall and Hitler barked in Germany and Mussolini yapped in Italy, the boys and girls at Denham were busy making fairy tales.

Baba took a look at her watch. Miss Duprez would be waiting for her tea. 'Time for me to scoot,' she said, giving Sabu's hand a squeeze. 'I'll be happy to run lines with you later, if you like.'

'There's not a lot of point,' said Sabu ruefully. 'The script's changed again.'

Baba set off back across the lot, taking care to steer clear of one of the sparks, who was watching her wolfishly with his pop eyes. She'd foolishly tried out her 'Lisa' persona on him one day, and that had been a big mistake because Popeye now ogled her lecherously everywhere she went.

As she passed by the 'harbour' where muscle-bound stuntmen in loincloths were furling sails and sliding down ropes, she found herself wondering why she had never bothered to try out her 'Lisa' persona on Sabu. He was too young for her, she knew, but it never did any harm to put in a little practice. And then she realized why. It was because she liked him too much to toy with his affections. She liked him too much to make a lapdog of him.

One Sunday morning as Baba sat on her little stool assiduously marking a list of props, Mr Korda himself appeared on the set, a huge Corona cigar between his teeth, and announced that there was to be an important radio broadcast. It was a surreal scene. June Duprez in her floaty pink pyjamas and Conrad Veidt in his red turban and Miles Malleson as the Sultan with his fake white whiskers, all congregated in the throne room of the princess's palace with strained, ashen faces. And Baba clutched Sabu's hand as Neville Chamberlain's voice came over the speakers and told them that Britain was at war with Germany.

When Baba returned home that evening she ran up to her room and dived under her eiderdown, awash with awful self-pity. She couldn't help it. The war was coming and all the young men would be called up to fight, and there'd be rationing, and drabness, and the only films that would be made would be dreary black-and-white propaganda ones, not glorious, expensive Technicolor fairy tales like *Thief*, and life wouldn't be worth living.

'Baba!' her grandfather called up to her from the hall below. 'There's a telephone call for you.'

It would be Dorothy, phoning to moan about the war. Well, hell's bells! At least she had a wedding to look forward to, and a new husband she could play happy families with. The Government was hardly likely to conscript married men unless things got really bad. As

Baba shrugged out from under her eiderdown, she wondered if maybe she *should* wangle a proposal out of Richard Napier. At least she'd have a future as the wife of someone with prospects. There'd be no other kind of future for her in bloody war-torn Britain.

She ran down three flights of stairs to where the phone sat on the console table in the hall.

'Hello?' she said into the receiver.

'Baba.'

It was Sabu's voice.

'Sabutage! Why are you phoning me at home?'

'I have news for you. I spoke with Mr Korda earlier. He filled me in on the future of the film.'

'It's being axed, isn't it?' She'd heard from her grandfather that the Prudential had withdrawn financial backing because Mr Korda had gone so precipitously over budget. The word 'hubris' was on everybody's lips.

'No. It's not being axed. It is being moved, lock, stock and barrel.'

Baba felt tears threaten. 'So you're phoning to say goodbye?'

'No. I'm phoning to offer you a job.'

'A job?'

'Yes. I decided that it was about time I used some film star clout and called a few shots. I told Mr Korda that I needed a personal assistant.'

'What's that got to do with me?'

'The job is yours if you want it.'

'You want me to be your personal assistant?'

'Yes. I've already been uprooted from my country, Baba, and since they expect me to go somewhere else where I have no family or friends, I decided it would be a good

53

idea to bring a friend with me – someone who will like me for myself, not just because I'm a big-shot movie star.

'So where are we going?'

Sabu paused dramatically, and there was a smile in his voice when he spoke again.

'Los Angeles,' he said. 'We're going to Hollywood, Baba.'

CHAPTER FIVE

JESSIE

PARIS 1919

'You know what to do?'

Jessie nodded. She knew for sure what to do. She'd done it gladly on countless occasions: but this was the first time she'd offered her services in exchange for payment.

Her workplace was a garret, sparsely furnished with ramshackle bits and pieces. The only exceptional item of furniture was the day bed. This had been the first thing she'd seen when she'd entered the room. It stood in the centre of the floor, richly upholstered in brocade, with gilded claw feet and plump tasselled cushions: fit for a Pompadour.

'You'll find a kimono behind the screen.'

He indicated with a peremptory nod the screen that stood in a corner of the room. It was Victorian, covered in cracked greyish-brown hide that had peeled away in places to expose the rotting jute beneath. It had a leprous look. Assuming a confidence she didn't feel, Jessie moved towards it, aware that his eyes were on her.

'I'd like your hair loose,' he added, jabbing a finger at her.

'As you wish.'

Behind the screen the kimono was draped over a bentwood chair. Of faded blue artificial silk, it bore a pattern of birds and butterflies and flowering cherry blossom, and it smelt of someone else.

The first item of clothing she removed was her straw cloche – the one she'd bought in Venice. She set it on the chair, then slipped out of her shoes and started to undo the buttons on her dress. Steeling herself, she pulled the frock over her head. There was no peg to hang it on, and she didn't want to drape it over the screen the way she knew some girls did. That would appear too provocative. Folding it neatly, she laid it on the chair alongside her hat. Underwear next. Garters, stockings, camiknickers . . .

Then – quickly! Into the kimono. As she slid her arms into the sleeves the scent of cheap perfume that still clung to the fabric was so overwhelming it almost made her gag.

Good Lord! How insane it was to think that not so long ago she wouldn't have bothered with either screen or kimono. She'd have discarded her clothes blithely and unselfconsciously because she'd discovered that nakedness held neither shame nor sin.

'Are you ready?' The voice was clinical, detached; but impatient.

'Not quite,' she replied.

Raising her hands, she began to unpin the chignon that she'd gone to some pains to construct that morning. What wouldn't she give to have her hair shingled! The weather had been stiflingly hot in Paris recently. But she knew that her hair was her chief asset. Apart, that is, from the obvious allure of her youth.

She dropped the hairpins into her shoe and uncoiled

the plait, and then she shut her eyes tight and brought her hands to her face, resisting the urge to cry out as she cast her mind back, remembering the way *he* had laughed and the shout of joy he would give when she discarded her clothes and loosened her hair, and how, muzzy with the wine they'd drunk at lunch, she would be sweetly compliant, holding the pose for hours on end until a craving for nicotine set in and she'd beg for a cigarette break.

A meaningful cough sounded: it was her cue.

Taking a deep breath, Jessie moved out from behind the screen and walked an imaginary tightrope across the bare floorboards: chin up, gaze direct, demeanour unflappable – even though she was shaky with nerves. When she reached the day bed, she paused.

'I'd like to examine the goods before we start, if you please.'

The goods. . . She'd never been made to feel like a commodity in her life before. But of course, that had been in her old life – before Finistère. She untied the sash, slipped the kimono from her shoulders and dropped it over the cushioned headrest.

The man moved towards her. She couldn't help but tense a little, waiting for his touch. If he touched her he had overstepped the mark and she would have to put her clothes back on and leave. But a surge of relief flooded through her when he stopped a yard or two distant and folded his arms.

'Turn around,' he said.

She did as he asked.

'And now back to me.' Another moment of scrutiny, and she held her breath and instinctively sucked in her tummy even though she knew she wasn't showing yet, and would not for some months. 'You'll do,' he said.

Thank God. Oh, thank God! She'd got away with it.

'Remove your rings, if you please,' he asked, directing his gaze to the third finger of her left hand. 'They're something of a giveaway.'

She slid first the narrow gold band with its single sapphire off her finger, then her plain gold wedding ring. There was something symbolic about the gesture. They would go to the pawn shop soon, as had her amber beads just last week, and her going-away suit, and the hounds-tooth coat that had been part of her trousseau. The whole lot had fetched just one hundred and fifty francs.

C'est fini, she thought, as she dropped the rings into the pocket of the kimono. *The jig's up and the final curtain's fallen – and hang it all, didn't I know it? Didn't I know in my heart that day in Finistère that it was over and that I would never see him again?*

'Now fan out your hair for me.'

She obliged.

'It's quite remarkable.' He reached out and lifted a hand-ful of her riotous hair, grinning as he saw her flinch. 'Don't worry, *jolie petite*. You're safe with me. I've never felt a smidgeon of attraction for the so-called "fairer" sex.' He let the mass of hair fall, then moved across the room. 'The Pre-Raphaelites would have envied me,' he remarked over his shoulder. 'Your hair is easily as glorious as Lizzie Siddal's. You know Millais's drowned Ophelia?'

'Yes.'

'She held that pose in a bath of cold water. Made herself so ill she nearly died. But don't worry,' he added, giving her a saturnine look before turning and moving back across the room. 'I shan't expect you to be quite so obliging as the divine Miss Siddal.'

The words of a letter she had written from Chambéry several weeks earlier came back to her.

Scotch has been very busy these last 2 or 3 days painting a divine Italian girl – he is absolutely mad on her, and no wonder, she's a real beauty – black hair and eyes, an olive skin, and a tall graceful lithe figure. He has begun another, a ripping one – in a black velvet dress, with a white ostrich feather fan in her hand . . .

That dress! The very texture of it made you want to reach out and touch. She remembered how it gleamed when the Italian girl moved, how the dewy blush of the rose tucked into her décolletage drew the eye there, how the dusky velvet set off the translucent sheen of her skin after dark, in the blue hour, the hour between dog and wolf . . .

'Ready to start?' The painter was standing next to the trestle table that bore the tools of his trade – palette, brushes, pencils, charcoal, knives. He was looking at her with a kind of resentment now, like a customer kept waiting too long to be served.

'Yes.'

'Then make yourself comfortable on the day bed, if you would be so kind. On your side.'

She did as he instructed, sliding automatically into a series of poses.

'Hm. No. No . . . Yes – that looks good,' he said, regarding her critically. 'Try leaning up on one elbow – that'll give me more of you.' He chewed on his bottom lip, considering. 'Good, good. Chin a little higher. Yes! Hold that. We're getting there, but there's something missing.'

'How about this?' She stretched a languorous leg. It was a pose she'd held successfully before, in that room in the Villa Balestri – the room with the view of the Arno and the Ponte Vecchio. The view he'd painted.

'No. I want a coquette, not a bloody *femme fatale*.'

This time she crooked her knee and arched a pretty foot. It would be a devil of a pose to hold, but she knew she was in no position to call the shots here.

'That's it! That's just what I'm after. Now – try looking away from me. To your right. And smile. God – no – not like that. Who d'you think you are? The Mona bloody Lisa?'

'Sorry.'

'A sweetheart look is what I'm after – d'you follow me? A Mary Pickford look – playful and sassy. Yeah. That's good. Lovely.' He held up a thumb and finger to measure perspective, then: 'Lovely,' he said again. Giving her a perfunctory nod of approval, he adjusted the angle of his easel a fraction, helped himself to a stick of charcoal and set to work.

Long minutes went by. It was stuffy in the studio despite the open casement, and she had to concentrate hard to stay awake. The air was redolent with the smell of oil paint mixed with a pungent odour of frying onions from the street stalls below, and the only sounds in the room were the scratch of charcoal on canvas, the whine of the occasional mosquito, and the sing-song cries of the traders that came drifting in through the window.

One call was familiar – *Madame Saprasti! Madame Saprasti! Diseuse de bon aventure!*

She'd been approached by the fortune-teller earlier, as

she'd made her way down the street looking for the artist's address. Madame Saprasti had offered to tell her what her future held for 'a mere' five francs. Jessie had shaken her head at the woman – five francs could get her a decent meal, after all – but part of her yearned *passionately* to know what the future held for her.

She remembered the cherry stone game she'd used to play as a child, the one that told you what class of man you might marry. Tinker, tailor, soldier, sailor. Rich man, poor man, beggar man, thief. Her mother had expected her to bag a rich man – what other kind *were* there, after all? – but she knew she'd never get any kind of a man now, a married woman, abandoned, and with a baby on the way.

A baby! The idea that she would be responsible soon for a living, breathing human infant made her nauseous with apprehension. If she hadn't been required to stay quite still, she'd have curled up in a foetal position the way she did every night now, wishing she could hibernate like some uncomplicated hedgerow creature and make real life with its anxieties and awful obstacles go away. She wasn't going to give birth, she wasn't going to give the 'gift' of life: sad bereft Jessie was going to inflict existence on another human being.

She'd spent many midnight hours recently lying awake, trying to garner a degree of comfort by praying to a God she no longer believed in. Mostly she prayed silently, but sometimes she murmured the words in a mantra. She'd have loved to shout them, on the really bad nights, but the walls of the boarding house were so thin they might have been rice paper and her neighbour was a grouchy fellow, a mad Serb who muttered endlessly to himself.

Oh, God, went her prayer, *make it a boy, please! It's got to*

*be a boy, a healthy boy, a bully boy, a little ox. Don't let it be a
girl! Don't let me bring a daughter into a world where men can
pick girls up and play with them like dolls and then throw them
away when a prettier popsy takes their fancy. Oh, God – please,
please make my baby a boy!*

What a sucker she'd been. What a mug! She remembered how she'd felt the day after Scotch had left her as
she'd sat by herself on the beach at Finistère with her arms
wrapped round her shins and her face on her knees, and
how, when she'd finally got up, the cotton of her skirt had
been stiff with salt. The wind had been as cold as a mother's
reprimand, and the sea and sky had been cracked pewter: so
grey that it was hard to believe that only the day before the
sun had been splitting the bright blue heavens, and she'd had
to take to the shade to finish writing her letter.

When she'd first arrived in Paris a week ago, Jessie had
hoped that one of Scotch's artist friends, a girl with whom
they'd stayed earlier that summer, might still be in
residence in the rue du Sommerard: but no. She had
headed north to Saint-Omer, where her architect fiancé
was working on the War Graves Commission. There had
been nothing for it but to find cheap lodgings elsewhere:
and, of course, the only legitimate work available to a
single woman fallen on hard times was as an artist's
model. That was how Jessie had ended up joining the
other hopeful destitutes on the carrefour Vavin, where
the models' fair was held every Monday morning. She had
hoped perhaps that she might run into a chum of Scotch,
someone who could provide her with a clue as to where he
might be, someone who might say: 'Jessie! There you are!
Thank God we've found you – Scotch has been searching
everywhere for you . . .'

But no-one had come looking for her, and she wasn't surprised: because every time she recalled the autocratic allure of the Italian girl, the oblique smiles she had shared with her husband, and the disdain with which her expressive sloe-black eyes had regarded his shabby little bride, Jessie knew how thoroughly she'd been duped. How long might she continue to fool herself, to live this lie? How long might she continue to deceive her parents, letting on that everything was tickety-boo, that she and Scotch were still basking in the warm glow of newly-wedded bliss and living *la vie en rose* in Montparnasse? How long might she continue to cling to the hope that he would come to Paris to find her, how long before she would have to return to the house in Mayfair as a jilted wife and hear her mother rail against her son-in-law: 'I *knew* it all happened too fast! Engaged within a month! I knew he was a ne'er-do-well . . .'

'Penny for your thoughts?' the painter asked, jolting her back to the present.

It took her a moment to reply. 'I'm thinking about the last time I sat for a portrait,' she replied.

'When was that?'

'Last month. On the beach at Raguenez, in Finistère . . .'

She'd said something to exasperate Scotch, that last afternoon. She couldn't remember what exactly – some facile remark about the PBIs who had come to the library in Rouen, to chat and flirt and read.

He had taken the drawing he was making of her and ripped it in two. 'What do you know about what goes on in the real world? What do you know about real men, about flesh and blood men, what do you know about the horror they endured in the trenches while you were toasting your toes by the library stove, engrossed in Jane Austen?' He reached into his knapsack and handed her a slim sketchbook – one she had not seen before. It had a bloodstain on the cover. 'This was made by one of the war artists. He died in the hospital in Rouen, poisoned by mustard gas. What you have there is a true record of the war, Jessie, one the Propaganda Bureau doesn't want you to see.'

Between the covers of the battered sketchbook had been images of the dead, the dying, the injured, the limbless. Page after page depicted atrocity: corpses trampled into mud, heaped into trenches, twisted at obscene angles. Some were unrecognizable as human; most had been mere boys. A poppy had been pressed between the last two pages of the book – the only splash of colour in a graphite record of hell.

Jessie and Scotch had stared at each other for a moment like two strangers on opposite sides of an abyss, and then Scotch had taken hold of her wrists, raised her hands to his face, and pressed them to his mouth.

'I'm sorry,' he whispered, and she had buried her face in her arms and sobbed until her face was red and blotchy and her throat ached, and then Scotch, at a loss for words for the first time since she had known him, had put the sketchbook away and changed the subject, and she had ended up prattling something silly, something inconsequential.

And now, as she lay on the couch in the artist's studio, Jessie realized that she had never had any real idea of what had been going on in her husband's mind. She had had no idea what horrors Scotch had seen in the years before she had come to Rouen to play at war work in the library; and no idea that every time she spoke of her privileged Cambridge education it might have irked him – really irked him. She had had no idea each time she rattled on about London and her shopping trips to Liberty or Harrods, and afternoon tea at the Savoy and visits to the West End to see the latest Somerset Maugham play, that it just might have had the effect of a chisel blow to the cement of their relationship.

Madame Saprasti! Diseuse de bon aventure! The fortune teller's chant recalled her to the here-and-now.

'I'm sorry – did you say something?' she asked the painter. 'I was miles away.'

'I asked you who he was. The artist you sat for.'

'I don't remember his name,' Jessie said quietly. 'He was nobody, after all. He was nobody very special.'

CHAPTER SIX

BABA

LONDON 1939

Before Baba embarked for Hollywood, Richard Napier took her to tea in the Palm Court, in the Ritz Hotel.

'I *love* this place!' said Baba, smiling at the waiter who had just finished pouring Lapsang Souchong. He returned the smile, made a small bow and backed away. 'It has the most soothing atmosphere of anywhere in London – and it has the most beautiful clientele, too. Even dog-faced women don't look so bad here – did you know that? It has something to do with the lighting, apparently. Dorothy told me that the Palm Court has the most flattering light of any tea room in Europe. Ha! No wonder she spends so much time hanging around here.'

Richard smiled at her indulgently as she reached over and selected a titbit from the three-tiered cake stand piled high with finger sandwiches, scones and miniature pastries.

'So, tell me. What do your grandparents have to say about you haring off to Hollywood?'

'They're quite keen on the idea, funnily enough. What with all the talk on the radio about evacuating children, they're glad that I have the chance to get out of the country.'

'But you're not a child. Don't you think you should stay and volunteer for ambulance work?'

'Richard! It's the opportunity of a lifetime! No girl in her right mind would turn down a chance to go to Hollywood.'

A pained expression crossed Richard's face. 'Hollywood! Even the name has a tawdry ring to it. You really want to be an actress that badly?'

'I don't want to be an actress, Richard,' said Baba. 'I want to be *somebody*. I want to wear shoes by Salvatore Ferragamo and evening gowns by Madame Grès and hats by Schiaparelli. I want to wear diamond earrings and dance Cuban rumbas and Hungarian waltzes. I want to be a star.' She bit crisply into her cucumber sandwich.

Richard put on his best sympathetic voice. 'I know you want to be somebody, darling, and I understand the reasons behind your compulsion, truly I do. Any little girl forsaken by her parents would—'

Baba looked away as if she'd just been slapped smartly on the cheek.

'I'm sorry. I'm sorry.' Richard put his head in his hands, sighed, then looked up again and tried another tack. 'I hate to drag you back to earth, my darling, but don't you think you're being a little naïve? There are millions of girls all over the world who have the same idea.'

'This isn't an *idea*, Richard. It's my dream. And it's not as if I'm going out there with no friends and no money. I'll have an income, and I'll know at least some of the crew members who are going, and Sabu will look after me.'

'Sabu! He's little more than a child himself! You need someone mature to look out for you, someone responsible.' Richard fiddled with his earlobe – a habit of

his when deliberating. 'I can let you have a letter of introduction to a friend of mine.'

'*You* know somebody working in Hollywood? Who?'

'A chap called Niven. He was at Stowe with me, in the
same house. We were in the chess club together – did a bit
of beagling, too. I understand he's doing walk-on parts out
there.'

'Niven! Not *David* Niven?'

'That's the fellow.'

'Why didn't you tell me before?'

'It didn't seem important.'

'But don't you know he's doing more than just walk-on
parts? He had a supporting role in *The Prisoner of Zenda*,
and now he's starring in *Raffles*! Oh – could you please get
in touch with him for me, Richard? That would be just
peachy!'

Richard gave Baba the kind of indulgent smile you
might reserve for a pet. Then he leaned back in his chair,
steepled his fingers, and looked at her over his beautifully
manicured fingernails. This made him appear even more
grown-up than he already was, and Baba was convinced he
did it deliberately.

'I don't mean to put a damper on things,' he said, 'but
the odds of you being plucked from the ranks and given a
speaking role are infinitesimal, darling.'

'Richard. I know you don't understand, but the movies
are my *future*! I *have* to do this.'

'You have such a theatrical streak, Baba. It's really rather
endearing.' He gave her that indulgent smile again. 'You do
know that I'm fearfully fond of you, don't you?'

'Of course I do.'

'And that I probably know you better than anyone?'

Baba bridled a little. 'Allow me a modicum of mystique, please!'

'And allow me to remind you that I've lived next door to you nearly all my life. I'll never forget the day I first saw you – up a tree in Grosvenor Square, hanging upside down like a monkey, with those funny sticky-out plaits.'

'And you shouted "Hey, you! Get out of here! It's private land!"'

He had the good grace to look abashed. 'Oh, Lord. I was a pompous little boy, wasn't I?'

Baba took a sip of her tea to hide her smile. The truth was that Richard still had plenty of pompous moments.

He continued to regard her over his steepled fingers. 'Heavens. Who would have thought to look at you back then that you'd turn out to be so . . .' For once, he appeared lost for words.

'Grown up?' supplied Baba.

'Grown up. That'll do.'

'Is that a compliment, Richard?'

'It most certainly is a compliment.'

'Thank you!' Since Carole Lombard had said in her 'Introduction to Charm' in *Film Pictorial* that it was always more seemly to acknowledge a compliment than not, Baba gave Richard a winsome smile, then lowered her eyes and surveyed the cake stand. She'd have loved to scoff one of the delicious little chocolate éclairs that the Palm Court did so well, but she had her figure to think of now that Hollywood was on the horizon, and her girdle could only achieve so much. She'd be better off sticking to sandwiches, and the miniature smoked salmon ones were irresistible.

She popped one into her mouth. When she raised her

eyes, Richard was still looking at her: immediately she knew what was coming. She felt her heart go into a kind of skid as he reached into his pocket, produced a box, and set it on the table in front of her.

'You know what that is,' he said.

Baba nodded. It would have been disingenuous to pretend she didn't.

'What is it?' he asked.

She chewed and finally swallowed her sandwich with an effort. 'Why – it's a ring.'

'Aren't you going to open the box?'

Baba sent him a pleading look. 'No, Richard. Please don't ask me to.'

'Why not?'

'Because I can't marry you.'

'You say that now. But we're living in troubled times. This war is going to be fast and furious, Baba, and the most stable institution that we can cling to will be the institution of marriage.'

Oh, God! How could he describe marriage as an 'institution'? The words just didn't belong together.

'But—'

'Listen to me! Just hear me out. If you marry me, Baba, I can offer you all the security you need. I'm wealthy, and I have prospects. As you know, I have my own Chambers – and I'm extremely well connected politically. I'm in negotiation with the diplomatic corps; I intend to make politics my career. At the highest level. I don't want to appear arrogant, but I know that one day there will be a place in the Cabinet for me.' He smiled. 'How does the idea of being Prime Minister's wife appeal to you?'

Baba floundered around for a spanner to jam into the

works. 'But – but how could a Prime Minister have an actress as a wife? It's unheard of.'

Richard reached across the table and took her hands in his. 'That would be the one sacrifice I'd have to ask you to make,' he said. 'I don't expect you to give up your dream of going to Hollywood – of course I don't – but when things don't work out for you there you may be very glad to give up any notions about going into films, and decide to return home and marry me.'

'But I—'

'Shh!' Richard touched Baba's lips with a forefinger. 'Don't say anything just yet. Just think about what I've said. And open the box.'

She shouldn't have. She knew she shouldn't have opened it, but she couldn't resist it, any more than she had resisted that smoked salmon sandwich.

It was a diamond. It was the prettiest darn diamond she had ever seen – set in platinum – and she knew that it must have cost Richard a great deal of money.

She looked at the diamond, and then she looked back at Richard, and steeled herself to form the words, 'I'm sorry, Richard, I just can't.' But there was such a happy, puppy-dog look about him that was so at variance with the grown-up way he usually looked that Baba felt a sudden great tug of sympathy for him – sympathy, and something else. Neither ardour, nor lust . . . just a profound, sisterly affection. 'Why do you want to marry me?' she asked, genuinely curious.

'Because I love you.'

'*How* can you love me?'

Richard smiled at her. And then he did something that was so un-Richard that Baba was completely taken aback.

He took her hands between his and began to recite Elizabeth Barrett Browning's 'How Do I Love Thee?'

'How do I love thee?' he said. 'Let me count the ways . . .
I love thee with the breath,
Smiles, tears, of all my life! – and, if God choose,
I shall but love thee better after death.'

And all the while, his eyes never left her face. She felt that nobody in her life before had spoken to her with such artless sincerity, and her tears took her by surprise.

'Oh! Now look! You're making me cry. My mascara will run.'

Without hesitation Richard produced a pristine handkerchief from his breast pocket, and Baba couldn't help but laugh at how quickly he had resumed character. She blew her nose and dabbed carefully at her eyes, and then she looked down at the monogrammed handkerchief between her fingers, twisting it and thinking very hard about what to say.

What to say? The last thing she wanted to do was hurt this man, who had always been there for her. He was her friend, her confidant, her stalwart. Baba pictured herself as a married woman in a dream kitchen wearing a frilly apron and pureéing baby food, and she pictured herself at some dreary state dinner surrounded by dignitaries, and she pictured herself in bed in a Winceyette nightgown, Richard in stripy pyjamas, both of them reading their books, and she knew that, while this might be a vision of domestic bliss for another girl, it simply was not for her. What she craved was fun and adventure and glamour, and a life free from responsibility. She would not find it with Richard.

Finally she looked up at him and said: 'I can't promise to marry you, Richard. But I can promise you that I will think about it.'

'Thinking about it is a beginning,' he said with a smile.

And before she could say anything else, Richard took the ring from her and raised her left hand to his lips before sliding the gleaming circlet onto the third finger. As though on cue, the two ladies at the next table pitter-pattered their hands together and beamed affably at the happy couple.

'How lovely,' said one, 'to know that love's young dream continues to flourish even in the face of war!'

Baba had the decency to blush, a little.

CHAPTER SEVEN

JESSIE

PARIS 1919

Every day Jessie got dressed, walked across the river to the studio in Montmartre and disrobed. Every day she struck an ever-more challenging pose, and every day her muscles grew stronger while her spirit grew feebler. She knew her despondency showed in her demeanour, and she suspected that if she didn't buck up her artist would soon send her packing: but the grim irony was that the more he exhorted her to smile, the more she felt like crying. After several hours she would put her clothes back on, pocket the twenty francs the artist counted out and go back to her room in the Hôtel des Trois Moineaux. She walked the two miles quickly, with her head down, taking care to avoid the eyes of the prostitutes she passed on the streets in the Latin Quarter – those raddled absinthe girls who were suspicious of her youth and beauty, and keen to see her off their patch. Some evenings she'd go and sit by a statue in the Jardin du Luxembourg that lovers tended to use as a meeting point. Jessie persuaded herself that perhaps, *perhaps* Scotch might turn up there, looking for her. Once she had thought she'd seen him striding along an avenue, that distinctive rangy silhouette moving swiftly through the shadows cast by plane trees. Her heart had somersaulted and she'd leapt to her feet to call out to him – but when the gentleman raised his right hand to tip his hat at a passing lady, Jessie had turned and blundered her way through the congregation of courting couples, back to the rue du Coq d'Or. Some evenings she'd buy something to eat from one of the street vendors on the way, some evenings she'd boil up macaroni or potatoes on the little meths stove she kept in her room, and some evenings she'd skulk in a corner of the bistro, hoping that yellow-haired Adèle wouldn't drop by.

She was wary of Adèle. The woman had befriended her on the very first day she'd moved into the hotel, and always greeted her with a jocular 'Bonjour, Mam'zelle!' when they passed each other on the street. But there was something – something *bogus* about her that made Jessie want to keep her distance . . .

On her first night in Paris, Jessie had been sitting on her own at a corner table in the bistro that took up most of the ground floor of the Trois Moineaux. She was dawdling over a modest supper of bread and cheese, determined to make it last, when a blowsy woman strolled up to her, introduced herself and asked if she might buy Mam'zelle a glass of absinthe. Jessie dithered a little before smiling and saying '*Merci, Madame. Comme vous êtes gentille*.'

Baring broken teeth, Adèle returned the smile, then slid herself onto the banquette next to Jessie, called for two glasses and a *pichet*, and poured. '*Santé!*' she said, then knocked the green liquid back in one.

'*Santé*.' Jessie mirrored the gesture. It was the only way to drink absinthe; that way you didn't notice quite how vile it was. The slow burn in your gut was well worth the wormwoody aftertaste, though, as was the lovely muzzy feeling.

Adèle poured again. 'You're British, yeah?'

Jessie nodded.

'A city girl?'

'London.'

Adèle sucked on her teeth, then leaned back against the pitted wood of the banquette and narrowed her eyes speculatively. 'Look, kid,' she announced in a pally way. 'Mind if I offer you a little friendly advice? I've been watching you all evening. You want to know why? I'm intrigued. Here you are dining on hard bread and cheese when I've reason to suspect you're used to better fare. Am I right?'

Reluctant to give too much away, Jessie shrugged.

'It's all right. You don't have to tell me anything you don't want to. But it's clear that you've fallen on hard times. You've been used to the finer things in life, yes? You're an English milady, through and through, *non*? I can tell by your bearing, and by your clothes. They were good once – quality stuff. But now you've learned to mend your own stockings and stuff newspaper into your shoes to keep the wet out, like the rest of us. I know how hard it is. *C'est dommage, mignonne.*' Adèle sighed heavily, and shook her head. 'I myself come from a properous farming family. We had over a hundred acres in Brittany, near Saint-Malo, and I wanted for nothing growing up. But I lost my entire family during the war.'

'Oh. I am sorry.'

'*C'est la vie.* You lost somebody, too?' Adèle directed a meaningful look at Jessie's ring finger, which still bore the pale indentation left by her wedding band. The sapphire had joined the charm on the ribbon around her neck, to keep it safe. 'A husband?'

'I – Yes.'

'Tch tch tch.' Adèle made that sucking noise again, and Jessie flinched. 'Well, kid, I just want to let you know that I'm here for you. I've been living in the city for three years now, and I know the way of things. You need any help, you come to Adèle. We single gals gotta look out for each other, *hein?*'

'Thank you.'

'You OK for funds, kid?'

'Yes. Yes, I'm fine,' lied Jessie.

Adèle gave her an appraising look, and Jessie knew she'd been rumbled. 'Well, that's good to hear,' said her new friend, with a small smile of collusion. 'But any time you're strapped, give me a shout. There are ways and means in this town, kid. Ways and means. And I don't mean rag-picking.'

Adèle had been right to be sceptical about Jessie's claim that she was flush. Money was scarce, and it was getting scarcer. Jessie had taken to frequenting the pawnbroker's near the Gare Montparnasse so often that she felt like spitting at the motto carved into the stone above the entrance. *Liberté. Égalité. Fraternité.* What a joke!

Her watch had gone, and her Venetian glass beads, and her cashmere coat and – finally – her wedding ring. It had fetched fifty francs, which barely covered the rent on her room for a week. It had been a mistake, she realized now, to have pawned her coat. It had been a benign autumn so far, but winter was just around the corner. How would she manage without an overcoat?

Every week she pawned another item, and every week

her self-esteem sank lower as she handed her pledge to the clerk and took a place on one of the long benches alongside the dozens of other desperate-eyed souls who sat just as she did, watching their hands twist in their laps as they waited for the announcement that would determine how well they'd eat that evening. 'Numéro 32. Will you take forty francs for this?' 'Numéro 33. Ten francs?' 'Numéro 34. One hundred francs.' One hundred! The eyes of the hapless cases would follow the lucky dog as he scuttled out, carefully stowing the wad of notes where no slippery-fingers could get at it. Jessie had long since taken the precaution of sewing her money into her suspender belt when she got back to her room.

Her room was worse – far worse – than the lowest of the low-down places she'd stayed in with Scotch. She had tried hard to make it as homely as she could, but it was disheartening to see how depleted her possessions were. When she'd first moved in she had arranged her books and knick-knacks on the shelf above her bed: the pretty china flasks they'd bought in Certosa, and the silver Apostle spoons Scotch had haggled over in Siena – she'd even festooned the shelf with the handmade lace she'd collected on their travels. But everything was gone now.

Most evenings she'd haul the washstand across the floorboards of the room to barricade the door for the night, before sitting cross-legged on the thin, lumpy mattress and devising works of fiction to send home to her parents. The bed, along with a washstand (for which basic bathing facility she paid the *patronne* extra), a small chest of drawers and a rickety bentwood chair, comprised the sole furnishings of this so-called *chambre meublée*. She'd discovered that the seat of the chair was easy to prise out, and when propped on her knees it doubled nicely as a writing desk.

Her letters home were full of lies about how well she and Scotch were set up – although she always added: *'send letters still to Thos. Cook's in case we should change our address'*. She was teaching herself to cook, she told her mother, and getting better at it all the time.

Fantasizing about food was one of Jessie's favourite ways of passing the time these evenings. She concocted lavish imaginary dinners: soups of carrots and potatoes and leeks enriched with butter and cream, followed by roast chicken or an escalope of veal with *pommes rissolées* and *petits pois*. Or perhaps a *cassoulet* – garlicky pork sausage layered with smoked bacon under creamy, golden-crusted haricot beans and fragrant herbs, served with red wine and a green salad, with cheese or fruit to finish, or perhaps a lemon soufflé. A lemon soufflé! The mere idea of it made her mouth water.

It was ironic to think that just months ago she'd received letters from friends in England concerned about whether she was finding the living too hard on the Continent in the aftermath of the Great War. Was the living too *hard*?! Six months ago they'd stayed in the Pensione Balestri in Florence, where Signora Balestri had prepared the most glorious three-course luncheons from fresh produce. Jessie remembered, too, the afternoon that she and Scotch had feasted on biscuits and chocolate and cherries that they'd carted in their picnic basket all the way up the steep pathway to the monastery on the hill near Galluzzo. And afterwards they'd treated themselves to an aromatic liquor distilled from herbs grown by the Cistercian monks who lived and worked there. That liquor was nectar compared to the nasty absinthe that she drank occasionally now, to help blur the edges.

There'd be no absinthe this evening: she couldn't afford it. The rent was due tomorrow, and she'd have to find something else to pawn. Jessie signed *Love to you both*, then set aside her letter, dragged her suitcase out from under the bed and surveyed the contents. She knew it was useless to try to pawn the silver cigarette case that had been a wedding present from Tuppenny, her best friend back in England, because it had her initials engraved on it. Oh, how she wished that she had her twenty-first-birthday pearls! But they were at home in Mayfair, in a jewellery box in her bedroom – that pretty, airy room with its sprigged wallpaper and chintz curtains and feather bed with the counterpane that smelt of lavender, and, curled up on the pillow, her little cat, Purdy . . .

Her evening dress? Could she pawn that?

The mass of silk from Liberty lay in a drawstring bag at the bottom of the case. It might be worth as much as fifty francs. Why had she not considered pawning it before? She knew why. As she hooked her fingers around the shoulder straps and rose to her feet, the full length of the dress unfurled, the scent of Chypre emerged from its folds, and she remembered how Scotch had brushed aside the tendrils of hair at the nape of her neck so that she could put the finishing touches to her toilette – a ribbon for her neck, from which hung the Egyptian charm. He'd bought for her in the flea market in Rouen because the stall-holder had insisted it would bring them luck, and had presented it to her that Christmas along with her engagement ring. And after she'd adjusted the length of the ribbon to ensure that it accentuated the tantalizing dip between her breasts,

Scotch had re-pinned a curl that had come loose and kissed the hollow behind her ear.

Jessie let the silk gown drop back into the case. She would take it to the pawnbroker tomorrow. That, and the ring with the cabochon sapphire – and maybe the charm, too. It had scarcity value, if nothing else – she'd never seen another like it. Perhaps she should cross the river and ask someone in the Musée du Louvre to have a look at it? It was quite possibly worth a great deal more than Scotch had paid for it, and she should be glad to get rid of it, for it did not seem to bring her luck. In fact, she thought mirthlessly, it had not brought her any luck at all.

CHAPTER EIGHT

BABA

AMERICA 1939

The team that was to put the finishing touches to *The Thief of Bagdad* in Hollywood was transported across the Atlantic in the SS *Duchess of Bedford*. Crossing the ocean was a tortuous business because of the risk of being targeted by German submarines, and the *Duchess* zigzagged her way drunkenly around the coast of Greenland, dodging icebergs and careering up and down in the swells like some colossal fairground ride.

Virtually everyone on board was laid low by seasickness, and for those passengers who were still standing the only topics of conversation were the blasted war, or the likelihood of the ship being torpedoed.

Sabu and Baba took to patrolling the decks together, parading their sea legs past the rows of the afflicted who were marooned on their deckchairs swathed in blankets, and who were obliged to make the occasional undignified dash to the rails to throw up. During their promenades the two friends amused each other by painting word pictures of their childhoods. Sabu conjured India for Baba by describing smells and tastes and colours, and he sang the praises of the elephants he'd cared for, telling her how much wiser and kinder they were than many of the humans he'd known. When she asked him what the defining moment of his boyhood had been, he was unequivocal. 'It was when Robert O'Flaherty cast me in *Elephant Boy*,' he told her. 'I loved that man. He was like a father to me after my own had died. And he was one of the greatest storytellers I have ever met.'

They had reached the end of the companionway. Baba automatically turned to retrace their steps, but Sabu laid a hand on her arm. 'Why not take a breather? It's your turn now, Baba. Tell me how you ended up living with your grandparents.'

'It's a long story.'

'Since we are on a seemingly endless voyage,' he replied, nodding towards the charcoal line of the horizon, 'you have all the time in the world.'

She shrugged. 'I guess.'

'So – "Once upon a time . . ."' prompted Sabu.

'Once upon a time,' she began, 'when I was very little, I lived in France with a couple I called Maman and Papa. They were very kind. They were . . . normal. But they weren't my real parents – I just lived on their farm. I only ever spent a couple of months a year with my real mother, in a villa there.' Baba found herself smiling. 'They were golden – those summers. Really golden. It was a kind of Garden of Eden, everything shimmering in a haze of heat, and the villa seemed like the centre of the world.' She could see it now, as if through the lens of a child's kaleidoscope. 'It was on a hillside, and the garden was always bright with great splotches of colour – mimosa and peonies and lavender – and there were tangerines to eat straight off the trees, and at night it was lit up with lanterns, and if you went down to the sea wall you could hear the wash of the waves below, and there seemed always to be the smell of burning eucalyptus because there were wildfires in summer. And up on the top terrace you'd see where my mother and her friends would congregate around a big table with wicker chairs and an enormous beach parasol – a vivid blue parasol against the pink façade of the house. There seemed always to be people sitting round that table, as if life was one continuous mealtime – a bit like the Mad Hatter's tea party. And sometimes I was allowed wine, and it tasted of sweet meadows so I guess it must have been a Muscat. And everyone smelt of coconut oil, which I shall always associate with sand and sun and sea. It was a sea that was a kind of aching empty blue – nothing like this wretched dull grey ocean.' Baba looked down over the taffrail at the beaten pewter of the Atlantic, and then said, 'I remember one day in particular. Mama was wearing a white tuberose in her hair, and her skin was nearly as brown as yours, Sabu, from all the sunbathing, and she seemed so brimming over with life. They were drinking champagne to celebrate someone's birthday and I remember – I remember going to the bathroom and finding two girls there half naked and giggling, and they told me that they'd spilled wine on their clothes but I know now that they must have been making love. Oh, Sabu – I haven't shocked you, have I?'

He shook his head and gave a wry smile. 'Nothing can shock me after seeing the antics that some of the crew got up to at the wrap party in Denham.'

'Yes. That wasn't elegant. But these girls *were* elegant, somehow.' Baba looked speculative. 'I guess a lot of sex went on in that villa. People were always flirting and dancing, and there was always music playing – the same tune was on the Victrola from morning until night – it was Noël Coward's "Poor Little Rich Girl."'

Sabu gave her his great smile. 'Was she pretty? Your mother.'

'Pretty's the wrong word. She had . . . mystique, I guess you'd call it.'

'What happened to her, Baba?'

'I don't know. Nobody ever told me.' Baba looked down at her hand in Sabu's and started to play with his fingers. 'I was sent away to England, and that was the last night I remember ever having her all to myself. I spent a long time sitting on her lap by the bedroom window, watching the garden turn a darker and darker shade of blue. The moon looked so close that you felt you might unhook it from heaven if you could only stretch your fingers an inch or so higher. And sparrows were squabbling, and she told me that they were squabbling over who had laid the prettiest egg, because nobody had laid a prettier egg than the one I hatched out of. And then she read me the story of the Little Mermaid which I loved because it was so happy and so sad at the same time. And the next day it seemed to me that summer was over because the blue sea had turned grey, and the wind – the mistral – came howling down from the Alps. That was when I was told that my grandpa and grandma wanted to meet me, which was strange because no-one had ever spoken of them before.'

'So that's how you ended up living in London?'

'Yes. But it wasn't long before Grandma got sick of me, and sent me off to boarding school.'

A silence stretched between them, then Sabu said: 'That was a companionable silence, wasn't it? They always call them "companionable silences" in books.'

Baba laughed, then gave a shiver and said: 'Let's go and play snooker. It's too cold to stay out here any more.' She released Sabu's fingers, then linked his arm, and together they strolled in the direction of the games room.

'A companionable silence,' continued Sabu, 'means that we are soulmates. It's funny, isn't it? We come from such completely different backgrounds, yet here we are flung together by fate – the way Abu and the princess in *Thief* were.' He looked up again at the grey sky where big clouds were, like them, scudding westward. 'I wonder what the future holds for us, Baba? What do you hope we may find there?'

'In America?'

'Yes.'

'I hope,' she said, 'that we'll find what Abu goes in search of.'

Sabu smiled. '"Some fun and adventure at last"?'

'You've got it in one, Sabu. Some fun and adventure at last.'

Baba's first abiding memory of Los Angeles was the fluted stone and chrome art deco buildings on Sunset and Wilshire – so modern! so sophisticated! – and her second was of a giant orange with a window cut in it to serve juice through. She was to find that such discrepancies in taste were commonplace in California.

She had been booked into the Beverly Hills Hotel along with Sabu, where she was to stay until she found a place of her own. On the way there, the driver pointed out landmarks: Grauman's Chinese Theater where the stars' hand- and footprints were immortalized on the forecourt, the Café Montmartre – 'Where everyone goes to see and be seen' – and last and most magnificent of all, the Gillette mansion which Gloria Swanson had bought when she was just twenty-three years old. Baba vowed that one day she, too, would live in a dream house like that.

The Beverly Hills was an extravagant, sprawling village of a hotel, and for two days Baba resided in style, looking down on the beautiful villas that lined the drives and avenues on the surrounding hillside. Sadly, her new home was at the other end of the spectrum to these opulent palaces. It was an apartment – not much bigger than her stateroom on the *Duchess* – but it had the advantage of being within walking distance of the studio. And there was a swimming pool in the garden! It was tiny, but for Baba any pool was synonymous with glamour.

The apartment also boasted a small kitchen, which meant that she could save money by catering for herself. Before the war, she and Dorothy had had fun experimenting with Countess Morphy's eclectic cookbook, *Recipes of All Nations*, but in Hollywood, because she had to be mindful of her figure, Baba got by on cottage cheese, radishes and saltines while fantasizing about the countess's Chicken Marengo and Pont Neuf potatoes. She'd read in *Screen Book*'s Lowdown Chart that Carole Lombard, who – at 5′ 5½″ – was exactly the same height as her, weighed in at 112 lb, and Baba was determined to get there too.

CHAPTER NINE

JESSIE

PARIS 1919

Adèle was leaning against the blistered wooden door of the bistro on the ground floor of the Hôtel des Trois Moineaux as Jessie trudged by with a bundle under her arm. Jessie pretended not to see her, but she could hardly ignore the woman when she called out a greeting in her raucous accent. 'Hey! Where are you off to with that bundle, Milady? The laundry? Or the pawnshop?'

Jessie paused. She knew that there was no point in maintaining her veneer of dignity. 'You guessed right second time,' she admitted.

'Tch, tch, tch. Didn't I tell you to come to Adèle if times got hard? Drop in here later and I'll stand you an absinthe.'

Jessie gave her a pallid smile and continued on her way, past the red-sashed workmen and Arab navvies and the rag-pickers and vociferous hawkers and barefoot children chasing orange peel over the cobbles, past the reeking refuse-carts. Sometimes she felt as though she were walking through one of Pieter Breughel's nightmare landscapes, and she wondered if ever again she would dally in Arcadian surroundings or stroll through Constable Country.

She stopped short as she rounded the corner onto the Rue Mouffetard. A small man, dark of hair and sallow of skin, was sitting on the terrace of a café nursing a pastis and talking animatedly to a handsome, saturnine-looking gentleman. She had no idea who the gentleman was, but she had met the small man before.

They had first encountered Count Demetrios in Siena, in the Pensione Saciaro – a former Renaissance palace. She and Scotch had arrived there one evening in the aftermath of an electric storm, and the gardens of the palace had been full of fireflies. Jessie had stepped out onto the balcony of her bedroom to admire the view, and caught sight of a little girl in a white frock performing dance steps on the lawn. She was humming a melody as an accompaniment to her dance, and when Jessie stopped to listen she realized that the song was 'Greensleeves'. When the child had finished she dropped a curtsey, looked up at the balcony and announced in solemn tones: 'An English song for a beautiful English lady.'

Jessie laughed and clapped her hands. 'Thank you kindly,' she called down to the child, and then Count Demetrios had risen from the bench on which he had been sitting and smiled up at her. 'Good evening, Madame,' he said, removing his hat and executing a neat bow. 'Would you care to join me and my daughter for a refreshment?'

'How did your little girl guess that I was English?' Jessie asked him as they sat together at the wrought-iron table in the garden ten minutes later. She and Scotch had been exchanging pleasantries with him over a carafe of Chianti, and had found out that this middle-aged aristocrat was, like them, travelling through Europe on a painting holiday. He appeared to be a most erudite man, and was very impressed upon learning that Jesse had studied English at Cambridge.

'Coincidentally, I myself am married to a member of a Cambridgeshire family, he told her.'

'Your wife is British?' said Jessie, surprised. 'Is she here?'

'Alas, no. She remains in Greece.' The count shook his head sorrowfully. 'She is unable to travel. She suffers from heart disease.'

'Oh – how dreadful! She must miss you and her daughter terribly.'

'Carlotta is, in fact, not our real daughter – although of course we consider her to be part of the family.' He gazed fondly across the garden at Carlotta, who was kneeling on the path constructing a racetrack for snails from pebbles.

'She is a remarkably beautiful child,' said Jessie.

'The face of an angel, indeed. But an angel with a tragic history.' The count sighed lugubriously.

'Oh?' Jessie was instantly curious.

'Yes, indeed. Her mother and her father – a dear friend – went missing at the beginning of the war, and the baby was taken to Greece where she was given over to my wife and my good self. The poor mite was suffering from malnutrition, but we nursed her back to health and have cared for her ever since.'

'You're clearly a good father to her, sir,' observed Scotch. 'She has exquisite manners.'

'Aha! She can be a little minx, though, that Carlotta. And it is past her bedtime.' The count glanced at his fob watch, then took up his cane and raised it to attract the child's attention. 'Carlotta!' he called. 'Desist from your snail racing and come and say goodnight to our new friends.'

The child looked up from her game and gave her angelic smile. 'All right, naughty boy,' she called back in her sweetly accented voice. 'I'll come in a minute.'

'What did she call you?' asked Scotch, amused.

'It's her nickname for me – and for any man she takes a fancy to,' said the count. 'She calls us all "naughty boys".' He knocked back the remains of his Chianti, rose to his feet and tucked his cane under his arm. 'Carlotta,' he said, in rather firmer tones. 'Bedtime. Now.'

On the rue Mouffetard, Demetrios was sitting in half-profile with his back to her, but there was no mistaking his identity. The monocle, which magnified the glint in his hooded eyes. The hair sleeked back from his high forehead with pomade. The silver-topped cane that he customarily placed between his legs to lean upon as he spoke – all these affectations were present and correct, and all of them were familiar to Jessie.

She stood in a doorway, clutching her bundle to her chest. Demetrios had been good to her and Scotch, although there had been something about him that they had found unsettling. She remembered how she'd described him in a letter to her parents:

The Greek is a queer fish – very autocratic and yet artistic. He speaks familiarly about all sorts of people all over Europe and, we think, is an exile from Greece owing to political trouble.

But Demetrios had connections. He might be in a position to help Jessie now, find her some kind of employment that would pay well enough to liberate her from the hellhole that was the Hôtel des Trois Moineaux.

She studied him from her vantage point in the shop doorway. He looked prosperous, dapper, well-fed. His younger companion, too, looked prosperous, but unlike Demetrios, he was no dandy. If anything, his appearance verged on the negligent. The angle of his hat, the careless way his tie was knotted, the cigarette ash on his lapel were the sartorial equivalent of a Gallic shrug.

As Jessie watched, he rose to his feet and bade Demetrios farewell. Oh God, oh God – what should she do? Should she approach the count? Would he remember her if she did? She knew her appearance had altered almost beyond recognition. Weeks of a hand-to-mouth existence had robbed her of the bloom of a woman in love, the bloom she had taken for granted last month. She looked haggard now, she knew, even a little disreputable. Demetrios might find it embarrassing to be accosted on the street by a woman who at a push could be mistaken for a beggar.

The younger gentleman had moved off. Demetrios was settling up with the *garçon*. It was now or never. Jessie pinched her cheeks to lend them a little colour, adjusted the brim of her hat and raised her chin, then stepped jauntily out along the pavement.

Demetrios was retrieving his cane from where he had leaned it against the back of his chair just as Jessie drew abreast of him. 'Count Demetrios!' she exclaimed in a delighted voice. 'What a pleasant surprise!'

The count turned, tucking his cane under his arm. 'Mademoiselle?' he said in a note of polite enquiry, then recognition dawned on his face. '*Mais, non! C'est Madame, naturellement.* Charmed to see you again.'

He executed a neat bow and extended his hand. Before she took it, Jessie saw the count's sharp eyes flicker with interest, and knew he had registered her missing wedding ring. He scooped up her right hand and raised it to his lips.

'How well you look,' he said, gallantly. 'Please – take a seat. Might you be so kind as to partake of a little refreshment?'

'That would be delightful, Count,' she said.

He raised a hand, snapped his fingers imperiously. '*Garçon! Encore ici, s'il vous plaît.* What will you have, Madame?'

Jessie sat down in the chair the waiter drew out for her. 'A brandy and soda would be very welcome.'

'*Deux fines à l'eau,*' Count Demetrios told the waiter. Then he dropped into the chair opposite her and gave her a speculative look before leaning forward with both hands wrapped round the silver knob of his cane. 'Well, Madame,' he said, with an urbane smile. 'It would seem that your circumstances have changed since we last met. Would you care to tell Count Demetrios all about it?'

CHAPTER TEN

BABA

HOLLYWOOD 1939

'Sabu!' said Baba, picking up the phone. 'I was just about to call you! Answer this for me. Who is the very successful star whose restless spirit of adventure took him to strange places?'

'What?'

'I'm doing a quiz in *Silver Screen*. I can win a Wittnauer's watch worth twenty-five dollars.'

'Forget about that. I'm calling with news for you. Ziggy Stein is looking for a new leading lady. A British one.'

Baba dropped her magazine. 'No kidding!'

'No kidding. Apparently he's fed up with having to borrow English stars from other studios so he's decided to create one of his own.'

'How do I get to meet him?'

'He's giving a pool party tomorrow. I'm invited, and so are you.'

'Sabutage! You angel.'

'I'll have my driver pick you up around one o'clock, OK?'

'You betcha!'

'And Baba?'

'Yeah?'

'Try to refrain from saying things like "No kidding!" and "You betcha!" You've got to sound British.'

'Very well, Sabu. What marvellous weather we're having.'

'That's more like it. See you tomorrow.'

Baba smiled as she put the phone down.

Ziggy Stein! Ziggy Stein was one of the most powerful players in Hollywood. When he'd arrived in LA back in the twenties he had been an assistant producer of B-feature westerns, but because he had devised a way of shooting two pictures simultaneously – thereby slicing production costs almost in half and endearing himself to the money men – he had risen through the ranks and formed his own production company, Orion, in 1931. Baba had, of course, sent a mug shot to Orion, but then she'd sent mug shots to all the major studios and hadn't heard back from any of them.

However, what Sabu had told her made sense. British stars were the latest accessory for a Hollywood hotshot. Selznick had Vivien Leigh; Korda, Merle Oberon, and Stromberg had just signed Maureen O'Sullivan for *Pride and Prejudice*.

Baba looked out her most alluring bathing suit, shaved her armpits, did her calisthenics, cold-creamed her face and had an early night.

She wore the bathing suit under floral-printed cropped slacks, teamed with a pair of high cork sandals and a white bolero jacket. And then she changed her mind and substituted a rather more demure pleated skirt for the slacks, flat pumps for the platforms, and added a string of pearls. English girls had a reputation for being demure, after all, and if Mr Stein was looking for glamour, she'd be able to give him a taste of *that* once he saw her by his pool in her bathing suit.

Sabu picked her up in his chauffeur-driven Cadillac, and they headed for the Hollywood Hills in the golden-yellow California sunshine.

'It's like the Pink Palace in *Thief*,' Sabu remarked, as they rolled up the driveway of Mr Stein's house. And indeed, the house was the last word in ersatz oriental glamour, with stuccoed walls and turrets and minarets everywhere.

Limousines lined the driveway. 'Look, look!' cried Baba, as a stout man with an enormous cigar between his teeth emerged from a white Packard Sedan. 'He's *got* to be some-one important.'

'Every man you meet here today will claim to be some-one important, Baba. They'll tell you that they have the perfect role for you – even if they've never set foot in a studio in their lives. They'll suggest some publicity shots of you in your bathing suit, and then they'll invite you out to dinner. And after dinner they'll want you to join them for a nightcap in their apartment.'

'How do you know? Surely you can't have had people come on to you?'

Sabu gave her an old-fashioned look. 'At least I'm in the fortunate position of being able to tell them to get lost. Be warned, Baba. You're a gazelle in the sights of a hunter.' He leaned forward to address the chauffeur. 'You can let us out here, please,' he said.

'Yes, sir,' said the chauffeur, and not for the first time Baba smiled at the notion of her fifteen-year-old friend being called 'sir'.

The moment Sabu emerged from the car, he was hauled

off by someone who wanted him to meet the columnist for the *LA Times*, so, trying to look casual, Baba walked into the grand hallway of the house, which was full of people drinking and talking and laughing. So determined was she to find some opportunity to impress the great Ziggy Stein, that she decided the best thing to do was to brazen things out and not allow herself to be fazed.

Since it was a pool party, Baba told herself it would be logical to find Mr Stein by the pool. She hadn't a clue where the pool might be, but, having seen a photograph of Ziggy Stein at the Oscars sporting a tux and a bow tie, she had a vague idea what he looked like: middle-aged, overweight, avuncular and balding. But, she realized as she looked around now, there were an awful lot of middle-aged, overweight, avuncular, balding men at this party. Which one was the legendary Ziggy?

She meandered through a succession of rooms – a billiard room, a parlour and a library – before spotting a pair of enormous latticed windows that opened onto the poolside. All around the pool people in swimming costumes were jumping in and out of the water, splashing and shouting and showing off. Baba felt ridiculously out of place in her pleated skirt and pearls, but she carried on until she happened upon a waiter. 'Excuse me, would you happen to know if Mr Stein is here?' she asked.

The waiter turned and flashed her a grin before producing a horn from behind his back, tooting it in her face, waggling his tongue at her and scarpering.

'Ha ha ha!' trilled a girl wearing a satin bathing costume trimmed with artificial flowers. 'You just got pranked by Harpo Marx!'

Baba gave a wan smile, then went back into the house

and walked upstairs. In all the bedrooms gaggles of beautiful girls were powdering their noses and applying lipstick and babbling like brooks – but Baba ignored them with as much feigned indifference as they ignored her. After negotiating a maze of corridors, she made her way back to the grand staircase that led down to the hall. There was no sign of Mr Stein anywhere, and she was starting to lose her nerve. Should she just give up and go home?

Out in the garden she thought she had to be dreaming as she walked past the tennis court. There was Ronald Colman knocking a ball about with Joan Fontaine! She was so overwhelmed that she couldn't help herself. 'Look who it is!' she said in an awed voice to a man in baggy swim trunks and a sun hat who was spraying bougainvillaea with a hosepipe.

The man turned to her and smiled. 'I guess that underneath it all stars are just regular folks, Miss, like you and me.'

'It's funny, isn't it? Five minutes ago I mistook Harpo Marx for a waiter.'

'You ain't seen nothin' yet,' he said. 'Carole Lombard's up next, playing with David Niven.'

Baba's hands flew to her mouth. 'Carole Lombard?' she squeaked. 'And David *Niven*? My fiancé was at school with him. They used to go beagling together.'

'Beagling?'

'Yes – you know, the dogs. It's like fox-hunting, only for hares. I always thought it was awfully cruel, until I heard that the Mitfords hunted their own children.'

The gardener looked aghast. 'With beagles?'

'With bloodhounds, actually. For fun.'

'You British sure have a strange sense of humour. You *are* British, right?'

'Yes.'

'This your first time in America?'

Baba nodded. 'I came over with *The Thief of Bagdad*, Mr Korda's film.'

'So you're an actress?'

'I'd like to be, but I've only been on stage once, in a production of *As You Like It*.' The gardener looked blank, so Baba added, 'That's Shakespeare.'

'The guy who wrote "to be or not to be"?'

'Yes. We had to learn all of Hamlet's soliloquies by heart at school.'

'Lucky you.'

Baba gave him a sceptical look, but he clearly wasn't joking, because he added, 'I never had the benefit of a regular education, Miss.'

'Oh, I wouldn't worry about that. It's not all it's cracked up to be, you know. I'd much rather have learned something useful, like gardening. What a spiffing job you have, out in the California sunshine all day.'

The gardener looked tickled pink. 'We're all gardeners in life, Miss. The best place to find God is in a garden.'

On the tennis court, Ronald Colman served an ace.

'Oh – good shot!' cried Baba.

'You fancy seeing Miss Fontaine's new film, Miss?' said the gardener.

'*Rebecca*? I should love to see it.'

'There's an advance screening later today, in the projection room.'

'Thanks so much for the tip-off.' She glanced at her

watch. 'I must find my friend, and tell him. It's a pleasure to have met you.'

'Goodbye, Miss.' The gardener winked and tipped his hat at her, then went on with his watering.

Sabu was sitting in a pergola talking to a woman wearing an outrageous cartwheel of straw on her head. Baba hovered, hoping that he'd catch sight of her in his peripheral vision. Just as his companion was rising regally to her feet, he beckoned Baba over.

She approached, stapling on a smile. The woman turned towards her and Baba recognized her immediately.

Hedda Hopper was a pretty, autocratic woman of around fifty years old, so thin it looked as if you could break her in half. She was also the most important person Baba had yet met in Hollywood. The woman could make or break an actor's career with a single stroke of her pen.

'Miss Hedda Hopper, may I present—'

'Lisa La Touche,' Baba interjected. She didn't want Sabu to introduce her as Baba McLeod. It was time for Lisa to take centre stage. 'I'm charmed to meet you, Miss Hopper.' She extended a hand, trying to make her handshake just right – firm, but not too firm.

'Likewise,' said Miss Hopper, raking her eyes over Baba, as if taking a mental photograph. 'You're British?'

'Yes,' said Baba. 'From London.'

'I adore London,' Hedda remarked. 'It's an absolutely marvellous city. The British Museum. Buckingham Palace.'

'Indeed,' Baba replied uncertainly.

'Well, welcome to Hollywood,' said Hedda, not sounding welcoming at all. 'I suppose you'll be joining the Hollywood Raj.'

'I beg your pardon?'

'The Hollywood Raj. It's a club for ex-pat British actors. They celebrate St George's Day, play cricket, that kind of thing. David Niven's a member – you should talk to him. He's here today.'

'Thank you so much for the advice, Miss Hopper!'

'Good luck. You'll need it. It was delightful to meet you, Sabu,' she added, before turning and marching off magisterially across the croquet lawn. Her high heels left little pockmarks in the grass as she walked, as if she was stabbing it with daggers.

Lisa and Sabu exchanged looks of mock-trepidation, then clutched each other and burst out laughing.

Later, they joined Hollywood royalty in Mr Stein's projection room. Down from the ceiling the screen came, and as Baba was looking around with awe at the stars sitting around like everyday folk, the door opened and the gardener walked in. Except this time he wasn't wearing swimming trunks and a sun hat, he was wearing dark pleated trousers and a silk shirt that had to be from Sulka.

'What's the gardener doing here?' Baba asked Sabu.

'That's not the gardener,' Sabu told her. 'That's Ziggy Stein.'

CHAPTER ELEVEN

JESSIE

PARIS 1919

Over brandy and sodas and fragrant Turkish cigarettes Jessie told Count Demetrios her tale of woe: how she'd woken in the Hôtel Simonet in Finistère one grey morning at the end of summer to find Scotch gone.

'Gone? You mean he abandoned you?'

'Yes.'

'Despicable! That kind of conduct's beneath contempt. Where did he go?'

'I haven't an idea.' That was a lie. She knew only too well that Scotch had gone to Chambéry, to the Italian girl.

'And why did you decide to come here to Paris, instead of returning to your family in England?'

'I – I suppose I rather hoped that Scotch might drift back here.'

'Unlikely. My guess would be that he has gone to Corfu. He expressed an inordinate interest when I suggested that I could introduce him to some patrons there. There's money to be made in the wake of the war, if you know where to look for it, and he knows that the mere mention of my name will open doors for him. Do your parents know that you are alone in Paris, Madame?'

'No.'

'Why haven't you told them?'

'I couldn't bear the shame, Count. My mother had warned me against marrying Scotch, and I didn't listen to her.'

'Why didn't she want you to marry him?'

'Because we're from completely different backgrounds. She said I'd regret it, and sadly, it would appear that she was right.'

'Have you taken a job of work?'

'Yes. As an artist's model, for twenty francs a day.'

The count sucked in his breath. 'Twenty francs! *Tiens!* How do you manage?'

Jessie shrugged. 'I don't know. I've been living on bread and cheese and *Bouillon Zip*.'

'*Bouillon Zip?* That disgusting packet soup?'

'It's cheap.'

The count gave her a look of assessment, then raised his hand and clicked his fingers peremptorily. '*Garçon!* The menu, if you please.' He turned back to Jessie. 'Now, Madame. What would you care to eat?'

'Oh, really – I couldn't accept—'

'You must. I insist.'

Jessie bit her lip. The image of her most cherished fantasy meal – escalope of veal with *pommes rissolés* and *petits pois* – swam before her mind's eye. Oh, God! She realized now that she hadn't had a decent meal for months – not since Florence. She'd been too sick with worry when Scotch had fallen ill in Chambéry to look after herself properly; her chief concern then had been to make sure that *he'd* been well fed.

A waiter was approaching with a menu. Another bore

aloft a dish of *boeuf bourguignon* so aromatic that Jessie thought she might pass out. Her pride insisted that she couldn't accept the count's hospitality, but her stomach was begging her to. It felt as if it was turning inside out with hunger. With an encouraging smile, Count Demetrios slid the menu across the table, and to her horror she found herself bursting into tears.

'My dear! What's wrong?' asked the count.

'I'm pregnant,' she blurted out. 'I'm expecting Scotch's baby.'

Demetrios said nothing for a moment or two. He gave her a pensive look, then gently laid his hand over hers. 'Then you most certainly cannot refuse my offer of a square meal,' he said, 'if you are eating for two.'

'Oh!' His solicitude made her want to cry harder.

'There, there, *pauvre petite*. Dry your tears.' Count Demetrios handed her a big linen handkerchief. And when she'd cried herself out and blown her nose, he leaned back in his chair, shook his head mournfully and said: 'Things have come to a pretty pass. It is imperative that we get some food inside you – and none of your protests,' he added, as she made to object once more. 'I am putting my foot down, as they say. *Garçon!*'

Jessie consulted the menu briefly, avidly, and then, remembering her manners, requested the count to order for her. *Bouillabaisse*, to be followed by *fricandeau* of veal, with sorrel and asparagus.

'And bring some spinach,' the count instructed the waiter, before resuming his scrutiny of her. 'You look peaky, young lady. You must not allow yourself to become deficient in iron.'

'You're so kind,' she said. 'So very, very kind.'

'*De rien.*' He raised his glass. 'Here's to you – and to your baby. When are you due?'

'In April.' Jessie made a little moue. 'I'll start to show in a couple of months, and that will be bad news.'

'How so?'

'I'll be out of a job – and out of lodgings as well. Madame Perron, the *patronne* of my hotel, allows no women with children to lodge there. As soon as she finds out I'm expecting, I'll be out on the street.'

'Well, we simply cannot allow that to happen. Where are you residing?'

'In the Hôtel des Trois Moineaux, on the rue du Coq d'Or.'

'That dosshouse!' Count Demetrios looked genuinely aghast. 'Forgive my language, Madame, but that is no place for a young gentlewoman like you. We must get you out of there at once.'

'But I can't afford anywhere better.'

He looked at her thoughtfully, and his eyes appeared more hooded than ever. 'I have a suggestion to make, Madame—'

'Jessie, please.'

'Jessie.' He acknowledged her Christian name with a small incline of his head. 'I may be in a position to procure some rather more lucrative work for you.'

She gave him a sceptical look. 'What kind of lucrative work can a woman with child expect to get?'

The count tapped the side of his nose. 'You'd be surprised. I have a friend – a very talented young artist – who has expressed dissatisfaction with his recent work. He goes from one commission to the next, earning a lot of money in the process, but he is currently suffering from feelings of *ennui* and chronic disillusion. He has had enough of "churning out" – as he calls it – the society portraits that *le tout Paris* is clamouring for, and he's looking for someone fresh and unspoiled to sit for him. I think I might persuade Monsieur Lantier—'

Jessie's jaw dropped. 'Not Gervaise Lantier?'

'Yes. You know him?'

'No, but I know *of* him. Scotch told me that he sells every canvas almost before it's touch-dry. Is that an exaggeration?'

'That is no exaggeration – Monsieur Lantier is a wealthy man. But is he a happy man? That remains to be seen.' Amused at her incredulity, the count lit up a cigarette and blew out a plume of smoke. 'Coincidentally, I met Monsieur earlier today, and he extended an invitation to me to come to a soirée this evening, at the Boulevard Péreire. Might you care to join me?'

She looked doubtful. 'What kind of a soirée?'

'The comtesse de Valéry holds a salon in her apartment on the first Friday of every month. Many of the cultural and intellectual élite of Paris attend.'

'So it's a very swagger event?' she asked.

'Black tie.'

That settled it, then. She could not go, simply because she had nothing to wear.

'I have no —' she began, then her gaze fell on the bundle at her feet which contained the silk gown that she had last worn at Christmas.

She remembered how they'd cleared the hotel sitting room of furniture that night in Rouen – there'd been charades and singing and musical chairs – and decorated it with Chinese lanterns and paper festoons and holly and mistletoe. And they'd danced until they were breathless – old-fashioned dances like waltzes and lancers and reels – and the silk of her gown had swirled round her in a blur of colour and motion. Much later, Scotch had taken her out into the garden for air and his breath had been a brush stroke of spectral mist in the freezing night as he'd leaned down to kiss her mouth . . .

Jessie bit her lip. Would the gown pass muster at such a sophisticated gathering? For the first time since she'd arrived in Paris she had an opportunity to earn decent money and make important contacts. If she declined the count's invitation she'd be back in the Hôtel des Trois Moineaux, breathing in the stench that wafted through the narrow corridors, and listening to the racking bark of the consumptive youth who lived on the floor above.

She couldn't do it. She *couldn't* go back to a place where cockroaches were her room-mates, and where there was fighting in the street outside her window every night. She couldn't go back to a place where lecherous wet-lipped types ogled her every time she passed them on the stairs, and where her Serbian neighbour had taken to burning sulphur to drive off his lice. Her Scripture teacher at school had told her that hell smelt of sulphur, and Jessie was sick to death of living in hell.

She smiled across the table at Count Demetrios. 'I think,' she said, 'that I should be delighted to accompany you this evening.'

An hour later Jessie had finished her soup, her veal, her vegetables, and her heavenly pineapple fritters.

'Thank you from the bottom of my heart,' she told the

count. 'I've been dreaming about that kind of food for ages.'

'I'm delighted you enjoyed it.' He gave her a brief smile, then signalled for the bill. When he had settled up he turned back to her, and Jessie noticed with a pang of apprehension that his expression was grave. 'Madame,' he said. 'I do not know how to ask this question without appearing discourteous – ill-bred, even – but ask it I must. It is clear that you have fallen on extremely hard times. May I enquire as to whether you have the correct attire for a social event of the kind to which I am to escort you?'

Jessie faltered. The Dutch courage instilled by the cognac was beginning to desert her. 'I have – an evening dress. It is of the finest silk from Liberty of London.'

'A most elegant establishment.' The count directed his gaze at her tanned legs.

'But I have no . . . no stockings.'

'Well,' said the count. 'We must remedy that. Let us make our way to the Boulevard Saint-Germain to do a little shopping.'

'I have no money, Count!'

'Allow me to make a gift of the stockings to you.'

'No!'

His eyes narrowed, and he assumed his autocratic air. 'Madame. You must permit me at this stage of the game to assist you in any way that I can. I myself shall look upon the purchase of stockings for you as an investment. If I say so myself, I predict a successful outcome to this little experiment of mine.'

'Experiment?'

'Monsieur Lantier is a young man, Madame. But already his palate is jaded. I told you I intend to whet his appetite for something fresh and new. If you refuse my help, I cannot interest him in employing you because, Madame, if you have no stockings, you cannot go where polite society congregates. It is as simple as that.'

Jessie frowned, considering.

'Madame, Madame!' He was leaning towards her, hands clasped over the handle of his cane, and his tone was hectoring, now. 'You can repay me any money I expend in your interest another time. Right now, we must strike while the iron is hot. Otherwise you are – as they say – in the soup, are you not?'

The truth of his words was undeniable. She'd have to accept for there was no alternative. If it transpired that there was anything duplicitous about the 'game' he was playing, she would finally admit defeat, go home, have her baby and live in that mausoleum in Mayfair for the rest of her life. In the meantime, she had to make good use of any opportunities that came her way.

'You are very kind, Count Demetrios. And I vow that I will pay you back one day. I mean that.'

The count waved a dismissive hand. '*Que sera, sera.* But I have one more question, Madame, if you can forgive me for this gross intrusion. I may hazard a guess that you no longer have any jewellery?'

She gave a wry smile. 'Not even paste. Apart from my engagement ring, and that doesn't count as jewellery.' She had been loath to pawn the ring, since that and the charm were the only gifts she had ever received from Scotch. But she no longer had room for sentimentality in her life. 'It's a cabochon sapphire.'

He took hold of her left hand. 'But your wedding ring is gone.'

'Yes.'

'In that case, may I make a suggestion, Madame?'

'Of course you may, Count.'

'With your permission, I shall introduce you tomorrow evening as Mademoiselle Beaufoy. Beaufoy was your maiden name, as I recall?'

'Yes.'

'Then, if you have no objection, I think we may concoct a small fiction concerning your marital status.'

'But when my baby starts to show—'

'Trust me. We'll play that card when we have to.' He rose from his seat and as he held his arm out to her his eyes lit upon the little jade charm that rested upon her breast-bone. 'What an unusual amulet,' he said. 'It is a replica of the god Anubis, is it not?'

'I've no idea,' confessed Jessie. 'I don't know much about Egyptian mythology.'

'It is he,' pronounced the count. 'He is the only god with the head of a jackal.'

'And he represents . . . ?'

The count gave her a look of mock trepidation. 'He was their revered mortuary god, Mademoiselle Beaufoy.' he said. 'Anubis was the ancient Egyptian god of the Dead.'

He took her to the Boulevard Saint-Germain to buy her stockings. And because Jessie confessed that she had no shoes other than the down-at-heel T-bars she was wearing, he bought her a pair of kid dancing pumps, and a small embroidered evening bag to go with them.

Afterwards they stood on the pavement and the count jotted down on the back of his calling card details of where they were to meet the following evening. Jessie watched the *boulevardiers* passing on their way to *thés dansants*, or matinées or concerts, and she felt like a spectator at a glittering carnival. She could have been a million miles away from the Dickensian slums she had sloped through just hours earlier.

'I will repay you some day,' promised Jessie, as she pocketed his card. 'Some day I will make sure you are rewarded for your generosity.'

To which the count's gallant response was again, *'Que sera, sera.'*

Just then, a motor car passed, a gleaming green Bugatti. At the wheel sat a woman with flame-red hair, shingled in the latest fashion. Her style was somewhere between louche and patrician. Her complexion was chalk-white, her lips vermilion, her emerald eyes were rimmed thickly with black kohl. She wore a chartreuse velvet cinema cape and a matching turban, the tasselled ends of which were artlessly swathed around her neck.

Count Demetrios raised his hat to her, and the woman acknowledged the gesture with a peremptory incline of her head.

'Who is she?' enquired a stupefied Jessie.

'The Marchesa Casati. Lantier painted her portrait last month.'

'She's an example of the kind of women Monsieur Lantier has been painting?'

The count looked down at her and quirked an eyebrow. 'Not for much longer, Mademoiselle Beaufoy,' he said, tucking his cane under his arm and crooking an elbow for her to take. 'Not if your humble servant has anything to do with it.'

Jessie smiled back at him as they stepped out along the

pavement. Perhaps, *perhaps* her luck was changing? Earlier today she had left the Hôtel des Trois Moineaux prepared to swap the last of her valuables for the price of a decent meal. Now her belly was full, she was nicely warm and fuzzy with wine, and she had stockings, at last! Brand new silk stockings *de premier choix*! And shoes to dance in, and a little bag to match!

Tonight she would wear again the gown that had been made specially for her from yards and yards of exquisitely patterned silk crêpe-de-Chine. The last time she had worn it – just weeks after the Armistice – the words on everyone's lips had been *liberté, égalité, fraternité*. Equality and fraternity were no longer priority; her socialist principles belonged to to the past. But liberty – the freedom to start anew, to take another course in life – *that* mattered. A year ago Jessie had been an unmarried woman; she was, to all intents and purposes, an unmarried woman now and today she had been given an opportunity for advancement.

Her hand went to her throat, and as she fingered the trinket chanced upon by Scotch in a Rouen curiosity shop, Jessie prayed that it might bring good fortune, after all.

CHAPTER TWELVE

BABA

HOLLYWOOD 1939

After the screening of *Rebecca*, Baba braced herself to approach Mr Stein.

'I'm frightfully sorry, sir, for twittering on at you earlier,' she said with a rueful smile. 'I'm afraid to say I didn't recognize you.'

'That's the first time anyone's talked to me without trying to brown-nose me for *years*!' Mr Stein sucked on his cigar and gave her an appraising look. 'Tell me this. Can you swim, kid?'

'Yes sir, I can.'

'You're not just bullshitting me, are you?'

'Why would I do that, sir?'

'Most actresses would claim they can juggle and sing an aria while riding a horse bareback and blindfolded.'

'I can put my hand on my heart and say that I've been swimming since an early age, sir. My doctor prescribed it when I was diagnosed with scoliosis of the spine. *Mild* scoliosis,' she added quickly, as she saw Ziggy's eyes take in her posture.

'Scoliosis, hmm? My daughter has that, but she's scared of the water.'

'Try telling her the story of the Little Mermaid. I used to imagine I was a mermaid when I took swimming lessons.'

'I might just do that. It's clearly worked for you.' Reaching into his pocket, he handed her a card. 'Phone my secretary tomorrow,' he said. 'Ask her to get some sides off to you in the mail.'

'I'm sorry, sir, I don't know what you mean by sides.'

'Sides are script pages for test purposes.'

Baba looked blank.

'You *are* interested in being in movies, ain't ya?'

'Oh, yes – I most certainly am, sir!'

'I'll tell her to set up a test for you some time next week.' Mr Stein turned on his heel, shot his cuffs, and was collared at once by a Lana Turner lookalike who had been loitering with intent.

Reeling, Baba turned to find herself face to face with an elegant gentleman of military bearing.

'Good evening,' he said in an impeccable upper-crust drawl. 'Allow me to introduce myself. I'm—'

'David Niven,' she supplied.

'And if I am not mistaken you are young Baba MacLeod, come all the way from London. Richard told me to look out for the new Brit in town, and you're positively wet behind the ears.'

'Actually, Mr Niven, I've changed my name.'

'Oh? Richard didn't mention that.'

'He doesn't know yet.'

'I see. And what might your *nom de guerre* be?'

'Lisa La Touche. You don't think it's silly?'

'It's no sillier than any other you might have chosen.

115

Indeed, I've heard a lot sillier. Vivien Leigh's agent wanted to call her "April Morn". Welcome to Hollywood, Miss La Touche.'

'Thank you. Please call me Lisa.'

'And you may call me David. Now we're perfectly cosy. You must have tea with me some day soon, and I'll fill you in on all the ex-pat gossip.'

'I'd love that!'

'Here's a nugget for openers. Did you know that Larry Olivier has such skinny legs that he has to pad them when he wears tights?'

'No!'

'And Merle Oberon had to sterilize her face after doing love scenes with him? And that Claudette Colbert insists on only ever being filmed from the left because she thinks her right profile is ugly?'

'Oh!' said Baba with a laugh. 'It's going to be such fun knowing you!'

'You have Richard to thank for that. I don't look out for just anyone, you know. Your fiancé was the only person at Stowe who didn't tease me about my ears. You're engaged to a thoroughly decent chap.'

'Yes, I am,' Lisa agreed meekly.

David Niven caught the eye of a passing flunkey, and their champagne saucers were instantly replenished.

'Now that we've been introduced,' he said, chinking his glass against hers, 'let's get down to brass tacks. Have you found work yet?'

'No. But I have an audition next week with Mr Stein.'

'Congratulations. When I first came here, I was labelled Anglo-Saxon Type Number 2008 in Central Casting. I hope you're aiming a little higher than that.'

'Goodness, I'd consider myself very lucky to even get work as an extra.'

'I received some very good advice early on in my career. From no less than the King himself.'

'You mean, Mr Gable?'

'Yes,' he said, handing her his card. 'He's never taken his success for granted and he's a great believer in reciprocity. So any time you need the benefit of my words of wisdom, I'd be glad to help.'

'Thank you! Everybody's been so kind to me today.'

'Milk it for all it's worth. Those kind of days are rare here.'

'I'll remember that,' said Lisa earnestly.

'You're sweet.' And David gave her an amused look and bade her farewell before rejoining his glamorous tennis partner, Carole Lombard, who had changed into the kind of halter-necked satin lounging pyjamas that Lisa had always dreamed of wearing.

She took a thoughtful sip of champagne. Imagine being tagged 'Anglo-Saxon Type Number 2008', or lumped with a name like 'April Morn'! Imagine being as beautiful as Claudette Colbert and yet be panicky about the way you photographed! Dorothy might have written off Baba's persona as being vulgor, but nobody here had scoffed at her yet. So far – touch wood – Lisa La Touche seemed to have a canny knack for turning base metal into gold.

The picture Lisa was to test for was called *Crimson Lake*, a 'B' feature set in the roaring twenties with a screenplay by some has-been called Scott Fitzgerald. The 'sides' she received read as follows:

INT. GABRIEL'S STUDIO. DAY.

A comfortable room, but functional, too. The day bed boasts an intricately wrought Turkish counterpane; there are canvases stacked against the walls. On a side table two crystal glasses stand beside a bottle of wine. SUNLIGHT streams through the skylight into the room. From outside, we hear the crash of the OCEAN. DAPHNE and GABRIEL are at work – Daphne holding a pose. GABRIEL is standing at his easel, alongside which is a trestle table littered with painterly paraphernalia.

GABRIEL

You've held that pose for forty minutes now, and we're losing light. Perhaps it's time we finished for the day. Wine?

DAPHNE

Thank you.

[DAPHNE stretches as GABRIEL moves to the side table and pours wine. He hands DAPHNE a glass, then moves to the day bed.]

DAPHNE

Mud in your eye.

[She drinks.]

GABRIEL

You sure can put it away, honey. You must have been liquored to the ears the other evening.

DAPHNE

Never seen a girl do cartwheels before?

GABRIEL

I've never seen a duchess do cartwheels before. And certainly not along a sea wall.

DAPHNE

Easy peasy. Anyway, I'm not a duchess, I'm a countess.

[GABRIEL reaches out a hand and proceeds to unravel her coiffure.]

GABRIEL

Your hair is magnificent – though I'm not sure I have the colour right yet. I'll need to mix in a little more Raw Sienna. I trust you've never considered having it bobbed?

DAPHNE

Are you crazy? Daphne Bolingbroke doesn't follow trends, she sets them.

[GABRIEL smiles. He leans in and kisses her lightly on the lips.]

DAPHNE

Can't you stop that damn ocean outside?

GABRIEL sets down his glass. They kiss again, with increasing ardour. He breaks the kiss and they look at each other for a long moment, registering their powerful mutual attraction.

[DISSOLVE TO:]

* * *

Lisa hadn't a clue what the scene dissolved to, and cared less. Her entire focus was on those half dozen lines – or, more importantly, their subtext.

For the next few days, she studied the script over and over and allowed herself to hope. She had all the qualifications for the role of Daphne: she had the hair, the accent – and she thought she just might have the talent.

On the morning of the test she checked in to Hair and Make-up. Her hair was plaited and pinned, her face painted with pale foundation, her eyes rimmed with heavy kohl, and the curve of her lips emphasized with the ruby red Max Factor.

In Wardrobe she was kitted out in slinky bias-cut satin, the kind Jean Harlow had made famous. So close-fitting was the gown that it was clear that she could not wear her girdle underneath. In fact, the wardrobe girl advised her, it would be better if she wore no undergarments at all. Displaying a nonchalance she did not feel, Lisa returned to her changing cubicle and peeled off her underclothes.

The dress was a little tight over her breasts – and it was still warm from the previous actress who had tested. Lisa wondered how many other hopefuls were being considered for the role. Again and again she went over her lines, convinced that nerves would send them spinning from her brain; again and again she replayed in her head the advice that Amy, Mr Stein's secretary, had given her:

'The money's in the kiss. The kiss is how they gauge screen chemistry, honey,' she'd told her over the phone. 'You want this part, you're going to have to kiss like Theda Bara and Greta Garbo and Vivien Leigh rolled into one sweet package.'

What made things even more nerve-racking was that the

120

actor she was to kiss was quite damnably attractive. His name was Lochlan Kinnear, and he had recently starred in an aviation feature that was doing great things at the box office. *Photoplay* had carried an interview with him in which he'd been quoted as saying that he performed all his own stunts because he liked taking risks.

Lisa looked at herself now as she stood in front of the full-length mirror in Wardrobe, naked but for a sheath of satin and a shaky smile.

She turned to the wardrobe girl, hoping for some words of reassurance. The girl's eyes flicked over her with manifest unconcern.

'You need to lose ten pounds,' she said.

And then Lisa found herself on set, where an indifferent director was instructing an indifferent cameraman. An indifferent lighting man was tweaking lamps, and an indifferent props man was setting up Gabriel's 'easel' while a make-up girl gossiped with the script girl. Lisa thought that if she stripped to her pett and recited 'The Wreck of the Hesperus' none of them would look twice.

But Lochlan Kinnear had been watching her very closely from the shadows of the sound stage, and when he strolled into the pool of light and fixed on her the full beam of his attention, everything else receded. It was as though he had conjured some special effect: suddenly they were the only two people in the plywood construct of the phoney artist's studio.

'Don't worry about any of it,' he told her in a low voice: 'lines or camera angles. I'll cover for you if you fluff, and I'll make sure the camera favours you. Play the scene as if it's a dance – a beguine. Just follow my lead. '

That was all Lisa needed to hear. It was as if he had held

out his arms for her to fall into from a height. Together they segued into the scene – synchronizing glances, mirroring gestures – and when she spoke the final line – *Can't you stop that damn ocean outside?* – Lochlan's smile told her that their footwork had paid off. He reached out a hand and pushed aside her hair, allowing a finger to trail down her neck. His mouth was so close that she could feel his breath merge with hers, and his hand was hard against the back of her head as he drew her face in to his.

Nothing had prepared Lisa for the intensity. She had never been kissed like this by anybody in her life before. She found herself responding – hesitantly at first, then – as per the stage directions – with increasing ardour. Finally, Lochlan broke the kiss and they gazed at each other for a long moment, registering their powerful mutual desire.

'And – *cut!*' commanded the director.

Lochlan swept her off to the Sunset Tower Hotel, where a poker-faced concierge palmed a twenty-dollar bill.

A couple of hours later, slick with sweat and rosy with consummated lust, Lisa lay back against the pillows and said: 'I have never done anything like this before. I promise you I haven't. I know this sounds feeble, but I'm just not that kind of girl.'

'I've never done anything like this before either,' confessed Lochlan.

'Then how did you know to sweeten the concierge?' She regretted the words the minute they'd been uttered. What business was it of hers?

But Lochlan didn't seem to be remotely fazed. 'It was one of the first lessons my agent taught me,' he replied, turning candid eyes on her. 'He presented me with a list of guidelines if I ever became involved in what he termed an "indiscretion". And I reckon that what happened between us on Sound Stage B this morning was about as indiscreet as it gets, Miss La Touche.'

'Was there chemistry?' she asked, with a disingenuous smile.

'*Boy*, was there chemistry!' Their smiles broadened as they lay looking at each other, then Lochlan reached out a hand to caress a strand of her gloriously dishevelled hair and closed his eyes. She watched his expression change as he uttered two words in such a low voice that she had to ask him to repeat them.

'I'm married,' he said.

It took her a couple of moments to respond. 'But . . . *how* can you be married?' she asked, feeling numb and very, very stupid. 'I'm sure – I'm *sure* I read in *Photoplay* that you were single.'

'I married on the q.t., a week ago in Vegas. It was a shot-gun wedding; she's pregnant. The reason the press haven't cottoned on to it yet is because I told Sheilah Graham she could have an exclusive. She interviewed me last week for *Hollywood Today*.'

'Oh.' Lisa sat up, hugged her knees to her chest, and laid her forehead on them. She didn't want to look at him.

'I'm sorry.'

She felt his hand on her shoulder, and she shrugged it off, but he was persistent.

'I'm truly sorry, Lisa. I never dreamed that anything like this would happen.'

'What *has* happened?' she said, tension making her shrill.

'A thunderbolt, is what has happened.'

'A thunderbolt? A kick to the head, more like.' Lisa really did feel as though she'd been slapped. The sensuality in which she'd taken such pleasure earlier was shameful to her now; she felt dirty, used. She got out of bed and found her clothes. 'How very, very unfortunate,' she said, in her best finishing school tones, trying to pull on some dignity along with her garments, 'that you neglected to tell me you were a married man.'

'Would that have made a difference?'

She didn't answer.

'Would that have made a difference, Lisa?' He got to his feet and grabbed her shoulders, searching her face, forcing her to look at him.

'No,' she admitted in a very small voice. They regarded each other with uncertain eyes, then: 'What shall we do?' she asked.

'I don't know.' He hit himself, hard, on the forehead with the heel of his hand. 'What *bloody* disastrous timing,' he said. 'My apologies. Please, excuse my French.'

'Who is she?'

'She's nobody. I was extremely drunk and *monumentally* stupid one night, and . . . it just happened.' Lochlan gave a hopeless shrug, and sat down heavily on the bed. 'She threatened to go to the papers if I wouldn't make an "honest woman" of her. So I went to my agent, asked for his advice. He told me I'd painted myself into a corner and the only thing to do was to marry her. Then, once the baby's born and enough time has elapsed for us to cite "irreconcilable differences", she'll walk away with a hefty divorce settlement. It's standard procedure in this town. I'm sorry – I'm so sorry. I feel like she's taken me for a dupe, and there's nothing I can do about it.'

Lisa was astonished to realize that Lochlan was on the verge of tears. She had never seen a man cry before, and she found it distressing. Crouching down beside him, she took his hands in hers. 'Please don't feel so bad,' she said, earnestly. 'I'm no saint either. I have a fiancé back home in London.'

And then she remembered the tender expression in Richard's eyes as he had slid the diamond solitaire onto her finger in the Palm Court of the Ritz Hotel that September afternoon, and she was so covered in shame that she hid her face.

'He's on the other side of the world, sweetheart; there's a war on, and engagements are ended easily. You could do it tomorrow. But to actually be married is something very different indeed.' He slumped, putting his head in his hands. 'And to be married to somebody you despise is about as bad as it gets.'

Lisa perked up a little. 'Do you really despise her?'

'Yes. She's mad as the devil. I just wish I'd seen you coming first. You were a real bolt from the blue.'

'Poor, poor Lochlan.'

She reached out a hand to stroke his hair and, catching hold of it, he pressed the palm hard against his lips.

A bolt from the blue – did he mean it? Oh yes – she could tell by the dazed look in his eyes that he'd been caught off guard just as she had by what had happened between them when the camera had started to roll. Anyone who had witnessed their screen kiss could testify to the electricity they'd generated. It had been so palpable that after the director had shouted 'Cut!' there'd been a round of spontaneous applause from the crew, and catcalls and wolf whistles galore.

'You've got to get this part, Lisa.'

'Oh, Lochlan! There must be hundreds of girls—'

'I've tested dozens. You're the one I want.'

'But what if Mr Stein—'

'Ziggy owes me a favour.' He looked away, eyes narrowed suddenly, jaw set, his mouth a determined line. 'Hell. As far as I'm concerned, the part's yours. It's my gift to you because . . .' He faltered, as though lost for words.

'Because?'

'Because I think I might be falling in love with you.' Lochlan looked deep into her eyes, the way he had earlier when the cameras had been rolling. Then he brushed a strand of hair tenderly away from her face and smiled. 'We're going to be doing a lot of rehearsal, angel. We might as well start now.'

CHAPTER THIRTEEN

JESSIE

PARIS 1919

'Fire! *Fire!* Clear the building!'

Jessie had laid out her evening dress on the bed, and had just finished washing when the cry came up from the ground floor of the Hôtel des Trois Moineaux.

'*Fire!*'

There was no word in the world more galvanizing. The entire building, which had been dozing through an uneventful *heure bleue*, came suddenly to life. Next door she heard the mad Serb fall out of his bed, lumber across his room and out onto the landing. From overhead came the inchoate sounds of an imminent stampede. *Fire!* The cries were multiplying now, echoing from floor to floor of the building, interspersed with panicky shrieks and shouted commands to remain calm.

Jessie threw aside her towel and lunged for her shabby peignoir. There was no time to worry about undergarments or shoes – she just wanted something to cover her nakedness. She found herself struggling with the sleeves, in her haste confusing left with right, and it seemed that the more frantically she tried to disentangle her arms, the more she found herself in a straitjacket of her own making. Calm, calm, *calm* – she told herself, taking a deep breath, forcing herself to slow down, slow down and *think*. As she fumbled with the sash, someone passing banged on the door of her room.

'Hurry! Hurry! Fire! Fire! Fire!' she heard.

Jessie threw a quick look at the case where she kept her precious things. Did she have time to drag it out from under her bed? No, no – getting out was her priority. The golden rule was that you never dithered in a burning building. Unhooking her raincoat from its peg, she swung through the door, pulling it to behind her.

Already the corridor was jammed with bodies jostling, swarming towards the rickety staircase that led to safety. Jessie braced herself, then propelled herself forward. An elbow hit her savagely in the chest, someone pushed her from behind, the consumptive youth from upstairs barged past her with astonishing force. The 'ladies first' ethos was clearly unheard of in the Hôtel des Trois Moineaux.

Outside on the street there was chaos. Neighbours and children had come running when they'd heard the alarm, dogs were barking in excitement, and a squadron of cavalry was clopping down the middle of the street, shouting to the crowd to let them through. The cavalry was not popular among the denizens of the rue du Coq d'Or, and already they were being subjected to a barrage of insults.

Jessie made her way with difficulty through the throng to the opposite side of the street and stood looking up at the building, expecting at any moment to see smoke billowing from the windows. As curious observers converged to witness the spectacle of the Trois Moineaux going up in flames, so the more panicky inmates of the hotel fled.

Jessie's instinct was to run with them, to put as much

distance as she could between herself and this imminent conflagration – the hotel was constructed from *matchwood*, after all! But she couldn't rid herself of the notion that the alarm might have been a hoax. What if some sneak thief was systematically going from bedroom to bedroom, helping himself? It had been known to happen, and the last thing she needed was for her meagre savings to be sticky-fingered. She stood poised between fright and flight, hugging herself and performing small dance steps on the spot to keep warm.

'Where did the fire start?' one woman asked of a gaping scullery maid. 'In the kitchen?'

The skivvy shrugged. 'I seen nothing,' she said. 'Nor smelt nothing, neither.'

Some of the crowd oohed, some catcalled at the cavalry officer who, having reached the door of the hotel dismounted and, donning his most officious air, proceeded to grill Madame Perron who was standing there, gesticulating angrily. Jessie could tell that she was shouting, but couldn't hear what was being said above the excited din and the clanging of approaching klaxons. Finally, a couple of *poilus* who had entered the building re-emerged, and consulted with their captain. It appeared that there had been no fire at all. The brouhaha had either been engineered as a diversionary tactic, or the alarm had been raised by mistake.

Within minutes the crowd had dispersed – the urchins to their street games, the shopkeepers to their trades, and the inmates of the hotel to the cells that Madame Perron had the nerve to call *chambres meublées*. Jessie joined them, anxious to return to her room. But when she reached the third floor it was to find her door hanging open. The room had been pillaged – ransacked. The covers had been pulled from her bed, her mattress had been overturned and the floorboard under which she kept her passport had been prised up. All the drawers in her chest had been pulled out and their contents scattered. And of course – of *course* – her case had been dragged into the middle of the room and forced open.

Jessie stepped across the threshold and looked down at the suitcase to which she had consigned her most precious possessions. It was empty. The silver cigarette case that dear Tuppenny had given her was gone. The kid evening pumps and bag and the stockings that Count Demetrios had bought her were gone, and as her eyes registered the despoliation, she saw that the secret pocket on her suspender belt into which she took such care to sew her handful of francs every evening had been slit open, and her money was gone too.

But all this counted for nothing when she saw the slashed drawstrings on the cambric bag lying by the door. It had contained the garment that would gain her entrée into society this evening: the Liberty silk evening dress.

For many moments Jessie stood there frozen, with her hands clamped over her mouth and her eyes fixed on the looted bag at her bare feet. Then she started to hyperventilate, gasping for air as though she were drowning. She lurched across the room and flung open the casement, trying desperately to drag air into her lungs. This was worse – far worse – than the night the Serb next door had burned sulphur.

Below her, the cobblestoned street glistened with damp. She closed her eyes, and when she opened them again it occurred to her that the surface of the street looked like the flank of a great sea monster, rolling over in its sleep. How easy it would be to dive in there, how easy to topple from this height and fall to her death by drowning. Except, of course, she wouldn't drown. If she dived, she would hit the ground with such force that her skull would shatter, and then all her thoughts, her worries and troubles would spill out along with her brains onto the stinking pavement of the rue du Coq d'Or, and that would be an end to yet one more wretched life on this wretched street, and she could sleep easy at last.

Pulling herself up, clinging to the window frame, she eased herself onto the sill. It was difficult to stand upright: the belt of her raincoat had caught on the handle of the casement. She had just managed to unhook it, when something made her stop. Her parents. How would they feel when they learned that their beautiful girl – their only child – had ended up a suicide in a wretched hotel? All those letters she had written home, all those letters full of lies about how happy they were, she and Scotch, and how they planned to maybe move into an even finer apartment. What would happen if they came to find her and stayed on in Paris indefinitely, and the trail led to the Hôtel des Trois Moineaux, and they discovered the truth about their daughter's sordid secret life? Oh, God! She couldn't do that to them. She couldn't. But what *could* she do?

Tears started to flow down Jessie's face, and she must have given a cry of despair, because there came the sound of footsteps in the corridor, and suddenly someone was in the room with her and strong arms were around her waist, restraining her, pulling her back . . .

And then she was on the floor of her room, weeping

131

and weeping and someone was smoothing her hair and saying in a rough but reassuring voice: 'There, there, Mam'zelle. It's all right. You're safe now, and everything is going to be fine. You come with me, and I'll buy you a drink and before you can say Jack Robinson you'll be feeling chipper again and wondering what had you in such a state. There's no better girl than the Green Fairy to cure a case of the horrors. You come with me, Milady. You come with Adèle.'

'My friend!' said Adèle, pouring a second shot of absinthe into Jessie's glass. 'What were you thinking? What is the loss of a few francs to the loss of a life? And the life of one so beautiful, so young, with so much to live for?'

'I've nothing to live for.'

'Shame on you!'

They were sitting at Adèle's favourite table in the bistro on the ground floor of the Hôtel des Trois Moineaux – the one opposite the framed photograph of a funeral that hung behind the bar, bearing the legend '*Crédit est mort*.' Jessie's unlikely Good Samaritan had been right – the liquor had eased her pain a little, as had the non-stop litany of platitudes that Adèle had been murmuring since she'd helped Jessie pick her way downstairs in her unshod feet. It was funny, Jessie thought, how very soothing platitudes could be: from the moment Adèle had stroked her hair and told her that everything was going to be fine, she'd half believed her. She supposed nothing could ever be as bad again as the few insane moments she'd spent clinging to the window ledge upstairs, preparing herself to jump.

'To friendship, Milady!' said Adèle, raising her tumbler.

Jessie mirrored the toast and found herself mumbling 'To friendship!' before downing the second shot in one. Oh, how good the liquor was! It burned a line all the way down to her stomach. Setting the glass on the table, she leaned back against the banquette, and closed her eyes. How sweet it would be to stay here in the muggy atmosphere of the bistro and drink absinthe until she fell asleep and could forget all her troubles! How much sweeter still if she were to open her eyes and find herself back in Finistère with Scotch, in the Hôtel Simonet . . . She would stretch like a cat, and then she would pinch him awake so that she could tell him about the vile nightmare she'd just had – and how they'd laugh that anything could mar their happiness!

The clink of carafe against glass made her blink and refocus. Adèle was regarding her with concern. This woman had turned out to be a true friend after all. In spite of her rough edge and her vulgarity there was something oddly maternal about Adèle ... Oh, God – how Jessie wanted her parents now! She needed them more than she'd ever done – even that time in Chambéry when Scotch had nearly died and she'd written home – what had she written?

I am feeling so young and incapable-like, and oh Lord! I wish I were in England . . .

'I wish I were in England,' she told Adèle.

Adèle nodded. 'We must find some way of getting you back there, safe and sound. And a way for you to earn some money fast, kid. You need clothes, shoes. Was every stitch you own taken?'

133

'Yes. But I don't care. The only thing I care about is the dress.'

'What dress?'

'An evening dress. I was going to wear it tonight.'

'Where were you off to?'

'A soirée. On the Boulevard Péreire.'

'Swanky.'

'Yes.'

'You can't go now. The state of you! What was this dress like?'

'Beautiful. Silk.'

'A silk dress, eh? I've a friend could lend you one. Shoes, too. Have you a gentleman waiting for you?'

'Yes. We were to meet at eight o'clock.'

'Ach. It's nearly nine now. No gallivanting for you tonight. A silk dress ...' Adèle gave Jessie a long look of appraisal. 'D'you know something? I've just thought of a way that might earn you good money, Milady – with your clothes on.'

'What do you mean?' asked Jessie.

'You've been posing in your pelt, haven't you?' said Adèle, with a wink. 'Word gets around fast in these parts.'

'It's artistic!' Jessie protested. 'There's nothing sordid about it – nothing shameful.'

'Be that as it may,' said Adèle. 'Where I come from, a woman of your breeding does not permit a man to see her naked until her wedding night.'

There was bound to be an answer to that, but Jessie couldn't think of it. She struggled to find the right words, then gave up and looked rather too pointedly at the carafe.

Adèle poured immediately, then signalled to the garçon to bring another. 'Personally,' she added, 'I can think of ways in which a girl can earn better money without removing a stitch.'

Jessie took a sip of absinthe, made a face, then threw it back. 'Oh?' she said. 'What have you in mind?'

Adèle leaned her elbows on the table. 'There is, I am sure you know, a class of man whose work takes him to town from time to time, and who seeks in the evenings a little – erm – how to describe it? A little . . . distraction, a little pleasure.' Jessie stiffened and Adèle gave her an affronted look. 'My friend!' she said. 'You don't have faith in me? Listen to me: let me explain. These men want women to accompany them to dinner, women who are not just lovely to look at, but who are refined and who know how to talk of lofty subjects. A genteel person like yourself – why, such men would be happy to pay for the pleasure of your company over a good dinner and a bottle of fine wine.'

'You mean men *pay* to take a girl out to dinner?'

'*Bien sûr*, Milady!'

'And that's all it would entail? Having dinner?'

Adèle nodded. 'Trust me. These men are lonely, they are away from home, they do not want to spend an evening after a hard day's selling or travelling, having dinner on their own. They want the company of a woman who will amuse them and who will in turn laugh at their jokes. Men are simple creatures, Mam'zelle, and have on the whole simple requirements.'

Jessie looked dubious. 'There's no catch?' she asked.

'None. I take the booking, reserve the table – and of course I take a small cut.' Adèle leaned back and looked at Jessie with curiosity. 'This work you do for your artist – how much does it pay you? Forgive me for asking.'

'Twenty francs a day.'

'Twenty francs a day! *Non!*' Adèle went off into a peal of merriment. 'Excuse me, kid. It's rude to laugh, I know, but hell's bells! Twenty francs a day to sit starkers in front of a man! If you allow me to take care of things, I could net you fifty. That way you could have your fare back to good old Blighty earned in, let's say . . . a month.'

'A *month*?'

'What's the alternative, kid? Walking to Calais barefoot and begging the price of a ticket?'

The garçon had arrived with the carafe. Adèle gave Jessie a motherly smile, and patted her hand. 'Help yourself,' she told her. 'You've had a shock. A little more of the Green Fairy won't do you any harm.' Then she turned away to confab with the boy.

Jessie allowed her mind to drift, looking into the depths of the murky greenish liquid, making shapes: a leaf, a fish, a wing, a baby's fist ... She wondered how the baby inside her was changing shape, how it was growing. She shouldn't be drinking rotgut – she should be drinking milk, eating fruit and fresh vegetables and red meat. But how could she afford it? Just last night she had seen a skivvy here in the bistro cramming a leftover piece of ham into her mouth. She'd picked it up off the floor – and she seemed glad of it. Jessie hadn't sunk that low. She didn't – couldn't – add 'yet'.

'*Ma chère amie*, you are in luck!' Adèle's voice interrupted her reverie. 'Jacques knows who took your dress! I have sent him off to fetch it. It will cost you to get it back, but we can deduct that from your fee. I'll set you up with a client tonight, and then you are that small bit closer to raising the money for your fare. Let's not allow the grass to grow under our feet.'

Jessie looked blank.

'You want to start work as soon as possible, don't you?'

'Yes, but—'

'Good. I will endeavour to arrange a rendezvous for you every night this week. I'll keep a record of your earnings and pay you on Friday. If you wish to continue stripping for your artist friend during the day, that's your lookout.'

Adèle took a small notebook from her pocket and started doing calculations. 'Of course you could earn the price of your fare in less than a month if you were prepared to offer additional services. I've known girls set themselves up in business with the money they've earned. Just think how dandy it would be to have your own little hat shop, eh?' She smiled at Jessie and began to croon a popular music hall song. '*Elle a perdu son pantalon, la la la la . . .*'

A hat shop? What was the woman thinking of? What would Jessie want with a hat shop?

'*Tout en dansant le cancan, la la ti da . . .* Ah! Here's Jacques with your finery!'

Jacques dumped a duffel bag on the table and pulled the dress from it with grubby fingers. As it unfurled, it gleamed like a pennant in the surrounding gloom. Jessie rose unsteadily from the table and reached for it.

'That's right,' said Adèle, with an encouraging smile, 'take it now, and go and change. By the time you come back downstairs, I will have gentlemen queuing to escort you to dinner. Dinner – just think! And maybe the *Folies* afterwards!'

Jessie was confused. What gentlemen? What *Folies*? She was feeling sick now, from the absinthe.

'Mademoiselle Beaufoy!'

Looking up, Jessie made out a figure approaching their table through the fug in the bistro. It was Count Demetrios. She stumbled as she took a step towards him.

'I have been looking for you everywhere,' he said, roughly. 'Come with me at once. Come on!'

'Count Demetrios,' began Jessie, realizing to her shame that the syllables were slurred. 'I'm sorry. I owe you an explanation. My friend has—'

The count didn't bother to throw so much as a glance in Adèle's direction. He took the dress from Jessie and began to steer her forcefully towards the door.

'Hey! Hey – that's my property!' she heard Adèle shout. 'Give it back!'

'Get out. Just get *out!*' commanded the count. 'This is no place for a gentlewoman like you.'

Jacques had nipped between the tables and was blocking their way. 'A gentlewoman?' he sneered. 'That *poivrotte*? Pay up, mister. Pay what you owe us. The dress is worth a lot of money.'

Demetrios sent a handful of coins spinning, and as Jacques went scrambling for them Jessie looked back and saw Adèle spit in her direction. Her face was twisted and ugly with fury. 'I don't know why I bother my arse with ungrateful little bitches like you!' she screeched. 'I'll be glad to see the back of you!'

'Keep moving,' said the count, gripping her elbow. 'Keep moving.'

'Fuck off!' Jessie heard from behind her. 'Fuck off with your fancy pimp and don't come looking to me for help again, you scrounging little tart.'

They had reached the door. The count pulled it open and stood back to allow Jessie to precede him. She was confused still, disoriented by the liquor. She cast a look over her shoulder. Adèle was lighting a cigarette. She sucked hard hard on the end, blew out the match, then snapped a familiar silver case shut.

'Count Demetrios!' Jessie tugged at his arm as the door shut behind them. 'She has my cigarette case!'

'No matter. Have you any idea how lucky you are to have escaped the clutches of that abominable woman? Her kind is notorious, Mademoiselle. If you *ever* tell the authorities that you suspect her of larceny, she will not hesitate to send one of the many cut-throats she has in her employ after you post-haste, and the very *least* you can expect is a lacerated face.'

Jessie gave him an uncertain look.

'You have the gown – that's all that matters. Go and change. I will settle your bill with the *patronne*.'

'But Adèle took everything I own! She—'

'Mademoiselle Beaufoy, if you go back in there I shall not answer for the consequences.' The count's eyes were boring into hers. '*I shall not answer for the consequences*,' he repeated. 'Do you understand me?' He very deliberately removed his hand from hers, then stepped back. 'I am in a position to help you, and I shall do all in my power to pro-tect you, but if you will not take my advice – *hélas*.' He gave an eloquent shrug. 'You are the mistress of your own destiny, Mademoiselle. You alone must make the decision.'

CHAPTER FOURTEEN

LISA

HOLLYWOOD 1940

Lisa got the part of Daphne Bolingbroke. She also got a congratulatory telegram from Richard and two massive bouquets – one from Lochlan, the other from Ziggy Stein. But before she signed the contract that was being drawn up for her, Lisa got in touch with David Niven, who invited her to lunch at his house on North Linden Drive.

'Now, my little chickadee,' said David as they settled down to shrimp cocktail. 'Since I gave my solemn word to Richard that I would look after you, I want to know how you have been getting on.'

Lisa told him about her screen test and how well it had gone, and how pleased Ziggy was, and how over the moon she felt.

'This is all good,' said David. 'Mr Stein is one of the more genial souls in Hollywood. He's happily married, devoted to his wife and his kids, and he isn't likely to jeopardize that domestic bliss by screwing around with his starlets. Excuse my French. He looks on his stable as family, too, so don't let him down.'

It wasn't the first time Lisa had heard movie actors referred to as belonging to a 'stable'. Privately she hated it, but she knew she was going to have to get over it.

'It seems that you, Lisa,' continued David, 'are ready for representation. Allow me to recommend my agent, Phil Gersh. While he may not be up there with the big guns like Selznick or Wasserman, he's hard-working, keen and honest. Mark my words, Lisa – that's a big deal in a town where most people don't know how to spell the word "integrity", let alone define it. Who's written the screen-play, incidentally?'

'A chap called Scott Fitzgerald. Apparently he and his wife were famous, back in the twenties, but he's a lush now. Have you heard of him?'

'My dear! Haven't you read *The Great Gatsby*?'

'No.'

David gave her a look of reprimand, then moved to the bookcase, scanned the spines, and took down a well-thumbed volume. 'Here,' he said. 'You may borrow this. And this . . . and this. Have you read any of them?'

'I've heard of them,' said Lisa, leafing through the pages of Voltaire's *Candide*. 'And I've seen some of the films. *A Tale of Two Cities* was awfully good.'

'Hardly the same thing. Read the books. When you have finished, return them and we'll have a little chat.'

Lisa looked baffled. 'A chat about *books*?'

'Yes indeed. I'm going to educate you, my dear.'

'Why?'

'To stop me from going mad with boredom. Oxymorons amuse me.'

'Where's the oxymoron?'

'In this instance, "well-read" and "starlet",' said David.

The next day, along with another floral tribute from

Lochlan, Lisa accepted delivery of a Morocco-leather-bound dictionary from Mr Niven, along with a signed copy of F. Scott Fitzgerald's short stories. The cover was adorned with dancing jazz-age couples, and Lisa settled down to what she assumed would be an undemanding read. The first story wasn't at all undemanding; it made her think. And by the end of the afternoon, she had finished all eleven stories in the book and was ready to start on the novels.

Phil Gersh signed Lisa, and got her a little-above-bog-standard contract with Ziggy Stein. She bought a second-hand fire-engine red Chrysler coupé and moved out of her tiny apartment into a marginally bigger one in the Westwood area, north of Sunset Boulevard.

And she and Lochlan saw each other as often as they could manage it.

If anyone in the studio knew that a torrid affair was burgeoning under their noses, they didn't let on. Yet it befitted the star-crossed lovers to tread carefully, for while such liaisons were unremarkable among the jaded denizens of Hollywood, extra-marital antics between artistes were an abomination according to the code laid down by the all-powerful Hays office, and an outrage in the eyes of a brainwashed public who believed the marriages of their screen gods and goddesses to be apple-pie wholesome.

Producers went to extreme lengths to ensure that reputations remained spotless. For the preview of *Gone with the Wind* David Selznick had insisted that Vivien Leigh and Laurence Olivier take separate planes to Atlanta and stay in separate hotels, even though they had been lovers for nearly four years. It was rumoured that Louis B. Mayer had paid Clark Gable's ex-wife one hundred thousand dollars if she promised not to cite Carole Lombard as co-respondent. And Joan Crawford had become box office poison after speculation about her less than perfect marriage to Franchot Tone. Press agents were kept busy sweeping up the shards of careers that had been shattered by the bogeyman infidelity, and consigning them to the trash.

The PR woman assigned to Lisa was called Myra Blake. She took Lisa to lunch and interviewed her, then came up with a press release to circulate amongst all the fan magazines. A couple of weeks later, Lisa came across an article in *Screen Book* along with a publicity photograph of her wearing a dress by Molyneux that the studio had lent her. She skimmed through it, wincing at each outright lie or half-truth she happened upon, then rang Myra in a tizzy.

'Myra?' she said. 'I'm afraid you have got rather a lot of things wrong about me in your press release.'

'Oh? Like what?'

'Well, my father isn't an earl.'

'Earl, schmearl. What are your aristocratic credentials, then?'

'One of my ancestors was a baronet.'

'That'll do. So what's your pa?'

'I never knew him.'

'We'll stick with what's there. The great American public don't want to know that. Any other quibbles?'

'I'm not athletic.'

'Yeah. I just made that up.'

'I don't use Nulava shampoo.'

'They paid me to say that.'

'And I don't do needlepoint and I haven't read the complete works of Dickens.'

'Well, you'd better get cracking, sugar!'

Myra put the phone down, and Lisa did likewise. She would have loved to pick it up again, to call Lochlan, but of course that was out of the question in case his wife answered.

She and Lochlan had taken every opportunity they could for what he called their 'trysts'. Lisa adored that he used such a romantic word, a word so redolent of the gallant knights of the Round Table and their lady loves. Sometimes he visited her apartment, sometimes they drove out to the hills to make love, and once he had been so overcome by passion that he had taken her rather roughly in her dressing room. 'Never again,' he'd said afterwards. 'If anyone had walked in on us, our careers would be over, angel.'

Such circumspection didn't come easily to Lisa, who longed to be able to announce her feelings to the entire world. It was especially difficult when she was confronted with pictures of her lover and his wife, Judy, in the trade papers. Judy wasn't even particularly cute or glamorous: she was *homely* looking. Lisa felt so sorry for Lochlan, trapped in a loveless marriage. *Silver Screen* had recently published an interview with him in which he'd expounded on the 'Invaluable Lessons' he'd learned since marrying Judy, referring to her as 'his other half', and Lisa had cried when she'd read it.

'The first thing I intend doing when this shoot is finished is go to Shwab's and lay into strawberry shortcake and a malted. I have never been so miserably hungry in my life.'

'Well, you know what they say. You've got to suffer for your art, angel.'

Lochlan and Lisa were sitting in the Orion commissary having lunch. Lochlan was tucking into pasta, while Lisa made do with a paltry salad of grated carrot and cottage cheese so that she could fit into her second-skin negligees and swimsuits: she had been on a perpetual diet since the day she had donned the satin gown for her screen test. It was the end of the second week of shooting: *Crimson Lake* was behind schedule because the entire second unit had had to be hospitalized for three days, having come down with a bad case of poison ivy after shooting exteriors at Del Monte up the Californian coast.

'What on earth do *top* stars have to complain about?'

Lochlan raised an eyebrow. 'They may be working gods and goddesses, but it's a tough life. Stardom is a form of drudgery. All those celebrities might spend their working day hanging out in a trailer decked out like an empress's boudoir, but the bottom line is that actors in this town are just glorified wage slaves. I mean – get a load of what you had to do earlier today. You spent an hour leaning up against a bloody board.'

Lisa had felt like an idiot when she'd first used the 'slant board', a device that actresses were obliged to rest on between takes so as not to crease their costumes by sitting down in them. Resting on the board was the dullest thing Lisa had ever had to endure. She had heard that Lana Turner insisted the studio hire a girl whose sole requirement was to turn over the records that the star liked to listen to on occasions when she had to spend time on *her* slant board, and she wondered if she'd ever have enough clout to make a similar request. Movie-making, she had discovered, really could get fearfully boring.

'This is your official salutary warning,' Lochlan told her. 'Normal folk leave the job behind when they clock off for the day, but once you become a bona fide star, you've nowhere to escape to. You might go to London or New York or Paris, but Hollywood stays right there with you. You might nip outside to pick your paper off the stoop, but you better make sure you're in full make-up when you do it. Fancy a Danish?'

'No. I've got to suffer for my art.'

Despite all the suffering, stardom still held an irresistible allure for Lisa. Every time she drove through the famed art deco gate of the studios she pretended that the autograph seekers gathered there were hoping to get a peek at *her*. When she received her first fan letter – addressed simply to 'the strawberry blonde in the Chrysler coupé' – she pasted it into a scrapbook, hoping it would be the first of many. She was thrilled to become one of half a dozen starlets picked to endorse a brand of soda (the copy read: 'a cooling relief from the hot Klieg lights'), and she was over the moon when *Modern Screen* ran a feature on her swimming prowess for which she posed in a bathing costume alongside the Tarzan actor Johnny Weissmuller and Cheeta the chimp. (She cut Cheeta out of the photograph when she added it to her scrapbook.)

This photo opportunity had been set up by Myra, who was glad to know that one of the skills listed on Lisa's CV was actually genuine. Her swimming prowess really had been pivotal in landing her this role, because *Crimson Lake* included a scene in which a tipsy Daphne performs a swan dive over the edge of a cliff. This necessitated hours floundering around in a tank on the back lot with the actress playing the lead, Mabel Philips. Mabel had been a star of the Ziegfeld Follies a decade ago, and still possessed a blowsy glamour.

'I'm milking it for what it's worth, kid,' she told Lisa. 'If I lay off the booze I might have another year or two left.'

'What happens then?' asked Lisa.

Mabel laughed. 'People write you off,' she said. 'You become a nobody.'

And Lisa thought of poor Scott Fitzgerald's wife, Zelda, on whom the lead role was said to be based, her looks ruined, her dancing days over. She thought too about the time she'd been surprised by her own nondescript reflection in the mirror in Sefridge's, and how terrified she had been that she might be perceived as a nobody, how she had considered it a fate worse than death. Now, as the weeks wore on, Lisa came to realize that Lochlan had been right when he'd warned her about the downside of work-ing in the industry. The lustre wore off – literally as well as figuratively. Her skin and hair took heavy abuse – not just from the gallons of bleach that were added to the water in the tank, but also because of the numerous tweaks she had to endure from hair and make-up. Ziggy wasn't happy with the script, and every day she was presented with fresh pages to memorize – each new line of dialogue, to her mind, worse than the last. The original screenplay was by now virtually unrecognizable, and when poor Scott Fitzgerald died of a massive heart attack, nobody was really surprised.

However, as the movie evolved under a new committee of writers, so too did Lisa's role. From being a cameo, the character of Daphne grew to play a more pivotal part in the drama. Lisa welcomed the opportunity to make an impression, but the promotion had little financial impact, for, being a contract player, she was not paid for the extra time she worked. She was on call six days a week, setting her alarm for 5 a.m. to be in the studio before seven. Rehearsals started at nine and often she didn't get to leave the studio until midnight or even later, occasionally opting to sleep in the dressing room rather than drive home.

By the end of her next film – a convoluted thriller shot hot on the heels of *Crimson Lake* – Lisa was so exhausted that the studio doctor was administering daily shots of thyroid extract and vitamin B-12. She lost weight without even trying, make-up and hair were working overtime, and she was too tired to make love. She lived in fear that Lochlan would tire of her – especially now that he had a bouncing baby boy in his life, courtesy of 'his other half.'

The headline in *Silver Screen* had read: *THE CARDINAL RULES OF MARRIED LOVE – Hollywood's Happiest Husband Tells How He Stays That Way.*

CHAPTER FIFTEEN

JESSIE

PARIS 1919

Jessie and Count Demetrios were in an open horse-drawn cab, bowling down the rue du Coq d'Or. Jessie had changed into her evening dress and was curled against the leather upholstery, shabby raincoat over her shoulders, bare feet tucked beneath her.

'Where to?' asked the driver.

'Boulevard Péreire,' the count told him.

'You can't be serious!' Jessie protested. 'I can't go there! I look like a vagabond.'

'A *vagabonde*!' The count smiled. 'A perfect conceit – like the heroine of a novel by Colette. I shall tell Monsieur Lantier that I happened upon you in the Tuileries Gardens, wandering barefoot and confused, entirely lost, with no idea how you got there.'

It was hardly a conceit. Jessie really did feel confused and lost. 'I don't understand,' she said. 'What do you hope to achieve by such pretetense?'

'You're reinventing yourself. Why not? The war has changed everything. *Anything* is possible.'

'It's preposterous, Count!'

'Precisely. I want a shock effect. The impact you make

this evening shall resound among *le tout Paris* tomorrow.'

'But—'

He held up a hand to forestall her. 'You asked me to help you. It is not an exaggeration to say that I saved your life, Mademoiselle. Now, *you do as I say*. Let your hair down.'

Jessie's hair had been damp when she'd twisted it up earlier that evening. When she released it, it rippled over her shoulders lending her the appearance of some wild fairy-tale creature.

'Perfect!' he said. 'A Pre-Raphaelite Venus.' Reaching into the pocket of his opera cloak, he took out a cigar, cut the end with a silver pocket knife and lit it, inhaling deeply as he studied her. 'Have no fear that you can't carry it off. I observed you last summer playing charades in the salon of the palazzo Saciaro – a game at which you excelled. Now it is time to play the game for real.' He reached for her hand and gave her a reassuring smile. 'What name shall we fabricate for the role you are to play? A fairy-tale name.'

'Perdita,' said Jessie without hesitation. It was the name of the stray kitten she had taken in as a child. 'It's from *The Winter's Tale*. It means "lost soul".'

'Lost soul,' echoed the count. 'Perfect. The name, the hair, the dress – all a little bizarre, all more than a little intriguing.'

The carriage had drawn up outside an imposing building. Count Demetrios produced a large silk handkerchief and handed it over to the coachman along with the fare. 'Take this,' he instructed, 'and soak it in that drinking fountain – see there? Across the road.'

The coachman set off, and was back in a moment with the square of wet silk.

'Perhaps,' said the count, 'you would assist the lady to alight.'

The coachman obliged. Jessie could tell by the way he was avoiding her eyes that he could scarcely believe the audacity of a woman who stepped barefoot and bareheaded onto the pavement outside one of the most prestigious addresses in Paris.

She followed the count to the steps that led to the front door, and then he did a most surprising thing. He knelt down and gently took first her left foot, then her right between his hands, and wiped them carefully with the handkerchief. 'It is one thing,' he said, 'to go social climbing in bare feet. But it is quite another thing to do it in dirty feet.'

He removed the raincoat from her shoulders, handed it to the coachman, then crooked his elbow, inviting her to take his arm. '*Courage*, Perdita,' he said.

The comtesse de Valéry's apartment was on the top floor of the building. The lobby was all understated chic, in tones of eau de Nil and rose and gilt, and the salon beyond was peopled by the most outlandish individuals Jessie had ever laid eyes upon.

The women were of the type she had seen on the Boulevard Saint-Germain when the count had taken her shopping. No female face in that room was unpainted – bar her own. The women's complexions were clown white, their mouths scarlet gashes, their eyebrows surprised circumflexes. Some resembled exotic birds preening in peacock and marabou and ostrich feathers, some were oriental princesses in embroidered Turkish trousers of looped silk chiffon and boleros of silver lamé, and some were beautiful barbarians trailing trains fashioned from leopards' skins and serpents' scales. And the colours! The room seethed in an orgiastic riot of colour: violent harmonies of incandescent reds and jewel-bright emerald, clashes of vermilion and purple, and an explosion of exuberant azure and opulent indigo.

The moment she and Count Demetrios stepped hand in hand over the threshold, the level of the hullabaloo and the chattering in the salon plummeted. It was replaced by a chorus of little gasps and squeaks and titters of embarrassment and astonishment. 'Who is *she*?' Jessie heard. 'How very . . . quaint!' 'How very *gauche*!' 'How very *outré*!'

How very *outré*! That was rich, thought Jessie, coming as it did from the lipsticked mouth of a woman who had a geyser of bird-of-paradise feathers erupting from her head and whose legs were hobbled by tiers of shocking pink tulle. A small smile began to play around her lips.

Count Demetrios strolled through the room, his eyes flickering over the assembly, searching for – searching for *whom*? Jessie could not remember what she was doing here, and she suddenly didn't care. Armoured by the absinthe she'd downed earlier, impervious to the sniggers that were continuing like bursts of machine-gun fire, she held her head high, moving with the careless grace of a dancer, surveying her audience with a kind of cavalier amusement.

At the other side of the long salon, beyond floor to ceiling French windows draped in dove grey velvet, two men in evening attire were standing on a balcony, deep in conversation. One was leaning against the balustrade, smoking a cigarette. In contrast to the strict penguin suits of the other male guests, he appeared in a state of virtual undress: his jacket was slung over his shoulder, he sported unlinked French cuffs and unknotted tie, and his hair hung like a lopped raven's wing over one eye. Jessie recognized him as the raffish man to whom the count had been talking yesterday on the terrace of the café on the rue Mouffetard. This must be Gervaise Lantier.

Alerted to the charged atmosphere in the room by the sudden drop in decibel level and witchy hisses, Lantier looked up. Count Demetrios paused on the threshold of the open French windows, released Jessie's hand, and gestured to her to advance a pace or two.

'Monsieur Lantier!' he announced in tones that could not fail to be overheard by the entire salon. 'You told me just today that you were seeking a new muse.'

The artist raised an eyebrow.

'I hope you will not consider it presumptuous of me, Monsieur,' continued the count, 'but I fancy I may have found her. May I introduce you? Her name is Perdita.'

And then the count did something so outrageous that, as he predicted, it sent shock waves around *le tout Paris* that same night, and for many, many nights and weeks afterwards. He produced from his jacket pocket his gleaming silver pocket knife, took a pace forward, and with two deft movements, he slashed the straps of Jessie's gown before backing away in the manner of a magician who has just completed an astonishing demonstration of legerdemain.

A small exclamation of surprise escaped her. She took a step forward onto the balcony, catching hold of the silk and clasping it to her before it could slide over her hips. But the modesty of the gesture contrived to make her appear infinitely more desirable than if she were stark naked. She stood motionless for a moment, silhouetted in the lamplight that streamed through the windows of the salon, then, knowing that the only alternative was ignominious flight, decided to brave it out. She resumed her erect stance and adopted the dispassionate expression she often assumed when sitting; one that would reflect whatever emotion the artist wished to project upon it.

Lantier's expression was equally unreadable. Tossing his cigarette over the balustrade, he moved towards her and draped his jacket around her. Then he took her face between his hands. She watched as his eyes assimilated every detail, tracing, mapping, learning her by heart. Artist's eyes, she thought. When he finally looked directly at her he gave a smile of recognition, and something told her that she could keep few secrets from this man: her face had revealed more than any curriculum vitae could have done. He leaned down and murmured in her ear.

'Perdita. I should very much like to paint you. And I should like to do it now,' he said. 'Will you allow me?'

Jessie lowered her gaze, as if considering. She let a moment go by, then another, before she favoured him with an oblique look. 'For sure,' she said. 'I shall allow you to paint me with pleasure, Monsieur.'

Then Gervaise Lantier took his new muse by the hand and led her from the balcony and down the green-carpeted length of the salon, impervious to the cicada-like, rasping whispers of the astonished assembly.

His eyes agleam with cupidity, Count Demetrios watched them go.

CHAPTER SIXTEEN

LISA

HOLLYWOOD 1941

For the premiere of the first film in which she played a leading role – a costume drama that again starred Lochlan – Lisa wore a gold lamé gown and wedge evening shoes in gold kid and red satin by Salvatore Ferragamo. The gown was yet another loan from the studio and she could have borrowed footwear, too (the shoe department was a fetishist's paradise) but she wanted to glide up the red carpet in her own heels. Hadn't she *told* Richard Napier she'd wear Salvatore Ferragamo one day!

The event was held at the Hawaii Theatre, a B-movie showcase on Hollywood Boulevard, and her companion for the evening – randomly picked by Myra from a list of celebrity escorts – was Fred Crane, who'd had a small part in *Gone with the Wind*.

'We're just good friends!' Lisa told a reporter from *Photoplay* magazine as they strolled up the carpet arm in arm. 'Be sure to quote me on that – I don't want my fiancé in England to think otherwise! He sent me this corsage, by the way.' She was sporting a jewel-like arrangement of dwarf orchids that Richard had gone to enormous pains to have delivered, along with a note attached that read: *Twinkle, twinkle . . .*

The engagement ring that she sported on the third finger of her left hand had kept the sleazier studio executives off her case – especially after David Niven had put it about that Lisa's fiancé was a chum of his. It also kept reporters off the scent of her raging affair with Lochlan.

He attended the premiere with his wife, and they all posed happily together under the awning of the theatre – Judy with a proprietorial hand on Lochlan's arm, Lisa with a smile too wide to be true.

Lochlan sat next to her in the auditorium, and at one point during the screening he brushed a hand along her lamé-clad thigh. She knew he'd done it deliberately, to make her shiver, and she longed to be able to touch him back, but she suspected that Judy's eyes were all-seeing – even in the flickering half-light from the screen.

She still hadn't got used to seeing her face up there, fifty times larger than life. Thanks to the artistry of the lighting cameraman and her make-up and hair people, Lisa barely recognized herself. Her skin was luminescent, her hair a gleaming cascade, her smile radiant. During the love scenes between her and Lochlan, little 'oohs' and 'aahs' came from the female members of the audience, and she even fancied she heard a sniff or two during the schmaltzy bits. As she glided down the aisle to take her bow after the credits had rolled, there came applause that was gratifyingly sustained.

'They like you,' Lochlan told her in an aside as they bowed and smiled and posed for more photographs. 'I'm not surprised. How I would love to peel that dress off you and cover you with kisses right now.'

Oh, God! How she wanted him. She wanted to gaze at him, to touch him, to hear his voice intimate in her ear: but he didn't even make it to the post-premiere party. Judy allegedly missed her new baby so badly that she'd persuaded Lochlan not to attend.

In Ciro's after the screening, Lisa drowned her sorrows with the help of champagne and Fred Crane. She couldn't take her eyes off Lana Turner, who was sitting at her table at the bottom of the staircase, blowing kisses to a favoured few, and nodding like a potentate.

'You screen-kiss beautifully,' Fred told her. 'You and Lochlan have terrific screen chemistry. It's the second time Ziggy has teamed you, isn't it?'

'Yes.'

'He'll want to do it again. You better watch your ass if that happens, Lisa. The press will have a field day, fiancé or no fiancé.' And the way he tapped the side of his nose made Lisa wonder if he'd seen Lochlan caress her thigh earlier.

The film received fairly mediocre reviews, but Lisa didn't care, because her performance attracted mostly raves. The one she loved most she read over and over.

Miss La Touche was costumed exquisitely. The drama of her first appearance on screen is heightened by the effect of having her sit in a darkened carriage, giving the audience the sense of an apparition beyond life, a mysterious creature in the dark. When she finally does lean forward into the light – and the Technicolor – audiences were not jerked rudely back to earth. She simply was unreal. A proper goddess.

Ziggy was very happy with the impact she was having on cinema-goers. He upped her salary to $250 a week and, as Fred Crane had predicted, immediately started searching for another vehicle in which to team Lisa and Lochlan. Louella Parsons was intrigued enough to summon Lisa to her house for an exclusive. Having heard so many horror stories about the hack, Lisa was more than a little apprehensive – but her press agent was dogged.

'You gotta play ball in this town, girl,' said Myra. 'Paulette Goddard and Frances Farmer are universally loathed because they're so stuck-up about the press. That's what lost Paulette the role of Scarlett O'Hara.'

'Are you serious?'

'Yep. Her tests were terrific, and word around the industry was that Scarlett was hers. But her snooty attitude made the MGM press chief decide to count her out. You turn down an invitation to talk to Louella or Hedda or Sheilah Graham and you're shafted, honey. You might as well roll up that film script and invite them to shove it up your royal British ass.'

Lisa winced. She still hadn't got used to the way most people in Hollywood spoke.

'You'd do well to heed my advice,' continued Myra. 'This is Ziggy Stein's Hollywood, not King George's England, and you're not the only Brit in town. Greer Garson and Ama Lee and Deborah Kerr are easily as plummy and beautiful as you, and there's a new girl arriving every day from some posh finishing school. So you take care to mind your Ps and Qs, whatever they are.'

'Very well, Myra,' Lisa said, meekly.

'And another thing. Louella's style of journalism may be of the rubbishy variety, but don't let that persuade you that she's not a sharp cookie. Don't try to bullshit her. She won't thank you for it.'

So Lisa screwed her courage to the sticking place, and went to lionize the lioness in her den in Beverly Hills, bearing a massive bouquet of hothouse flowers.

Miss Parsons's maid showed Lisa into the living room. It was the last word in vulgarity, boasting a cocktail bar so crammed with highball, champagne and wine goblets it resembled a glassware shop. On the wall, resplendent in a gilt frame worthy of an Old Master, a *Time* magazine cover was flanked by votive candles. It featured Louella talking on a white telephone, wearing a pearly evening dress, kid gloves and a diamond crucifix. Her grinning mouth resembled a red-painted letter box.

The real Louella was sitting on a throne-like armchair, scanning the press release that Myra had sent her. 'Take a seat,' she commanded, and as she flounced an arm at her, Lisa smelt whisky in the air.

Sitting down obediently on a tasselled couch, she waited until Louella had finished reading the litany of lies that the publicity department had dreamed up. The hack finally set the press release aside, took a cigarette from an enamel box and lit it with a silver table lighter in the shape of a horse. 'I guess you'll want tea?' she asked, giving Lisa a look of assessment.

Lisa was on the verge of saying: 'Tea would be lovely, thank you,' when something made her think twice. 'Perhaps I could have something a little stronger, just to help me relax? I may as well tell you that I'm nervous as anything, Miss Parsons. It's such an honour to be interviewed by you.'

Louella threw her a smile as she rose to her feet and moved to the bar. 'No need to be nervous. Under the hard-bitten exterior I'm soft as an ice-cream sundae. What'll you have?' she asked, reaching for a bottle of Seagram's VO.

It was only two o'clock in the afternoon and Lisa hated whisky, but she sensed that it would be a good idea to follow the example set by her hostess. 'Whatever you're having would be lovely, Miss Parsons,' she said politely.

'Call me Louella,' said Louella, pouring whisky into a glass and handing it over in the manner of someone bestowing a precious gift. 'That'll put hair on your chest. Bottoms up! That's what you Brits say, isn't it?'

'Yes. Bottoms up!' Lisa took a pull and managed not to gag.

Louella resumed her throne. 'So. You wanna be a star, Lisa?'

'Well, yes!' she said brightly.

'You think you got what it takes?'

'I hope so, Miss – Louella.'

'There's been a flurry of British actresses fighting it out for stardom in recent years. I know that little Miss Vivien Leigh had her heart set on landing the lead in *Rebecca*. Tell me, Lisa.' Louella regarded her shrewdly. 'How did you feel about Joan Fontaine getting the part? Isn't that the role all you English gals would've killed for?'

Lisa had heard that Joan Fontaine and Louella Parsons were as thick as thieves. She would have to tread carefully.

'I was thrilled for Joan,' she enthused. 'Really thrilled. She and Larry Olivier made a splendid on-screen couple. Joan is a fabulously talented actress, and everyone tells me she's a lovely person.'

It was the right answer. Louella nodded and helped herself to a cigarette. 'What's Ziggy lined up for you next?' she asked.

'A contemporary version of *The Lady with the Little Dog*. It's a short story by Chekhov.'

'Chekhov, schmeckhov. Who's the screenwriter?'

'Anita Loos.'

'Smart choice. Who's co-starring?'

'Lochlan Kinnear.' Lisa made sure her voice was deadpan.

Louella looked thoughtful, and for an apprehensive moment Lisa thought she might be given the third degree about her co-star. But instead Louella picked up a short-hand pad and propelling pencil and said, 'OK, Lisa. It's time for you to spin me your spiel. Tell me what you think you've got that makes you different to all the other Great British Hopefuls who've invaded Hollywood.'

What had Myra told her? *Don't try to bullshit her.*

'Well, Louella,' she said. 'I'm very much a woman, and I'm not afraid to say that I enjoy it. Womanliness is a gift from God, and I believe that God's gifts should be put to good use on this earth. Otherwise it's disrespectful to Him.' She put a little emphasis on the word 'Him' to make sure the capital letter registered. She had heard that Louella kept a five-foot-high illuminated statue of the Virgin Mary in her back garden.

Louella gave a robust laugh. 'Good girl! Honest injun – I am so sick to death of coy actresses. Sex sells: we all know that, and it's refreshing to hear someone tell it like it is. 'Oomph' girls and 'It' girls and 'Sweater' girls! For Christ's sake! What's wrong with being plain sexy?'

'My guess is that the Hays Office is afraid of women, Louella. They'd rather keep us in the kitchen or put us up on pedestals than admit that women enjoy being women as much as men enjoy being men.'

'Great stuff!' remarked Louella, scribbling on her pad. 'Carry on, honey. Be as candid as you like – and don't worry that you'll say too much. I have a great talent for dreaming up euphemisms.'

'Well, it seems to me that one of the greatest advantages of being put on a pedestal is that men haven't yet realized that women can give orders better from there.'

'Ha ha ha!'

'I firmly believe that the quality of womanliness comes from within, Louella. It doesn't have much to do with physical attributes. And the secret is not just what you got – it's what people *think* you've got.' Lisa prayed Louella wouldn't suss that this hooey was a rehash from a Sheilah Graham column.

'Very good. Very clever,' Louella pronounced. 'Fancy another drink?'

'Sure. I'd love one!'

So Lisa spent the next couple of hours schmoozing and knocking back whisky with Lolly Parsons, and by the time she reeled out into the blazing sunshine that nailed down onto Beverly Hills, she'd made a new best friend.

The hangover she had to endure was worth it. The piece that appeared in Louella's column in the *Hollywood Reporter* was a virtual hagiography:

I recently spent two delightful hours in the company of the beautiful Miss Lisa La Touche, over fragrant Earl Grey Tea. Miss La Touche is one of the newer British actresses to arrive in Hollywood, but already she has earned her place on a pedestal. Yes – something tells me that Lisa is set to rise through the ranks to Goddess status. She has the beautiful manners one takes for granted from the English aristocracy (unlike some of our 'aristocracy' here in Hollywood: Take heed, our Nightclub 'Queen'!) She has been presented at court, and is engaged to be married to a viscount, which means that one day she will be genuine nobility!

Like most of the English aristocracy, Lisa loves to ride and is an accomplished horsewoman . . .

Hell's bells! thought Lisa.

. . . Mr Stein says of his protegée: 'Miss La Touche's career is mine to build and protect exactly as I have done that of my other stars, and I should be disappointed if she is not a very great star for the next ten or fifteen years.' Her next picture will be *The Lady with the Little Dog*, to be scripted by one of our wittiest screenwriters, Miss Anita Loos. She will co-star with Lochlan Kinnear . . .

Ten or fifteen years of stardom? Top marks, thought Lisa. That wasn't bad going in a profession that held youth and beauty in such high esteem that actresses over thirty were considered past it. She fetched a pair of scissors and started cutting out the interview to join the others in her scrapbook. As she turned the page to apply the adhesive, a headline caught her eye. 'Mabel Philips found dead,' she read. 'Ziegfeld girl in suspected suicide.'

CHAPTER SEVENTEEN

JESSIE

PARIS 1919

'Who was responsible for the preposterous charade? You or Demetrios?'

In a saffron-washed bedroom, on the top floor of the Montparnasse townhouse where Gervaise Lantier had his studio, Gervaise and Jessie were lying between sheets that were tempestuously tumbled. They had been there for nearly twenty-four hours, leaving the bed only to fetch food or wine – and once so that Gervaise could test her prowess as a model.

'It was the count's idea,' confessed Jessie. 'The story is that he found me wandering barefoot in the Tuileries Gardens suffering from amnesia.'

'How very convenient! *La belle dame sans mémoire*.'

'And *sans* baggage. The evening dress is the only item of clothing I possess.'

Gervaise smiled. 'The *beau monde* will be itching with curiosity. Who is the beautiful, feral waif that Gervaise Lantier has plucked from obscurity to become his muse and bedfellow?'

'So I've passed the test? I am to be your model?' Jessie lowered her eyes so that he would not read the desperation in them as she awaited his answer.

Since the previous evening – from the moment she had been presented to Gervaise at that swagger apartment in the boulevard Péreire – she had sensed that she was under scrutiny, like an actress auditioning for a role. Around noon, with the sun at its zenith, the artist had positioned her beneath the skylight that latticed the ceiling and reached for his sketchbook, and Jessie knew then that going to bed with him had been but a curtain-raiser to the main event. The words of the painter who'd picked her up on the carrefour Vavin came back to her: *I'd like to examine the goods before we start* . . . That's exactly what Jessie had become. The goods.

She had followed his direction to the letter, biting down on the inside of her lip with pain as she segued into pose after pose, each one tougher than the last: a more elegant elevation of her thigh, a more sensual curve of her arm, a more sinuous twist of her spine. She struck each attitude with apparent ease; defying gravity even when cramp threatened and sweat began to trickle down her ribcage, until at last dusk infiltrated the room.

Gervaise still hadn't answered her question. A moment went by, then another.

'A prima ballerina might have found those poses arduous,' Gervaise said, finally. 'The job's yours.'

Thank Heaven. Oh, thank Heaven! This would keep her going until ... Until when? Until she'd earned enough money to make a fresh start, or until her pregnancy started to show? She wouldn't think about that now. She couldn't tell him yet that she was carrying a child. She'd keep going until Gervaise got wise to the fact, and then . . .

'When is your baby due?'

Oh, God. 'You mean – you've guessed?'

'Of course I have. I'm an artist. I see things that other people don't.'

Jessie felt horribly deflated. She sat up and pulled the sheet over her breasts. 'I'm sorry.'

'Why do you say that?'

'My condition – well, it will make problems for you, won't it?'

'On the contrary. Your condition is a bonus; I'll get an entire series out of your changing shape.' He reached for an orange and began to toss it casually from hand to hand. 'I'd mentioned to Demetrios just recently that I had planned a series of Violetta when she was pregnant, but she wouldn't countenance it. She hated the idea of getting fat.'

'Violetta?'

'My last model but one. Also my ex-wife. After our divorce she had the nerve to ask me if I'd paint a portrait of her wearing the Vanderbilt diamonds.'

'She's a Vanderbilt?'

'She is now. But even though she snared herself a millionaire, I'm still liable for our daughter's upkeep.' Gervaise dug his fingernails into the orange, and started to peel away the skin. 'I take it the father of your child is past history?'

Past history . . . She thought of the words she'd pledged – the promise she'd made to love, honour and obey. She couldn't ever stop loving Scotch – her love for him was part of her, as fundamental and immutable as the three primary colours: but since he hadn't bothered to keep his side of the bargain, why should she concern herself about honour? As for obeying! The only imperative now was to obey the instinct for survival that told her how lucky she was to have been thrown a lifeline in the form of Gervaise Lantier.

'Yes,' she confirmed. 'He's past history.'

'You're sure?'

'I'm sure.'

'Good. I should hate to think that he might turn up and reveal your true identity. Elitist imbeciles like the ones at last night's party tend to recoil from impostors. They don't like the idea that they may have been gulled.' He was dividing the orange into quarters, regarding her from under the wing of dark hair that fell across his forehead. 'You've successfully bluffed your way into high society, *Perdita*. Let's go a step further and *épater le bourgeois*. You know what that means?'

'Yes, I do.' It's what she had done when she'd pursued an education, embraced socialism, supported the Suffragettes and married a bohemian. Now something one of the molls on the carrefour Varis had said came back to her: when a girl is without fortune or profession, what can she do but keep her mouth shut, take what she can get, and thank God for it? 'Have you ever known what it's like to be really, really hungry?' she asked.

'No. I'm almost ashamed to say that I've led a reasonably privileged life.'

'Hunger is a great leveller. I now know the literal meaning of "earning a crust".' She tore off a segment from the fruit Gervaise handed her and slid it into her mouth. 'I know it's vulgar to talk about money, Gervaise, but I have to ask how much—'

'You're absolutely right: it is in*eff*ably vulgar to talk

167

about money. Suffice it to say that the higher the price I can command for my paintings, the happier Demetrios will be.'

'Demetrios? Why?'

'He curates my work. It's in his interest to turn a profit.'

'Does he take a percentage of your earnings?'

'Yes. I don't begrudge him; he makes us both a great deal of money. He's very astute.'

'Machiavellian?'

'If you like. His type thrives on chaos. He's clever enough to realize that the unorthodox times we're living in call for unorthodox behaviour.' Stretching out a hand for his cigarettes, Gervaise lit two, then handed her one. 'I have to warn you that if you agree to become my muse, I make the rules. In return, you shall have all the privileges of a *maîtresse en titre*.'

'Wasn't the *maîtresse en titre* the chief mistress of the King of France?'

He nodded, regarding her with lazy, interested eyes. 'You strike me as the emancipated type, Perdita, so you may consider that to be a retrograde step. However, you should know that in bygone years courtesans were highly respected. They were educated, beautiful, and – as a result of their connections – extremely wealthy.'

'So I am to be your muse, model and mistress?'

'You make it sound like a song.' He smiled, but his tone was businesslike as he set about enumerating his require-ments on elegant fingers. 'Firstly, you are to be sexually available to me at all times – until your pregnancy starts to show.'

She caught the inference. He wouldn't want to have sex with her when she was big with another man's child. That was hardly a drawback – so long as he continued to support her. Gervaise was a skilled love-maker, which made her role of ardent bedfellow less burdensome, but she had no appetite for intimacy with anyone who wasn't Scotch.

'Secondly,' he continued, 'I shall expect you to be inspirational, compliant, resilient and hard-working. And thirdly, I shall want you to keep me amused. A sense of humour is an essential trait in a *maîtresse en titre*. Violetta regrettably lost hers when Ghislaine was born.'

'Ghislaine is your daughter?'

'Yes.' Gervaise plucked the cigarette from between her fingers and stubbed it out, before extinguishing his own. Then, leaning on an elbow, he turned to look down at her. 'What do you say, Perdita? I think that between us we shall make a very elegant couple. And if we fail, we shall fail with panache.'

Jessie took a moment to assess the validity of this. It was cut and dried: failing with panache was infinitely preferable to failing abjectly. Here she was lying on Irish linen, with duck-down pillows supporting her head and a glass of vintage Bordeaux within arm's reach. The alternative was a room where she was obliged to sprinkle pepper between the threadbare bed-sheets to rid them of bugs, and a dank cellar where Adèle and the Green Fairy held sway. She returned Gervaise's smile.

'We shan't fail,' she said, with decision. 'When do I start?'

'You've already started.'

He drew the sheet aside, and as he readied her for love-making, Jessie vowed that she would make herself indispensable to him. She, Perdita, the construct who'd wandered barefoot into Parisian society, would master the strategy made famous by Machiavelli, and she would damn well win. Gervaise was rich already – she could make him richer. Jessie was determined that she and her baby would want for nothing.

CHAPTER EIGHTEEN

LISA

HOLLYWOOD 1942

One day, Ziggy Stein summoned Lisa to his office and uttered the sweetest seven words she'd ever heard. They were: 'You're ready for the big time, kid.'

If Ziggy weren't so ugly, Lisa might have kissed him.

'I'm casting you as a plucky young British nanny on board *The City of Benares*.'

'*The City of Benares?* Isn't that the liner that was torpedoed last year?'

'Yup. It's time we got on the war propaganda bandwagon.'

Ziggy lit up a fat cigar, and Lisa tried not to show her distaste. *The City of Benares* had, tragically, been carrying a cargo of hundreds of British children to safety in America when the Nazi U-boats had attacked. Privately she thought it crass that so recent a tragedy should be the subject of a major motion picture, and wondered if she shouldn't try to get out of it.

'Lochlan will play your love interest.' Smoke plumed from Ziggy's mouth as he eyed her knowingly, and Lisa demurely lowered her eyelids. 'You make a great couple. On screen.' The emphasis was on the noun. 'If you can

promise me to keep your reputation squeaky clean . . .'
Lisa inclined her head '. . . I have other plans for you. See
that painting?' He waved a hand towards a portrait on the
wall that showed a woman with her skirts bunched up
around her thighs, treading grapes. 'That painting is by a
famous French artist called Lantier.' He pronounced it
'Lanteer', his accent clumsy. 'I have invited Mister Lanteer
to come to LA. Columbia got that British painter Sir
Laverty—'

Lisa refrained from pointing out that 'Laverty' was
actually Sir John Lavery, and that he was Irish, not British.

'—to paint Loretta Young and Maureen O'Sullivan. The
guys at Twentieth Century got a portrait of Anna Lee, by
some other fucking British lord. So I'm going to go one
better and have a French artist paint my English rose.'

Lisa tried not to wince. She hated being described as
being an 'English Rose' almost as much as she hated Myra
going around telling the ladies and gentlemen of the press
that she was an accomplished horsewoman.

'That's wonderful news, Mr Stein. I'm so honoured.'

'You should be. It don't come cheap, commissioning a
famous artist to travel all the way from France and shack
up in the Chateau Marmont.'

'When is he arriving?'

'Next week. So you'd better help yourself to something
from Wardrobe.'

She had hoped that she might pose for her portrait in
something glamorous by one of the legendary Orion
costume designers, but Ziggy was insistent on the English
Rose image, and Lisa knew he was right. Recently Dorothy
had written to tell her that there was a growing backlash in

Britain against ex-pat film stars, with headlines such as 'COME BACK YOU SHIRKERS' emblazoned on newspapers. It wouldn't do to offend British moviegoers by dressing ostentatiously, so Lisa ended up wearing a simple buttercup-print frock and a straw hat. It was decided that the location for the portrait should be equally unpretentious, and that's how she found herself on Sound Stage 4 one warm November day in a 'barn', where she was required to recline against a stack of hay bales.

'I'm allergic to hay,' she told Myra, as make-up Max-Factored her mouth, and hair-tonged her strawberry blonde tresses. 'It brings me out in a rash.'

'We'll Pan-Stik over it. Consider yourself lucky we didn't bring along some smelly old hens and a pig or two.'

'Or a goat. Ha ha ha.'

Lisa turned to see the rotund figure of Ziggy Stein framed in the entrance to the barn. Next to him stood a tall man wearing a Homburg hat. The distinctive smell of French tobacco drifted towards her on the air. 'Ladies!' boomed Ziggy. 'May I present Mister Gervaise Lanteer.'

Lisa watched as the artist tossed aside his cigarette and strolled across the floor, his gaze focused entirely on her. When he drew level with her, he scooped up her hand and brushed his lips against her fingers.

'It is a pleasure to make your acquaintance, Mademoiselle.' Lantier's voice was velvet, slightly accented. His gaze was so intense it seduced Lisa into believing momentarily that they were the only two people in that cavernous place.

'What do you think of her, Gervaise?' breezed Ziggy, breaking the spell and making Lisa feel like horseflesh all over again. 'Ain't she a little doll?'

Lantier raised an amused eyebrow. 'In France we would say *mignonne*.' He circled her, assessing. '*Très mignonne*.'

'*Mignonne*,' echoed Ziggy in his execrable French accent, looking very pleased with himself.

Lantier turned to the women grouped around Lisa. 'So, *mesdames*, which of you is responsible for the *maquillage*?'

This drew a blank.

'Make-up,' translated Lisa.

Dawn, the make-up girl, stepped forward.

'Might you be so kind as to tone it down a little?'

Ziggy nodded self-importantly. 'Mister Lanteer agrees with me that Miss La Touche should look as artless as possible.'

Dawn stapled on a smile. 'Sure,' she said, reaching for a pot of Cremine.

As Dawn started work on her face, Lisa watched Lantier and Ziggy turn and stroll down the corridor of sunlight that streamed through the open barn doors. She wondered if she was the subject – or rather, the *object* – under discussion. What might they be saying about her? Might Ziggy be making further equine references? Praising her as a breeder might a prize mare? She felt herself bristle as Dawn peeled off her false eyelashes, and rubbed spit along the line where the glue had been. She was fed up with being poked and prodded by Make-up and Wardrobe, fed up with being told what to do and exactly how to do it, fed up with simpering at Ziggy and his cronies and smiling at cameras. *Mignonne!* What did this Lantier fellow think she was? Some kind of lamebrain?

Once the revamp was finished, Dawn asked Ziggy's PA to summon the menfolk. 'Well, gentlemen? How's that?' she fluted, as they approached.

Lisa rose to her feet to present her face for inspection. Lantier gave her the once-over, and then she saw his eyes go to her feet. She was sporting a pair of peeptoe platform shoes with a buttercup yellow trim.

'Remove your footwear, Mademoiselle, if you would be so kind.'

Lisa stepped out of her shoes, feeling ridiculously vulnerable. 'Your stockings, too,' Lantier told her, and she saw Myra smirk. Turning away, she lifted the hem of her frock and unrolled first one stocking, then the other, before balling them and handing them to the wardrobe girl.

Lantier took a step back, narrowed his eyes at her, then smiled. 'Better,' he said. 'We can get to work now.'

'Myra. Bring Mister Lanteer anything he needs,' commanded Ziggy. 'Mister Lanteer, I look forward to seeing the finished product.'

'Thank you.'

'Might you care to join me for dinner tonight? My wife does a mean meatloaf.'

'I regret that I am otherwise engaged.'

'Another time, then.'

'That would be delightful.'

'You be good, now, Lisa!' Ziggy ran an avuncular eye over his pet starlet, adding, 'Have fun, girls!' Then he turned and strode out of the barn, his PA scurrying behind him.

The remaining 'girls' stood to attention, polite smiles in place.

'Can I fetch you anything, Mister Lanteer?' asked Myra.

'No. A boy is bringing my equipment.'

'Then how may I help you? Make-up and Wardrobe are

175

happy to stay on until everything is to your satisfaction.'

The wardrobe girl flashed Lantier a flirtatious smile before plonking the straw hat back on Lisa's head.

'I need no help. And remove the hat, please.'

Wardrobe obliged, and then Hair stepped forward with a comb and a can of spray.

Lantier held up a hand. 'No further grooming is necessary. There is a supply of water, yes?'

'Yes,' said Myra. 'I can arrange for food, too.'

'No food, thank you.'

All right for some, thought Lisa, who'd restricted her breakfast to a small bowl of fruit.

Lantier strolled towards the phalanx of Klieg lights, threw a couple of switches and began angling them adroitly. 'Perfect,' he said, finally, returning his attention to Lisa. 'Now, you may all go.'

'Are you sure, Mister Lanteer?'

'Quite sure, thank you.'

The team of women looked relieved as they gathered up the tricks of their various trades and backed off, Myra reminding Lisa to 'return the frock to Wardrobe once you're through.'

She stood perfectly still as she listened to the clack of retreating heels and stifled giggles. She knew that within an hour the news that Miss La Touche had had to take her stockings off in front of Ziggy Stein would be all over the studio commissary. She suddenly felt more self-conscious than she had ever felt in her life, more so even than when she had stepped in front of a camera for her first wardrobe test.

Lantier turned back to Lisa. He was still wearing his hat, which she considered not a little rude. It must have shown

176

in her expression, because, 'Forgive me,' he said, removing it and setting it on a packing case. 'Have you posed for a portrait before, Miss La Touche?'

'For photographic ones only,' Lisa told him. 'And please call me Lisa.'

'It is your real name, or one adopted for the screen?'

'I'm coy about that,' she said.

'Most actresses are coy about their real names, aren't they? I suppose it's one way of forging a new identity.'

'What do you mean?'

'Isn't a new identity part of the job?'

'Sometimes. Especially if your given name stinks.'

Gervaise smiled.

'Anyway,' Lisa went on, 'La Touche is a kind of family name. We're in Debrett's. Oh, I guess you don't know what Debrett's is.'

'On the contrary. I'm familiar with many of your British institutions.' He glanced at his watch. 'Are you ready to start?'

She nodded.

'Posing for a painter is very different to posing for a photograph, and very hard work. But if you are compliant and do as I tell you, we should be finished within the week.' He turned to survey the hay bales. 'I would of course prefer natural light, but Mr Stein does not want your fair skin to burn. I would like you to try some poses for me, if you would be so kind.'

As Lisa tried vainly to make herself comfortable (the hay was very prickly against her bare legs), a studio runner arrived lugging a trolley on which were piled an easel, a canvas, a knapsack and a wooden paintbox. Lantier tossed the boy a coin, glanced at his watch and said, 'Come back at four o'clock.' The boy touched his cap, then disappeared into the shadows beyond the circle of light.

'I'd like you to loosen your hair a little more,' Lantier told her. Lisa was aware of his eyes on her as she shook her hair out, running her fingers through the mane that had taken hapless Phyllis in the Hair Department nearly an hour to coax into shape. 'That's better,' he said. Then he turned away and opened his paintbox. The smell that emerged, a woody combination of linseed oil and eucalyptus, sent Lisa's mind reeling back in time, to the villa in France where her mother had swung with her on a hammock on the terrace, redolent with the scent of—

'Chypre,' she said.

Lantier gave her a quizzical look.

'It's the perfume my mother used to wear.'

He remained silent for several moments, studying Lisa's face. Then: 'Think of her,' he said, 'while I paint you. The expression is perfect.'

'Do you want me to talk about her?'

'No. I prefer silence while I paint. You can tell me all about yourself when the portrait is finished.'

'There's not much to tell.' This was Lisa's standard response when she was talking to somebody off the record, and not parroting Myra's litany of fabrications.

Gervaise sent her a brief smile. 'We all of us have stories. But for the time being, you can keep them to yourself.'

Sitting for Gervaise proved to be surprisingly therapeutic. Lisa was used to photographers and their assistants adjusting lamps and climbing ladders and fiddling around with light meters while Hair and Wardrobe tweaked and prodded.

For five days she lay on her mattress of straw and thought about her mother, and her schooldays and her grandparents in London, and about Richard Napier and the life she might have had, and she wished she were able to telephone home, to talk to her darling Gramps, or to Dorothy. But transatlantic telephone calls were out of the question during wartime.

Lisa wondered now how her family and friends were surviving the war, and if they had enough to eat, and she remembered how her grandfather's eyes had misted over when he had seen her off in Southampton, and she wanted to weep in return for all her loved ones.

On the fifth day, the artist turned to her with a smile and said, 'It's finished.'

Lisa's thoughts were dragged back to the here and now, to the cavernous interior of the sound stage, the heat of the lights, the itch of the hay on her skin, and the smell of oil paint. 'May I see?' she asked.

'Of course.'

The portrait was stunning. There was about it an ingenuous quality reminiscent of a world pre-war, where a lovely girl could loll barefoot and bareheaded, and day-dream. Lisa gazed and gazed at it, and then, with tears in her eyes, she turned to Lantier. 'Thank you,' she said. 'It is the most beautiful image that anyone has ever made of me. It's me as I really am. How did you know?'

'It's what I saw in your expression. That is why I don't like my subjects to talk to me while I work. People are generally more eloquent when they keep their mouths shut. But I should be delighted to listen now. Perhaps I could take you to dinner? You've certainly earned it.'

'It's late, and I rather think *you've* earned it. If you don't mind slumming it, I'd be more than happy to cook something for you in my apartment. I've just moved in, and I'm dying to show it off.'

Lisa's all-white 'Moderne' style duplex boasted a bar in the spacious living area, three bedrooms, four bathrooms, a walk-in wardrobe, a cantilevered staircase and her own small kidney-shaped swimming pool. Apart from an eye mask, some skincare products and a bottle of Dom Pérignon, the fridge was virtually empty, but she could rustle up a mean spaghetti Alfredo in minutes. The notion of having to dress up and make an entrance into some fancy eatery fatigued her, and she sensed that Gervaise felt the same.

'You cook?' Gervaise sounded surprised.

'Yes. And just in case you're wondering, I don't do meatloaf. Is pasta OK?'

'Pasta would be perfect.'

'And just in case you're wondering some more, if I say I'm going to slip into something more comfortable, I'm not making a move on you.'

Gervaise laughed. 'Poor Lisa. Do you always feel obliged to add that proviso when you invite a friend into your home?'

'I don't have many friends in Hollywood.' She smiled up at him. 'Will you travel with me in my roadster? I can take you by the scenic or by the tourist route.'

But before Gervaise could make a decision either way, there came the sound of urgent footsteps, and a runner arrived, breathless and red-faced.

'There's a telegram for you, Mister Lanteer,' he said.

The telegram had been from France, telling Gervaise that his brother was dying. That same evening he packed his bags, and checked out of the Château Marmont.

The next day, flowers were delivered to Lisa's apartment accompanied by a card that read: 'Gervaise Lantier. Villa Perdita, Cap d'Antibes, France'. On the back, in a bold black cursive script, was the following: 'If ever you should want a break from La La Land, I know the perfect place. Keep in touch. G.'

Lisa learned later that the ship transporting him back to Europe had narrowly missed being torpedoed.

'Miss La Touche?'

'Yes?'

'My name is Johnny Meyer. I got your number from Myra Blake. I'm calling on behalf of my boss.'

Lisa sat up very straight on her couch. She knew what was coming. Johnny Meyer procured for Howard Hughes. 'Ye-es?' she said.

'Mr Hughes saw you in *The Lady with the Little Dog* and admired your performance and all that jazz. He wants to take you to dinner at the Cocoanut Grove in the Ambassador Hotel. This evening, OK?'

She couldn't turn down an opportunity to meet Howard Hughes! Dorothy would shoot her dead if she did.

'That's terribly kind of Mr Hughes,' Lisa said. 'Just let me check my diary.' She set down the receiver and counted to twenty. Then she picked it up again. 'Yes. I just happen to be free this evening.'

'I'll send a car. Seven-thirty,' said Johnny Meyer. 'And be sure to speak up.'

'I beg your pardon?'

'Mr Hughes is a little hard of hearing,' said Johnny Meyer. And he hung up.

Lisa went straight to an incredibly exclusive dress shop on Hollywood Boulevard, and bought a black silk chiffon and Chantilly lace gown that cost her an entire week's salary. But it was worth it.

When she made her entrance into the Cocoanut Grove five hours later, the cameras of the press photographers who haunted the hotspot went into overdrive.

'That gown is Howard Greer, isn't it?' said a gallant Mr Hughes after he'd introduced himself.

'Yes,' she said, surprised. 'Not many men would know that.'

'And not many women can carry off his look. You do so with great style.'

'Thank you.' Lisa sat down in the chair that the *maître d'* was holding out for her.

'Champagne?'

'Yes, please.'

Fizz was poured, and glasses raised.

'Here's to you,' Howard said in his low, clipped Texan voice. 'That was some entrance you made. You've succeeded in making quite an impact on Hollywood, Miss La Touche.'

'Please call me Lisa. And I've been rehearsing that entrance for years.'

Hughes gave a gratifying laugh. 'You're knockout, Lisa. And I simply love your English accent. Shall we order?'

As she consulted her menu, Lisa studied her date out of the corner of her eye. He was about forty years old, tall, handsome, with a rakish moustache and a debonair manner. As well as being a movie-maker, he built and flew his own planes! How sexy was that?

'Is that an engagement ring you're wearing?' Howard

asked, after the waiter had brought their food. The 'usual' Howard had requested turned out to be strip loin steak and peas – twelve of them – geometrically lined up.

'Yes,' she replied, resisting the impulse to lean over with her fork and ruin the symmetry of his plate. 'My fiancée—'

'Is a barrister called Richard Napier, I know. Since you're engaged to him, what are you doing playing around with Lochlan Kinnear?'

Lisa dropped her fork. 'Goodness! What a thing to say! I – my relationship with Mr Kinnear is purely professional.'

'Don't bullshit me, Lisa. If we are to be friends, I would appreciate the courtesy of an honest reply.' She started to protest, but he raised a cautionary finger. 'Because when your affair is over, you're going to need a shoulder to cry on. I've been around the block a few times, and I'm very good at listening.'

Lisa was so astonished that she almost did burst into tears. Since the very beginning of her affair, she had confided in nobody – not even Dorothy, in the letters she occasionally wrote. Lochlan had instilled such paranoia in her about the press that she was terrified her mail would be intercepted – a commonplace enough occurrence in wartime. She couldn't talk to her hairdresser the way most women did, or the wardrobe girls, or any of the other chatterboxes she met during the course of her working day. She couldn't talk to Sabu because she feared his opprobrium, or to David because he'd gone back to Blighty to enlist, and any female friends she had made were far too fairweather to trust.

'Why not spill some beans?' said Howard.

So she told him about Lochlan, and about how he'd

been tricked into marrying Judy. She told him how Lochlan had to allow a decent interval before he could initiate divorce proceedings, and about how they planned to marry at the soonest opportunity thereafter. She told him how envious she was of Judy's baby, and how she longed for a child of her own.

'And how does Mr Napier feel about this?' asked Howard, when she'd finished.

Lisa felt herself turning bright red. 'He doesn't know.'

'Not very tidy behaviour, Lisa.'

'No.'

'I'm not one to stand in judgement, but you might want to set about some spring-cleaning. It wouldn't do your reputation any good to ditch your British fiancé while there's a war on, but you need to drop Kinnear like a ton of bricks.'

'But I love him!'

'Sure you do. But once your fling hits the headlines, you're on the ropes.'

'Do people suspect?' she whispered.

'Sure.'

'What can I do?'

'Stop seeing him.'

'I can't!'

'Don't be stupid, Lisa. You want your career to move forward, you listen to what I have to say. Your agent's Phil Gersh, right?'

'Yes.'

'I'll give him a call.' Howard pushed his plate away as the orchestra swung into 'In the Mood'. 'Let's dance,' he said with a smile. 'Sometimes it's the only thing to do, whether you're in the mood or not.'

The next day Miss La Touche accepted delivery of so many dozens of gardenias – compliments of Mr Hughes – that she ran out of vases.

On the morning of the grand unveiling of her portrait, Lisa stumbled into one of her streamlined Moderne style bathrooms, crouched down on the gleaming white tiles, pushed back her hair, and threw up into the lavatory. It was the sixth consecutive day that she had been violently sick; she had not had a period in over two months. Hauling herself off the floor, she peered into the glass above the porcelain basin. She looked peaky – gaunt, even. Her Max Factor free complexion was patchy; there was a burgeoning pimple just above her upper lip. She needed no consultation with a doctor to tell her that she was pregnant.

From the sitting room came the jangle of the telephone bell. It would be Myra, calling to fill her in on the press interviews that were lined up for today. She had another gruelling schedule to look forward to, culminating this evening in the official unveiling of the Lantier painting.

The studio had decreed that she wear an Adrian gown for the occasion, even though Maria, her dresser on *Lady and the Little Dog*, had told her that the zipper on the dress was faulty, and it had acquired a permanent taint of sweat after being loaned out to actresses in the talent department for social engagements. With a sinking heart, Lisa remembered the full-length body stocking she would be required to wear underneath, and how problematic it would make visiting the bathroom. For recently Lisa had felt an increasingly urgent and frequent need to pee. She remembered how poor Maria had used to lunge towards the bathroom door with her hand clutched to her crotch, whimpering lest she might not make it in time. The dresser had given birth to a stillborn baby in a corner of the wardrobe block some weeks later, fenced off by costume rails laden with antebellum crinolines.

The phone stopped ringing, then started again. Pulling her negligee tighter around her, Lisa moved into the sitting room, managing a quick do-ray-me to warm up her vocal cords before answering.

'Good morning!' she said, brightly.

'Get your ass over to the Biltmore by midday,' barked Myra. 'You're talking to *Collier's*, *Modern Screen* and *Click*. They'll be through with you by two-thirty.'

'The Biltmore, midday,' said Lisa, trying to sound businesslike. 'Is there a suite booked?'

'Who do think you are? Olivia de Havilland? They'll look after you in the lobby. Order tea: Lord Grey or whatever that English shit is. No liquor – not even if the hack offers.'

Liquor at midday! Lisa was about to riposte; then remembered that Myra routinely splashed gin into her tea from nine o'clock in the morning onward. 'I'll call by the studio and pay a visit to Make-up first, shall I?' she volunteered.

'Bob has no time for you in Make-up until after six o'clock. He's a dozen new girls testing.'

'But—'

'Don't "but" me. We'll supply the mags with studio pics, OK? Once you're through rendez-vooing get on over to Barney's Bowls for a ribbon-cutting: bring a change of clothes with you. Something sporty – socks and loafers and a kilt or something.' A kilt! What was Myra thinking?

'And a tight sweater.' The photographers liked them tight. It would have to be the baby blue angora again, teamed with her pleated rayon.

'Will I have time to get something to—'

'Put her on hold, Olive.' Myra's voice over the line was muffled, suddenly. 'On second thoughts, tell her I'm out of the office until next week.'

Lisa wondered what poor sap was being given the brush-off, and decided against asking Myra if she'd have time to eat. She didn't want to antagonize her. Anyway, missing a meal would be good for her: she'd want a perfectly flat stomach this evening.

'Next item,' resumed Myra. 'Your gown will be ready for you in Wardrobe when you're through at Barney's. Make-up's scheduled for six-thirty; Bob'll throw a fit if you're any earlier. There'll be a car, and diamonds courtesy of Cartier—'

'Cartier!'

'Make sure you return them to the goon at the end of the evening.'

'Will it be a late night?'

'Hey! I said *black* coffee, asshole!' Myra wasn't listening.

Lisa tried again. 'Will the car take me back to studio at the end of the evening, Myra? I'll need to change.'

'You think those overworked gals in Wardrobe wanna hang around waiting for Cinderella to get back from the ball? Not a chance, sweetie.'

'But how will I get out of the gown? The zipper's faulty – I'll have to be sewn into it.'

'Not my problem. I'm sure the goon'll be happy to oblige.'

'But—'

'Biltmore, midday. Don't be late.'

There was a click on the end of the line, and Myra was gone.

Shambling into the bathroom, Lisa fetched a cloth from under the basin, got down on her hands and knees and wiped vomit from the floor.

CHAPTER NINETEEN

JESSIE

PARIS 1919

'These are so *good*! D'you know, I never tasted croissants until after the war.'

Jessie and Gervaise were sitting cross-legged at a low
table in his apartment, breakfasting on fruit, croissants
and apricot conserve. It was the first time she had emerged
from the bedroom to explore her new home. There was
something louche about it, something of the kasbah. The
furniture was intricately carved, the windows draped in
heavy, oriental silk. Embriodered cushions were heaped
on vast couches and faded Turkish rugs carpeted the floors.
On a wall, handpainted gesso panels depicted couples
engaged in acts from the Kama Sutra.

Jessie was sporting nothing but one of Gervaise's
shirts, haphazardly buttoned. She reached for her
third croissant, and spread it with lavish amounts of
butter.

'That shirt looks very fetching on you,' he remarked. 'But
have you given any thought to what you might wear when
you venture out?'

'No.' She furrowed her brow. She really hadn't an idea
what was currently in vogue, but if the glad rags sported by

the gargoyles in the boulevard Péreire the other night were anything to go by, she wasn't impressed. After months of living like a vagabond, blissfully free from sartorial constraints, the simpler the get-up the better, as far as she was concerned.

'In that case I shall have to take you shopping,' said Gervaise.

'I can hardly go shopping wearing nothing but a shirt.'

'I have something I can kit you out with.' He left the room, and came back a couple of minutes later with a suit on a hanger.

'I can't wear that!' she said.

'Why not?'

'It's – well it's a sailor suit, isn't it?'

'It is. It was a prop for the marquis de Villeparisis. His mother insisted I paint him as a jaunty *matelot*. It was one of the most fiendishly difficult portraits I've ever had to do.'

Jessie held the suit at arm's length and frowned.

'The only alternative is a dressing gown. Coco's emancipated enough to have ditched her corset, but even she might draw the line at receiving a lady sporting a *robe de chambre*.'

'Who's Coco?'

'Coco Chanel is the mistress of a friend of mine – Boy Capel. She's a dressmaker, and she's just opened a *maison de couture* on the rue Cambon. We'll pay her a visit today.' Pulling the sailor suit off the hanger, he tossed it across to her. 'Go get changed. I rather fancy the notion of you dressed as a cabin boy.'

Jessie looked dubious. 'What about my hair?'

'There's a beret in the pocket. You can stuff it under that.'

'Will I have to go barefoot again?'

'No. The other indignity forced upon the hapless *comte* was a pair of girlish patent pumps. They'll do you for today, until we can get you properly shod.'

'You make me sound like a pony.'

'There's a joke there somewhere, but I won't be coarse enough to put it into words. What did you think of the style on parade at my sister's soirée, incidentally?'

'I thought it was hideous.'

'I agree. That's what makes me think that you and Coco will get along famously. She's considered more than a little bohemian by her rival modistes.'

'Bohemian, how?'

'Let's just say that she has a healthy disregard for convention – like you.' Gervaise grinned. 'Bring on those society beldames with their chain-mail couture and their painted visors and their pomaded helmets of hair. You and Coco'll knock 'em for six, Perdie dear.'

Jessie crammed the rest of her croissant into her mouth, then moved in the direction of Gervaise's bedroom, shrugging off his shirt as she went. She was glad that she had no qualms about nudity. If Scotch had taught her one thing, it was that the human body was to be celebrated, not shrouded in shame.

Once she had secured the last button on the jacket, she raised her head and regarded her reflection in the cheval glass. The sailor suit fitted her almost perfectly. It was a touch tight over the breasts, but that only had the effect of flattening them and making her figure appear more boyish.

Another successful disguise! she thought, stuffing her hair up under the beret. She, Perdita, was becoming a veritable mistress of them.

*　　*　　*

Chez Chanel on the rue Cambon, Gervaise and Jessie followed a chic salesgirl upstairs to a suite of rooms on the second floor. The furnishings were sparse, but exquisite: Madame Chanel evidently had excellent taste. A statue of a blackamoor stood sentinel in a corner, an elaborate crystal chandelier was reflected in an ornate gilt mirror, a screen had been angled just so, to display its lacquered panels.

Silhouetted against a window with her back to them, a woman knelt on a suede-upholstered ottoman, clearly pre-occupied in taking measurements of the casement.

'Madame? *Voici* Monsieur Lantier,' announced the sales-girl, then bobbed a curtsey before backing out of the room.

Madame Chanel – who, Jessie judged, was in her early thirties – was quite ravishingly pretty. Her face – framed by soft bangs and devoid of make-up – boasted the kind of cheekbones Scotch had raved about. Her eyes beneath slanting brows were candid; her nose a perfect retroussé and her mouth curved in a wide smile. She was wearing a shift dress made from unstructured black jersey that fell in supple folds to mid-calf, and Jessie realized that Gervaise had been right when he'd said that Coco Chanel was unconventional – to construct a dress from fabric that hitherto had been reserved for men's underclothing was nothing short of revolutionary. Over the dress Madame wore a tabard of embroidered silk; a single strand of pearls was her only adornment. The effect was breathtakingly art-less.

'Gervaise!' said Madame. 'What a pleasure to see you!' With nimble fingers, she rolled up the tape measure, then tossed it into a corner. 'Forgive me – I'm measuring the windows for drapes. I shall want yards upon yards of velvet.' Extending a hand to be kissed, she turned her attention to Jessie. 'Bonjour, Monsieur.'

Gervaise laughed. 'Coco, it is with pleasure that I introduce you to. . . Perdita.' Turning to Jessie, he said: 'Perdita, you may remove your hat.'

Jessie reached up and pulled off the beret, whereupon her hair tumbled over the collar of her sailor suit in a mass of unruly waves. Madame Chanel looked nonplussed, momentarily, then clapped her hands together and crowed with glee.

'Of course! You are the girl who caused such a sensation at the salon in the boulevard Péreire the other evening! And now you show up here dressed as a cabin boy! How I applaud your audacity!'

'Thank you, Madame.'

'Coco, please. And I shall call you Perdita.' Moving across to a fluted sconce, Madame unhooked a speaking tube. 'Rose! A bottle of Veuve Clicquot, if you would be so kind.'

Gervaise took a seat on the ottoman, stretching his long legs out in front of him. 'As you may have guessed, I brought Perdita here to be kitted out.'

'Will my clothes appear in your paintings?'

'I rather think not,' said Gervaise, with a smile. 'I'm embarking on a series of nudes.'

'No matter. I will have my secretary write to the important magazines. That way, word will soon spread that the new muse of Lantier favours Chanel.' She turned back to Jessie and touched her lightly on the arm. 'Please don't be afraid to say "no" to anything you don't care for, by the way, Perdita. It stands to reason that you should feel as comfortable in my clothes as you do in your pelt.'

How disarming and ingenuous was this woman! Jessie felt as if she'd met up with an old friend to whom she could talk about anything. 'Is this design your own?' she asked, indicating the tabard.

'But of course!'

'I truly love it.'

'What impeccable taste you have. Isn't the embroidery exquisite? Gervaise – help yourself to champagne when it arrives. I'll have your protégée try on a half-dozen or so outfits, then send her back to show them off to you. Come with me, Perdita.'

They arrived in a room that smelt of fresh paint and new fabric. There were no furnishings, just row upon row of costume rails draped in dust-sheets.

'This is a temporary arrangement,' Coco told Jessie. 'Before the year is out, the apartment will be refurbished as a dedicated salon. It is going to be *so* beautiful! You and Gervaise must come to our first party. In fact – why not dine tonight with me and my beau? I'm sure Gervaise told you about Monsieur Capel? Gervaise and my Boy are great friends.' Taking hold of a corner of one of the dust-sheets, Coco pulled smartly in the manner of a magician performing the tablecloth trick.

'Oh, heaven!' said Jessie, when she saw what had been unveiled. 'What *exquisite* clothes!'

Coco smiled at her. 'You like? That gladdens me. Go on, rummage – rummage! I can tell your fingers are itching to!'

But these clothes were too precious to be handled in anything but a reverent manner. Feeling apprehensive lest she soil the garments, Jessie wiped the palms of her hands on the hips of her sailor's bell-bottoms, then took from the rail a hanger from which was suspended a tunic and matching skirt. Like the dress that Coco was wearing, the garments were deceptively unstructured – but the opulence of the embroidery made up for the schoolgirl simplicity of the line.

'Look here, at the little peacocks. Aren't they darling!' Coco took hold of the hem of the tunic, around which paraded a procession of minuscule silken peacocks worked in jewel-coloured chain stitch and herringbone, and dotted here and there with French knots.

'I've never seen anything so pretty,' exclaimed Jessie. 'Not even in the needlework department in Liberty!'

Coco looked smug. 'Try it on.'

'May I?'

'Of course! And – let's see . . .' She took down a black crêpe-de-Chine dress that boasted panels of equally intricate embroidery, and passed it over. 'The square décolletage is most becoming. You'll need a coat, naturally: this one is superb – a work of art. And I *love* this jersey skirt and jacket ensemble – it looks like nothing on the hanger, but in motion it is as elegant as a poem.'

Jessie regarded her benefactress gravely over the exotic fabric that had been heaped into her arms. 'Coco – how can I repay you?'

'That's easy, *mon amie*,' said Coco, with an eloquent shrug. 'Everywhere – but everywhere you go in Paris, you will wear my clothes. You will be a walking advertisement for my *maison de couture*.'

'But I'm not a socialite! I'm nobody – nobody important. My real name is Jessie—'

'Hush!' Coco touched a finger to her lips. 'I don't need to know your identity. To me – to anyone who matters – you are Perdita.'

Feeling defeated suddenly, Jessie slumped. The bravado that had kept her buoyant since she donned her new persona had deserted her. 'I can't carry this charade off! I've never been a fashion plate – never will be.'

'But don't you see? *this* – this is not fashion. Fashion goes out of style. It is style alone that endures. Audacity and style combined are most effective weapons – I should know! And – forgive me, my dear, but it would appear that you have no option other than to be audacious. Gervaise told me earlier on the telephone that his new protégée is destitute. Is this true?'

Jessie nodded. 'Yes, it's true. If Count Demetrios had not come to my rescue—'

'Demetrios? You know him?'

'He was responsible for staging that stunt in the Boulevard Péreire.'

'*Tiens!* Take care, *petite*. The count is a dangerous man. You are lucky that it was a gentleman he delivered you to, not some debauchee who would gobble you whole and spit you out. Gervaise is a good man. He will be a protector to you, as my Boy has been to me.'

Jessie looked down at the pattern of hearts and flowers that embellished the neckline of the crêpe-de-Chine dress, and then looked back at her new friend. 'May I ask you a personal question, Coco?'

'You may. You'll find that I am not easily offended.'

'Do you – do you *love* your Boy?'

'Whether or not I do is irrelevant. Love doesn't enter the equation in arrangements such as ours. You must know that fortune has smiled on you. To be a *succès de scandale* is not something every woman welcomes, but the clever ones make it work to their advantage. I've worked hard to get to where I am today – look! Just look at my apartment. But all this beauty comes at a price. You know the analogy of the swan?'

Jessie shook her head.

'So beautiful on the surface – so unruffled, so serene! But underneath the water, what is she doing? She is paddling like the very devil to make headway. That is how women like you and I must always appear, Perdita. Outwardly insouciant, carefree and sparkling: inwardly striving, toiling, forever thrusting ourselves forward, forever elbowing the opposition out of the way. The Great War may be over, but the war for the emancipation of women continues.'

'I've always considered myself to be emancipated,' said Jessie. 'I've always associated with freethinkers and liberals and—'

'Listen to me. Something tells me that your outlook on the world is a trifle naïve, Perdita. Something tells me that up until now you have led a comfortable, happy, reasonably privileged life. Am I right?'

'Yes.'

Coco smiled. 'Let me tell you a little about myself. My father was an itinerant peddler. My mother died when I was twelve. I was brought up in an orphanage, I wore second-hand boots. When I was twenty I passed round the hat in a music hall in Moulins. Now? Now I have all this.' With an expansive arm, she indicated her surroundings. 'Do you think it just fell into my lap?'

'No, I don't.'

'Believe me – you make your own luck, Mademoiselle Perdita. You make your own fate. You grab it with both hands and you wrest it into shape. You've been given a god-sent opportunity. Make the most of it – hit your mark, centre stage. If you don't, you'll find there are a thousand more Perditas waiting in the wings.' She raised a cautionary eyebrow. 'Now – go try on my beautiful clothes, and I will have Rose bring you a glass of champagne. We'll toast to our mutual success, *oui*?'

And with a sideways smile and a switch of her hip, Coco Chanel turned and left Jessie to it.

CHAPTER TWENTY

LISA

HOLLYWOOD 1942

Lisa was in the back of a limousine, gliding toward the Pacific Palisades, where the unveiling of the Lantier painting was to take place in the Riviera Country Club. A flunkey handed her a champagne glass as she entered the Grand Ballroom, and Fred Crane sprang forward with a light for her cigarette. On a dais stood an easel, swathed in spangled midnight-blue velvet: the portrait, waiting to be unveiled. Lisa made her way towards Ziggy Stein, who was holding court on a Louis XIV sofa, a Havana cigar jammed between his teeth, a battalion of fedora-wearing press photographers surrounding him. As she glided across the floor, silk chiffon drifting in her wake, several B-movie starlets bared their teeth at her. Envious eyes followed her progress; swanlike necks snaked towards each other to hiss venom in bejewelled ears, slim shoulders were shrugged in affected indifference.

'Here's my leading lady!' Ziggy drew his protegée down beside him and slung an arm around her. Sending practised smiles at the cameras that flashed and popped until her head swam, Lisa accepted compliments and fielded invitations and laughed at unremarkable *bons mots* from junketeers, all the time scanning the crowd for Lochlan.

Finally she located him. He was framed in the arc of one of the ceiling-high French windows that led onto the terrace, talking to a gimlet-eyed Lolly Parsons. As Lisa watched she saw Judy join him, saw her reach for her husband's hand and entwine her fingers in his. Encircling her slender waist with his arm, Lochlan smiled down at his wife, whereupon Louella's calculating expression broadened into one of beneficence, as if bestowing a price-less gift upon the happy pair.

Lisa couldn't bear it. Smiling up at Ziggy, she said: 'Mind if I inveigle Lochlan outside, so that the boys can get some shots of us together?'

'Good idea,' said Ziggy. He turned back to the assembled hacks and raised a hand. 'Ladies and gentlemen of the press – there's a photo op waiting for you across the room, if you can persuade Mr Kinnear to peel himself away from his lovely wife. May I suggest the terrace, with the ocean as a backdrop?'

Lisa gathered up her skirts and rose gracefully to her feet. As she headed towards the French windows, questions were fired at her by the accompanying hacks. Exchanging her empty champagne glass for a fresh one, she took another hit of Moët before approaching Lochlan and his coterie. Then, feeling faintly ridiculous, she waited for an opportunity to attract his attention. She saw Judy throw her a glance.

'Why, Lochlan,' she observed drily. 'Here's your leading light.'

Lochlan turned and looked Lisa directly in the eye. It was a hard look, charged with warning. 'Lisa!' he said. 'You look utterly ravishing. You've met Judy, of course—'

Judy blew a plume of smoke in her direction.

'—and you know Miss Parsons, too, I think?'

'Indeed. Delighted to meet you again, Miss Parsons.'

'Likewise, dear Lisa.'

'Mr Kinnear?' A photographer stepped forward. '*Photoplay* magazine. May I trouble you and Miss La Touche for a picture on the terrace?'

'Happy to oblige,' said Lochlan, smoothly. With a gracious smile at Miss Parsons and an indulgent one at Judy, Lochlan moved towards Lisa and placed a mannerly hand on the small of her back. 'How're things?' he asked in an undertone, guiding her through the French windows.

'I need to talk to you,' she murmured, as the press pack clustered around, exhorting them to 'Smile!' Draping chiffon becomingly over the balustrade, Lisa sent a doe-eyed look at the *Photoplay* photographer.

'That's swell!' the photographer enthused. 'But would you mind please moving a little to the right, so I get that palm tree in?'

Lochlan shifted sideways, and directed his most charming smile at the lens. Lisa could feel his fingers cool against the inside of her elbow as together they segued effortlessly into a camera-friendly pose.

'Terrific! Say cheese!'

'What's on your mind, honey?' queried Lochlan, out of the corner of his mouth.

'Not here,' Lisa told him. 'Can't we find somewhere private?'

'This is as private as it gets at an event like this. You wanna talk, just keep looking down the lens.'

'It doesn't feel right.'

'It's too dangerous for us to meet up anywhere. Louella's on our case.'

'How do you know?'

'She just sent me a coded message. I sent her one straight back.'

'What kind of a message?'

'She hinted that life was imitating art. That our on-screen romance might have off-screen repercussions.'

'Miss La Touche? Can I ask you to shake back your hair?'

Lisa obliged, then murmured, 'But we've been so careful.'

'I told you Louella has spies everywhere.'

Not in my john, she hasn't, Lisa thought, as an image rose before her mind's eye of her wan reflection in her bathroom that morning and the morning before and the morning before that . . . And then the enormity of her predicament hit her with the force of a blow to the solar plexus, and she knew she had to share the news with Lochlan, right there, right now, otherwise she would find herself reeling around the Riviera Country Club, scream-ing it out loud to the entire assembly.

'I'm pregnant,' she said.

Lochlan's fingers jerked away from her arm as though he'd been burnt; she heard him suck in his breath.

'Smile!' cajoled a freelance jerk she recognized. The last shoot they'd done, he'd spent way too long rearranging her décolletage.

'Did you hear me, Lochlan?'

'I heard you.'

She allowed him a moment to process the news, then turned to him with a tentative smile. 'I know it's happened sooner than we'd planned, but—'

'Get rid of it,' he said.

'Get *rid* of it?'

'I don't have room for another baby in my life. Judy's expecting again.'

'*Judy*? How—'

'You're going to have to see a doctor.'

'I know, but not for a few months yet. I can—'

'Not that kind of doctor, you dumb broad. Use your loaf.'

'*Lisa! Over here!*'

Turning automatically, she waited for the flash. Then: 'You're asking me to have an abortion?'

'I'm not asking you, Lisa. I'm telling you. Because if you don't, your career is over. Check the morals clause in your contract.'

'My career? I don't care about that! It's you I care about – you and our baby.'

'Who says it's our baby?'

'Of course it's ours!'

'Keep your voice down.'

'Miss La Touche? Mr Kinnear? Can you turn and look out to sea?' A snapper from *Silver Screen* was eyeballing them through his aperture. 'Ahoy there!'

'Ahoy there!' she echoed, pointing towards the horizon.

'There's nothing to prove it's mine,' resumed Lochlan, following the direction of her gaze and speaking through pearly white teeth, like a ventriloquist. For the first time, Lisa noticed that the canines were prominent, lending him the appearance of Bela Lugosi in the Dracula film.

'Whose could it be? You're the only—'

'Come on, sweetheart. We all play charades in this town.

203

Don't tell me you haven't spent time in Ziggy's office down on all fours?'

'That's disgusting!'

'And a little bird tells me you've been seen out and about with Howard Hughes.'

'*Ahoy there*, again!'

'Ahoy there!' they carolled.

'I've heard he prefers oral,' resumed Lochlan, sending the photographer a jaunty salute. 'But I'm sure he wasn't averse to giving your hot little hole a poke from time to time.'

Lisa couldn't believe the filth that was pouring from the mouth of the man she loved. Who was this person? This wasn't the man who had wooed and worshipped her, who had described his love for her as a bolt from the blue, the man whose kisses she had returned with such abandon.

'Say cheese again, Miss La Touche,' exhorted a grinning hyena. 'We love cheese!'

'Toss your hair!' urged *Motion Picture* magazine.

'Laugh!' commanded *Screen Book*.

'So, you don't love me?' Lisa's voice was so faint she could barely hear herself.

'Sweetheart,' Lochlan told her, 'this is the most cynical city in the world. It's all charade. No-one – but *no-one* – means what they say in LA. You've lived here long enough to know that.'

'Miss La Touche? One on your own, please.'

Lisa moved a little to her left, to oblige. Lochlan was right: she had lived here long enough to know that 'Hollywood's Happiest Husband' was a lying cheat – as he smilingly reminded her when she rejoined him for more photographs.

'Tomorrow the great cinema-going public will be overwhelmed with joy when they open the *Los Angeles Examiner* and find out that my beloved wife is expecting our second child. In their eyes, Lisa, I am a happily married man.'

'So our baby means nothing to you?'

'Your baby, Lisa, your problem. I will deny to hell and back that it's anything to do with me, and the powers that be will support me, while *you* will be denounced as a strumpet gold-digger, the whore of Babylon. The Hays Office and the studio executives will see to it that you're stripped naked and dragged kicking and screaming through every fanzine on the planet. If that's what you want, go ahead and commit professional suicide. If not, then I suggest you go talk to Lana.'

'Lochlan, you can't mean this.'

'I have never been more serious in my life. As I said, talk to Lana. She can tell you which backstreet quack will oblige.' Abruptly, he disengaged. 'OK, folks,' he said, flashing his famous smile, 'it's time for me to rejoin my lady wife. And allow me to share a secret with you. Judy and I will be hearing the patter of tiny feet again in the not-too-distant future.'

A collective intake of breath met this pronouncement, and pencils scribbled faster in notebooks.

Lochlan winked. 'I'm saying nothing else. Just pick up a copy of the *Examiner* tomorrow, and you can read all about it. Louella has the exclusive.'

The second-stringer shot him a resentful look, clearly miffed that she hadn't got the scoop.

'Thank you for your time, ladies and gentlemen. Enjoy the rest of your evening.' With that Lochlan strolled off, pausing here and there to sign an autograph.

The spotlight no longer on her, Lisa stumbled down the steps that led to the gardens. Feeling her heels becoming mired in the sprinkler-soaked lawn, she tugged them off and veered towards the car park where her car was waiting. She was about to call out to the chauffeur who was sharing a smoke with a fellow driver, when she ran slap bang into Myra.

'Where do think you're going?' demanded Myra.

'I'm not well. I have to get home.'

Myra grabbed her wrist. 'You're not going anywhere, sweetie. This is a unique publicity opportunity, and you're going to grab it with both hands.'

'But I'm unwell – really unwell. I can't face any more press tonight.' Lisa realized that tears were streaming down her face.

'If you had tertiary syphilis it would cut no dice,' Myra told her crisply. 'You're a professional now, sweetie, not some spoilt princess. So get your royal British ass into the bathroom, wipe that mud off your heels, and do something with your face. The portrait's being unveiled in five.'

The next morning Lisa awoke, and wished that she hadn't. She wanted to sleep for ever; she craved oblivion. How could she have been so naïve, so *stupid*? How many people knew about her affair with Lochlan, and had been laughing up their sleeves at her all the time? How many of his friends had he boasted to about his conquest, in the changing room of the golf club or over a card game? What kind of unsavoury detail might he have gone into?

Lisa felt sick, and it wasn't just down to her condition. She was sick with herself. Her 'stolen moments' with

Lochlan now appeared to her as the shabbiest, most tawdry of her life. Oh, God! They'd made love in an alleyway once, and once in a public lavatory, and twice in a motel room where she knew the sheets hadn't been changed, and many, many times on the rear seat of his car. Except it hadn't been 'making love', Lisa knew now. Lochlan had been fucking her, and she'd allowed herself to be fucked.

She lay a while, curled with her arms wrapped round her tummy, postponing what she knew she had to do. Then, reaching for the phone, she dialled Lana Turner's private number.

The story about a seventeen-year-old Lana being discovered in Schwab's Soda Fountain sipping chocolate malted through a straw was – as Louella had told Lisa – a myth concocted by MGM. In truth, the original 'Sweater Girl' had been just fifteen-going-on-sixteen; she'd been discovered in the Top Hat Soda Shop across the road from Hollywood High, and she had been drinking a Coca-Cola because she couldn't afford malted. Now Lana, at the age of twenty-two, was all grown up. She'd featured in half a dozen movies, been affianced to one man and married to another, and – as Lisa had inferred from Lochlan last night – had undergone that most terrifying test of endurance, now routine in Hollywood: an abortion.

Lisa had met her twice. The first time Lana had remained aloof and suspicious, clearly perceiving Lisa as a rival. But once it was established that Lisa was to be marketed as an archetypal English Rose and posed no threat, Lana's attitude changed. She had publicly embraced Ziggy's new star, and had even confided in the Powder Room at the Brown Derby (after several

Manhattans) that her marriage to bandleader *du jour* Artie Shaw had been a complete mess. Lisa wondered if Artie had been responsible for the pregnancy that had been terminated.

As the phone rang, Lisa found herself desperately wondering what she might say. She could hardly mention the 'A' word; abortion was, after all, a criminal act. She wished she could spool back time like a cinema reel and go home to London and her grandparents, and her stalwart, Richard. She wished it were Dorothy on the other end of the phone line, not—

'Lana speaking,' Lana's husky voice drifted over the receiver.

'Hi there, Lana! It's Lisa, Lisa La Touche.' Lisa spoke with a confidence she did not feel. 'You told me to get in touch if I needed help and, well . . . May I buy you lunch?'

'I don't eat lunch, Lisa. That's how I keep my figure. But I'm happy to talk to you now.'

Lisa's fake confidence evaporated. 'This is difficult, Lana . . . I'm so sorry; I have a problem.'

'This is Hollywood, sweetheart; we all have problems. I'm kept real busy with my own and Mr Mayer requires the pleasure of my company in thirty minutes, so if you want me to help you, you'd better come straight out with it.'

'I'm pregnant.'

Lana gave a small, world-weary sigh, but evinced not the slightest shock. 'Who's the father?'

'Lochlan Kinnear.'

'I might have guessed it.'

'It was *that* obvious?'

'There are few surprises in Hollywood, darling. And Lochlan has done this before.'

If she'd had a glass in her hand, Lisa would have dashed it against the wall. 'Oh! Oh, God how I hate him!'

'You and half a dozen others.'

'I've been so stupid – so naïve!'

'We were all naïve once, Lisa, but you grow up fast here.'

In the background, Lisa heard a voice calling. There was a muffled response as Lana put her hand over the receiver, then resumed the conversation in brisker tones. 'OK. Let's cut to the chase. You know Lochlan won't leave his wife. That means you have two choices. Get Ziggy to sort you out with a lavender marriage—'

'I beg your pardon?'

'A lavender marriage. Haven't you heard the expression before?'

'No.'

'Ziggy will get his hands on a faggot for you: a man you can marry without sex being part of the deal. That means you've a bona fide father for the baby and you can play-act at being happy families.'

'I couldn't do that!'

'Which brings us to option number two. I can give you an address, a private house downtown. It ain't the Ritz, but if you won't consider an arranged set-up it's the only option available to you – unless you want to end up on the streets. Do you have a pen and paper handy?'

'Yes.'

Lana dictated an address; it was in an insalubrious area downtown.

'Do you know what the . . . procedure involves?' asked Lisa.

'Yeah.' Over the phone line, Lisa heard a sound as of fingernails drumming a tattoo on a hard surface. 'I have

. . . a friend who had it done. You'll have a fluid injected into your cervix and be told to rest for an hour. Then you're advised to go home and drink gallons of coffee until you pass the foetus.'

'Is it painful?'

'Is it painful. *Is* it painful.' A brusque inhalation told Lisa that Lana had lit up a cigarette. 'Do you suffer from period cramps?' she asked.

'Sometimes.'

'OK. Imagine your worst period ever and multiply it by ten – by a hundred. In my – in my friend's case, she thought she was going to die. She went through excruciating pain for twenty-four hours before calling the quack for help. Without anaesthetic, without so much as an aspirin, he scraped her out. She had to stifle the screams with a washcloth. There was blood everywhere. My friend felt as if her insides were being ripped out before she went unconscious. It took her a long time to recover, even though she was young and strong. As young and strong as I am.' Lisa heard Lana take another long draw of her cigarette. 'As young and strong as I am,' she repeated, and Lisa knew that of course there was no 'friend', that this story was Lana's own.

'I don't have much choice, then,' she said.

'We none of us do. It's a man's world. Not even Louella and Hedda could stand up to the might of bastards like Louis B. Mayer.'

'Lana! Your car's here!'

The voice in the background was over-enunciated and louder than necessary: clearly a cue for Lana to end the conversation.

'Coming,' she called.

'Thank you so much for your help, Lana,' said Lisa.

'You're welcome. Whatever you decide to do, I hope it works out for you.'

Lisa put the phone down and looked at the contact details she had scribbled down. Then she folded the sheet of paper and tucked it into the address book she had brought with her from home, a book patterned with forget-me-nots that contained the names of dozens of people from the past, people she knew she would never see again.

She started to turn the pages. Rajendra, her Indian schoolfriend, had drawn hearts around her name, and one of the Kylemore girls had done that thing of adding 'Connemara, Galway, Ireland, Europe, The World, The Universe'. Some of the names she'd filed meant nothing to her, and some were brand new entries: her make-up man, her dermatologist, the secretary of her fan club. And there, under 'R', was, in a nondescript, roundish hand, the name of her cousin Róisín from Ireland, who was married now to a D'Arcy, or a de Courcy maybe – one of the more common Connemara names, Lisa couldn't remember which.

Róisín! Lisa hadn't thought of her cousin in years. She remembered a ruddy-cheeked, laughing girl with a pronounced Irish accent; she remembered the family mimicking her own posh voice; she remembered playing 'Mammies', she and Róisín, with a rag dolly and a knitted thing that could have been either a cat or a bear. Because Róisín was the older cousin, she'd always bagged the dolly, and Lisa had had to make do with the knitted thing; but when the babbies were swaddled in bits of flannel it didn't make any difference. They were burped and given medicine and put to bed without supper, which gave the

211

mammies more time to make mud pies and shoo away the hens.

Lisa shut the address book and turned her attention to her mail. She wanted something to distract her from the image of the knitted thing that had been her baby: she was scared she might dream about it tonight.

As her fame had grown, so too had Lisa's mailbag. Aside from the usual begging letters and entreaties for signed photographs there were, now that America had joined the war, plenty of requests for appearances at morale-boosting events. Lisa was at a loss how to handle these requests. She couldn't dance or sing, like Betty Grable or Rita Hayworth. She was no ambassadress, like Marlene Dietrich. All the talk in Hollywood was of propaganda films and the selling of war bonds, and many of her American colleagues – including Sabu – had joined the forces. But Lisa couldn't even do that, since – unlike Sabu – she had not taken out American citizenship.

She was growing increasingly worried about her grand-parents, having had no word from them for some time. Aside from the disruption to international mail and telephone services, the escalating hostilities meant that travel between continents had become more perilous than ever. Hundreds of British ex-pats had returned home in the immediate aftermath of Pearl Harbor.

But Lisa's contract kept her shackled to Tinseltown.

For the next few days she took no action. She slept a lot, wrote a short guest column for *Click* magazine, and tuned into the World Service for news of home any time she could. Then one evening the distinctive warm voice of Sam Browne came over the airwaves, crooning 'Keep the Home Fires Burning' live from London.

London! Her home! Her family, her friends – were they still there, in a city half-destroyed by German bombs? What was she, Lisa, doing *here* in this shiny, vapid, pantomime place?

Pouring a large drink, she knocked it straight back. Then she grabbed her address book, flicked through the listing to 'H', and picked up the phone.

'Mr Hughes, please,' she told Johnny Meyer.

'What do you want? Flying lessons?' Johnny laughed down the line – a little nastily, Lisa thought, and there was silence for several moments. Thinking she'd been cut off, Lisa was just about to put the receiver down, when Howard's gentle voice came on.

'What can I do for you, baby?' he asked.

'Howard – I'm sorry. You're the only person I feel I can ask for help.'

'Fire ahead.'

'I'm awfully worried about my grandparents. I haven't heard from them in months, and I need to get home.'

'I thought you had a film lined up? The one about the ship?'

'*The City of Benares.* It's not happening – the attack on Pearl Harbor's changed everything. I'm going to ask Ziggy for a temporary release from my contract.'

'He's not going to want to do that, Lisa.'

'But Ziggy has no use for me – I'm no good for anything here.' Lisa started to cry. 'I'm sorry. I'm really desperate.'

'Shh, shh, honey. I hate to hear a dame cry. Leave it to me. I'll have a word with Phil Gersh tomorrow. We'll negotiate some kind of sweetheart deal.'

'A what?'

'Don't worry your pretty head about it. Allow us to do the talking for you.'

'Thank you!' Lisa didn't care about sweetheart deals and negotiations with agents and studio executives. She just wanted to hold her grandfather's hand again, and hear him call her his princess. 'Howard, do you think you could do anything about getting me to London?'

'Sure. If you don't mind taking a roundabout route you can hitch a ride with one of my pilots. I have a seaplane scheduled for Ireland via Newfoundland.'

'Why Ireland?'

'Right now, it has the biggest civilian airport in Europe. I've still got business interests there, and a licence to land. Once there, you're just a shuttle away from London.'

'Oh, thank you, Howard – thank you so much!' In her gratitude she cried even harder, and after another in-effectual 'Shh, shh, honey', Howard deftly made his excuses and hung up.

The wireless was still on low: she could hear Vera Lynn singing 'We'll Meet Again' and she yearned now as she never had for the long-forgotten names in her address book, and for Richard and her poor, bewildered grandparents, and for the mother she could barely remember.

CHAPTER TWENTY-ONE

JESSIE

PARIS 1919

The evening after Coco had put the finishing touches to Jessie's wardrobe, Gervaise and Jessie took cocktails with the couturier and her lover, Boy Capel, in the Ritz bar. Jessie had never tasted a cocktail before and she'd felt just like a child let loose in a sweetshop – she'd sampled a gin sling and a sidecar *and* a martini! And then they'd all piled into Gervaise's Buick and motored off to the quartier Bas-Meudon for dinner in la Pêche Miraculeuse, a restaurant that – Gervaise told her – was frequented by both established and up-and-coming artists.

Jessie was wearing one of Coco's little black dresses with fluted sleeves and an asymmetric hemline that showed to advantage her shapely ankles and calves encased in silk stockings; Coco was sporting another svelte jersey ensemble.

The *maître d'* was all obsequious smiles and bows as he took their coats. Clicking his fingers at a waiter, indicating for menus to be brought *tout d'suite*, he led the way to the most prominent table in the restaurant – one that commanded a view of the rest of the room. Other diners gawped openly, glanced surreptitiously, or pretended very hard indeed not to look as the party took their seats. There were one or two sniggers, and Jessie heard a man murmur: 'What outlandish get-up' – which was ironic, since his dining companion had what looked like a velveteen fruit bowl on her head.

'Good work, Coco,' said Boy, as the waiters fussed around them, unfurling napkins and pouring water. 'That was some entrance. Ignore the nay-sayers – between the two of you, you'll soon have Paris at your perfectly shod feet.'

Boy Capel was a handsome, athletic man with glittering dark eyes, a raffish moustache and a devil-may-care manner that made him most attractive – the appreciative sidelong glances that Jessie had seen being directed at him during the cocktail hour had been testimony to that. But Boy had eyes only for Coco. He quite clearly adored her.

'I told you *chez* Chanel would be an excellent invest-ment,' Coco said with mock-hauteur, producing a cigarette from a little lacquer case and waiting for Boy to light it. Then, blowing an elegant plume of smoke into the air, she turned to Jessie. 'Boy has been my financial backer since the business was in its infancy. What blind faith he had in me then! Do you know – the assistants I employed in my very first shop in Deauville couldn't even sew! And now I'm dressing all kinds of women: actresses and opera singers – and artists' muses, of course,' she added with a smile.

'And she'll be branching out again soon,' Boy told Jessie, with manifest pride, 'into fragrance.'

'I hope you outsell Guerlain,' remarked Gervaise. 'I'm sick of the smell of Mitsouko. The Ritz positively reeked of it this evening.'

Jessie was just about to make some observation about the smell of Mitsouko in the Ritz bar being infinitely preferable to the stench that clung to the inhabitants of the Hôtel des Trois Moineaux: then stopped herself just in time. Perdita – who'd been found romantically wandering around a rose garden in the Tuileries – had no business in a dump like the Trois Moineaux.

'Has the parfumier delivered yet?' asked Boy.

'Yes. I've narrowed the samples down to six.' Looking thoughtful, Coco tapped ash into the ashtray. 'The fifth is my favourite, I think.'

'What's so special about it?' asked Jessie.

'The base notes – vetiver and vanilla. I'm going to call it something beginning with the letter "V", to reflect that.'

'"V"?' said Boy, looking up from the wine list. 'How about "Virgin"?'

'Don't be facile, darling.'

'Why not call it "Velvet"?' suggested Gervaise. 'Since you work with fabric?'

'No.' Coco shook her head. 'The word "velvet" is too luxe. I want something quite different and quite, quite plain.'

'Why don't you just call it "V", then?' said Jessie. 'As in the Roman numeral?'

'I rather like that conceit,' said Coco, holding her cigarette as though it were a pen and describing the symbol in the air. 'Chanel – Number Five.'

'It'll never work,' scoffed Boy.

Coco raised an autocratic eyebrow at him. 'It will if I want it to,' she said.

Jessie laughed. 'In England, we use two fingers – instead

of your French single one – to cock a snook. It's called the "V" sign. That should appeal to your subversive streak, Coco.'

'Five it is, then! Oh – Pablo! *Bonsoir!*'

'*Bonsoir, messieurs et dames.*' The man looking down at them had wicked, Spanish-looking eyes. 'Will you introduce me, if you would be so kind, Gervaise? I understand this lady is your new model.'

'Word travels fast,' said Gervaise. 'Who the devil told you?'

'Marie Laurençin heard it from the Cunard woman.'

'Hell's teeth! Demetrios must have been on the blower to every hostess of every salon in town this morning.' Turning to Jessie, Gervaise effected a perfunctory introduction. 'Perdita, this is Pablo Picasso.'

'*Enchanté*, Mademoiselle.' Jessie felt a fingertip graze her palm before Monsieur Picasso relinquished it. 'Perhaps, Gervaise, you might think about sharing your new girl? She has . . . a quality. As I sat at my table there in the corner, I took the liberty of making some sketches.' Taking a page from the breast pocket of his jacket, he unfolded it and tossed it onto the table. The page was covered in little head and shoulder pencil sketches of Jessie looking animated.

'They're a very good likeness,' said Jessie with a smile. 'But I'm not sure that I could trust you to confine yourself to my head and shoulders in the privacy of your studio, Monsieur.'

With a laugh, Coco reached for the drawing. 'Tch, tch, Pablo,' she said. 'You've neglected to sign it.' Unclasping her evening purse, she extracted a pen and passed it over along with the sheet of paper.

The artist scribbled his signature on the bottom left-hand corner, then handed it to Jessie with a flourish. 'If ever you should change your mind, Mademoiselle, I should be more than happy to welcome you to my studio. Until then, I shall just have to make do with admiring you from afar, or in the paintings Gervaise makes of you. When do you intend to show, Gervaise?'

'The Galérie Pierre is available in April. I hope to have a new series ready by then.'

'*Tiens*. That will take some work.'

'Perdita isn't afraid of hard work.'

'I wish I could say the same for my wife. She has me eating out of the palm of her hand because it saves on the washing up. Sorry – that was a feeble joke.'

And Monsieur Picasso bade farewell with a shallow bow before returning to his table in the corner of the restaurant where a beautiful, heavily pregnant redhead sat, looking sulky.

'Is that Madame Picasso?' Jessie asked Coco.

'Yes. She's a Russian ballerina, née Khoklova.'

'Rather an unfortunate name,' observed Jessie, 'if she were English.'

'Perdita! You rogue!' Coco hid her smile behind her menu, then twinkled her fingers at Boy. 'Come, come, *mon beau mec*. You've been perusing that wine list for ages. Isn't it time we ordered?' Leaning in to Jessie, she murmured in an undertone. 'By the way . . . you've just made yourself a lot of money, *mon amie*. Hang on to that sketch of Pablo's. I guarantee you it will be worth thousands of francs in years to come.'

Thousands of francs . . . What couldn't she and Scotch have done with thousands of francs six months ago, when they'd been so broke that she'd had to petition her father for the wherewithal to visit Venice!

As Jessie studied the appetizing list of *hors d'oeuvres*, she wondered how Scotch was faring with his Italian girl. Gervaise had told her that he'd want her to start sitting for him tomorrow, after he'd paid a visit to Sennelier, the artists' suppliers on the Left Bank. Perhaps, when the series was finished, Scotch would come across reproductions of Gervaise's work in the press: images of her, 'Perdita', posing for one of the most sought-after portraitists in France. Might he then realize his mistake and come looking for her? Might he beg her to return to England with him and they could set up home in the house Pawpey had promised them, and live happily ever after with their baby? Perhaps—

'*Du vin, Madame?*'

'Oh! *Merci.*'

The sommelier – who had arrived with the *réserve spéciale* they had ordered – poured, and Boy Capel raised his glass. '*Santé!*' he said.

'*Santé!*' echoed the company, mirroring Boy's gesture and continuing with their perusal of the menu.

Jessie's eyes scanned a variety of fish dishes that once would have sent her into a swoon; the waiter set upon the table a basket of bread that could have kept her going for a week; the label on the wine bottle spoke of resplendent châteaux and lush valleys. Raising the glass to her lips, she took a sip of wine that probably cost as much as the most extravagant meal she and Scotch had ever shared.

On the other side of the restaurant, Monsieur Picasso slid his sketchpad from his pocket and proceeded to execute a series of rapid pencil strokes. It took him just moments to record Perdita's bereft expression for posterity.

CHAPTER TWENTY-TWO

LISA

EUROPE 1943

Lisa flew into Foynes on the south bank of the Shannon Estuary in an airboat captained by a dashing pilot who was pleased to accept an autographed photograph and a kiss. She was scheduled to leave for London the next day, but in the meantime she requested that a car take her – at great expense, due to petrol rationing – to the small town of Clifden in Connemara. There she knocked on the door of an unprepossessing two up, two down on the main street.

Róisín answered, uttered a shriek at the sight of her cousin, then fell silent for a long moment, taking in Lisa's travelling clothes: her tailored waistcoat, her slacks and boxy jacket, her smart snakeskin clutch, the sheepskin coat she had draped around her shoulders. Róisín was plump and motherly, with rosy cheeks. She was smaller than Lisa: the last time they'd met, Róisín had been the taller of the two.

'I'm sorry,' Lisa said. 'Weren't you expecting me? I did send a telegram.'

'I got it,' Róisín managed, finally. 'But I still can't believe it. What a vision of elegance you are. Come in, come in.'

'Thank you.' Lisa followed Róisín into a narrow hallway

that boasted just two doors off. Róisín opened the one on the left. It led into a small sitting room where a fire burned brightly and a table was set for tea. The smell of turf mingled with an aroma of baking, and Lisa felt an overwhelming sense of homecoming as she dropped into the armchair indicated by her cousin.

'It must have been a terrible journey you had.' Róisín was regarding her, wonder still evident in her eyes. 'Flying all that way.'

'It was tiring. It's so good to be here, Róisín. What a pretty room!'

'Thank you. Let me bring you refreshments – you must be starving.'

'That would be lovely.'

'You'll excuse the tea, I hope. We haven't had real tea since rationing began. We use ground-up blackberry leaves instead.'

'I wish I'd known – I could have brought you some.'

'We've got used to making do.'

With a smile, Róisín backed through the door, leaving Lisa to study her surroundings. The room was painted in pastels, with sprigged wallpaper beneath the picture rail. There were two armchairs, a small sofa, and a footstool drawn up by the fire, upon which a large cat was snoozing. Several framed watercolours adorned the walls, and photographs were on display atop a bookcase that contained the complete works of Shakespeare, the complete works of Dickens, and the *Encyclopaedia Britannica*, all bound in battered Morocco leather. Randomly, Lisa reached for one of the photographs.

It showed a smiling Róisín on a stretch of golden sand, flanked by a handsome dark-haired man and a pretty girl of about five or six. So, her cousin had a daughter. On the back of the photograph, pencilled in careful script, were the words Dónal, Róisín, Caoimhe. Gurteen Strand, March 1941.

The sound of the door opening made Lisa turn. Róisín was carrying a tray laden with sandwiches, scones and thick slices of barmbrack.

'Oh, my!' Lisa moved to help her cousin set plates on the table. 'What trouble you've gone to. You shouldn't have – I know things are terribly scarce.'

'Sit yourself down. Here in Ireland we've plenty enough to eat, although petrol's fierce expensive. We have a pony and trap for transport.'

'That must be fun for your little girl.' Something in Róisín's expression told Lisa she had made a faux pas. 'The child in the photograph? Isn't she your daughter?'

'She was my foster child.'

Lisa registered the past tense, and stiffened. 'Oh. I am so sorry.'

'Don't take me up wrong – she hasn't passed away; it's just that she's not here with us any more. Molly – her mammy – had been living a while in a Magdalene laundry. She came back for her.'

'A laundry?'

'They're institutions run by the nuns for what they call "fallen" women. Pregnant girls are sent there to have their babbies, and then the babbies are taken from them, and the girls set to work. I took Caoimhe, and promised Molly I'd look after her until she was able to rear her herself. After five years in that hellhole she couldn't take any more. She said the nuns were worse than the Gestapo. So she ran away, and came to claim her little Caoimhe.' Róisín pronounced it 'Kwee-va'.

'It must have been very difficult for you to give her up.'

'It broke my heart. In Irish, Caoimhe means "gentle, beautiful, precious". She was all that, and more, to me. Especially precious.'

'Couldn't you have fought to keep her?'

'She wasn't mine to keep. She belonged to Molly. And Molly had suffered so much in that awful place, her hands raw from washing the sheets of the very priests who raped her.'

Lisa gave Róisín a look of horror.

'Yes. They raped and beat her and called her a vile sinner. And when she got pregnant at the age of fifteen, they sent her to that evil place to do penance on her knees for those so-called sins.' Róisín's expression was one of uncharacteristic bitterness. 'That's when I lost my faith. I haven't received the sacrament since I heard Molly's story in the hospital, when I was delivering Caoimhe.'

'You helped at the birth?'

'I did. I'm a nurse. I've brought hundreds of babbies into this world, but nary a one of my own.'

'You can't . . . ?'

'No. And it's not for the want of trying.'

'Oh, Róisín! I'm sorry.'

'Ah, sure. I had her a good while. And wasn't I blessed to have had her at all?'

'Yes,' said Lisa. 'You were.'

Róisín managed a smile, then set about pouring tea.

London wasn't London any more. It was a city mired in rubble. In the West End, many of the theatres had been shut down or bombed. The civilians on the streets were clad in shapeless, worn-out garments and down-at-heel shoes: fashion was a thing of the past. On their side of Grosvenor Square, her grandparents' house was one of a handful that hadn't been hit.

Gramps answered the door in his carpet slippers, a woollen blanket wrapped around his shoulders. He was unshaven, and looked many years older than when she had last seen him. He said nothing, simply took Lisa in his arms on the top doorstep and held her for a long time. When he released her, Lisa clasped his hand and led him into the drawing room, instructing the cab driver to leave her baggage in the hall. The tall windows were boarded up, and flanked by heavy blackout curtains. There was a smell of damp and drains, and every surface was covered in a layer of grime.

Gramps made a helpless gesture. 'I'm sorry you had to come home to this,' he said. And then he slumped down upon the old leather chesterfield and started to cry.

Taking a handkerchief from her clutch bag, Lisa wiped Gramps's cheeks and told him gently to blow his nose. 'Is it Grandma?' she asked, when he'd finished sobbing.

'Yes. She died last week, Baba. We buried her the day before yesterday.'

Lisa took her grandfather's face between her hands and pressed her lips to his forehead. Then she took off her sheepskin coat and laid it over his lap.

'How did she go?'

'Very peacefully, in her sleep.'

'Here?'

Gramps shook his head. 'In a home, not far from here.'

'You mean, a residential home?'

226

'It was more of a hospital, really. It had got to the stage where I couldn't look after her, Baba. She took to wandering, and refused to go into the air-raid shelter. She'd just bolt from the house when the sirens started. I was terrified that she'd end up hurt, or dead. So I had her committed.'

'Oh, poor, poor Gramps. How long ago?'

'Nearly a year now.'

'Why didn't you tell me?'

'I couldn't upset you, Baba. I knew you'd want to come back at once, and everything was going so well for you over there. There was nothing you could have done for her, anyway. She wouldn't have known you.'

'I could have helped you!'

'I have Eva to look after me. She moved in when her house was destroyed.'

'So Great-Aunt Eva's living here now?'

'Yes. She's gone out, to the grocer's. She'll be a while – the queues are endless.' He sniffed, then managed a wry smile. 'Don't imagine we'll be feasting on chicken or beef this evening. You might get a vegetable hotpot, if you're lucky.'

'Things really are that bad?'

'Yes. Though we've been lucky, Eva and I. The house is still standing, and our hens are thriving.'

'Hens?'

'There's a hutch in the back garden where the summerhouse used to be. We have an Anderson shelter out there as well, but nowadays we tend to go to the Underground to take cover. The Anderson floods so easily.'

'What's the Underground like?'

'One puts up with it.'

It was clear that Gramps didn't want to talk about

227

conditions in the Underground. Lisa changed the subject.

'So the summerhouse is gone?' She had fond memories of the pretty trellised pagoda, all grown over with Virginia Creeper, where she'd sneak off and lose herself in a book, knowing that her grandmother was unlikely to find her there and rail at her for being lazy.

'We demolished it so that we could use the wood for fuel. Look – we managed to get in some coal for your homecoming.'

Gramps indicated the paltry fire burning in the grate, and Lisa thought of the fine turf fire in Róisín's cosy house in Connemara, and the sandwiches and freshly baked barmbrack, and the wild strawberries they'd picked as they rambled down a boreen near Clifden, chatting until sundown came and it was time for Lisa to return to Foynes.

'I brought you oranges from California.'

'Oranges! I've forgotten what they taste like.'

'And razors.'

Gramps managed a smile. 'What luxury. The last ones have had to do me for six weeks.'

'Wait here.' Lisa moved to the hall, where the driver had left her bags.

Undoing the straps of her suitcase, she accessed the compartment that contained the luxury items she'd brought with her from LA. The cigarettes and nylon stockings that she'd bought for friends had been donated to a delighted Róisín, but she had fine French milled soap, still, wrapped in tissue paper, and shampoo that had been intended for Grandma, and silk socks and razors and oranges for Gramps, as well as a bottle of Tanqueray gin.

Returning to the drawing room, Lisa sat down next to

Gramps and pressed an orange into his hand. 'Smell that,' she told him.

He held the orange to his face, closed his eyes and breathed in. 'Brings me back to happier times. Picnics on Hampstead Heath with you and your grandmother.'

'Funny how smells do that. The smell of eucalyptus always reminds me of the house I lived in, in France – the one Grandma never allowed me to talk about.'

'I'm sorry. It must have been awful for you, a little girl growing up, that your own mother was a taboo subject.' Gramps looked down at his orange and started to peel it the way a child might who had never seen one before. 'The tragedy was that there was nothing to tell you, since I knew so very little about her final years. She stopped writing to us then. All I know is that she fell in with a bad crowd.'

A bad crowd . . . The beautiful girls kissing in the bathroom; her mother, smiling at her over the rim of a champagne coupe, her mouth a crimson curve; the balmy nights when Lisa would lie listening to laughter rising from the terrace, voices singing along to the Victrola, the swishing of silk and the tip-tapping of heels passing her bedroom door, the murmured endearments, the sighs as lovers drifted from liaison to liaison . . . A bad crowd? Her grandmother had always led her to believe that her birth father had been the bad lot. Just how bad could *he* have been?

It was time for Lisa to ask the question she had always wanted to, but had never dared. Her paternity had always been a cause for embarrassment in the family: her grandparents used to freeze any time Lisa had touched on it when she was little, and she had learned never to upset her grandmother by asking questions. 'Whatever happened to Scotch, Gramps?'

'Scotch?'

'You told me that my father's nickname was Scotch.'

Gramps peeled away a segment of orange. 'We never found out. We presumed that he abandoned Jessie when he found out she was expecting. He was too much of a vagabond to settle down and rear a family, even though he'd promised before God to love and honour her till death. Here.' Gramps handed her the orange segment, and Lisa shook her head.

'No. They're all for you, my pet. You need your Vitamin C. I have oranges every day in California.'

Actually, she thought, she too would have to supplement her Vitamin C while she was here. And her calcium and iron and fish oils: all essential to growing a healthy baby.

'I'm glad we got to keep you, in the end,' Gramps told her.

'I'm not so sure how happy Grandma was. I always felt she thought I was tainted – illegitimate somehow.'

'She started asking for you, shortly before she died. Thought you were up at Cambridge, like Jessie in her final year before she went to Rouen.'

'You must miss her awfully.'

'She died for me a long time ago, Baba, when she began losing her mind. It was as if I were married to a different woman. She was happier, I think, towards the end. All her anger seemed to have ebbed away. I found some of Jessie's letters to her, by the way, in an old box. Some of them were destroyed by rain – a loose slate in the corner of the tank room – but I managed to salvage a couple of dozen.'

Gramps rose stiffly to his feet and moved across to the walnut chiffonier.

'Grandma told me years ago that she'd burned them all.'

'I think she forgot where she put them.' From the depths of a cupboard, he produced a battered hatbox and passed it to Lisa. It had *Millinery Modes* emblazoned upon it in an elaborate font. 'Why don't you read them now, while I take a nap?'

'I'd rather talk to you, Gramps. I want to hear all about what's been happening here.'

Even though she was travel weary, Lisa was avid for news of friends and family and neighbours. As well as that, she felt awfully guilty that she had not once enquired after the man to whom she was affianced. She wanted news of Richard.

'We'll talk over dinner this evening. I need my afternoon snooze. I'm an old man now, my dearest heart. You'll find me very dull company after your movie star friends.'

'Nonsense. They're much duller than you. In LA, we go to bed at half past eight and get up at half past four in the morning. We're all walking zombies.'

Lisa accompanied her grandfather to the door, and watched as he climbed the stairs. He had a noticeable limp, the bald patch on the back of his head had spread, and his shoulders were hunched. It was too, too pitiful. Lisa couldn't bear it. She turned away, and went back into the drawing room. There, she sat down in the middle of the floor and opened the box that had once contained a hat made by *Millinery Modes*, and now contained the vestiges of Jessie's life story.

The letters were mostly still in their envelopes. Some had French stamps, and some Italian. Some were dated 1918, some the following year. She picked one at random, and slid out the thin paper. It was the first time she'd seen her mother's handwriting. It was an untidy hand, impatient – as if the pen hadn't been able to keep up with all the thoughts that were racing through her mind; all the emotions that she wanted to convey, all the news that she had to spill on to the page.

The letter was dated 13 June 1919, and it had been posted from San Gimignano in Italy.

Last evening our friends the foreign artists – of the real bohemian type who go without collars and drink nearly all day long – took us along to a low-down Café, to a Socialist meeting. The Frenchman called for a guitar, and we sang the most glorious songs – and they were the most disreputable, dirtiest, down-and-outest sort of looking men you ever saw, and <u>never</u> *have we spent such a ripping evening . . .*

The idea of her mama, young, carefree, fraternizing with socialist types in a low-down café astonished her. Any memories of Mama were fixed in her mind in that beautiful villa in the South of France. This girl of the letters was a free-spirited hellion.

Rummaging among the envelopes, she picked out another.

I've never told you about our Greek count. He is an art <u>dealer</u> and has been living here in the pension with a little girl of 6 whom he has adopted. She is the most charming little creature – a little fairy – so small and dainty and just pure spirit – you can't describe her anyhow else. In fact, she is so ethereal that it makes you frightened she'll never grow up.

She has had an awfully sad history, but was rescued by our Greek and he has brought her up here for the last 5 years as his own child – he is a most efficient nurse and he dresses, washes and altogether looks after her. All men she likes she calls Naughty Boys, in the sweetest accent. We play innumerable games of pretending – she puts a little statue we have to bed, and calls Scotch –

Scotch? Her father!

– and she calls Scotch the Fly Man because he chases her when he has a campaign against the flies which swarm in our room.

Scotch. The 'Fly Man'. Lisa felt jealous, so jealous of this fairy-like six-year-old who had spent time with *her* father larking and joking and playing make-believe. She, Lisa, didn't even know what 'Scotch' looked like . . .

As she sorted randomly through the letters, trying to make chronological sense of them, she worked out that the very first one had been written shortly after her mama had arrived in Rouen, where she was on active service with the British Expeditionary Force:

We little lot – 7 of us – live in a hotel, each have our own room and have a small sitting-room. One man is an artist, with one arm, the other withered or something. He is very 'alive', and is always racing about somewhere – he has a perfect knowledge of the town, knows all the streets and buildings, shops and cafés. This afternoon we went to the Opera together – good way of starting war-work in France, eh? I think I shall like the whole thing – so don't worry about

me, darlings. And everybody looks after me – I think they
imagine I am too young to be out alone!

From reading between the lines it was clear to her that
her mama had fallen in love at first sight. No wonder
Grandma had worried about her so. To let her only
daughter go off on her own to France in wartime, and to
realize that she was falling for an artist – a 'Scotch' artist at
that, an amputee, and probably penniless – must have
alarmed her terribly.

Lisa put the fragile pages back in their paper cocoon,
then picked up another envelope, and another. She sifted
through them all, fascinated, mouthing the words as she
read them, devouring letter after letter then discarding
them until she was the centre of a little reef of envelopes.
Some of the letters were full of a wild, gay abandon, some
were wistful and a little homesick, but all of them were
resonant with the love her mother had felt for the man she
called Scotch.

And, as she read, bit by bit she managed to construct the
story of Mama before she became mama to Baba. As far as
she could tell, the last letter had been written in August
1919 on a beach in Finistère. It made her cry because she
felt as if her mother was talking directly to her across a gap
in time of nearly a quarter of a century.

Why had Scotch left her? It seemed impossible that the
strength of the love Mama had felt for him had not been
reciprocated. What had she done when she found herself
alone on the north coast of France? Why had she not
returned home to London? Lisa's birth certificate told her
that she had been born in Paris. Had her mother been on
her own then? Had she been friendless? When had she

travelled to the Riviera? How had she ended up in that beautiful villa, surrounded by bright young things, leading such a hedonistic lifestyle?

But Lisa knew that it hadn't always been a rainbow clutter in that house. There had been dark times, too, when Lisa would wake late at night and find her mother hunched over her desk, sobbing and scribbling frantically – not on writing paper, but in books with hard red covers – and in the mornings the books would be gone. What had she been writing? Who had she been writing to? Was that where the secrets were kept – between the pages of those red books? Because Lisa sensed that her mother had been keeping secrets, and there was something that did not add up. It all came back to Scotch. Why had he abandoned the love of his life; why had he abandoned his child?

At the very bottom of the box she came upon a photograph: a studio portrait of Jessie in a simple wooden frame, signed by the photographer and dated Rouen, 1918. It showed her mother in sepia, her shoulders bare, her abundant hair twisted into a loose chignon, tendrils of which skimmed an elegant neck. It was, Lisa thought, not unlike the head shot that Myra had organized for publicity purposes, the one that she signed routinely and put into SAEs for fans. It was the only photograph of her mother that she had ever seen.

Lisa recovered the tissue paper in which the French soap had been wrapped, and carefully swathed the photograph in it. Then she put the letters away – but not in the dilapidated hatbox. Instead she fetched a biscuit tin up from the pantry – one with a pretty pattern of peony roses on the lid. She didn't want to run the risk of another accident happening to those precious souvenirs.

* * *

Later, in the kitchen, Lisa helped Great-Aunt Eva prepare the evening meal, chopping potatoes and parsnips, and sloshing gin into glasses.

'Gin! Real Tanqueray gin!' said Eva, adding a few drops of Angostura Bitters and taking an appreciative sip. 'There's been nothing but synthetic since the distillery got shelled. I wish I had a slice of lime, and lots of ice cubes. As for quinine tonic! I dream of it, sometimes.'

'I'm so spoiled in LA,' said Lisa, apologetically. 'I have a bar fully stocked with all the liquor you could ever want.'

'How gloriously vulgar, darling.' Eva pulled a gas mask from a box, and started fiddling with the straps.

'Why are you putting that on?' asked an alarmed Lisa. 'Is there an emergency?'

'No, no,' Eva assured her. 'But it's jolly handy when you're chopping onions. I was lucky to get one – they're scarce these days.'

'Gas masks?'

'No. Onions.'

'How long did you have to stand in line for?'

'Stand in line?'

'I mean, queue.'

'Of course – you're American now. Over two hours.'

'For a handful of vegetables? Oh, Eva – that's shocking!'

'It's commonplace, darling. Welcome to wartime Britain.'

It felt utterly bizarre to Lisa to stand in the kitchen of her childhood home, conversing with a once sophisticated woman who was wearing a gas mask, a baggy tweed skirt, an Aran cardigan and matching tam o'shanter. She had still been an elegant woman in her early fifties when Lisa left London: her farewell present to her grand-niece had been a chamois leather jewellery roll. But now Eva had joined the legions of women who valued warmth and comfort over high fashion.

'Have you seen anything of the Napiers?' asked Lisa. 'I noticed their house was bomb-damaged.'

'Oh, my darling.' Eva reached up and unfastened the mask. Her face, when revealed, was ashen. 'When did you last hear from Richard?'

'Not for ages. Sea mail takes months sometimes, you know – they say that half of it ends up on the ocean floor – and telephoning's just impossible.'

'Richard joined up, Lisa,' Eva told her.

'But he was working in the diplomatic corps!'

'It was considered a soft option, rather, when so many able-bodied young men were enlisting. He kept getting white feathers sent to him anonymously. In the end, he couldn't take the shame. He went off to France.'

Lisa knew at once. She set down the kitchen knife. 'He's dead, isn't he?'

'Yes. He was shot down over Antwerp during his first week on duty.'

Lisa gripped the edge of the table and looked down at the solitaire diamond set in gleaming platinum that Richard had given her on one of the last occasions they'd met, in the Palm Court of the Ritz a whole wartime ago. She remembered his expression, of such puppy-dog hopefulness that she hadn't been able to turn him down. Sliding the ring off her finger, she pressed it to her lips.

'Are his parents alive?' she asked Eva.

'Yes. They're living next door, still.'

'This belongs to them,' said Lisa.

Then she took a hit of gin, untied her apron, and made for the stairs.

Later that evening, Lisa took herself up to the room that had been hers until she had gone sailing off to Hollywood with the *Thief of Bagdad*. It was still redolent of her former life – a trunk full of old toys and back issues of *Film Pictorial*, a set of Arthur Mee's *Children's Encyclopaedias*, her swimming trophies, a box that played 'The Sugar Plum Fairy' when you opened the lid.

Inside the box were amassed trinkets: a coral necklace, a cameo brooch, an enamel buckle, a set of carved ivory buttons, a tiny porcelain monkey. She remembered the jewels she'd been loaned in Hollywood, the collars and cuffs of glittering gemstones, the heavy chandelier earrings that had tugged at her earlobes, the Cartier diamonds she had been terrified of losing.

Alarmed suddenly that she might not find the item she was searching for, she riffled through the contents; but there it was, nestled into the padded satin lining: the ring that her miscreant father had given her mother on Christmas Day 1918.

The stone was a polished cabochon sapphire. What excellent taste Scotch had had! It had come with her from France when, as a tiny child, she had been delivered to her grandparents in Dover. The small suitcase that had accompanied her had also contained clothes quite unsuitable for autumn in England, along with her birth certificate and the little porcelain monkey. The ring had been far too big for her, of course, and had been consigned to the music box with the monkey, which had since lost a paw.

It fitted her now. She slid it onto the third finger of her left hand, covering the white strip left by Richard's diamond. Then she set the framed photograph of her mother upon her bedside locker, and beside it one of Richard, which he had given her before she had left for Hollywood. She had neglected to pack it; it had gathered dust in her bedroom ever since.

It had been taken at his graduation. Wearing his cap and gown, he was regarding the camera with an expression she knew well: an expression that could be construed as complacent, but that Lisa knew was simply that of a person who believed he was – like Voltaire's Candide – living in the best of all possible worlds, an eternal optimist. She hoped he had never suffered disillusion, she hoped that Richard Napier had believed until the very end that the war he was fighting was good and true and just.

Lisa turned off the nightlight, and then she slid beneath the eiderdown and started to cry.

In the morning she awoke feeling tired still, wiped out by the demands of her growing baby and the endless travelling, and a night spent half awake, waiting for air raid sirens to sound. But after a breakfast of porridge, dried egg and tinned tomatoes, she pulled on a smile and set about visiting neighbours with Eva, filling everyone in on life in America, and answering their questions about Hollywood. She was glad she'd come home, even though she suspected that Gramps was anxious at her being here rather than in the comparative safety of Los Angeles. But she had had to come. Gramps was the only family she had.

She'd had an idea that she could make herself useful here doing some kind of war work, but she felt as redundant in London as she had in Hollywood. Dorothy had gone off to Ceylon, with rumour rife that her work for the Field Ambulance Service was a cover for Special Operations. Special Operations! Lisa might as well resign herself to the fact that she could not make any kind of contribution to the war effort until after her baby was born. And then what?

She knew of course that thousands of brave women had lost their husbands since the beginning of the war, and were rearing their families single-handed. But Lisa had no husband, dead or alive, and she was not brave enough to face the opprobrium of the Legion of Decency in America, or the censure of the Hays Office, or the poison pens of Louella and Hedda. Lachlan had been right about one thing: it was professional suicide to have a baby outside wedlock. If she kept her child, she would never, ever be able to go back to her old life in LA. Lisa did not especially want to go back to her old life, but she had no choice. She needed to earn a living, she needed to be self-sufficient. She had no room in her life for a baby just yet – but Róisín did.

Before Lisa left for Connemara, Pawpey and Eva took her to dine in the Savoy Grill, where, despite its restricted wartime menu, the dress code was still formal. Wishing to remain as anonymous as possible, Lisa insisted on a corner table, and sat with her back to the restaurant. Eva gave her a running commentary on the various celebrities, who were dining as insouciantly as if the war was not happening. 'Goodness – it's Mr Churchill! Is that Lady Diana Cooper? Oh, look! There's one of the Mitford girls!' Lisa resisted the impulse to turn around and stare, and, once the meal was finished, she tried to make her exit as unobtrusively as possible.

But somebody must have seen her, because *The People* duly reported that: 'Miss Lisa La Touche, Britain's latest export to Hollywood, was seen dining in the Grill Room at the Savoy Hotel last Saturday. Miss La Touche was the personification of elegance in a clinging, dove-grey bias-cut cocktail dress.'

The invitations started to arrive: Lisa had been unearthed. She didn't bother to respond. She knew that if she accepted an invitation to cocktails or a Saturday-to-Monday or a fund-raising gala, she wouldn't be wearing clinging frocks. Her figure would be subject to scrutiny, and before long word would get back to Ziggy and her keepers in Hollywood. So, without further delay, she composed and sent a generic telegram to those concerned:

```
DETAINED IN EUROPE DUE TO BEREAVEMENT
STOP SEEKING TEMP RELEASE FROM CONTRACT
ON COMPASSIONATE GROUNDS STOP WILL
RETURN WHEN POSS STOP LISA LA TOUCHE
```

She couldn't get out of London fast enough.

In Connemara, the living was easy. Anxious for Lisa's baby to be as robust and healthy as possible, Róisín reserved for her cousin the best of everything. The parlour was converted into a bedroom for her, she was served breakfast there, and fed on the freshest produce available. Lisa craved fish, and Dónal, Róisín's husband, returned from his fishing trips with bucket-loads of mackerel. Lisa tried to do her fair share of the housework, insisting she needed the activity and the distraction, but Róisín refused every offer of help, and encouraged her instead to take gentle exercise outdoors.

It rained a lot that summer, but Lisa was glad of the unseasonable weather. It meant she could wrap herself in layers of loose clothing, to disguise her condition lest anyone recognize her. However, after the initial curiosity, nobody took much notice of the reserved, rather over-weight woman – 'a cousin from England' – who had taken up residence in the de Courcy household. So Lisa spent her days ambling along nearby beaches and boreens, through fields and on the shores of the salt lakes just outside the town, or on the riverbank, listening to the plashing of water, watching the fish leap and enjoying the unfamiliar sensation of the rain on her face.

At night they would sit around the kitchen table, cosy in the warmth of the wood-burning stove, and Dónal would take out his fiddle and play lively Irish jigs and reels with names like 'Toss the Feathers' and 'The Walls of Limerick'. Other times he would play heart-achingly sad laments which brought tears to Lisa's eyes, and once in a while he would put his fiddle down and entertain them with 'pishrogues' – tales of the fairy folk; of Tír na nÓg and the Pooka, of the Banshee and the Fir Darrig and the mischief they'd get up to. And Lisa learned that the Irish freedom fighters had loved their country so much that they had given it the name of a beautiful woman with the walk of a queen, Caitlín ni Houlihan. So Lisa decided to call her baby Caitlín if she was a girl, and Patrick – after the country's patron saint – if he was a boy.

One day, Dónal took them in the pony and trap to visit Kylemore Abbey. As they rounded a bend in the road, Lisa was greeted by the view that still had the power to take her breath away. The castle that had been her home from home fronted on to a lake, its turrets and parapets and castellations glimmering upside-down in the smooth, mirror-like surface of the water. Lisa remembered the camaraderie she had shared with the other boarders: the midnight swims, the illicit picnics in the woods, the ghost stories after dark in the dorm.

And she turned to Róisín, and said: 'If the baby is a girl, I should like her to be educated here, as I was.'

Róisín had her conditions, too. The de Courcy surname was to appear on the birth certificate and Lisa was required to give Róisín her word that she would not return to Ireland until the child's age of majority had been reached, lest she decide to claim it as her own and abscond back to LA. Since she had already had a daughter taken from her, Róisín was determined that it would not happen again. Lisa would be permitted to keep in touch by letter, but she was to be known as 'aunt' Lisa. In return, the child would be encouraged to look upon Miss La Touche as a benefactress and Róisín would keep Lisa up to date with all developments concerning the well-being of her offspring.

On 24th July, in the small hours of the morning, Caitlín – immediately known as little Cat – entered the world. With her unblinking slate blue eyes and autocratic expression, it seemed as if she had been here before, knew all there was to know, and would set about getting her own way as soon as ever she could. While Róisín assured Lisa it had been an easy birth, Lisa's memory of the event was rather different. However, once the infant was cleaned and swaddled and tucked into bed beside her mother, the pain that she had suffered seemed as nothing. Gazing at her sleeping baby, Lisa fell hopelessly in love.

She spent a week in bed with her darling girl, and then she donned her travelling clothes, packed her bags, and fed her daughter for the last time. Before taking leave of Róisín, she carefully wrote down details of the standing order she had set up for her cousin in the bank in Clifden. Then she said goodbye to a sleepy, milk-glutted Cat, kissing her tiny fists and her perfect ears and her peach-bloom cheeks before wrapping her in a shawl of rose pink wool, and placing her in Róisín's arms.

This time there was no car to take her to Foynes: she couldn't spare the money for the fare. Instead, Dónal took her to the airport in the pony trap.

Lisa wept throughout the journey, nonstop.

CHAPTER TWENTY-THREE

JESSIE

PARIS 1919

Jessie was holding a particularly arduous pose for 'Perdita Treading Grapes', with her breasts exposed and her skirt ruched up round her thighs. The pose was fiendishly difficult, one that required her to keep one leg raised and her head thrown back – the one that she'd demonstrated to Gervaise on the first evening they'd met.

'Look at those lissom legs!' said Gervaise. 'Look at those clever feet! You are the hardest-working model I've ever had the privilege to paint.'

'It's all to do with balance,' Jessie told him. 'And I've always been supple. When I was little, I dreamed of becoming an acrobat.'

'I know *exactly* how supple you are, beloved.' Gervaise narrowed appreciative eyes at the canvas, then stepped back from it. 'That's that section done. You can take a break now.'

'Thanks.' Jessie eased her arms into a stretch, then strolled across the studio floor to help herself to a fig. She sang a little song as she split it. 'I wish I could shimmy like my sister Kate, she shakes it like a bowl of jelly on a plate—'

'You're not going to be doing much more shimmying for a while, darling,' he said. 'You're starting to show. Even those drop-waist dresses of Coco's aren't going to disguise your shape for much longer. The painting I embark on next will have to be called *Perdita Enceinte*.'

An Expectant Perdita . . .

She and Gervaise rarely discussed the child she was carrying. The due date was still several months away, and there was a tacit understanding between them that they'd deal with that side of life when they had to. What mattered right now was Gervaise's work. Since he'd starting turning down commissions, it was important to establish him as eminently collectible, and he and Jessie were working flat out. Her pregnancy meant that she tired sooner than she might have once upon a time, but she soldiered on.

Since moving in with Gervaise, 'Perdita' had – as per Coco's prediction – become the talk of the playground that was post-war Paris. Together they patronized night-clubs – Le Boeuf sur le Toit, or Zelli's and El Garron in Montmartre. They were inundated with invitations to lunches, art shows, dinners, cocktails, fancy-dress balls, premieres, and Saturday-to-Mondays in the country houses of Gervaise's moneyed patrons. At one party the King of Spain had tried to put his hand up Jessie's dress, at another Augustus John had rashly tried to 'poach' her away from Gervaise, and at a gallery opening the writer Colette told her she was going to immortalize 'Perdita' in a book.

It seemed to Jessie that they were seldom sober; they frequently stayed out until dawn tinged the sky over Saint-Sulpice with chartreuse yellow. Then they would head to

Les Halles for the best onion soup in Paris before reeling back to Gervaise's apartment, blurred at the edges from want of sleep. Jessie loved the feeling of time going by in a giddy, kaleidoscopic haze. It meant that there was no time to dwell on the past.

The fact that their set-up was so unorthodox only added to the rather outré glamour they exuded. Hostesses competed to be on first name terms with the charming couple but Gervaise cocked a bit of a snook by being very picky about which social events he deigned to attend. Invitations to lunches and dinners were seldom taken up, because the idea of being placed next to 'some footling, stupid goose of a socialite' gave him the horrors. And of course, such an air of exclusivity only had the effect of making their presence at a 'do' even more desirable.

This suited Jessie, who lived in terror of being unmasked as an impostor. She knew that not everybody was convinced by her 'Perdita' persona, and that many of the women she met would take malicious delight in exposing her as a fake and charlatan if the opportunity arose.

She saw Count Demetrios occasionally, at the opera or the theatre, and he always asked solicitously after her health. She knew that this was a subtle reference to her pregnancy, and she wished she had never blurted out to him the fact that she was carrying Scotch's child. But then, she reasoned, if she had not done that, maybe she would still be a prisoner in the Hôtel des Trois Moineaux with the debauched Adèle as her gaoler, and that was unthinkable . . .

And then one day in late December, Gervaise received a

telephone call from Antoinette Chanel, Coco's aunt, to say that Boy Capel had been killed in an automobile accident on the road to the Riviera.

CHAPTER TWENTY-FOUR

LISA

HOLLYWOOD 1946–1949

'Ziggy's angry with me,' Lisa told Sabu.

She was sitting poolside with him, scanning page after page of execrable dialogue.

'How do you know?'

'He's refused to sell my contract to RKO, even though Mr Hughes upped the ante. And he's cast me in another skid. I'd rather play a Bearded Lady than do this script.'

Lisa tossed aside the typescript that had been delivered earlier. She had taken up temporary residence in David Niven's house. The quintessential gentleman – who was working in the UK – had kindly told their mutual agent that Lisa was welcome to stay *chez lui* until she started earning again. Because, 'compassionate leave' notwithstanding, since she had turned her back on Hollywood while still under contract, Lisa had been put on suspension, loaned out to second-rate studios and – most humiliatingly of all – asked to test for each potential role. Now she badly needed money.

'Have you managed to see Mr Stein yet?' asked Sabu.

'Finally. He kept me waiting for over a fortnight this time. I guess my days as his pet English Rose are over.'

Sabu took a sip of iced tea. 'If you want to get back in his good books, you're going to have to bite the bullet and do what you're told,' he said. 'I did, when I signed up for those rubbishy Maria Montez flicks. Never forget, Lisa, that we are just commodities.'

'I know, I know, I know!' She was fed up with hearing it. 'But honestly, Sabu, this takes the biscuit.' Picking up the typescript, she thrust it at her friend. 'Here – have a look.'

Sabu turned over a couple of pages, and then: 'Oh Lord, Lisa!' he exclaimed. 'They've given you a four-year-old son!'

'Isn't it the absolute end?' Lisa slumped back on the sofa. 'I'm already too old to play juves, Sabu, and my career has barely started.'

'Tch, tch. You're far too young to be playing mothers!' he pronounced, loyally.

'Thank you.'

But not too young to actually *be* a mother, Lisa thought, feigning interest in a trail of ants negotiating the grouting beneath her feet. She hadn't told Sabu about her baby. She didn't think that he would have a problem with Cat's illegitimate status but, since he was one of the most principled people Lisa had ever met, she sensed he would be genuinely shocked by the fact that the father of her child was a married man. Especially one as meretricious as Lochlan.

He gave her a sympathetic look. 'Cheer up, darling. At least they haven't sent you off to San Fernando to do cut-price westerns.'

'Yet,' she added gloomily. 'It'll be Saturday matinée serials next.'

'Maybe you'll bag a sugar daddy.'

'I couldn't sleep with somebody I didn't love, however rich he was.'

'Some girls don't seem to have a problem with it. Look at Marion Davies.'

'Yes – but look who she has to go to bed with every night. Randolph Hearst. Ick!'

Lisa slid her sunglasses on and picked up *Modern Screen*.

'Have you ever been in love, Lisa?' asked Sabu.

'No,' she said, truthfully.

The only creature on the planet with whom she had ever been in love was little Cat. Since the war had ended, and communications with Europe had been re-established on a less erratic footing, Lisa had received photographs of her daughter from Róisín. She was extremely glad to see that the child had inherited her genes rather than Lochlan's. The photographs were in black and white, but Róisín told her in her letters that Cat had red-gold hair and aquamarine eyes, transparent, milky skin and the sweetest, most infectious laugh of any girleen in the whole of Ireland. Strangers stopped to admire her, Dónal was in thrall to her, and a local fiddle-player had composed a tune dedicated to her. Cat, Róisín claimed, was a queen of Connemara in miniature. And every time a new photograph arrived, Lisa mounted it in a brocade-covered album kept specially for the purpose, before retiring to bed for the rest of the day so that she could gaze upon her daughter's beauty, and weep.

'I've heard rumours . . .' continued Sabu.

'What rumours?'

'That you've been seeing Mr Howard Hughes.'

'I have been *seeing* him, Sabu. And why not? He's a charming, generous and most attractive man.'

'You ought to watch out, Lisa. You think it's bad being

251

part of Ziggy's stable? If you get involved with Howard Hughes you won't just be part of a stable, you'll be part of a harem. Don't you know he has a string of girls that he keeps in apartments and houses all over Beverly Hills?'

Lisa shrugged. 'Models.'

'*Actresses*, Lisa. Real, talented actresses, who could have made it big. Except once he signs them, he doesn't allow them to work. He keeps them locked up. That man is a serial collector of women.'

'How come you know so much about him? Oh look – here's an advertisement for a thingie that rolls away your fat. Listen to this, Sabutage. "'Rollette' makes it possible for you to rid yourself of unsightly pounds of fat and have a beautiful slender form without strenuous diets, dangerous drugs or exercise."'

'Stop making excuses not to listen to me, Lisa. I know a lot more than you think, about many things.'

'Fiddle-dee-dee! I'm definitely getting one of these.'

'And I'm much more grown up than you in many ways, as well.'

'What thundering rot.'

But on looking sideways into her beautiful friend's beautiful, wise eyes, Lisa knew that it was true.

That night Lisa had a dream. She was back in Connemara, sitting by a lake shore, nursing her baby, and suddenly the baby was gone. The cry of a hawk made her look up. There, on the top of a hill was little Cat – except she wasn't little any more. She could have been any age – a sprite, an elfin creature – with a laughing face and coltish legs and wild, sun-bleached hair.

'Hi,' called Lisa, and 'Hi back,' came the response. And

then her daughter was flitting down the heather-purple hillside, and Lisa was holding her arms out to her, yearning. She had waited for ever for this reunion, this embrace.

And then she woke. She could still smell the scent of her child, still feel the place where she had kissed her on her cheek, near to the hollow formed by her jawbone, just by her ear, still hear her laugh.

Lisa accepted the wretched role of the mother. And then she accepted a role as a discarded mistress. And then she accepted a role as a wife and 'mommy' of *three* children, with below-the-title billing. Lisa's star was not only in descent, it was plummeting.

She'd heard horror stories about other stars whose careers had gone off the rails. Frances Farmer had been arrested for drunken driving and vagrancy, and been committed to a mental institution. Louise Brooks had ended up working as a salesgirl in Saks Fifth Avenue (rumour had it that it wasn't just gowns she was selling), and Sabu had learned that the fragrant June Duprez – erstwhile pink-pyjama-clad star of *The Thief of Bagdad* – had become so impoverished that she was subsisting on a diet of dog biscuits spread with marmalade.

One day, having been obliged by his return from the UK to move out of David Niven's sumptuous house, Lisa found herself sitting in the kitchen of an apartment infested not by ants, but by cockroaches. Her closets were crammed with classic couture gowns and fabulous shoes, but she could barely afford to shop in JC Penney. She was on first-name terms with the *maître d*'s of the most exclusive restaurants in town, but had taken to frequenting

cut-price diners. Recently, she had seen Faith Domergue –
one of Howard's girls – dressed to the nines behind the
wheel of a nifty red roadster, and she knew that a life like
that could be hers if she was prepared to be just that little
bit nicer to him. Howard would look after her, Howard
would see to it that she never slipped on a liquor slick, or
sloped off to suburbia, or slept rough on Skid Row. So
what if freedom was the price she had to pay? She had
been disenfranchised years ago, when she had signed away
her life to Orion Pictures.

But before she dialled Howard's number and steeled
herself to crawl to Johnny Meyer, she picked up the phone
to Phil Gersh, just in case. *Just in case . . .*

'I was about to call you,' he told her. 'There's an offer in
for you.'

'What is it this time?' she said, trying not to get her
hopes up. 'Down-at-heel mother of eight?'

'Don't be smart, sweetheart. I've had a long chat with
Ziggy. He's prepared to loan you out—'

'To Mr Hughes?'

'No. We're not looking at a major player here, but it's a
role you may be interested in. Classy.'

'Tell me more.'

'How does Madame Bovary sound to you?'

'Oh!'

'I thought that'd make you sit up and take notice.' There
was a smile in Phil's voice.

'Well, of course it does!' Emma Bovary, tragic *femme
fatale*, was a dream role for any actress. Still, there had to
be a catch somewhere. Lisa's rampant insecurity prompted
her to add, 'You *are* talking about the role of Emma,
aren't you?' Knowing her luck, she was probably under

consideration for the part of a raddled whore, or woman of the roads or some such.

'For sure they want you for Emma.'

'Oh, Phil! If you weren't on the other end of the line, I'd kiss you! Who's directing?'

'Emile Legrandin.'

So there *was* a catch. 'Emile Legrandin? Hasn't he been blacklisted by the HUAC?'

'Yes. But he's relocating to France.'

Lisa guessed that relocating to France was the only recourse for a maverick *auteur* such as Legrandin. Once any Hollywood player came under scrutiny by the House Un-American Activities Committee and was suspected of leftist sympathies, their career in Tinseltown was over. However, since the end of the war, movie-making was no longer confined to the backlots of Orion or MGM or Universal: the entire world was now a director's oyster, and new horizons beckoned north, south, east and west.

'He wants authentic locations,' continued Phil.

'Nothing to do with politics, then,' deadpanned Lisa.

'Politics and art don't mix. Never have, never will.'

'So I'd have to go to Europe.'

'Yep. No hardship in your case, I'd have thought. You can catch up with family.'

'True.' She'd be able to travel to London to see Gramps and Eva, and catch up with Dorothy. Róisín might even bring Cat to her there for a visit! 'What about finance?'

'There's a backer. It's not a huge budget, but in terms of kudos you can't go wrong.'

Phil was right. If she stayed on in LA, she'd end up playing grannies soon. Emma Bovary was a peach of a part, and it was high time she proved that she could give serious actresses a run for their money.

'Will I be based in Paris?'

'No. Rouen.'

'Rouen! Of course – the novel's set near there.'

'You mean you've actually read it?'

'Yes.'

How proud she was to be able to say that! Since David Niven had made himself responsible for her education, Lisa could now consider herself reasonably well read. While she might not have managed the complete works of Dickens, as once claimed by Myra Blake, she had at least read some of the abridged versions.

'I'll get a script over to you, Lisa,' said Phil.

' "*Madame Bovary, c'est moi*",' she murmured.

'What?'

'It's something the author said about his novel,' she said. 'It means, "I *am* Madame Bovary."'

'I wouldn't make that claim until you've signed the contract.'

'Pragmatist.'

After she had put down the phone to Phil, Lisa went to her wardrobe and took out the biscuit tin with the pattern of peonies on it, the one in which she had stored her mother's letters, and selected one dated November 1918, postmarked Rouen.

She'd be visiting the town where her mother had met her father, where they had fallen in love and become engaged after just one month. How could she say no?

CHAPTER TWENTY-FIVE

JESSIE

CAP D'ANTIBES 1920

Typically, Gervaise decided not to mourn Boy, but to celebrate his life in a pilgrimage: he and Jessie would drive to the south coast.

'We'll run away for a while,' he told her, after the funeral. 'Make ourselves scarce. It's time to get out of Paris, anyway. It's starting to madden me.'

'Where shall we stay?'

Gervaise narrowed his eyes speculatively. Then he touched the tip of his index finger to her nose and said: 'I know exactly where we shall stay.'

'Where?'

'It's a surprise. Let me call in some favours.' He smiled at her expression of frustration. 'Trust me,' he said.

'But I never trust *anyone* who says "Trust me"!'

'Allow me the privilege,' he said, 'of being the exception that proves the rule.'

For the remainder of the day Gervaise was infuriatingly enigmatic. He wrote letters, made telephone calls, sent for messenger boys, and finally left the apartment without telling her where he was going. When he returned later that evening she was dressing to go out to dinner.

'Let's not go out tonight,' he said, dropping a kiss on the nape of her neck as she hooked on her earrings. 'Let's eat in.'

'That suits me. I'm whacked.'

'Come with me,' said Gervaise, taking hold of her hand and pulling her to her feet. 'I've brought home a surprise.'

He led her into the main body of the atelier, where she saw to her astonishment that the table had already been set. It was most unlike Gervaise to be so domesticated! But – but—

'What on earth?' she exclaimed, as she approached the table.

The plate he'd set for her – a Georgian silver salver – displayed a work of art, a seascape in collage. The sea was represented by a mass of dried and crumbled lavender flowers, and a narrow white trail of crystalline salt marked the shoreline. The beach was of pale golden sand, scattered here and there with Lilliputian shells and tiny dried petals like miniature sea pinks.

Jessie turned uncomprehending eyes on him. 'What does it mean?' she asked. 'Have you gone stark, staring mad, Gervaise?'

He took a handful of fine sand, and his smile was wicked as he trickled it onto her palm and closed her fingers over it.

'It's your escape,' he said. 'It's your very own beach. Your piece of paradise. It's the most beautiful place in the world, it's called Salamander Cove, and it's on the Riviera, near Antibes. It has a rather splendid villa attached. And I'm offering it to you on a plate.'

The Villa Salamander – soon to be renamed the Villa Perdita – had belonged to Gervaise's brother-in-law, the comte de Valéry, scion of an important banking family. However, since the war, the comte had fallen on hard times, and had been obliged to retrench. He and Gervaise had agreed a fair price.

Gervaise and Jessie motored south in his Buick, and Jessie kept him entertained as he drove, with stories of growing up in England and her Cambridge days. She taught him English slang and laughed at his blustering accent when he repeated phrases like 'by Jove!' and 'what the deuce!' and 'Great Scott!' and she told him about her charming little cat Purdy, and invented a comic saga that kept him entertained from Beaune to Montélimar – a journey of some three hours.

And at the end of the journey, Gervaise took her face between his hands and said: 'I would never have been able to do that drive without you,' and she knew that on the bend of the road where the tyre on his roadster had burst, the ghost of Boy Capel had been in the car with them.

Salamander Cove was a pocket Venus of a beach, small, but perfectly formed. The first thing they did upon arrival was take off their clothes and dive into the sea, despite the wintry weather. And afterwards they towelled each other dry and ran the length of the strand and back, over and over until they got warm. And then they sat together on the steps that led to the villa, taking nips of brandy from Gervaise's hip flask, and Jessie hugged her knees to her chest and smiled; but when Gervaise asked her what she was smiling about, she gave him a sphinxy look and said, 'Nothing!' because she didn't want him to know that she was planning, after the baby was born, to present him with a little Purdy cat of his own – a Siamese, maybe, like the one Jean Cocteau had.

The villa was in a state of disrepair, but still habitable. It was set back from the road behind wrought-iron gates intricate as cobwebs, and it wore an air of faded grandeur that Jessie found achingly romantic. The terraced garden at the rear of the house was overgrown with nettles and brambles and bindweed, and wild honeysuckle had almost strangled the bougainvillaea that had once been abundant: but ever since Jessie had read *The Secret Garden* as a child she had harboured a desire to bring such a place back to life. She explored with childlike glee. An ivy-covered pergola afforded a breathtaking view of the Mediterranean, a table for al fresco dining ran the length of one of the terraces – its marble surface cracked and bleached by sun and sea air – and a crumbling neo-Gothic angel, pinions poised for flight, stood guard over a weed-choked lily pond. The garden enchanted her.

As did the house. Inside, a dusty chandelier hung from the ceiling of the hall, where a cantilevered staircase unfurled upward to the first floor.

While Gervaise set about opening windows, Jessie wandered from room to room, pulling dust-sheets away from furniture. Most of the furnishings were of the formal variety: rigid occasional chairs and sofas in the drawing room, self-important escritoires in the library. In the dining room she uncovered a gargantuan sideboard and a table that could have accommodated a platoon of guests. In a niche in one of the smaller salons, a Louis XVI bust of some stoic-looking Greek gazed heavenward with vacant marble eyes. She was reminded of her parents' house in Mayfair, with its heavy Victorian chiffoniers and whatnots, and overstuffed armchairs.

Upstairs, a grandfather clock stood sentinel on a landing that opened onto bedrooms swagged with tapestries and heavy velvet, shuttered and carpeted against winter draughts. The bathroom was preposterous, boasting a throne-like lavatory and stained-glass panels in the door, and plumbing so elaborate it might have been devised by Heath Robinson.

The only room in the house that lacked pretension was the kitchen. It was furnished with simple country pieces: a Provençal dresser, bentwood chairs, a scrubbed pine table, a bread press.

'We'll get rid of all the furniture,' Gervaise told her, 'clear the decks, and let some light in. We don't want to live in a *fin-de-siècle* mausoleum. We can kick up our heels here, invite friends to stay.'

'Let's not get rid of the grandfather clock! There's something incredibly soothing about the ticking of a clock.'

'And the wash of waves. That's soothing, too.'

They had wrapped themselves up warmly in eiderdowns purloined from the linen cupboard, and were sitting on the terrace drinking wine. It was getting dark, and the faint sound of the sea came to them from the beach below.

'Can we throw parties?' she asked.

'Why not? And when our guests have gone we shall laze like cats.'

Jessie smiled, and linked his arm. 'Smell the woodsmoke!' she said, breathing in. 'I wonder where it's coming from?'

'The farm, up above. It beats Parisian smog, that's for sure.'

'I wish we didn't ever have to go back. This place feels like home already.'

'It'll feel even more like home next time we come,' Gervaise told her. 'You can have free rein to play at being hausfrau, and do what you like with it.'

Jessie turned to him, astonished. 'You mean, decorate it?'

'Yes.'

'However I want?'

'Every single room. Apart from the one on the top floor: I'm bagging that as my studio.'

'What heaven! We shall make it a perfect dove of a house!' Jessie clapped her hands. 'And the garden, too? May I have carte blanche there?'

'You mean the jungle?' He gave her an indulgent smile. 'You'll need help.'

'We could hire a gardener.'

'And a housekeeper. And a cook.'

'Where will they all live?'

'There's a boathouse on the foreshore. It could be refurbished.'

Jessie had noticed the boathouse on the way to the beach earlier, and thought what an ideal hideout it would make for a child. She could convert it into a Wendy house for a little girl, a den for a boy. She could decorate it with a frieze of daisies, or of toy soldiers. It could be a repository for shrimping nets and beach balls and buckets and spades and kites! Maybe one day there'd be other children, half brothers or sisters for the child she was carrying. Jessie slid a glance at Gervaise. She knew she couldn't prevaricate any longer, that it was time to broach the subject neither of them cared to talk about.

She took a deep breath. 'Which room shall we use as the nursery?' she asked.

Gervaise didn't speak for a long time. By the time he did – in a very grave voice – Jessie's mouth had gone dry and her nails were digging like poniards into the palms of her hands.

'Jessie,' he said. 'I've thought about this a lot, and I'm very glad you brought the subject up now, because I've outlined a plan that I think will suit both of us. I would like you to give the baby over to foster care—'

'Foster care? But why? The baby has a mother and a . . .'

'I know what you were going to say. The baby has *no* father, Jessie. The baby's father might as well be dead.'

'No!'

'I can't be a father to a child that is not mine.'

'Oh! Oh, God – Gervaise—'

'Hear me out. It's not uncommon – I know lots of women who have left their babies with foster parents in order to pursue their own lives, and personally, I'm not sentimental about children. They're hardy little buggers.'

'But—'

'Listen to me, Jessie! I'm not suggesting that you abandon your child – don't get me wrong. What I am suggesting is that he – or she – comes to live in Provence. It's far healthier for a child to grow up in the clean air of the countryside – can you imagine the poor creature stuck in Montparnasse in the smoky heart of Paris? And then, when we come here to escape from the city – which I have no doubt we shall want to do regularly – you can see it as often as you wish. You're in the fortunate position of being able to have the thing reared without inconvenience; most women who find themselves solitaire can't afford that luxury.'

The *thing*.

Oh, God. Jessie felt as if she'd been kicked in the gut. White-faced, she stared at him. 'You called my baby a "thing".'

'Well, it *is* a "thing", darling. Until it – until the birth we haven't a clue what the gender might be.'

'I hope it's a boy!' she hurled at him. 'Men can do whatever they like in this world, it seems to me. I'm a so-called "emancipated" woman, but I'm still expected to be a good girl and do as I'm told!'

Gervaise sighed. 'I'm not *telling* you to do anything, Jessie. I'm simply being pragmatic, and outlining my thoughts on the subject – which is more than you've ever done.'

'I thought you were open-minded about such things,' she retaliated.

Gervaise gave an incredulous laugh. 'Open-minded! You come into my life pregnant with another man's child and blithely assume that I'm comfortable with the idea! Don't you think that smacks a little of presumption? Oh, Christ! Please don't cry.'

'I can't help it. I can't help it!' Sobbing, she stood up from the table and stumbled to the sea wall. Her baby! The child she and Scotch had made when they loved each other still, before Finistère . . .

But wait. He *hadn't* loved her then. He'd known full well that he was going to betray her. Scotch hadn't loved her since Chambéry, since the Italian girl. He had called Jessie his elixir of life while she had been his muse and lover, but he'd clearly drunk his fill of that particular elixir.

How had he left her? Had he looked down on her sleeping face before he'd walked out of the room on the top floor of the Hôtel Simonet? Had he tiptoed out like a coward, terrified that she would wake and confront him?

He hadn't loved her then. The child she was carrying was not a love child. But she could feel the flutter and pulse of life in her womb, and some instinct told her that the baby they had conceived together would thrive and flourish in spite of everything.

Jessie clutched the balustrade until her knuckles went bone white, gazing down at the churning sea below, feeling as though she'd been set adrift. She and all the other lost souls, the walking wounded, all the ghosts of the bloody corpses scattered about Europe in the aftermath of the war, all the weeping widows and pale, hungry children. How to go on living in such a world where men began wars, men would not end wars, men were stupid enough to mythologise wars: men who were motivated solely by greed and power and money. Jessie suddenly felt strangled by the need for Scotch; just to hear his voice might bring some ease. She had sunk so low and now she was sinking again, deeper and deeper, because to relinquish her baby meant that she was cutting for ever the ties that bound her to him.

But she couldn't look back. It hurt too much to look back. Gervaise was right. She knew in her heart of hearts that she couldn't expect him to be a father to a child who was not his. She forced herself to think rationally, forced herself to be objective. What had he said, when he first offered 'Perdita' the job? *I shall want you to keep me amused. A sense of humour is an essential trait in a* maîtresse en titre . . .' He had ditched his former muse, Violetta, and his own daughter Ghislaine. He might not have any qualms about ditching her, too.

'If I refuse to give my baby up, what will happen, Gervaise?' she asked, trying to sound dispassionate.

'I think you know the answer to that.'

Jessie could hazard a guess. If she refused to relinquish her child, she would have to renounce her privileged, very lucrative position as muse to a major artist, and once that happened she and her child would be quite destitute. They would fetch up in some dosshouse as bad or worse than the Trois Moineaux, some place reeking of unwashed bodies and the sour miasma of drunkenness, in a street where tank wagons emptied the cesspools by night and couples copulated on corners.

'You say I may see my baby as often as I wish when we come here?' she asked, without turning to him.

'Of course.'

'Could – he – she – stay here at the villa while we're in residence?'

There was a pause while Gervaise considered. 'I don't see why not. As long as it doesn't get in my way.'

'And may I ask you for a gift to bequeath the child? I couldn't bear to think that – should anything happen to me – the poor creature would have no inheritance.'

'Of course. What do you want?'

'I want one of your Picassos.'

Gervaise whistled through his teeth. 'Astute girl. Which one?'

'I want the blue pierrot.'

He didn't hesitate. 'It's yours,' he said. He joined her by the balustrade and kissed her, first on the forehead, then more passionately on her mouth. When he broke the kiss, he took her by the hand and drew her back to the table where they'd been sitting over their wine. Refilling her

266

glass, he gave her a sympathetic look. 'I am sorry to have given you this ultimatum. I know it can't have been an easy decision to make.'

With an effort Jessie smiled, then raised her glass to her lips to hide the fact that her smile had faltered. She hadn't made any decision, she thought as she sipped the red wine that had come from the vineyards of a revered local château. That luxury had been denied her. She had simply had no choice.

CHAPTER TWENTY-SIX

LISA

FRANCE 1949

In Paris, in the Hotel George V, Lisa met her director Emile Legrandin for the first time. It was a trying experience: Legrandin appeared so indifferent to Lisa as to be offhand, and she found herself doing all the small talk, and asking all the questions.

'What is likely to be the duration of shooting?' she enquired, trying to appear business-like.

Legrandin gave a Gallic shrug.

'As you know, I'm contracted for three months, not including weather cover. But my agent can renegotiate, if you feel you need more time.'

'*Non. Ça marche.*'

'When might I meet my fellow actors?'

'In Rouen.'

'Oh. I thought a small party might be a good idea, in order for me to become acquainted—'

'No party will be necessary.' An assistant entered the room and passed Legrandin a note. He scanned it briefly, then rose to his feet. 'Enjoy your stay in Paris, Mademoiselle. A car will collect you from the hotel and take you to Normandy on Monday. We start shooting on Tuesday morning.'

And that was it.

The following few days were spent undergoing make-up tests at the hands of a supercilious *maquilleuse*. Costumes and wigs had been hired rather than made to measure, so at least she didn't have to spend too much time under the scrutiny of Wardrobe, who just gave her a perfunctory once-over before dismissing her and lapsing once more into trilling, songbird French. Lisa zoned out: she didn't want to know what these women were saying about her.

She spent a lonely weekend wandering through Montmartre and the Latin Quarter, ducking into museums when the rain became too relentless, retracing the path that her mother had taken with Scotch in the early days of their honeymoon, referring constantly to her letters.

How different – how very different – had her mother's life been back then! Blithe, buoyant, irresponsible – Jessie and Scotch had been jazz-age gypsies, free to travel where and when they wanted, unconstrained by finances simply because they had so little.

And when Lisa returned to her hotel room with its over-sized four-poster bed and pink marble bathroom and view of the grand Avenue George V, she wondered why she was feeling so damnably miserable.

Rouen bore no resemblance to the busy, vibrant town described by Jessie in her letters home. It had been badly hit in the Second World War, and the citizens had a hopeless, beleaguered air about them. Lisa was reminded of London the last time she had visited, and wondered how long it would be before life in Europe returned to any semblance of normality.

The movie was to be shot in colour, but it might as well

have been in black and white, so grey was the landscape and so funereal the lighting. Lisa needn't have drawn attention to the weather cover clause in her contract, because Legrandin's misanthropic perspective made it redundant. He wanted his film to have an earthy realism, and took a perverse delight in sending his cast out in rain, hail and sleet. The actors were perpetually bedraggled, bad-tempered and muddy; Lisa's boots were so soaked through that she feared she was in danger of developing trench foot.

Few of them spoke English. When Lisa questioned this, she was told it was no matter; their voices would be dubbed post-production. So while Lisa's lines were scripted in English, the rest of the cast spoke theirs in French, which only added to her confusion and increased her stress levels. Even the dog that was assigned to her – a little greyhound called Djali – hated her, and bared its pearly fangs every time she approached.

In the evenings she would retire to her hotel room and write to Róisín, hungry for news of her daughter. Her cousin's letters were all she had to look forward to, and she read and reread them avidly. From Róisín, Lisa learned that Cat was intelligent beyond her years and wickedly charming. She had her own hen, who laid a brown egg for her every day, she had a kitten that slept in her bed and a pet lamb that followed her everywhere ('just like Mary!' Róisín wrote). Róisín enclosed with her letters photographs of a sweetie-pie with curls like a miniature Rita Hayworth, a drawing in crayon of a donkey that showed a precocious talent, and on one occasion a lock of red-gold hair fell from between the folded sheets of paper. Lisa promptly visited a jeweller's shop in Rouen, and bought a locket in which to safeguard the precious keepsake.

On the day filming wrapped – a week ahead of schedule – she quit the set shivering in camisole and starched linen petticoats, suffering a blinding headache from the wig that was cruelly pinned to her scalp, nursing a nip from Djali and beard rash from the actor playing Rodolphe. When she left Rouen, streaming with a cold and running a temperature, neither Legrandin nor any of her fellow actors turned out to say goodbye to her.

At a loose end in Paris, Lisa cast around for some way of keeping herself amused. She thought of going to London, but because she was so under the weather she did not wish to be an additional burden on Eva, who was still getting by on meagre post-war rations. She thought of maybe travelling south to Italy, following in the footsteps of Jessie and Scotch, but lacked the energy to arrange the itinerary. She would have loved more than anything to make an impromptu visit to Ireland, but she was bound by the promise she had made to Róisín, and besides, Cat had measles.

And then one day, as she was mooching past an art gallery on the rue Saint-Honoré, she saw a painting in the window, a portrait of a woman in a simple peasant skirt and blouse, recumbent in the shade of a fig tree. It bore all the hallmarks of a Lantier.

She remembered the words written on the back of the card that had accompanied his farewell flowers: *If ever you should want a break from La La Land, I know the perfect place* . . .

What better place to go, to recover from ill health, she thought, than the French Riviera?

* * *

That night Lisa dreamed again about little Cat, the tousle-headed sprite dancing on the windswept hill. She called to her, but Cat did not hear. She just carried on dancing.

Lisa phoned the number that Gervaise had written on the back of the card, and was glad to hear the warmth in his voice as he told her she would be welcome to visit. Sadly, he would be unable to receive her himself as he had business elsewhere, but he would have his housekeeper meet her at Antibes. He would join her in the villa the following day.

She cabled Phil to tell him she was extending her stay in Europe, then took the Blue Train south. It would have been cheaper and quicker to fly, but after the wartime journey to Ireland that she had made in Howard Hughes's seaplane, Lisa's fear of flying bordered on the pathological.

In Paris she had bought a dozen postcards to send to Cat, intending to occupy herself throughout the journey by detailing what she saw through the window of the train. But, despite the sunshine, much of the countryside she passed was so dismal that she resorted to inventing the kind of imaginary landscape a small child might dream about, with unicorns grazing in fields and brilliantly coloured birds flying in a sky full of rainbows and bobbly white clouds. 'I know you can't read this by yourself, yet,' she wrote, 'but Mammy will help you, and I hope that she will give you an extra special big cuddly bear hug and lots and lots of kisses from your loving Auntie Lisa.'

The train stopped at the station in Cannes as she wrote these words, and she watched as a small girl, clearly under the stewardship of a nanny, ran laughing to throw her arms around a woman descending onto the platform.

'*Maman, Maman!*' Lisa heard. '*Tu n'étais jamais si belle!*' And as the woman scooped the child up to cover her with kisses, Lisa felt a pang of yearning so intense she had to look away.

CHAPTER TWENTY-SEVEN

JESSIE

PARIS 1920

Back in Paris some weeks after their trip south, Jessie continued to model for Gervaise, even as her shape changed. During their time in Antibes he had filled a sketchbook with drawings of the surrounding landscape, and these sketches informed the pastoral backgrounds against which the *Perdita* series was set.

A wash of French Ultramarine and Prussian Blue conjured a seascape; Hooker's Green and Indian Yellow delineated foliage; and skin tones were picked out in Raw Sienna – with minuscule brush strokes here and there of Crimson Lake. Touches of Chinese White created soft highlights on Perdita's face, breasts and rounded belly – lending her skin the lustre of peach-bloom – and Cerulean Blue traced the patterns on the soft fabrics with which he draped her.

The portrait she loved best was the one that showed her as she had first appeared to Gervaise, in her Liberty silk gown, her hair cascading over her shoulders. There was a hint of melancholy in her eyes, but her lips were curved in a smile. She knew, too, that this was the painting that meant most to him: the girl in the dress splashed with wild flowers, unadorned, bare of foot, as she had been when they had first met.

As her pregnancy advanced, the poses Jessie adopted became more languorous and lazy, as befitted her status as a woman heavy with child. The pastoral backgrounds were abandoned, and Jessie now reclined on chaise-longues and day beds draped with yards of seamless white linen. No more laborious treading of grapes for her – and no more making love. Gervaise seemed to view her with increasingly objective eyes, and she remembered his words to her the first time they'd slept together: *I shall require you to be sexually available to me at all times – until your pregnancy becomes too obvious to ignore* . . . Jessie guessed he had assignments with other women, but as long as she was the only one he was painting, her status as his *maîtresse en titre* was guaranteed. She continued to work hard; and she continued, as had been his stipulation, to keep him entertained, informed and amused. She read extensively – books and magazines and journals – she picked up titbits of delicious gossip at social gatherings, she made sure she was a delight at all times to the eye, sweetly scented, sanguine of temperament and cheerful of countenance. Above all, she made sure that Gervaise was never bored with her.

Gervaise had told her months ago that he would get an entire series from her changing shape, and he was as good as his word. The week before her baby was due, his *vernissage* was held in the Galérie Pierre on the rue La Boétie.

Jessie dressed for the occasion in a gown that Coco had designed specially for her. It was not unlike the gauzy *chitons* favoured by the dancer Isadora Duncan – and indeed the redoubtable Miss Duncan attended the exhibition opening, along with some members of her troupe, the Isadorables, and *le tout Paris*.

On the street outside the gallery, onlookers had gathered to gawk. Jessie was reminded of a motion picture premiere she'd attended some weeks earlier, when the *vedettes* had sailed like shimmering swans into the movie theatre along a carpet, nodding graciously and sending lip-sticked smiles at the fans who had congregated in the hope of bagging an autograph. The mob on the pavement this evening reminded Jessie of the destitute souls who had thronged the rue du Coq d'Or: the beggars, the prostitutes, the disabled war veterans on crutches or with eye-patches. Some called to her, all stared, some held out their hands for alms. Jessie would have obliged, but she had no purse.

'Leave it to me,' said Gervaise, 'I'll have a word with the commissionaire – see to it they get something.'

When Gervaise and Jessie made their entrance, little shrieks and squawks echoed round the gallery, along with a storm of applause. Gervaise was instantly surrounded by a sea of women.

'Gervaise! I *love* them!'

'They're fresh, they're delicate . . .'

'They're utterly charming!'

Gervaise inclined his head to right and left, acknowledging compliments as he moved through the room with Jessie by his side. She accepted a glass of champagne from a flunkey, and smiled enigmatically at each painted face that greeted her. 'Why,' she thought, 'there's probably more paint on all these faces than there is on one of Gervaise's canvases!' She smiled and sipped, sipped and smiled, and adopted an expression of profound gravity when the gallery owner launched into his speech.

'*Mesdames, messieurs* – may I welcome you here this evening to an exhibition of unabashedly sensual paintings. Unlike the exponents of modernism, Monsieur Lantier has the greatest respect for the beauty of the human form, and remains true to Hellenic principles in an age of aesthetic chaos. Monsieur Lantier is a consummate draughtsman in this way, and his best work loses nothing by comparison with earlier masters of the subject . . .'

'He clearly likes you,' said Jessie in an aside to Gervaise. 'But I'm awfully hot, and I need to sit down. Will you excuse me, *chéri*, for a few minutes?'

Skirting the crowd that was gazing with rapt and reverent attention at the gallery owner, Jessie made her way out to the foyer of the building, where hard-backed, mahogany chairs were ranged around the walls. Uncomfortable seating or not, Jessie badly needed to take the weight off her feet. She felt like a ripe fruit in danger of bursting. She had just perched herself heavily on the edge of one of the chairs, when the door to the gallery opened and someone slid through. It was Count Demetrios.

'Mademoiselle Perdita! How are you?'

'Count Demetrios!' Jessie held out her hand, which the count gallantly scooped up so as to drop the requisite kiss on the back of her fingers.

'I saw you slip out. You must need fresh air, yes? Not surprising in your condition.' His eyes slid to her belly. 'Your baby's arrival must be imminent.'

'Yes. It's due next week.' Jessie could barely keep the dejection out of her voice.

The count looked surprised. 'But why do you sound so despondent? You should be full of rejoicing, should you not?'

'Oh – I *am* happy – truly I am, Count. It's just that – well – I won't have the baby to myself for very long.'

'And why is that?'

'We – we shall be giving the baby into foster care,' she told him. 'We feel that Paris is an inappropriate place to rear a child, so he or she will be looked after by a couple who live on a farm in Provence. Gervaise has a villa there,' she added hastily, 'so of course we shall see the child every time we go south. And we plan to spend a lot of time there – even in the summer months – once the villa has been refurbished.'

'The summer months? But no fashionable person spends time in the South in the summer months!' The count seemed more surprised by this notion than by the news that Jessie had engaged foster parents for her baby.

Jessie shrugged. 'We plan to.'

'So.' His eyes slid towards her belly again. 'The baby will be a little Provençal, *hein*? How charming! What did your English poet, Keats say? *Dance and provençal song, and sunburnt mirth . . .*'

Those words had come to her, too, once she and Gervaise had found the ideal couple to foster her baby. The Reverdys were of solid stock, comfortably off. They lived on a farm just up the hill from the Villa Perdita, where they kept goats and pigs and chickens. They had three young children, so Jessie's baby would have playmates. And he – or she – would eat well. In the *boulangerie* in Antibes there were artichokes and asparagus and peas for sale, and potatoes and lettuce and spinach and oranges and figs and cherries and eggs – all the food Jessie had fantasized about during her miserable time in the Hôtel des Trois Moineaux, all piled up outside the shop like an elaborate still life by a Dutch Old Master. Provence was a cornucopia compared to dirty, rainy Paris. She had definitely done the right thing.

'Where is your villa situated?' the count asked her.

'On the Cap d'Antibes.'

'A most pleasant spot. My wife's family used to take a house there every autumn.'

'How is your wife? And your little girl?'

'*Hélas*, my wife is suffering still from tuberculosis—'

'Tuberculosis?' Jessie looked puzzled. 'I thought it was heart disease she suffered from.'

'Ah. That too. How she is afflicted! And Carlotta has gone back to her, to Greece. As for me, I still travel for my sins, like Pilgrim.'

'You must miss your family very much.'

'Yes, yes. I miss my poor wife, and our little girl.'

'And she must miss her naughty boy!'

The count gave her a swift sideways look, and then his mouth stretched in a smile. 'Her naughty boy, yes. I had forgotten that she used to call me that. So.' He tapped his cane against the parquet floor. 'You and Monsieur Lantier are happy together, yes?'

'Yes, we are. And I must thank you again, count, for effecting our introduction – even if it was a rather unorthodox one.'

He nodded. 'Sometimes, Mademoiselle, bold strokes are called for. The subtle approach is vastly overrated, to my mind.' He drew his fob watch from his breast pocket. 'Alas – I must go. It was wonderful to see you again, Mademoiselle. Please convey my kindest regards to Monsieur Lantier, and congratulate him on his magnificent new paintings.'

'I will.'

'And I wish you every happiness in Antibes, in your new villa. Does it have a name?'

'Yes,' she said. 'It's called the Villa Perdita.'

'The Villa Perdita,' mused the count, a small smile playing around his lips. 'The Villa Perdita. Home, sweet home. Isn't that a saying you English have?'

'Yes.'

He nodded again, and flashed his teeth at her. And then he did something quite shocking. He leaned forward and laid a hand on the mound of her belly.

'Safe journey, little one,' he said. 'I look forward to meeting you.' And with a swirl of his opera cape, he was gone.

Jessie sat motionless for some moments, appalled by the liberty the count had just taken. Then, with an effort, she got to her feet. She was halfway across the foyer when she felt the first jabbing contraction. Her baby was on its way.

CHAPTER TWENTY-EIGHT

LISA

CAP D'ANTIBES 1949

At Antibes, Lisa disembarked into blazing sunshine, feeling absurdly overdressed in her tailored travelling costume and high heels.

Hearing a shrill whistle, she turned to see a young woman at the other end of the platform. She was tall and rangy, dressed in loose linen trousers and shirt, her hair held back with a paisley-patterned scarf. A porter had sprung to attention, and was heading in Lisa's direction with a trolley.

'*Vos bagages*, Madame?' he asked, indicating the small pyramid of suitcases that had been unloaded from the baggage van.

'Yes. Thank you, you may take them all – apart from this one.' Lisa kept hold of her Vuitton beauty case. It had been a gift from Sabu, and she knew that it had cost him a small fortune.

The porter piled her luggage onto the trolley, and started pushing it in the direction of the woman who had commandeered him.

She made her way along the platform, feet aching in her tight shoes, past a newspaper vendor selling copies of

281

French *Vogue*, the cover featuring the new gamine haircut.

'Miss La Touche, welcome to Antibes,' said the rangy woman, extending a hand. 'My name is Hélène. I'm Gervaise's housekeeper.'

When Gervaise had told her that she would be met by his housekeeper, Lisa had envisaged an apple-cheeked, roly-poly type, not this willowy, Katharine Hepburn lookalike.

'How do you do,' she replied. 'Please call me Lisa.'

'Lisa. I have seen you in the movies.' Hélène tossed aside her cigarette and ground it under an espadrilled foot. Then she took Lisa's cosmetics case from her and led the way towards the exit. 'I did not imagine you would be quite so slight in real life,' she added, over her shoulder.

Lisa was about to say something about her perpetual diet, then realized that it would be in poor taste in a country that was still suffering wartime deprivation. At the main gate of the station they passed a stall selling *saucisson en brioche*, and Hélène saw Lisa look.

'You won't go hungry here. You'll find that we eat pretty well,' said Hélène. 'Even during the worst times there were ways of getting hold of BOF.' Her French was so rapid that Lisa had trouble keeping up; registering her perplexed expression, Hélène elaborated: '*Beurre, oeufs, fromage*.' She gestured toward a sleek navy blue cabriolet parked outside the station. 'You don't mind riding with the roof down?'

'Not at all. I prefer it. What a nifty roadster.'

'It doesn't belong to me, unfortunately.' Hélène slung Lisa's Vuitton case onto the back seat, while the porter loaded the rest of her luggage into the boot. 'It handles beautifully. Gervaise was lucky the Boche didn't take it along with the Buick.' Sliding behind the steering wheel, she leaned over to open the passenger door for Lisa.

'They took his car?'

'They took anything that moved. Horses, bicycles, even the touring canoe. They took paintings, too. Some of his finest work is probably now hanging on the wall of General Friedrich Wiese. We took care to conceal what we could, but it's difficult to keep your cool while looking down the snout of a Luger.'

The drive to the Villa Perdita took them along winding roads with treacherous hairpin bends and sheer drops to the right. On the passenger side, Lisa felt particularly vulnerable. At one point a man with a donkey cart nearly forced the car off the road, but the drivers merely saluted each other and laughed without bothering to remove the cigarettes from between their teeth.

As she drove, Hélène supplied a running commentary on the surrounding countryside.

'We were lucky not to have been hit directly by the hostilities, but you'll find that the war had a pretty devastating effect all the same. See how the farmsteads are run-down: people cannot afford to maintain them, and some are too old and dispirited to bother. They have lost their sons, and have no hope left for the future.'

'How many young men died?'

'Half a million.'

'How hellish.'

Hélène took a last, fierce pull of her cigarette, and tossed the butt onto the road. 'People nearly starved to death in Nice during the occupation. Here we can at least grow vegetables and wheat. Fish is plentiful, of course, and at this time of the year we don't have to worry about keeping warm. But the winters are tough. Here we are!'

The gates to the property were lying open. Upon their arrival, a great dog, which had been lolling in a patch of sunlight, lumbered to his feet and came to greet them.

'Are you at ease with dogs?' Hélène asked, taking Lisa's case from the back seat.

'Not all dogs,' said Lisa, remembering Djali. 'But he's a handsome boy.' She hunkered down to rub the dog's purply-velvet ears. 'What breed is he?'

'He's a Weimaraner, third generation. His name's Buster. Let me show you to your room.'

Hélène set off towards the house, Buster at her heels. They passed through the front door into an airy atrium where Hélène preceded Lisa up a cantilevered staircase, at the top of which stood a grandfather clock. The guest room was high-ceilinged, with tall windows flanked by muslin curtains opening onto a wrought-iron balcony.

Hélène dumped Lisa's case on the bed, and indicated a door to the right. 'You'll want to freshen up: your bathroom is en suite. I'll have your other bags brought up later.'

'Thank you. I'd love a shower.'

'The water pressure is not the best, unfortunately. The plumbing was installed back in the twenties. Perhaps you would care for a swim, beforehand?'

'You have a pool?'

'I meant in the sea.'

'Oh. I'm afraid I don't have a costume.'

Hélène looked her up and down, assessing. 'I'll see what I can do,' she said. Then she went back out through the door, and left Lisa to it.

The first thing Lisa did was to inspect her precious Vuitton case for signs of damage. Inside, she was glad to see the mirrored lid was intact: since she and the rest of the

284

world had just come to the end of several years of pretty lousy luck, she wasn't keen to extend it. Lifting the case with reverent hands, she placed it on the dressing table, and looked around.

The guest room was furnished in a style she recognized as Arts and Crafts: deceptively simple, more akin to American Shaker furnishings than the 'Moderne' apartments she had been used to in LA, and light years away from her grandparents' house in Mayfair which, before the war, had been crammed with Victoriana. Stepping onto the balcony with its view of azure sea beyond, Lisa kicked off her shoes and eased herself into a stretch, feeling knots of tension in her neck and shoulders bunch and relax.

Below her the sound of the sea was audible; above her white gulls wheeled and called. There was a scent of lavender in the air, and something else she recognized but could not identify. Honeysuckle? She felt at peace for the first time in months: no – years.

'Will this do?' Hélène had returned and was holding up a garment that bore, to Lisa's eye, little resemblance to a bathing costume. It was nothing like the glittering confections that were routinely paraded by starlets at the pool parties she'd attended, or the skintight satiny affairs in which she had posed for her cheesier publicity shots. However, it was certainly better than nothing at all.

'Thank you, Hélène. How did you happen to have it?'

'There have always been spare costumes for guests.'

Just then, a bird started to sing a fluting, utterly enchanting solo. It had been months since Lisa had heard birdsong: there seemed to be no birds in Brittany other than crows. 'Is it some kind of a thrush?' she asked.

'It's a nightingale,' said Hélène.

'I thought they only sang after dark.'

'They sing in the daytime, too. Their song stands out at night because so few other birds sing then. Listen out for him this evening.'

'Is he nesting nearby?' asked Lisa.

'In the stand of pines over there, see? Beyond that track. It's a right of way down to the beach.' Hélène draped the costume over the back of a chair. 'I will leave you to unpack. Or perhaps you would like to rest first? You must be tired after your journey.'

'Yes, thanks. I think I might lie down for half an hour.'

As the door shut behind Hélène, a bark drew Lisa to the window. Buster, followed by a man carrying a shotgun over his shoulder, was bounding along the beach below in pursuit of a stick. The man was wearing workman's boots and a worn suede jacket; a brace or two of quail hung from his belt.

Silhouettes of dog and man were attenuated on the sand, and now Lisa understood why so many artists came to settle here on the French Riviera: the light was incomparable. Unlike the sunlight in LA – which you sensed was always filtered through layers of smog – the air here was pellucid, limpid and, as day gave way to evening, languor-inducing. Now, as the time ticked down to what the French call l'heure bleue with dusk gathering overhead, the sky was a mesmerizing shade of indigo. Cicadas were warming up for vespers, and to the east a harvest moon was rising, looking so close that Lisa felt she might unhook it from heaven.

A sudden squabbling of sparrows under the eaves of the villa made Buster look up, and suddenly Lisa found herself remembering another dog from another era, and an earlier generation of sparrows in a garden. Déjà vu. Something told her she'd been here before.

It was dark. Lisa turned her head on the pillow to see through gauzy curtains the moon suspended high in the sky, round and golden as a pomegranate. Sitting up, she slid her legs over the side of the bed. Her travelling suit lay where she'd discarded it, her stockings were pooled on the floor. She rose to her feet and saw that a robe had been laid out for her on an ottoman: it was of fine lawn, embroidered with calla lilies. She shrugged into it and passed between the curtains on to the balcony, noticing that her cases were stacked just inside the bedroom door.

A tray had been left on the balcony table while she slept. It was set for supper: a wedge of Camembert and a bunch of grapes sat on a glazed platter beside a salad of tomatoes, avocado and red onion. A half-bottle of Burgundy had been uncorked, and on a small scalloped dish reposed a perfect peach. Wrapped in a gingham napkin was a demi-baguette.

Lisa realized that she was starving: she had had nothing to eat since her train journey. Pouring herself a glass of wine, she broke off a hunk of bread and spread it thickly with cheese. The salad had been drizzled with olive oil and was pungent with garlic; the avocado was firm and nutty, and she had never tasted anything so flavourful as the tomatoes – until, that is, she bit into the flesh of the peach.

Some fifteen minutes later, Lisa had devoured everything on the tray but the grapes. These she savoured while leaning over the balustrade, drinking in her surroundings.

The moonlight revealed a garden that had once, perhaps, been dedicated to pleasure but was now given over almost entirely to the cultivation of vegetables. The soil had been dug and turned and laid out in row upon row of drills. Lisa was no gardener, but she remembered how, as a child, her grandfather had held her hand as he led her between the narrow beds of scarlet runners and raspberry canes in the back garden of the house in Mayfair, how he'd taught her to identify which trees produced pears and apples every autumn and which produced cherries in the spring, how he'd allowed her to plunder the mulberry bushes for the purple fruit that used to explode on her tongue.

In her mind's eye she visualized tendrils curling around the bamboo canes that she could discern below, leaves unfurling as the sun climbed the sky, berries burgeoning forth. She remembered how excited she had been when the first of the summer strawberries were served up at high tea, how fragrant the greenhouse had been when tomatoes finally appeared, how mouthwatering the smell of chestnuts roasting on a grate ablaze with logs.

In Hollywood the embossed menus that had been set before her in the opulent surroundings of Ciro's or the Café Trocadero had invited her to partake of lobster and prawns dripping with brandy and cream, fillet of beef slathered in *pâté aux truffes* and enveloped in pastry, or chocolate mousse wrapped in cream cheese and studded with candied nuts. Dinner was usually preceded by Manhattans, and followed by Brandy Alexanders. Often after these meals Lisa had felt the need to retire to the restroom, to bring it all back up. Here, having finished a feast, she could have eaten the same all over again.

The sudden grating sound of a kick-start brought her back to the present: to the moonlit garden and the scent of tuberoses. An engine revved once, twice, and then, between the boles of the pine trees that bordered the property to the east, Lisa saw a light travel up the hill: it was, she conjectured, the headlamp of a motorbike. She followed it until it disappeared and the sound of the engine grew distant, and then something galvanized her. She wanted to swim, run, dance: her body craved exercise.

Taking a key from her purse, she unlocked her cabin trunk and opened the drawer that contained her casual clothes. A pair of cropped pants, a striped seersucker shirt, a pair of deck shoes. She took a quick shower and dressed, slinging a cashmere sweater around her shoulders in case it was chilly outside, then opened the door onto the landing. The only sound in the house was the sonorous tick of the grandfather clock.

Below in the atrium, beside the telephone on a console table, was a sheet of paper, folded once. It had her name written on it.

> *Good evening, Lisa! I hope you are well rested, and that you found everything necessary for your comfort. I did not wish to disturb you.*
>
> *If you should care to join me and my family, you are welcome to a small soirée in the farmhouse above, just off the main road. We are celebrating my niece's christening. However, if you are not feeling sociable, please help yourself to anything you need. There's an extensive collection of books in the library that may interest you.*
> *Hélène*

Lisa tried a door at random. It led to a reception room painted white, as her bedroom was, and likewise furnished with Arts and Crafts pieces. The second door she opened accessed the library. It lay beyond double louvred doors, its walls laddered with floor-to-ceiling bookshelves upon which hundreds of volumes were stacked. A deep linen-upholstered sofa – the kind you'd rather curl up in than sit on – faced onto the terrace, three or four Turkish rugs were strewn haphazardly on the parquet floor, and a butler's tray stacked with bottles and cocktail accoutrements stood in an alcove.

Gervaise owned an eclectic collection of books. Art books full of beautiful reproductions, and illustrated alphabets and bestiaries and flora; the *Erotica Universalis*. Poetry, biography and travel books in both French and English proliferated, and there were shelves upon shelves of fiction, arranged in alphabetical order. She wondered whose hands had assembled the literature with such care; the collection was as carefully compiled as David Niven's had been.

Scanning the spines, she reached randomly for a book. It was an English translation of Flaubert's *Madame Bovary*. Lisa slid it straight back on to the shelf between Forster's *Howards End* and a slim cloth-bound volume of short stories by . . . Zelda Fitzgerald. Lisa had not known that Scott's wife had had anything published other than a badly received novel. This collection was clearly the product of a vanity press: the title page bore the legend *The Girl the Prince Liked and Other Stories*, and the uncut pages told her that it had never been read. On the flyleaf was written, in a flamboyant hand: *For Gervaise, with love, Zelda*.

A sudden cry from beyond the French windows startled Lisa: an agitation of wings told her that some bird had been disturbed – a heron, perhaps, or a curlew.

Putting Zelda's book back on the library shelf, she stood for a moment, undecided. She glanced again at the sheet of paper in her hand.

You are welcome to a small soirée in the farmhouse above, just off the main road . . .

Why not? Tucking the note into the pocket of her slacks, Lisa left the library, pulling the double doors closed behind her.

CHAPTER TWENTY-NINE

JESSIE

PARIS 1920

Jessie's baby girl was beautiful! She weighed 8lb 13oz, and had arrived – a little Aries on the cusp of Taurus – after a mercifully short labour.

Since it was a stipulation of French law that her child's Christian name be that of a saint, Jessie left the designated space on the birth certificate blank, as had thousands of women in the wake of the war. She no longer believed in saints – not even in Jude, the redeemer of desperate cases. Noting her hesitation when it came to filling in the surname, the registrar told her that in the absence of a patronym the child would be deemed *bâtarde*, so Jessie entered Scotch's name. She did not want her child to go through life stamped with the stigma of illegitimacy.

Jessie felt such pride that the blood flowing through this scrumptious morsel of humanity coursed in her own veins, and that the milk that came rushing to her breasts when she heard her baby's demand to be fed – a lilting, musical sound – was helping her to become plumper and peachier and prettier each day.

She had an astonishing head of hair – clearly Jessie's legacy – but there was something of Scotch in her expression, and Jessie thought she had inherited his observant, artist's eyes. Every time she gazed into them, Jessie wanted to drown in their slate blue depths. But the child's eyes – beautiful as they were – had a knowing look, somehow, and Jessie felt awful pangs of guilt every time she put the baby to her breast, sick in the knowledge that soon her daughter would be fed by the wet nurse in Provence who had been engaged along with her foster mother. Jessie had placed a newspaper advertisement some months previously, and had stipulated that, as well as references, a photograph of the house in which her little girl was to grow up would be required. The picture of the farmhouse that the successful applicant had sent her reminded Jessie of one she'd seen in a picture book as a child, a house she'd fantasized about living in herself. It comforted her to know that her daughter would be reared in a dream home within a kilometre of the Villa Perdita.

However, before she and Gervaise could make the trip south, there was something imperative to be done: there was to be one last sitting.

It had been Gervaise's dream to call the final painting of the *Perdita Enceinte* series 'Mother and Child', depicting Jessie with her baby at her breast. Once Jessie was robust enough and she and the newborn had settled into a routine, he began to make preliminary sketches. Jessie hoped the painting would take for ever to complete. She wished that she could ward off the inevitable by erasing the brush strokes, just as clever Penelope had unravelled her tapestry on the isle of Ithaca, before her long-lost husband returned to her. But one day she heard the words that she'd been dreading.

'It's finished.' Gervaise took a step back from the canvas, then nodded in approval. 'It's finished,' he said again.

'Congratulations!' Jessie stapled on a bright smile. She gently removed her baby from her breast and set her on the day bed before wrapping herself in her gown. Blinking in surprise, the baby waved angry fists in the air and squawked in protest. 'Hush, hush, greedikins,' Jessie told her, scooping her up and inviting her to latch onto her nipple again.

She moved across the studio, joined Gervaise at his easel, and regarded the painting. It showed her as Perdita, reclining naked. She was holding her daughter to her breast, and gazing at her with an expression of such tenderness that Jessie felt a jolt go through her. How could she, who had been set adrift among strangers herself, contemplate handing her child over to someone she didn't know? *How could she?*

At her breast, the rhythmic suckling continued, and Jessie thought for the first time of the impending day when she would feed the infant for the very last time, when she would deliver her into the arms of another woman, when she would turn her back and walk away from her. Would she cry? Would she utter that oddly melodic, plaintive wail? Or would she howl in distress? Emitting a little moan of anguish, Jessie doubled over suddenly.

'What is it?' Gervaise crouched down beside her; she could feel his hands on her shoulders. 'What is it, Jessie? Are you in pain? Do you need a doctor?'

'Gervaise!' she blurted, shaking her head violently and gulping for air. 'I'm sorry! I can't do it! I can't give my baby away! How did I ever imagine I could?'

Gervaise's hand was on her chin, now, raising her face so that he could read her expression.

'I can't do it! I can't do it!' she cried, frantically. 'Can't you see that it's impossible?'

'Hush, hush, darling,' said Gervaise, taking her in his arms and drawing her head against his shoulder.

'I can't – I—'

'Try taking deep breaths, Jessie. You're panicking.'

'But how can I not panic? I'm abandoning my own daughter!'

'Come, come. You're doing no such thing. You're doing what's best for her, you know you are. It's an act of selflessness she'll thank you for one day.'

'She won't thank me! She'll revile me.'

'Nonsense. Nonsense, darling. I was sent away to boarding school when I was just four years of age, and I didn't hold it against my parents. And think of the fun you'll have together when we go south for holidays!'

Holidays? Squeezing her eyelids tight shut, feeling tears pool behind them, Jessie tried to conjure a picture of herself and her baby swaying in a hammock on the terrace of the Villa Perdita with that aching vista of blue sea below; she tried to imagine the pair of them paddling along the shoreline, gathering shells; she tried to visualize a game of hide-and-seek in the garden, grabbing a giggling girl and tickling her and saying 'Got you!'. . . And then another hellish thought struck her, and she felt a sob rise in her throat.

'What if she prefers her foster mother to me, Gervaise? She mightn't love me – she mightn't even like me.'

'Of course she'll love you, darling. Shh. Please stop

crying.' Gervaise held her closer, and began stroking her hair with an automatic hand.

'But I won't see her growing up!' Jessie was sobbing in earnest now. 'I won't see her taking her first steps!'

'There, there. There, *there*. Oh, calm down, Jessie, please calm down.'

'She'll call someone else *Maman*!'

'For heaven's sake! You're not—'

'I won't get to celebrate birthdays with her! Or Christmas. I won't be Santa Claus for her.'

'You're being utterly maudlin, now, darling.' Gervaise rose to his feet.

There was a long, long pause, in which the only sound in the studio was the sound of Jessie's sobs. And then the infant wriggled away from her mother's breast, and started to whimper.

'Oh! I'm upsetting her!' At once Jessie started to fuss, her own woes rendered insignificant in the light of her daughter's distress. 'There, there, sweetheart, there, my little lamb! Shh, shh, Mama's all better now. Come, come, finish your feed.'

Getting to her feet, Jessie guided the rosebud mouth back to her nipple, and wrapped her peignoir more closely around her. Then she shook back her dishevelled hair, wiped her face with her sleeve, and took a long, shuddery breath.

Gervaise was leaning against the paint-stained trestle table, watching her. Jessie turned imploring eyes on him. 'What am I to do?' she asked.

He looked back implacably, and then he said: 'You must decide for yourself, Jessie. I'm not your keeper.'

Oh! Jessie felt as if she'd been slapped across the face. What had she done? What had she *done*?

She'd just committed professional suicide, that's what she'd done. Because, in effect, Gervaise *was* her keeper. *I make the rules.* That's what he had told her, the day she'd consented to become his *maîtresse en titre*. *I shall want you to keep me amused* . . .

There had been *nothing* amusing about her behaviour just now. In just a few short minutes she had undone half a year's hard work. Over the course of the past months Jessie had made every effort to be entertaining, inspiring and witty, as per his requirements, and so far she'd never given him cause for complaint. Fear gripped her heart. She saw herself standing again on the rue Coq d'Or, this time with her baby in her arms, surrounded by the monstrous beings that peopled that quarter: the beggars whining for centimes; the drunks in the gutter; the dead-eyed prostitutes; Adèle with her gap-toothed grin.

Oh, God, oh God. She couldn't risk upsetting this man, couldn't risk being abandoned again. *Pull yourself together!*

'I'm sorry.' Swallowing hard, she managed a smile. 'I'm sorry,' she said again. 'That was schoolgirlish and mawkish. That was no way to behave.'

Gervaise smiled back, then moved towards her and dropped a kiss on her forehead. 'That's my girl. We'll pretend it never happened, shall we? But there must be no more tears. I find them . . . unsettling.'

'There won't be any more.'

'There's no need for them. You mustn't worry. Your daughter's well provided for.'

Jessie sent him a questioning look.

'The Picasso,' he said with laconic significance.

'You've done it, Gervaise? The Picasso is hers?'

'It will be one day. It's in the hands of my lawyer – he's adding a codicil to my will.'

'Thank you. Oh – thank you! You're most generous, Gervaise.' Bowing her head in grateful acknowledgement, Jessie looked down at her baby. 'And I apologize again – for the unseemly behaviour. I solemnly promise that those will be the last tears you'll ever see me shed.'

'I rather hope they may be. Your vulnerability was oddly . . . endearing. It would never do for me to fall in love with you.'

Slowly, Jessie raised her eyes to his. Gervaise was wearing his most inscrutable expression. 'Why would that be such a bad thing?' she asked.

'Because I know that you could never love me back.'

Turning to the still-wet canvas, Jessie thought fast. She would have to word her answer very carefully. She did not want to run the risk of him rescinding his promise of the Picasso.

'Gervaise . . .' she began

'You don't need to say anything,' he said, moving towards the door. 'I'm an artist, remember? You can't keep secrets from artists. We're mind-readers.'

He returned moments later with a furled canvas in his hands. 'It's just as well it needed re-stretching,' he remarked. 'It's more portable this way. Here. Here's the little girl's legacy.' He let go of a corner of the canvas so that the painting unfurled before her eyes. 'It's yours to safeguard for her,' he said, holding the painting out. 'Take it.'

Jessie was holding her daughter's future between her hands.

'Thank you, Gervaise,' she said. 'Thank you from the

bottom of my heart.' He had kept his side of the bargain: it was only fair that she should keep hers. 'May I have a minute to myself?' she asked.

She went into the bedroom and shut the door. Then she settled down on the bed and unwrapped the cashmere shawl that swaddled her baby. She gazed at her child in wonder: at the tiny, perfect nose, the rosebud mouth, the mother-of-pearl fingernails, the shell-like ears, the sable eyelashes, the infinitely blue eyes. She ran her hands over her rounded little belly, and squeezed her chubby legs, and stroked her velveteen head, and kissed the creases around her knees and elbows, and gently bit her toes. She learned the little girl by heart, so that she could worship her always in her heart. And then she held her daughter to her breast and breathed her in, the warm, sweet, baby smell of her mingling with the scent she had misted herself with that morning, and as she gazed at her she murmured the words of an old French nursery rhyme: *Y'a une pie dans l'poirier, j'entends la mère qui chante . . .*

And then a miraculous thing happened. Her daughter looked directly into her eyes and smiled.

Jessie sat there for many minutes, holding her baby, crooning to her and rocking her to and fro, crying and laughing. And then she rose from the bed, tucked her into the crib, and inspected her reflection in the looking glass. She pinched her cheeks to lend a rosy flush to her pallor, she smoothed her eyebrows with a little Vaseline, she arranged her hair, she practised a smile. Then she left the bedroom and went back to Gervaise's studio.

He was standing in front of the canvas, wiping his hands with a cloth. The air was redolent with the smell of linseed oil and turpentine.

Elevating her chin an inch, Jessie steeled herself. 'When do we go south?' she asked.

'Tomorrow,' he said.

CHAPTER THIRTY

LISA

CAP D'ANTIBES 1949

Lisa was glad the evening was cloudless, for without the lambent glow of the moon it would have been difficult to find her way. Once she reached the gates of the farm-yard, the sound of fiddle music told her that the party was being held in an adjacent barn.

The weathered doors were festooned with strings of paper chains and balloons, and a hand-painted banner announced *Bienvenue à la petite Sophie!* Inside, half a dozen musicians stood on a dais by a stack of hay bales, playing something lively, and the floor was crowded with dancing couples. Around the walls long trestle tables were piled with food: wine was being liberally poured from flagons. A man passing with a tray offered her a tumblerful, but Lisa declined politely. She'd already consumed nearly half a bottle with her meal.

All of a sudden the band launched into an impromptu version of 'When You Wish upon a Star', and Lisa realized she'd been spotted. Teenage boys were gawping, elderly matrons were regarding her curiously, young women were sliding oblique glances in her direction, and everyone was exchanging surreptitious whispers. *Lisa! C'est Lisa La Touche* . . .

'Lisa! Welcome!' She turned to see Hélène by her side. 'I'm so glad you came – the twins are dying to see you again.'

'The twins?'

Before Hélène had a chance to reply, a young woman with a gardenia in her hair leaned forward to kiss Lisa's cheek.

'Surprise! Don't you remember me? I'm Nicole.'

'My sister-in-law,' said Hélène. 'She is Nicole Poiret now. And here is Danielle, her twin, and her delicious daughter Sophie.'

Danielle was dandling a baby on her hip. The child was dressed in a broderie anglaise christening robe with a matching bonnet, and was sucking on a plump fist.

'What a beautiful baby!' said Lisa.

'I remember you, when you were the same age!' Nicole told Lisa.

'And now you're a big movie star in Hollywood!' said Danielle.

'We were so excited when *The Lady with the Little Dog* came out in France,' said Nicole. 'Your photographs were everywhere!'

'You look *so* like your mother. There's a portrait of her, in the villa – have you seen it? The resemblance is remarkable.'

Lisa felt as though she were watching a tennis match, switching her gaze from one identical face to the other.

'Stop bombarding her!' scolded Hélène. 'Poor Lisa may not even remember who you are.'

'I remember,' Lisa said, slowly. 'I remember now. This is where I lived, once.' The smell in the barn transported her back to when she was a toddler, chasing geese nearly as tall as she was, sneezing from the dust in the hay bales, playing 'catch the rat' with a black-and-white kitten and watching a dark-haired boy bait fishing-lines. 'Nicole, Danielle ... You were my family! That explains why everything – the villa, the garden – feels so familiar! Oh! Why didn't Gervaise tell me when he painted my portrait?'

'He didn't think you'd want somebody from the past turning up out of the blue in Hollywood.'

'Especially since you'd gone to the trouble of changing your name. I'm not surprised you changed it. Lisa La Touche is much more glamorous than Baba MacLeod.'

Baba MacLeod. Nobody had called her that for years. In Hollywood, Sabu and David Niven were the only people who even knew her real name. 'How did he make the connection?'

'A genealogist in the British Library did some research.'

'If only he'd said!' lamented Lisa. 'I would have come here sooner!'

Nicole touched her arm. 'He didn't want to intrude. He's very private, Gervaise, and he didn't consider himself family.'

'She's more family to him than his real daughter,' protested Danielle. 'Her name's Ghislaine,' she added on seeing Lisa's mounting confusion. 'She's his daughter by his first wife. He's never painted her. But he was dead set on painting you.'

Lisa remembered the portrait Lantier had made of her in the buttercup yellow frock, reclining on the palliasse, barefoot and bare of head, and how she had said to him: *It's me as I really am. How did you know?* He knew because Gervaise *was* family, just as these beautiful women, Nicole and Danielle, were family – of a sort. Family from a bygone era.

'If we'd had more time together in LA,' she said slowly, 'I guess I might have made the connection myself. But his brother took ill, and—'

'Gervaise doesn't have a brother,' said Hélène.

'But he got a telegram when he was in LA telling him to come back to France, that his brother was dying . . .'

'Pah. That was just Maquis code, to warn him that the Boche were sniffing around.'

The band had segued from a leisurely waltz into something upbeat. More couples were filing onto the dance floor, and the women were having to raise their voices to make themselves heard. Lisa recognized the slow-quick-quick, slow-quick-quick tempo of the foxtrot.

'You're probably itching to take to the floor,' Hélène remarked, 'but there is somebody you must meet first.'

'Nana,' said Danielle.

'Since she heard that you were coming she has been longing to see you again.'

'She's across in the house.'

'And Papa Reverdy? Is he there too?'

'Papa passed away back in 1926.'

'I'm sorry.'

A boy who had been hovering, ogling Lisa surreptitiously took a couple of steps forward. He had produced an autograph book, and Lisa knew that once she started signing, there would be no respite until everyone present had nabbed a trophy.

'Come,' said Nicole. 'Let's get out of here before they all start demanding to be introduced to you.'

'But I'd be glad to meet them!'

'Try telling me that after you've spent an hour stuck in a corner with Madame Boulanger and her cronies.'

An uproarious laugh from the other side of the room made Danielle look round. 'Uh-oh. That imbecile, Maurice. My husband,' she told Lisa, by way of explanation. 'I'd better grab him before he has much more to drink. *Au revoir*, Baba. I mean, Lisa!'

Lisa watched as Danielle made her way through the dancers to where a group of men were lounging by a table. One of them glanced up at her approach and made eye contact over Danielle's shoulder. Lisa was used to the way men looked at her: she generally dealt with it by adopting an aloof expression and staring them down. But this man did not look away: he held her gaze even as he slid a cigarette between his lips and lit it. Then he blew out a plume of smoke, narrowed his eyes, and smiled. Lisa looked away at once. There was something unnerving about the man's demeanour. She was used to a degree of deference from the opposite sex.

'How many grandchildren has Nana?' she asked, quickly returning her attention to Nicole and Hélène.

'Four,' said Hélène. 'She's waiting for me to produce the fifth.'

That meant, conjectured Lisa, that Hélène must be a daughter-in-law, married to the brother – the boy who had used to take her fishing when she was a small child, and who had taught her to swim. Raoul. She wondered where he was: she had not wished to ask in case he had been a casualty of the war.

'Come,' said Nicole, 'let's go and find Nana.'

In the kitchen of the farmhouse across the yard the stockpot simmered on the big range as it had every day when Lisa had been a child there, and a tortoiseshell kiten a descendant of the calico cat that had been her constant companion, was snoozing on an armchair.

'Nana!' called Nicole. 'Come and see who is here!'

There was the sound of a step on the stair and Madame Reverdy came into the room. She stopped when she saw Lisa, and her clasped hands flew to her face. 'My little girl!' she said. 'My Baba.'

And as Nana took Lisa by the hand and sat her down at the big table, Nicole discreetly withdrew. And then the film star and her erstwhile foster mother started to talk.

CHAPTER THIRTY-ONE

JESSIE

CAP D'ANTIBES 1920

The farmhouse where Jessie's baby was to be reared was a rambling affair, built of weathered red brick with bits that were clearly afterthoughts, and lots of chimneys and curious dormer windows and a cerulean-blue-painted front door. The only real difference between Jessie's dream farmhouse and this bucolic structure was that the picture-book one had roses growing around the door: in the Provençal version, there was bougainvillaea.

Gervaise left Jessie at the gate, and told her he'd come back for her in an hour. He'd done this, she knew, because he would not be able to cope if she broke down and started begging him to change his mind. But Jessie under-stood there could be no going back now. She had her future to think about, and that of her daughter.

Madame Reverdy, the farmer's wife, emerged from the farmhouse, drying her hands on a faded, floral-patterned apron as Jessie approached.

'Madame! How nice to see you again – and this time with the baby! Allow me to have a peek at her. Oh – but how pretty she is – how like her *maman*! What a head of hair for one so small! May I hold her?'

Jessie nodded, and handed her baby over. She didn't know whether to feel jealous or glad when Madame Reverdy said: 'Oh! I get a smile! Hello, *poupette* – what a pleasure it is to welcome you to our home! How would you like to meet your new brother and twin sisters? Raoul! Come here and help Madame with her bag.'

A boy of about six years old appeared, and took from Jessie the bag that she had packed with such care: the tiny baby clothes that she had shopped for so diligently in Paris; the little porcelain monkey that Gervaise had bought for her; her birth certificate; the cabochon sapphire ring that Scotch had given her – the only legacy the child would ever have from her birth father – and, most importantly, the blue Picasso pierrot, which Jessie had rolled up with careful fingers and inserted in a sturdy cardboard tube. She had included the Picasso because she was its custodian: Gervaise had entrusted the painting to her for safe keeping, after all. But Jessie had been clever: what if Gervaise dropped her for a more inspirational muse, the way Scotch had done? He might then change his mind, alter his will, and her daughter would never get the Picasso. It was safer to spirit it away here to the home of the child's foster parents, where Gervaise would never think to look for it.

They made their way towards the front door, Raoul loping beside his mother and craning his neck so that he could get a good look at his new baby sister.

'What's she called?' he asked.

'She doesn't have a name yet,' said Jessie. 'She's just "baby".'

Once inside the house, Madame Reverdy led the way to a sunny kitchen with a floor of warm terracotta tiles and a big range upon which an aromatic stockpot simmered. Beyond the open back door, Jessie could see chickens roaming. A ploughshare lay abandoned in front of a timberbuilt barn, which – to judge by the sounds coming from it – was home to a family of pigs. Troughs of bright geraniums bristled on every windowsill, a cock was crowing loudly from his perch on the half-door of an outbuilding, and a little cat was washing herself on the doorstep. She was the image of the kitty, Purdy, that had slept on Jessie's pillow every night at home in London.

Two identical little girls sporting pigtails came running across the yard. One carried a baby doll, the other a squirming puppy, and when one of them called out – 'Maman! Maman! Has our new sister arrived?' – Jessie knew that she could not have found a better home for her child.

She turned to Madame Reverdy and said: 'You will take great care of my daughter. I know you will.'

'But of course, Madame! Look at my bonny lad and lassies, how bursting with good health they are!'

'She's called Baby,' Raoul told his sisters importantly, indicating the bundle.

'Baby! You mean Baba. You can't just call her "Baby".' The girl gave her brother a disparaging look. 'Hello, little Baba! I'm Nicole! And this is Dannie—' Dannie leaned in and made little cooing noises '—and this is Cacahuète.' Nicole held out the puppy, and Baba reached out and wrapped her plump pink fingers around Cacahuète's tail. 'Look! They're friends already!'

Jessie sat down at the kitchen table and fed her daughter for the last time while her new family bustled around her. She bathed her, and changed her napkin, and dressed her in the tiny gown that had been hand-smocked by one of Coco's seamstresses. She accepted a bowl of vegetable soup and a heel of crusty bread and a cup of milk from Madame, and she watched the girls help their mother wind wool while Raoul trained the puppy to play 'fetch'.

And then a car horn sounded. Jessie turned to the window to see, at the end of the avenue leading up to the farmhouse, Gervaise at the wheel of the Buick. It was time to go back to Paris.

CHAPTER THIRTY-TWO

LISA

CAP D'ANTIBES 1949

In the farmhouse kichen, Nana and Lisa talked about the time Lisa had spent there as an infant: about Jessie and Gervaise and the glamorous jazz-age friends who had used to visit the Villa Perdita, and how carefree their lifestyle had been. Nana told Lisa how things had changed since: how Gervaise had become, in effect, a recluse; and how her own fortunes had suffered a setback since Monsieur Reverdy died, leaving her with another child to rear along with the three she had already. It had been tough, she told Lisa, but worth it – especially now that she had grand-children to dote upon.

'Can you tell me more about my mother?' Lisa asked the old lady. 'I know so little – just that she went missing here in France.'

Nana looked upset. 'There were rumours of foul play, but I never believed those preposterous stories.'

'What stories?'

'Oh, there was talk – stupid, stupid talk – of murder and abduction and all sorts of craziness. She left a shoe, you see – just a single shoe. They said that was symbolic, that she came into his life without shoes, with nothing, and that's how she left, with nothing but the clothes on her back. When the police questioned me, they asked if I thought that Monsieur Lantier might have had something to do with it – oh! It would have been wicked even to think such a thought.'

He loved her so much he nearly died of grief when she disappeared. He locked himself in the villa for months and barely ate – I used to bring him food. He hoped that maybe your father had come for her, but he knew she would never have left you. Never.' Nana put her head in her hands and started to cry.

Worried, Lisa rose from the table and went to the door. Outside in the yard, Hélène was scolding a small boy.

'Hélène!' she called. 'Can you help?'

'What's the matter?' Cuffing the child on the ear, Hélène advanced over the cobblestones, teetering a little in her dancing shoes.

'It's Nana,' Lisa told her. 'I've said something to upset her.'

'What about?'

'My mother,' said Lisa, in a low voice. 'I asked about what happened to her.'

Together they went back into the kitchen. Nana had opened a loose-leafed album, and was turning the pages.

'Here!' she said, wiping her eyes on her apron and sliding the album across the table towards Lisa. 'This is how it was reported, in the local paper.'

DISAPPEARANCE OF LANTIER MUSE

An event near Eden Roc has puzzled local gendarmerie. A woman known as 'Perdita', who was resident at the time in the nearby villa of the same name, has gone

312

missing. She was last seen on Thursday evening. Perdita is about 170 cm in height, of slight build with long auburn hair. She is said to have been wearing a silver-coloured dress of the low-waisted 'flapper' style with a 'handkerchief' hem and is thought to be barefoot. One of her shoes was recovered in the garden of the villa. Perdita is the British model and companion of the artist Gervaise Lantier. She has in the past been known to have suffered amnesia. Please report any sightings to the gendarmerie in Antibes.

'What does it mean?' asked Lisa.

'That is all we ever had to go on,' said Nana. The old woman's tears had dried, but her eyes and nose were red and swollen from the coarse fabric of her apron. 'I'm sorry for the outburst. You see, no body was ever recovered. Nothing was recovered. Just her shoe. Oh! Excuse me.' She wiped her eyes again, then retreated from the room, untying the strings of her apron as she went.

'Do people think that my mother committed suicide?' Lisa asked Hélène.

Hélène shrugged. 'Eden Roc is a common spot for such accidents. Just last week a boy fell from there.'

'Was she unhappy, do you know?'

'Nana says that she was the blithest creature – a perfect homemaker, a perfect hostess. And Gervaise adored her. You can tell from the painting he made of her. But then, I never showed Nana the journals.'

'Journals.' An image flashed before Lisa's mind's eye, of her mother covering page after page of lined paper with frantic scribbled words. 'I remember Mama used to write in red books – like schoolchildren's exercise books.'

'Yes. They're there, still, in the villa. I wanted to throw them away when I first came across them, but Raoul said no, that you might come back some day, and that they were yours by right.'

'You've read them?'

'I've . . . dipped into them. Forgive me. I will make sure that they are returned to you. I'm glad I took Raoul's advice – they were not mine to dispose of.'

Lisa turned the page of the scrapbook. There, gazing out at her was the sepia image of a woman, her face bronzed but only half visible under the brim of a straw hat. She recognised her at once. 'That's her!' she said. 'That's my mother. And that must be me.' Sprawled in Jessie's lap, dressed in a baggy striped jersey swimsuit, a miniature Lisa squinted at the camera. 'I remember that beach parasol.'

'And there you are again.' Hélène pointed at a snapshot on the opposite page. 'With Raoul! How cute you were!'

The photograph showed a lanky, dark-haired boy holding aloft a fish on the end of a line. Standing next to him, Lisa was saluting the trophy with a grin so broad she might have caught it herself.

'Raoul,' she said, with a smile. 'He taught me to swim.'

'How skinny he looks there!' remarked Hélène. 'Did you meet him earlier?'

'No.'

'We must remedy that.'

Lisa turned another page. Some postcards had been pasted in, and a small bunch of dried violets. There was a family photograph of the Reverdys and one of –

'The boathouse!' Lisa recognized a wooden structure, with a veranda and a gingerbread-style fascia and a wide slipway leading down to the beach. 'I remember playing there.'

'It looks rather different now.' There was a smile in Hélène's voice. 'It's had a facelift.'

But Lisa wasn't listening. She was examining a dog-eared photograph that had come away from its mount. It showed an attractive young couple in bathing suits sitting on the steps of the boathouse, she with bobbed hair looking challengingly down the lens, he focused on something beyond. Between them stood a fair-haired girl of about four or five years old, dressed in a sailor suit. On the back of the photograph was written in faded pencil: *Scott, Zelda, Scottie. The Plage, Salamander Cove, 1926.*

'Scottie!' exclaimed Lisa. 'That little girl – I remember her: we used to play at being cavemen together.' Looking at the photograph more closely, she noticed the assorted paraphernalia that surrounded the family: the dolly that Scottie was clutching between her hands, the soda siphon, the upturned cocktail glass. 'Scottie,' she said again, feeling as if she were putting together the pieces of some peculiar jigsaw. 'Scott and Zelda Fitzgerald's daughter. How extraordinary.'

A creak sounded on the stair, and Nana came back into the room. She had discarded her apron and tidied her hair, and she was carrying a stout cardboard cylinder. 'I'm sorry,' she said again, affecting a brisk assurance. 'It was stupid of me to be so maudlin. Of course, this should be a happy occasion.'

Laying the cylinder on the table, she went to the dresser and returned with a tray set with a bottle of Calvados and several small glasses etched with a pattern of vines.

'Go now, Hélène,' she said, 'and bring the family here. I would like to make a toast.'

'Calvados! You should feel honoured, Lisa,' Hélène said, as she rose from the table and made for the door. 'That's reserved for very special occasions. The last time we had it was at our wedding.' She flashed Nana a smile. 'Are you feeling better, my darling *belle-mère*?'

'Yes, yes. I'm fine. Now shoo, and be discreet about it. We don't want the entire *arrondissement* descending on the kitchen.'

Nana took a seat beside Lisa, easing herself onto it with an 'Ouf!', and reached for her spectacles. 'You've been looking through the album,' she observed.

'Yes. It's strange to see things and people that were so familiar once.' Lisa turned another page. 'Look! There's Papa Reverdy!'

'Pierre. God bless his soul. I haven't sat down with this book for a long time.'

'I'm so sorry, Nana, to hear that he died.'

'He left me with a bonny souvenir, all the same.' Nana took up a photograph that was lying loose between the pages, of a burly boy of about five.

'Your son?'

'Yes. My youngest, Bruno. He's in charge of the farm now.'

'I thought Raoul would have taken it over, being the eldest?'

'Raoul went to university instead. The Sorbonne.' Nana picked up another photograph. It showed a man leaning over a drawing board, shirtsleeves rolled to the elbow; a pencil tucked behind his ear, a cigarette between his fingers. 'This is him.'

Lisa recognized the man who had smiled at her from across the room earlier, and felt a little ridiculous. How snooty he must have thought her!

'He is an architect, now,' added Nana, proudly.

'That's some achievement!'

'Yes. Both my boys have done well. I am lucky to have them alive and with me still. So many of our Resistance fighters died.'

'They were part of the Resistance?'

'Yes. They were both *maquisards*. As was Monsieur Lantier. Ah – that reminds me – you must not forget this. It belongs to you.' Nana rolled the cardboard tube across the table towards Lisa.

'What is it?' asked Lisa.

'A painting. Your mother gave it to me for safe keeping.'

'Is it one of Gervaise – Monsieur Lantier's?'

'I don't know. I looked at it once, only. I did not care for it myself. However, your mother was insistent that you should have one day, and I am glad to be able to restore it at last to its rightful owner.'

Before Lisa could inspect the contents of the tube, Nana gave a little exclamation, and laid a hand on hers. 'You wear your mother's ring!' she said.

'Yes.' Lisa held out her hand so that Nana could inspect the gold circlet with the dark stone.

'Oh – it is the very same one! I am so glad you have it still! I remember, I put it in an envelope along with your birth certificate when you left us. And a little porcelain monkey.'

A sudden fracas from the courtyard announced the arrival of Danielle and Nicole. Baby Sophie's head was lolling on her mother's shoulder, and the flower in Nicole's hair was wilting. They were followed by Hélène and the man whom Lisa now knew to be Raoul. Then came a big, handsome fellow who was introduced as Bruno, and a trio of chattering children.

Nana called for silence. Then she, cleared her throat and handed the Calvados to Bruno, who solemnly uncorked the bottle and commenced pouring. 'I would like to make a speech. Today is memorable for all of us in this room, not just because it is the christening day of our darling Sophie, the newest addition to our family . . .'

At this, Danielle held a groggy Sophie aloft, and Bruno, who had just handed his sister a glass, said: 'Ick, Dannie! I think her napkin might need changing.'

'It is also the occasion of a very special reunion,' Nana resumed, sending Bruno a look of reprimand. 'I have gathered you around this table to welcome back a former family member. Please, all of you, raise a glass to Miss Lisa La Touche, whom we knew as Baba.'

The family toasted. 'To Baba!' said some, and 'To Lisa!' said others, and Lisa felt a strange sensation of being simultaneously a guest, and a cherished member of a family at last.

CHAPTER THIRTY-THREE

JESSIE

CAP D'ANTIBES 1921-1926

During the summer months spent at the Villa Perdita, Jessie hoped that Gervaise might execute another portrait of her and Baba, but he did not. The arrival of Scotch's child had changed something in the dynamic of their relationship.

As agreed, Gervaise had transferred all responsibility for the refurbishment of the villa to her. She replaced the mahogany chaise-longues and uncomfortable bergères with sofas loosely covered in pale linen and armchairs plump with squashy cushions. The heavy curtains and drapes, so essential when the villa had been a winter retreat, were ousted in favour of muslins and calico, and sailcloth in blue and white stripes. The opulent carpets were supplanted by simple rugs, the carved marble fire-places ripped out and refashioned into niches for *objets trouvés*. For these, Jessie trawled the flea markets and junk shops, as she and Scotch had done during their time spent in Rouen. She remembered how he had haggled for curios in his execrable French – always knowing what was genuine and what was not: a blue wooden rosary, a box inlaid with mother-of-pearl, an old silver buckle, an ivory paper knife, the tiny jade charm that she still wore on a silk ribbon around her neck.

The backstreets in Antibes yielded up all kinds of treasure to Jessie. She found a hammered-pewter-framed looking glass, a painted Russian birdcage, an oriental silk parasol. She found vases and jugs that she filled with flowers from the garden – peonies and roses and heliotrope. In the weekly market she acquired everyday objects that she made extraordinary: earthenware bottles into which she decanted expensive bath oils, wooden curtain rails which she festooned with silvery chimes. Wicker shopping baskets became repositories for scented soaps, while enamel basins from the *quincaillerie* were reinvented as punchbowls, and brushed steel flasks as cocktail shakers. Jessie was, she knew, making the kind of home she had once dreamed about settling down in with Scotch.

Gervaise spent much of his time sequestered in his studio, or sitting over pastis with his artist friends in Cannes and Antibes. Sometimes he would leave for Paris without her, and then she delighted in fetching Baba down from the Reverdys' farmhouse. As her daughter grew and learned to walk and talk, there were sandcastles on the beach, games of hide-and-seek in the garden, stories at bedtime, teddy bears' picnics, and lots and lots of kisses and cuddles and tickles and laughter.

Nicole and Dannie doted upon their foster sibling, but it was Raoul whom she worshipped. The boy had little time for his sisters, dismissing them as ninnies, but Baba was special because she had no fear of the water. He taught her to swim, and often took her fishing. Madame Reverdy frowned upon these activities, denouncing them as hoydenish, but Jessie loved to watch her daughter splashing about in the shallows in her vest and knickers, her tawny hair bleached into tiger stripes under the Mediterranean sun, her limbs burnt berry brown. Baba would help Raoul clear the beach of seaweed, too, dragging long strands of the stuff above the high-water line, where she would plunder it for crabs and shells and other treasure trove.

Periodically during July and August, Gervaise would come back from Paris with parties upon endless parties of people. Since the arrival in the Hôtel du Cap of Gerald Murphy and his wife – a couple of wealthy Americans who had come to Antibes with plans to build a villa – spending summer in the South of France, which had once been considered unthinkable, became fashionable overnight. A procession of socialites, artists, writers, musicians and hangers-on paraded through the Riviera and posed on the Promenade des Anglais. Scott and Zelda Fitzgerald drank their way through the afternoons and on into the early hours of the morning while Coco Chanel bought a plot of land to construct a retreat. Endless visitors 'dropped in' and stayed for days on end.

Jessie's life became a blur, a kind of hedonistic treadmill interspersed with the joyous, precious, increasingly infrequent moments she grabbed with Baba. Her daughter was not interested in the company of the adults who frequented the villa: when she wasn't pretending to be a pirate or a mermaid or a savage, she preferred to go back up the hill to the farmhouse, where there was a barn to play hide-and-seek in, and chickens to chase, and a kitten of her own to take to bed at night.

And that is when Jessie took to writing to Scotch in red hardbacked notebooks, with a bottle of wine to hand, late at night when guests had retired to collapse comatose or make illicit love.

I long & long to know about you, Scotch – where you have been; where you will go; how you are in health & spirit & what thoughts you have had about all sorts of things.

I love loving you, love having loved you. Lots of the time I feel quite isolated & afloat in an endless unknown sea – very very lonely – or, rather, alone & terrified of – I wish I was quite sure what. I know what death in life really is: I died on the beach at Finistère the day you left me, I died in that hellish hotel on the rue Coq d'Or, I died when Gervaise told me I must give up my – our – child. But this is a new high in lows.

I seem to be made of mist. And yet . . .

I have our daughter with me & no one can feel completely dead while someone so perfectly simple & beautiful is around – not so simple, either! Baba is quite the most wonderful character of a tiny girl & so lovable & attractive – I say this in a completely unbiased way! She is adorable, & such heavenly fun – trotting around after me & talking a lot of glorious jargon – a mix of French and English.

And then one day – after the departure of the renowned diva Mistinguett – another visitor arrived at Cap d'Antibes.

CHAPTER THIRTY-FOUR

LISA

CAP D'ANTIBES 1949

Later that evening, back in the barn, when the toasts had finished and Hélène and Nana had done the washing-up and little Sophie had been taken home to bed, Raoul approached Lisa. The smile he gave her was at once singularly charming and entirely self-assured.

'You've danced with my brother,' he said, 'and you've danced with Monsieur Dupois and young Homais and Rouault, who is the biggest womanizer in Antibes. Isn't it about time you danced with me?'

'I'd love to,' Lisa said, breathlessly. She had just come off the floor after having been swung about by a gangly boy who could not have been more than fifteen. Now, with Raoul leading her into the centre of the room and sliding a hand around her waist, she felt a little more . . . womanly.

The band was playing waltz time, and as Raoul guided her across the floor, Lisa realized that this was what a real celebration should be. Here there was no Hollywood artifice, no evoking glamour. Instead there were balloons and bunting and babies and pretty girls prinking in party frocks and teenage boys ogling them, and old men tapping their feet to the music and some of them taking to the floor with their wives and showing off how they could dance still, and dance better by far than them youngsters! And as Lisa turned and spun in the circle of Raoul's arms, it seemed to her that her senses were spinning too: she registered as in a dream the flushed faces, the victory rolls ruined in the heat, the bodies pressed close, the smell of soap that couldn't disguise a more animal smell, the pressure of his hand on her back, and the merry-go-round madness of it all – the music, the drum beat, the rhythm that rose through the floor and thrummed up through the soles of her feet and made her feel . . .

Sexy.

Lisa stopped mid-spin. At the edge of the dance floor somebody was bursting balloons and braying with laughter, and a party horn was being blown non-stop, and the tobacco smoke from a meerschaum pipe made her want to shut her eyes.

'Let's get out of here,' Raoul said authoritatively 'Do you have a coat?'

Lisa shook her head. She had left her pullover somewhere, she didn't care where.

'I'll take you back to the villa.'

'No. Please don't concern yourself – I can manage.'

'Come on.'

Outside in the yard, Raoul led her to where a motorbike was parked under a lean-to. 'Have you ridden pillion before?' he asked.

'No. Don't worry – I can walk. It's not far.'

'Don't be stupid. It's pitch dark out there.'

Raoul indicated the track that lay beyond the gate of the farmyard. The moon was hidden by cloud now, and a wind had got up. Lisa shivered. Slinging his leg easily over the machine, Raoul held out a hand to help her climb on behind him, and as she settled herself on the pillion, she felt like a small monkey clinging to the back of some sleek beast. There came a purr and then a roar as he kick-started the engine, and just as the motorbike leapt forward, the door to the farmhouse opened and Hélène came running out.

'Raoul!' she cried. 'Where are you off to?'

'I'm taking Lisa back to the villa.'

'Wait,' said Hélène. 'You must be freezing, Lisa. I'll get your pullover – you left it in the kitchen.'

She disappeared through the door, and returned with Lisa's cashmere sweater and the cardboard tube that contained the painting.

'Nana said to give you this,' she said, handing over the items. 'I'll see you in the morning. I'll be driving into Antibes to pick Gervaise up from the train – can I bring you anything?'

'No. Thank you so much for all your kindness. It really is not necessary, you know, for Raoul to drive me back. I'm sure I could manage perfectly well on my own.'

'But my *beau-frère* loves to help. He's a true chevalier. Drive safely, Raoul! Goodnight, Lisa! And make sure your shutters are closed tonight – there's rain on the way.'

Raoul gunned the machine, and as the motorbike set off down the bumpy track, Hélène's words sounded in Lisa's head. *My* beau-frère *loves to help . . . My* beau-frère *is a true chevalier . . .*

The phrase *beau-frère*, translated literally from the French as 'beautiful brother'. But its real meaning, Lisa knew, was 'brother-in-law'. Hélène Reverdy was married to Bruno, not Raoul.

During the short ride, she found herself concentrating very hard on staying on the back of the motorcycle without having to wrap her arms around Raoul. But the track was bumpy, and after a while she gave up trying.

Pulling up under the porte-cochère of the Villa Perdita Raoul killed the engine and helped her dismount. In the silence, the rustling song of the cicadas seemed amplified, the wash of the waves hypnotic.

'I'll come in with you. You're probably not familiar with the layout,' he said, aiming a booted foot at the kickstand.

The scent of jasmine mixed with petrol was strong in the air. Moving to the front door, Raoul opened it, holding it ajar for her to precede him. As she passed through into the atrium, he placed a hand lightly on the small of her back, making her horribly aware that she was wearing seersucker, not silk, and that she smelt of sweat, not Chanel. Once inside, he stepped back and threw a couple of switches on the wall. The light that sprang from the chandelier dazzled Lisa. Fearful that it was too harsh, she raised an automatic hand to coax into place the veil of hair she liked to hide behind when trying for an incognito look.

'Will you come in for a nightcap?' she asked, making for the double doors of the library.

'Thanks,' he said. 'Gervaise is due back tomorrow?'

'Yes.' Propping the painting in its cardboard tube against an ottoman, Lisa indicated the butler's tray. 'Help yourself. There seems to be just about every liquor under the sun.'

'You must be tired after all your travelling. An Elixir Végétal might do you good.'

'A what?'

'It's a kind of Chartreuse.' Lisa watched Raoul stroll over

326

to the laden tray and select a bottle. 'Carthusian monks attribute their longevity to it.' He poured an inch of emerald liquid into a glass, handed it to her, then reached for a brandy balloon and helped himself to a measure of cognac.

Since there were no mellow jazz records she could play to cover the silence, Lisa resorted to small talk. 'What a great party that was!' she said, perching on the edge of the ottoman.

'I dare say there'll be another one before long. Bruno told me this evening that Hélène is expecting.'

'Your mother will be thrilled.'

'Yes, she will.' Raoul swirled the brandy in his glass, then raised it. '*Santé.*'

'*Santé.*'

She took a cautious sip of Chartreuse. It was a heady blend of liquor and herbs, simultaneously aromatic and piquant and honeyed.

Raoul nodded at the cardboard tube at Lisa's feet. 'What's in there?' he asked.

Lisa picked up the tube. 'It's a painting.' A faded label pasted onto the side read: *Sennelier*. 'Perhaps that's the name of the artist.'

'It's an artists' supply shop in Paris.'

'Shame. I thought he might be somebody famous. Nana told me that she'd taken a peek at it, but it wasn't to her taste.'

'Have a look.'

Lisa eased the canvas carefully from the container. She unrolled it, laid it flat upon a table, and smoothed the surface while Raoul set a paperweight at each end. The painting depicted a pierrot embracing an infant.

'It's not one of Gervaise's,' she remarked, reaching for her drink.

'No,' said Raoul. 'It's one of Pablo's.'

'Never heard of him. It's quite good, though, isn't it? Is he a local painter?'

'You could say that. He's Spanish, but he has a house in Antibes.'

'I wonder is it worth anything.'

Raoul narrowed his eyes and looked at the painting speculatively. 'I should say it's worth around thirty thousand,' he said.

'Francs?'

'No. Dollars,' said Raoul.

After they had cleared up the Chartreuse that Lisa had in her astonishment spilled, they repaired to the garden at her suggestion to listen for the nightingale. She knew that what she really wanted was fresh air: her mind had been spinning non-stop since Raoul had told her the painting was a Picasso.

'Thirty thousand *dollars*! Golly gumdrops,' she said, settling herself on the cushioned swing seat on the terrace.

'What did you say?' asked Raoul.

'The painting. I can't believe its value—'

'No. You said 'golly' something.'

'Golly gumdrops.'

'What does that mean?'

'I don't really know. It's an expression of surprise. What do you French say when you're very surprised?'

'We say mostly, "*merde*". But if we were being polite, we might say "*saperlipopette*".'

'*Saperlipopette?*'

'Yes.'

'I like "*Saperlipopette*".'

They sat looking each other for a long moment, smiling, the swing seat rocking gently beneath them, and then Raoul said, 'What would you say if I kissed you?'

'I won't know until you try.'

He raised a hand and pushed a strand of Lisa's hair back from her face. Then he traced the whorl of her ear and the line of her jaw and the dimple just above her chin. 'You have a little touch of Chartreuse, just there,' he said, rubbing the corner of her mouth. 'May I taste it?'

'Be my guest.'

Several minutes later they broke the kiss. The nightingale was singing beyond the sea wall. Or maybe it was a skylark. Or a thrush, or a chaffinch, or a cormorant or something. Lisa hadn't a clue. She gave Raoul a look of mock surprise.

'*Saperlipopette*,' she said.

Lisa was lying on a bed, wearing nothing but a mass of white petticoats. She was aware of a man's voice urging her to stretch, to spread herself, and she found herself thinking that this was too much: she was displaying too much flesh. Her petticoats had been pulled up over her naked ass, her hair was dishevelled, she had lost an earring; her mascara was smudged, her mouth swollen, there was sweat trickling down her ribcage. And then her limbs became entangled in the yards of lace-trimmed linen which – she realized abstractedly – were sheets, not petticoats after all.

A voice was in her ear, telling her how soft she was, how succulent, how good she tasted; how he had wanted to have her from the moment he had led her on to the dance floor. Lisa sighed and laughed and lost herself, arching her back and snaking her arms around him, imploring him to ravish her. She was entirely in character as Emma Bovary, the shameless woman, the fallen wanton. And then zsomeone told her that the scene was over, that the cameras had stopped rolling, but she paid no heed because she was coming, and as she emerged from the dream she knew that if that had been a performance, she would have been up for an Oscar.

'Oh, beautiful, beautiful woman,' Raoul said, looking down at her with amused eyes.

Lisa tried to conjure up one of the glib remarks that she had used to make on the rare occasions when she spent a night with one of her leading men. But instead she just smiled stupidly. Raoul kissed her and rolled out of bed and said, as he buttoned himself into his trousers: 'Breakfast. My place. Fifteen minutes.'

'Where is your place?' Lisa asked drowsily, raising herself on an elbow.

'Do you remember the boathouse where we used to hang out when we were kids?'

'Yes.'

'That's my place,' he said. And then he was gone.

Outside, the rain that had fallen overnight had washed the landscape clean. All was blue; so blue she thought that if she could touch it, it would feel like paint. If she could smell it, it would smell of lavender and beeswax. If she could taste it, it would have the subtle sweetness of parma violets sprinkled with a little salt.

Along the track that led to the beach, wild garlic grew.

Trumpet-shaped flowers the colour of burnt orange proliferated. A riot of honeysuckle tumbled over a low stone wall. The smell of bacon wafted to her on the wind . . . Bacon? She wasn't expecting that. Jasmine, yes, or pine or seaweed – but bacon?

Taking the fork in the path that she knew would lead to the boathouse, she wondered how it might have weathered the storms since she had seen it last. If Raoul was living there now, she expected that it might have undergone some changes. But nothing prepared her for the structure that confronted her.

A long, low building had risen where the boathouse once stood. It was elegant, streamlined, pleasingly proportioned; it boasted a south-facing glass wall and a terrace of polished white concrete. It was not what one would expect to see at the foot of a cliff a stone's throw away from a secluded beach, yet there was nothing discordant or incongruous about it: it seemed part of the landscape.

A dog barked suddenly somewhere to her left, and then Buster came bounding up the path. As the animal approached, Lisa wasn't sure whether to turn tail or stand her ground. Instead, she barked back.

'Bravo!' said Raoul, emerging through one of the French windows and calling the dog to heel. 'Breakfast is ready. Come in.'

As he led her across the terrace, Lisa noticed that pebbles had been set into the smooth concrete to form the outline of a salamander. A wooden recliner painted in shades of sienna and yellow ochre afforded an uninterrupted view of the Mediterranean, and Lisa pictured herself lying there, contemplating sea and sky, happy as a sandboy. Some day she would do it, she decided. Some day she would be carefree and footloose, at liberty to bask in the sun and thumb her nose at Hollywood.

The glass doors led into an airy space – a sitting and dining room combined. The furnishings were minimal: a couch constructed from pale oak and upholstered in sage-green linen, a pair of comfortable-looking armchairs, two or three seagrass rugs, a refectory table. Sunlight flooded through the glass walls, and bounced off the sea beyond. Through a rectangular hatch in the far wall she could see a kitchen.

'I think the bacon's burning,' she remarked.

'*Merde*,' said Raoul, going to the rescue.

'What an amazing house.'

'I'll give you a guided tour later.'

'Did you design it yourself?'

'Yes.'

'You must be awfully clever.' Lisa moved towards the hatch and leaned her elbows on the counter, watching him scoop bacon off the grill pan with a fork. 'The kitchen's pretty impressive, too.'

'I designed it to the specifications of a professional chef. It's wasted on me.'

'Who's the chef?'

'Madame Raoul Reverdy. We're divorced now. That's my marital history in a nutshell.' Raoul moved to the sink, stuck the pan under the tap and looked ruefully at the blackened rashers. 'What a waste. That was worth half a week's rations to somebody. Coffee or tea?'

'Coffee, please.'

Clickedy claws on the living room floor announced the arrival of Buster.

'Don't trash that bacon,' said Lisa. 'Give it to the dog.'

Raoul tossed Buster a rasher. 'I was going to make pancakes. Americans love them for breakfast, don't they?'

'I'm not American, but yes, they do. Would you like me to take over?'

'That'd be a help.'

Following Buster into the kitchen, Lisa opened the big fridge and surveyed the contents. 'Goodness! Butter, cream, cheese. You wouldn't think rationing was still going on.'

'I'm lucky. I often get remunerated in victuals for the work I do.'

'You mean you get food in exchange for designing buildings?'

'No-one can afford architects any more,' said Raoul. 'We operate on a barter system here. I fix up people's houses and farmsteads in return for whatever they can afford to pay, plus food. I rarely go hungry.'

'That's a tidy arrangement.'

'Yes, it is.'

'I could make us an omelette,' she said.

'I'd murder one. I'm ravenous,' he confessed, dangling a rasher tantalizingly above the dog's nose. 'I'm not much of a cook. Sit, Buster! *Sit!* Good boy.'

Lisa looked around the kitchen. On a free-standing shelving unit bowls and plates were stacked. Pots and pans were suspended from a rack, utensils from stainless-steel hooks. A basin on the draining board contained eggs, a stoneware dish apples. On the windowsill above the sink, a row of polished pebbles had been aligned beside a perfectly formed nautilus shell.

Raoul tossed the dog another strip of bacon. 'Help yourself to whatever you need,' he told Lisa. 'There are tomatoes, mushrooms . . . maybe you could use up some cold potatoes?'

'Sure.'

As Lisa assembled ingredients, Raoul set about making coffee. While he waited for it to perk, he told her how they'd survived in this part of France since the end of the war. They were luckier here than elsewhere: there had been, as Hélène had told her, little collateral damage and the tourist industry had begun to pick up. The Riviera was still a fashionable place. It would always attract celebrities and the well-to-do and their hangers-on, and Raoul had no doubt that the economic climate could only get better.

'Pablo's back from Paris, with an exhibition in the Grimaldi museum,' Raoul said. 'He'll bring crowds flocking to Antibes.'

It felt strange to hear an artist as revered as Picasso being referred to by his first name. 'Do you know him?'

'Yes. He's a friend of Gervaise: they came to the Riviera at around the same time. He was part of the crowd that made summering here fashionable. Before that the place was full of moribund British milords and Russian princes.'

'Would he have known my mother, I wonder?'

'I don't doubt their paths crossed.'

Raoul poured the coffee while Lisa slid omelettes and the potatoes she'd sautéed onto plates, and set them on the kitchen table. They took a seat opposite each other and shared a smile, and then Raoul reached out a hand and touched her face.

'Golly gumdrops,' he said.

'*Saperlipopette.*'

'Can I take you to bed again?'

'Now?'

'Now sounds good.'

'We've only just got up. Eat your breakfast first.'

Picking up his fork, Raoul helped himself to a mouthful of omelette.

'Wow,' he said. 'You make a mean omelette.'

'I know,' she said, with justifiable smugness. 'My friend Dorothy and I went through a cooking phase when she was learning how to be married. She and I used to experiment with recipes. Find me an iguana and I'll make you a delicious fricassee.'

Raoul raised an eyebrow. 'I ate a lot of peculiar stuff during the occupation, but never lizard. The ones you find here are too small. I guess they might make good *amuses-bouches*.'

At Raoul's feet, Buster suddenly roused himself and pricked up his ears. Then, as the crunch of footsteps sounded on the path, he hurried off to investigate.

'*Bonjour mes amis*,' came a voice from outside. 'What's cooking in there? Your kitchen smells better than the Café Flore, Raoul.'

'I'm not cooking. Your house guest is,' replied Raoul.

Gervaise strolled into the kitchen, the dog at his heels. He was sporting a grizzled beard and he looked a little older, a little more careworn than when Lisa had last seen him. But then, she supposed they all did.

'Miss La Touche!' he said. 'You've arrived. Welcome to Salamander Cove. I suspected I might find you down by the beach. Have you been for a swim?'

'Not yet.'

He gave her an interested look, and Lisa was reminded of the way he had regarded her when she had sat for him. She wondered if he had looked at her mother in the same way; she wondered if he had held up an assertive hand to Jessie the way he had oftentimes to her, exhorting her to 'Hold that! That's beautiful!'. She wondered if he had instructed Jessie to think of her past as he had instructed Lisa, and if her mother too had spent day after day in a haze of golden nostalgia while she held her poses. How she would love to see the painting Donielle had spoken of.

'Take a seat, Gervaise,' said Raoul. 'How was Paris?'

'Vile. Dirty, crowded, full of venal people. Including my daughter.' His eyes fell upon the rashers that lay on the draining board. 'Is that bacon going begging?' he asked.

'It's burnt.'

'I don't care.'

'I could make you an omelette, if you like,' suggested Lisa.

'Did you make that?' Gervaise indicated the half-finished omelette on Lisa's plate: the perfectly golden potatoes, the tomatoes she had sprinkled with pepper and basil.

'Yes, I did.'

'I'm impressed.'

Somewhere beyond the living area, a phone rang.

'Excuse me,' said Raoul, getting to his feet. 'That'll be François. I'm going into Vallauris this afternoon, by the way,' he told Gervaise as he rounded the table. 'Need anything?'

'A case of Bordeaux, if you're going to the *cave*.'

'Sure. The usual?'

'Please.'

Raoul left the room, followed by Buster.

Alone with Gervaise, Lisa felt a little awkward. She wondered if his all-seeing eyes had registered the body

336

language between her and Raoul: the oblique looks, the give-away tension that would tell him that they had been to bed together. Rising from the table, she fetched a couple of eggs and broke them into a bowl.

'How long do you intend staying?' Gervaise asked.

'I don't have any definite plans.' What a joke. She didn't have any plans, full stop. 'I may do a bit of sightseeing around Europe. I don't want to impose on your hospitality, or get in the way.'

She was aware of him watching her as she finished whisking the eggs and turned them out into the pan.

'You're going to sit for me, aren't you, Lisa?'

'Again?'

'I'd feel more comfortable painting you in my studio than in the soulless environs of a Hollywood backlot.'

Lisa loosened the edge of the omelette with a spatula before responding. Then: 'I'd be happy to,' she said. She raised her eyes to his and returned his level look. 'I guess the real reason you want to paint me is because you painted my mother.'

'Madame Reverdy told you?'

'How could she not?'

He nodded. 'I'm glad.'

'Why didn't you tell me when you came to LA?'

'I didn't feel I had the right.'

Lisa turned back to the stove. 'I dare say I would have found out for myself before too long,' she mused, turning the omelette over. 'All the things from my old life and the places – seeing them all so new again, brought memories flooding back; especially when Nana showed me her photograph album.'

'Do you remember your mother?'

'Some things. I remember her smile. The scent she wore.'

'Chypre.'

'I remember the records she played, the stories she told. She used to read me 'The Little Mermaid' at bedtime. You never read to me, did you?'

'No.'

'Why should you have? You weren't my father, after all.'

Beyond the kitchen window, a gull screamed. Lisa saw it hang motionless in the air for a heartbeat, stark white against an incomparably blue sky, before plunging seaward. It emerged from the waves with a sleek fish held fast in its beak.

'There's a portrait of her above, in the villa,' said Gervaise.

'Danielle told me.'

'She's wearing the gown she wore when we first met. That's how I'd like to paint you. I'd like to make a companion piece.'

'What a lovely idea.'

'She would have thought so, too.'

Lisa set a plate in front of him, and Gervaise took a mouthful, then another. When he had finished, he set his fork down and gave Lisa an appreciative smile. 'What a revelation you have turned out to be: easy on the eye, an amusing companion, and now I discover you are a first-class cook. You, Miss La Touche, are welcome to stay in Salamander Cove for as long as you like.'

The sound of Buster's nails on seagrass told Lisa that Raoul had finished his phone call. She looked up to see him lounging against the door frame.

'I'll second that,' he said, with a smile.

CHAPTER THIRTY-FIVE

JESSIE

CAP D'ANTIBES, 1926

In her boudoir that evening, having given instructions to Marthe, the *bonne à tout faire*, about which rooms were to be made up for the next influx of house guests, Jessie took out her red journal. As she leafed through the pages she noticed that her skin smelt still of the soap she had used at Baba's bath time, mingled with her own perfume. After all these years, she still favoured Chypre. Maybe it was time to give in to Coco's entreaties to make No. 5 her signature scent?

She had not written in her journal for some weeks, and when she leafed through the book, the words she saw shocked her. The last entry read:

I know, finally & for certain, Scotch, that any bond you felt
for me must now be completely at an end & my tears fall that
a tiny link that once held all the pure wonder of life should
be so wholly broken.

Picking up her pen, Jessie sat deep in thought. What vain and idle fancies had consumed her? What was stopping her from reclaiming the pure wonder of life? Her story wasn't over yet! There were fresh links to be forged, further chapters to be written, new adventures to be had. She scored through the words with such force that the nib of her pen gouged the paper.

Outside on the landing, she heard the brisk step of Marthe. Crossing to the door, she opened it and called to her.

'Marthe! Could you bring me a dish of tomatoes?'

'Tomatoes, Madame?'

'Yes. Fresh tomatoes – no dressing.'

'As you wish, Madame.'

Marthe set a pile of towels on the credenza and made for the stairs, and as Jessie turned to go back into her room, she heard a voice call 'Mama!' in the tentative tones of a child who knows she's pushing her luck. She looked up to where Baba was peeking through the banisters.

'Hello, you! You should have been asleep ages ago!'

'It's Dolly's fault. I can sleep, but she can't. She's crying and wailing, and keeping me awake.'

'Why is she crying?'

'She thinks that you're going away again.' Baba hopped down the stairs towards her.

'Silly Dolly! Mama isn't going anywhere for the longest time.'

That was a lie. The summer was almost over, and soon she would have to close up the villa and deliver Baba back up the hill to the farmhouse.

'Sing that song again!' pleaded Baba, tugging on the sleeve of Jessie's peignoir. '*Y'a une pie dans le poirier* . . . .'

'*J'entends la mère qui chante,*' sang Jessie, scooping her daughter into her arms and swinging her ceiling-ward.

Baba crowed, and stretched out her arms, reaching for the chandelier.

'Higher!'

'No, sweetheart. It makes me too dizzy.' She slid the child down until they were nose-to-nose.

'Dolly says she needs a story.'

'*Another* one?'

'She wants 'The Little Mermaid'".'

'She'll have to have the short version. It's getting late and Mama has guests to entertain.'

'Stupid guests!'

'You're right,' agreed Jessie. 'Next summer we won't invite anyone. We'll have the villa all to ourselves.'

'Hooray! We won't need to mind our manners.'

'And we can play mermaids every day.'

Bearing her squirming daughter aloft, breathing in her bath-time scent, Jessie made for the nursery to console the fretful Dolly as the clock on the landing struck the hour.

CHAPTER THIRTY-SIX

LISA

CAP D'ANTIBES 1949

Later that day Raoul took Lisa in to Vallauris on his motorcycle. The road between the villa and the little town unwound like a ribbon beneath the wheels of the machine. This time Lisa didn't sit stiff and awkward on the pillion, as she had done the previous night. She leaned forward and eeled her arms around Raoul's waist, loving the feel of the cotton of his shirt against her breasts, savouring the sea breeze in her face.

They took lunch under the awning of a café, where they shared a *pichet* of wine, and feasted on *moules marinières* and hunks of bread dipped in garlic-rich olive oil. Afterwards, Raoul excused himself.

'You'll be content here on your own for a short time? I said I'd drop in on a friend.'

'Sure,' said Lisa with a smile. 'I'll have some coffee, and watch the world go by.'

She lit a cigarette, and did just that. Across the road, a girl was watering geraniums that burgeoned in bright splotches of colour from a window box. On the village square a group of elderly men were playing *boules*. Somewhere, someone was practising the clarinet. This was

342

a world away from LA, where people cut and thrust and moved and shook and never, ever stood still. This was life lived leisurely, the way it should be.

Beside her, two women were sitting over tea and cakes. One of them was leafing through *Paris Match*.

'Did you hear that Rita Hayworth is getting married to Aly Khan here next week?' she said to her friend.

'Here, in Vallauris?'

'Yes. They wanted to have the ceremony in the Château de l'Horizon, but of course they can't because of the law. They'll have to get married in the town hall, just like everybody else. That'll bring her down a peg or two!'

Lisa lowered the brim of her sun hat as she listened to the women gossip about Rita Hayworth's love life. What they didn't know was that sweet, shy Rita was being forced into a marriage she didn't want in order to escape from a life where crackpots threatened to kidnap her child and throw caustic soda in her face.

She sat for a while, deep in thought. She thought of poor Rita, menaced by grotesque threats. She thought of Judy Garland, whose wretched addiction to barbiturates and amphetamines had been connived at by the studios. She thought of Veronica Lake, an alcoholic has-been at the age of twenty-seven, of Vivien Leigh, whose fairy-tale marriage to Laurence Olivier was on the rocks, of Ingrid Bergman, whose illicit romance meant it was unlikely she could ever return to Hollywood.

But why would she *want* to go back? What was there for her, for any of them? They were none of them stars; they were all of them slaves.

'You look very thoughtful.' Raoul dropped into the chair next to her. 'And very beautiful.'

'Thank you.'

He kissed her cheek, and as he did, a gust of wind snatched her hat and sent it spinning along the terrace.

The women at the next table turned, and one of them exclaimed: 'My goodness! It's Rita Hayworth!'

'No, no!' hissed the other. 'It's Lisa La Touche!'

'You're mistaken,' Raoul corrected them politely as he retrieved the hat and helped Lisa to her feet. 'This lady is Baba MacLeod.'

'Who?' chimed the women, looking blank.

Lisa gave him a grateful smile. And as they stepped on to the pavement hand-in-hand, she realized with a lifting of her heart how uncommonly sweet it felt to be anonymous.

The next day, when Gervaise invited Lisa to his studio to sit for preliminary sketches, he led her first to an anteroom, where he showed her the portrait he had made of the woman he had called Perdita. It was, he told her, the only portrait that had been neither sold nor looted by the Boche: it was just the third time in her life that Lisa had laid eyes on an image of her mother.

In the black-and-white photograph she had found in the old hatbox, Jessie's hair had been arranged in a loose chignon; in the portrait it was unconfined, the abundant mass tumbling over her shoulders. She stood with her back to the viewer, glancing over her shoulder, lips parted in a half-smile. Her gown was of floral silk, splashed with primary colours. Lisa could tell at once it was from Liberty of London.

It felt strange to don the dress her mother had once worn, to feel the slither of the silk against her skin, the swirl of it as she moved. As she pulled it over her head, she caught the faint vestiges of Chypre.

In Gervaise's studio at the top of the house his easel had been set up, his paints mixed, his brushes aligned with military precision. A low table was set for lunch between a pair of easy chairs.

'Let's not go to work straight away,' he said, pouring her a glass of chilled Sancerre. 'I'm sure there is much you would like me to tell you, of your mother, and how we met.'

'I'd be very grateful,' Lisa said, settling down on an ottoman and tucking her legs beneath her. 'I should love to know more of her story. For me, it ends – with her last letter home from Finistère, when my father left her.'

So, as they ate, Gervaise told Lisa about how he and Jessie – or 'Perdita' – had set about making themselves notorious, the way so many bright young things had done in the years following the First World War. He told her of the gaiety and glamour of that short and radiant time they had spent together in Paris and here in Salamander Cove. He told her about the friends they had accumulated: Pablo and Olga and Coco and Boy and Scott and Zelda.

'The Fitzgeralds!' she said. 'I met him once: he wrote the screenplay of the first movie I ever made. It was set here, in the South of France.'

'Scott wrote a lot about the time he spent here. He was inebriated most of the time, as so many people were in that post-war era. In the words of your famous Noël Coward, it was a time of cocktails and laughter.'

The melody of the song came back to her, which had played over and over on the Victrola one summer evening: 'Poor Little Rich Girl'.

Gervaise poured more wine. 'There were tears too, though,' he said. 'It was a very turbulent time.'

'Nana told me.'

Gervaise's raised eyebrow invited elaboration.

'She told me about the night my mother disappeared. She said that nobody ever found out what became of her.'

Gervaise looked into his wine glass, then took a hit. 'As Perdita, Jessie had a great sense of drama,' he said. 'She would have enjoyed the idea of a making an exit shrouded in mystery.'

'Were there really no clues? No witnesses?'

'No. We thought that perhaps Zelda could shed light on what happened, but she was stewed to the gills that night.'

'Was Zelda very beautiful?'

'In that Southern Belle way, yes she was beautiful. But beauty and madness combined make a lethal cocktail – no wonder Scott was insecure. He even challenged Pablo to a duel once, when he was drunk.'

Lisa hesitated. She felt there was a clue somewhere, that someone knew what had happened to Jessie, and that that person was Zelda Fitzgerald. 'There's a collection of Zelda's stories, Gervaise, in the library, that seems to have been a present to you from her,' she said. 'Do you mind if I borrow it?'

'Be my guest.'

'Are you sure? It's never been opened – the pages are still uncut.'

'Absolutely. I'm never going to read it. I understand her

346

novel was second rate. They say that Pablo is in it, thinly disguised.'

'Did Pablo – Monsieur Picasso – ever paint my mother?'

'No. I was too jealous to permit him. Artists can be very proprietorial about their muses.'

'But she has – she did have – one of his paintings.'

'She did?'

'Yes – of a clown, all in blue, holding a baby. She gave it to Nana to safeguard.'

'So that's where it got to,' said Gervaise, with a laugh. 'I'd forgotten Jessie had spirited it away. How clever of her to have kept it hidden! You're a lucky woman, Lisa. It must be worth a lot more than I paid for it.'

'It's not mine, of course,' she protested. 'It belongs to you.'

'I'm a man of my word: a gentleman. I gave that painting to Jessie so that her daughter – so that *you*, my dear – would have a legacy.'

Lisa remembered something Nicole had said, about a daughter from a previous marriage.

'But surely your own daughter . . . I'm sorry. I don't know her name.'

'Ghislaine.'

'Ghislaine. Shouldn't it be hers, by rights?'

'Ghislaine is independently wealthy. She has never had to lift a finger or do a day's work in her life. You, on the other hand, have had to struggle for every cent you've earned – as did your mother, once upon a time. You deserve that Picasso more than Ghislaine does. It's yours, fair and square.'

'But—'

'No buts. Go ahead and sell it if you want. I can arrange

an appointment with my agent in Paris. He'll have the relevant documentation about provenance and all that jazz filed away somewhere.'

It was tempting, God knew it was! She hadn't a clue when she'd earn again. But Lisa felt that it was not right, somehow. She could have accepted the painting as a gift from her mother, but from Gervaise ...

'I'm not sure I could afford to have it insured. I—'

'Oh, stop prevaricating, woman!' said Gervaise. 'I'll have it framed for you. We'll hang it in the atrium. That way, every time you come and go, it'll remind you that it's yours to do as you want with, whenever you want it.'

'But I'm not staying here for very much longer.'

'That's what everybody says, who visits this part of the world.' Gervaise knocked back the remains of the wine in his glass and gave her a raffish smile. 'Now. Are you ready to go to work?'

CHAPTER THIRTY-SEVEN

JESSIE

CAP D'ANTIBES 1926

~~My tears fall that a tiny link that once held all the pure~~
~~wonder of life should be so wholly broken.~~

Jessie left the journal on her writing desk next to the depleted dish of tomatoes, and moved out onto the balcony. In the stand of pine trees beyond the garden, a nightingale was singing. The sky had mellowed from a dazzling, intense blue to an indigo so soft and warm you felt you could wrap yourself in it. A bee was working overtime in the honeysuckle that overhung the balcony, its somnolent buzzing belying its industry. From the open window above she could hear Baba singing her French nursery rhyme to Dolly; in the drawing room, someone was playing the piano, their foot on the soft pedal. The heady smell of burning eucalyptus came to her on a southerly breeze: there had been wildfires that summer.

This was the pure wonder of life. This is how things should be, how they were meant to be. Wherever Scotch was, whoever he was with, she hoped that he had found it too, this wondrous peace. She hoped he was happy.

The barking of a dog made Jessie look down. Below,

Gervaise was on the terrace, sharing a smoke with Scott. Their new pooch, a rowdy Weimaraner puppy, was chasing something between the flower beds – a rabbit, maybe. It was difficult to see. The low-slung sun cast rays of such intense gold upon the garden that all was a burnished blur.

There came the popping of a champagne cork from the further end of the terrace and Scott moved away in response. Gervaise took a long pull on his cigarette, then ground it into an ashtray. He looked sombre, introspective; she rarely saw him alone these days.

'Gervaise!' called Jessie.

Shading his eyes with his hand, he looked up. '*Bonsoir.* Is Baba in bed?'

'Yes.' As she reached for a strand of honeysuckle, the silk of her robe slithered over a shoulder. 'Why not come up?' she suggested, trailing the flower along the bare skin of her forearm.

Gervaise looked uncertain. This was clearly an in-vitation, and – since they had not made love for some weeks – a singular one.

'Come,' repeated Jessie.

'I can't now – I promised Scott I'd look over something he's written. Anyway, it's late. Why haven't you changed yet?'

'It's such a perfectly blue evening I didn't want to let it go. I thought I might wait until the evening star made her appearance; one so seldom sees her in the sky over Paris. But she's in no hurry this evening.'

Gervaise turned and scanned the horizon. 'There she is, divesting herself of a cloud.'

'She's left it rather late. She must have been detained somewhere. She was probably deciding what to wear.'

'Venus detained,' said Gervaise. 'It sounds like the subject of a painting.'

They regarded each other with contemplative interest.

'What does she wear in the end?' asked Jessie.

'Nothing,' said Gervaise. 'She is always her most beautiful with nothing on at all. See? She's cast off that last little wisp.'

To the south, Venus was all aglimmer, a cobweb of cloud trailing in her wake.

They smiled at each other, and then Jessie blew him a kiss and went back through the French windows. The journal was where she had left it on her desk, the line of black ink all but obscuring the last entry.

Jessie took up her fountain pen and wrote in careful capitals at the bottom of the page THE END. Putting the cap back she eased her arms and shoulders into a stretch. Tomorrow, she would take the red-backed books to the bonfire that the gardener kept smouldering beyond the sea wall, and burn them. She would help herself instead to one of the small black notebooks that Gervaise used for jottings and start her journals anew.

Slipping off her kimono, she moved into her Aladdin's cave of a closet. It had been designed for her by a master cabinet-maker, a friend of Gervaise's: it was Palladian in its simplicity and baroque in its cunning, lined with drawers and cubbyholes and niches to accommodate the wardrobe she had accumulated since embarking upon her career as muse to Gervaise Lantier. Her closet was so beautiful that when she had first seen it, she had burst into tears.

As she selected which garment to wear this evening, she could not resist pausing now and again to test the texture of a beaded collar, or run her hand along a satin sleeve, or

351

rub her face against a swathe of Shantung silk. She finally decided on a frock shimmery as moonshine, a scarf of silvery gauze and a pair of pearly shoes with Louis heels – a present from Coco that had been sent down with Mistinguett from Paris. They were dancing shoes, and though it was unlikely there would be dancing tonight, they were too pretty to resist.

She had just returned downstairs and was making for the drawing room to wind up the Victrola when a smooth voice made her freeze.

'Your daughter is a true *mignonne*,' said Count Demetrios, who had been sitting in the shadow of the cantilevered staircase.

Jessie gave a start, raising a hand to her chest to steady her heartbeat. 'Count! What brings you here?'

'I think perhaps that you and I should take a walk, Madame. We have important matters to discuss.'

She didn't want to discuss anything with the count, but since he acted for Gervaise and was responsible for their financial well-being, she felt it would be impolitic to decline. Demetrios extended an arm to her, and led her into the garden. As she passed the table on the terrace, she noticed that the big blue umbrella was flapping in the breeze, and found herself thinking abstractedly that she must ask the gardener to take it down.

They walked as far as the sea wall, and then the count adjusted his monocle and cleared his throat.

'You promised me once that you would do anything for me if I helped you,' he said. 'I don't think either of us can deny that you have achieved spectacular success, and that if it had not been for me, you would be dead now, of absinthe and of syphilis acquired from the "gentlemen" procured for you in that abominable hotel. And your child, too, would be dead of malnutrition, or worse. I, alas, lost my little girl, for whom I cared so dearly, and I am lonely without her.'

From further along the cliff top, Jessie heard Zelda's lilting, throaty laugh, and the low murmur of a man's voice.

The count continued, unperturbed. 'I am so lonely that I should like to relieve your daughter's foster parents of their charge, and adopt her as my own.'

Jessie stared at him wordlessly, and then she laughed out loud. 'Are you completely insane?'

An answering laugh came on the wind, to her right. 'Perdita – Perdie! Are you there? Come! Come swimming with me!'

'I am as perfectly sane, Madame, as you are clearly deluded. Sadly, as a kept woman, one might describe you as an unfit person for the duty of care you have relegated to the Reverdys. And, you see, I yearn so much for a little girl to call my own. I have had my solicitor draw up a contract—'

'You are mad. You *are* mad!'

'No, my dear. You are simply not listening to what I have to say. We made a bargain. I kept my side of it, now I must insist that it is time for you to do the same.'

'I made no bargain with you.'

'I *created* you. I washed your dirty little *feet* for you! Now, you owe me.'

'I owe you nothing -'

'*You owe me everything.*' The count's eyes were slits, his voice a rapier sheathed in velvet. 'If you will not do as my solicitor instructs, I will unmask you, "Perdita".'

'Perdie! Come! Come along!' came Zelda's exhortation again. 'It's a perfectly heavenly evening!'

'I don't care!' Jessie told him. 'I don't care if you unmask me. I'm fed up with this stupid charade. Act 5, scene 5, bring down the curtain! Do as you like.' Abruptly, she turned away from the count and started to move in the direction of Zelda's siren call.

But the count followed her, matching her step for step. 'If you don't grant me this request, you will no longer retain your prestigious position of muse to Monsieur Lantier,' he continued, conversationally. 'Do you know, I suspect he may be becoming more than a little bored with you. I hear that he has made no paintings of you lately. And when Lantier has no paintings to sell – *hélas!* – I make no money. But no matter, no matter! I have a beauty waiting in the wings, one who has an even more intriguing back-story than yours.'

'Leave me alone, Count.'

'What were you ever but a spoilt, silly girl masquerading as a bohemian? A girl who couldn't even keep a husband when all over Europe there are women who are desperate to be married?'

'Oh, you are evil!'

'There's always an understudy in the game of charades, Madame. Your time centre stage is over. And if you refuse to sign the papers my solicitor has drawn up, I will have no alternative than to write to your parents in Grosvenor Square, and tell them that their daughter is a whore and that their grandchild should be removed from her care.'

Jessie stopped, and turned fierce eyes on Demetrios.

'How did you—'

'I am clever, and I have connections. I procured for you what you wanted. And now I want the favour returned.'

The wind had got up. The waves below, which had

whispered seductively earlier in the summer, were haranguing her now into taking flight. And then came the sweetly cajoling voice of Zelda through the night air.

'Perdita, honey! Come.'

'Perdita!' echoed Demetrios, with a laugh. 'Your renown as a whore has spread far and wide. I recall the night of the *vernissage* in the Galérie Pierre when bystanders on the rue La Boétie stood agog as you waltzed in on your paramour's arm, with your pregnant belly on display. So flagrant! The women in the crowd whispered to each other behind their hands – and the men! The faces of the men were those of dogs who smell a bitch on heat.'

Jessie took two steps closer to the count. Then she slapped him, hard across the face, dislodging his monocle and leaving a livid patch on his sallow cheek. The expression in his eyes might have frightened her, or it might have made her laugh, but she did neither. Instead she kicked off her shoes, clambered up on to the sea wall and sprinted its length.

Zelda was sitting at the far end, bare legs dangling over the cliff face, a bottle of champagne beside her. There were two glasses, but one was empty. Whoever Zelda's companion had been, he had made himself scarce.

'Yes! You're here at last,' said Zelda, triumphantly. '*Santé!*' She sloshed Moët into the empty glass until it foamed over the rim, then handed it to Jessie.

'You're shaking,' she observed.

'I'm cold. That wind is chilly.'

'It bodes no good. That sounds neat, doesn't it? "Bodes". Have some champagne at once.'

Jessie hesitated.

'It eases the heart,' cajoled Zelda.

She was right, of course – the champagne would help numb the sting of Demetrios's words. Jessie downed it in one. It fizzed through her bloodstream, sending her head spinning, and Zelda promptly poured her another glass.

'I'm in love,' she told her. 'I'm in love with that French aviation officer who's taken a fancy to me. Isn't he divine? His face is full of the sun.'

Jessie wasn't surprised. The aviator was a beautiful young man, and Scott was too preoccupied with the novel he was working on to notice that his wife was infatuated.

'Who are you in love with?' Zelda asked. 'Gervaise? Or someone else? It's practically *de rigueur* to take a lover on the Riviera, after all, isn't it?'

Jessie turned to her and smiled. 'I don't have room in my heart for a lover. It's too full of love for Baba.'

Zelda gave her a thoughtful look. 'Love is such a big word, isn't it? You always feel you have to pronounce it with a capital letter.'

'Yes. Like Life and Death.'

'And Champagne. Too much is just enough, don't you think? Let's finish the bottle.' Zelda upended it into her glass. 'How funny that your daughter is the first person you conjure when you think of love. Weren't you disappointed when she turned out to be a girl? I was, with Scottie. She had hiccups when she was born, poor thing.' Zelda shuddered. 'I'd hate to be pregnant again.'

'I loved being pregnant.'

'Yuck. I got so enormously fat I thought I was having twins, even though I ate nothing but those little cucumbers.'

'Pickles?'

'Yes. I ate them morning, noon and night. Didn't you

have a hankering for weird food when you were expecting?'

'Yes,' said Jessie. When she had existed on Bouillon Zip and stale bread in the Hôtel des Trois Moineaux, she had hankered after *pommes rissolés* and *petits pois*. Now she hankered after tomatoes. She remembered the craving that had assaulted her earlier, for sweet tomatoes from the garden. She remembered the feeling of light-headedness, familiar from her previous pregnancy – a symptom she had in those days attributed to hunger.

'I was sorry Scottie wasn't a boy,' Zelda said again, maudlin now. 'When I found out I had a girl, I wished that she might be beautiful and a fool – a beautiful little fool.' Abruptly, she rose to her feet and stripped off her dress. Underneath she was wearing nothing but a thin, rose-coloured slip. 'I'm perfectly shellacked now,' she announced. 'Let's swim. It'll cleanse us, make us feel better.'

Jessie stood up, swaying a little in her bare feet.

'Careful,' said Zelda. 'You must've imbibed one too many cocktails at lunch.'

She had drunk no alcohol at lunch. She would have to get used to dizzy spells for the next few weeks, until she entered her second trimester. Then, if her new baby was as well behaved in her womb as Baba had been, she would feel perfectly healthy until the final month.

'Let me help you out of your frock.' Zelda undid hooks and eyes and allowed Jessie to slither out of silk. Beneath her dress, Jessie was stark naked. For some reason, she felt liberated, a butterfly emerging from a chrysalis, a snake shedding dead skin.

'Oh, look at you!' cried Zelda in delight. 'How beautiful you are! Like a fairy-tale girl! No wonder Gervaise loves you so much!'

'He does?' asked Jessie, confused. Tiny champagne bubbles were effervescing in her skull.

'Oh yes. You can tell by the way he looks at you, when your back's turned. He's completely besotted.'

'You're wrong, I think.'

'I'm never wrong,' Zelda told her, with hauteur. 'I have an unerring instinct for these things.'

Did Gervaise love her, then? Had she been misinterpreting the signals he sent out? Had she, in her preoccupation with Scotch and her beautiful, beloved Baba, alienated him, underestimated his affection for her? But now – now she could present him with a baby of his own – a boy! She could feel in her bones that she was carrying a boy. Gervaise would love a son – how could he not love a miniature version of himself? – and once she produced a child, he might relax his rules regarding Baba and invite her to be part of their family. They could be together, all four of them – they could leave the city and set up here for good!

She felt full of hope, suddenly, as she had earlier in the evening. The air on her naked skin felt like a benison: she was at one with the universe. She had so much to be thankful for! She had day upon wondrous day ahead of her reaching into the future, green days and blue days . . . Where had the words come from? A poem she had read on a beach somewhere, a lifetime ago, at the end of the earth. Something about birdsong and star-shine . . .

She turned to Zelda with a beatific smile. 'I know a poem,' she began.

'So do I,' said Zelda, strutting along the wall.

Out in the shimee sanatorium, she sang
The jazz mad nuts reside.

Out in the shimee sanatorium
I left my blushing bride.
She went and shook herself insane,
So let her shiver back again!

Jessie laughed, not because the poem amused her, but because Zelda Fitzgerald performing a Charleston along a sea wall in the South of France looked so bizarrely, insanely beautiful.

'The jazz-mad nuts! That's us, all right,' Zelda pronounced, slinging her glass over the cliff edge and looking down. 'I'll go first. The trick is to aim a little to the left. There are rocks on the right.'

All aflutter in her silk slip, Zelda raised her arms over her head and took a deep breath. 'Breathe! Breathe in the burning eucalyptus!' she cried. And then she executed a perfect swallow-dive over the cliff edge. Jessie heard her laughing all the way down to the water.

Jessie's eyes searched the sky until they lit upon her lodestar, Venus, gleaming in the blue beyond. Arms aloft in exhilaration, she raised herself on tiptoe and adopted Zelda's stance.

But as she prepared to launch herself into the air, she heard a voice come from the surrounding darkness, and it was saying: 'Scotch didn't love you, Madame MacLeod. You knew that: all along you knew in your heart that he married you for your family's money. But what you didn't know was that he ended by despising you. He was there that night on the rue La Boétie when your portraits were unveiled; he saw you parade as Perdita, he witnessed your shameless display.'

Disoriented, Jessie turned.

'You imagine Lantier loves you?' continued the voice, unruffled and inexorable. 'You're wrong. He has no love for you: you are nothing to him but a whore. As for the daughter you abandoned; if you died tomorrow, she would neither notice nor care.'

With a cry of distress, Jessie stumbled backward, losing her footing.

The monstrous words of Count Demetrios sounded in her head all the way down; before her mind's eye flashed the faces of all those souls she had loved: Pawpey and Mummy, and Purdy, and Tuppenny, and Scotch and Baba. And Gervaise.

CHAPTER THIRTY-EIGHT

LISA

CAP D'ANTIBES 1949

'Will you join me for supper?' asked Gervaise, when he and Lisa had finished for the day. A purple twilight had descended, the interval she had heard described by the French as 'the blue hour', less frequently as 'the hour between dog and wolf'.

'No, thank you. I have an engagement . . . elsewhere.'

'I'm glad you have company. In that case, I'll carry on working.'

'You can work without your model being present?'

'Sometimes it's easier to capture something of a person's essence without having them there, physically,' he explained. 'The expression goes dead after a few hours. The eyes glaze over and you can't see the soul behind them any more.'

Lisa's engagement was with Raoul. He had asked her to join him later that evening, for dinner at the house on the beach. It would be the third evening in a row that she had dined there since her arrival at Salamander Cove, and each night she had ended up in his plain white *bateau lit* and shared breakfast with him the next morning.

If Gervaise knew of her sleeping arrangements, he gave no indication.

After she left the studio, Lisa hung the Liberty silk gown back on its padded silk hanger and got into her day dress – a simple cotton halterneck she had bought in Vallauris. Then she went downstairs to the library and helped herself to the cloth-bound volume that had been inscribed to Gervaise, the one that contained the unpublished short stories of Zelda Fitzgerald. She cut the pages with an ivory-handled knife and leafed through the book with careful fingers.

The title of the third of Zelda's stories arrested her. It was called 'The Fairytale Girl'. Lisa curled up on the big cushions on the sofa that faced the French windows and devoured the tale of a beautiful young woman who had arrived from nowhere into the exuberant chaos of the jazz age, and who had departed without leaving a trace of her identity behind. Like Little Red Riding Hood, she had been lost in a forest and menaced by a Big Bad Wolf. Like Snow White, she had run away from danger and been rescued by a handsome prince. Like Cinderella, she had abandoned the most scintillating party of the century, leaving only a shoe behind. Like the Little Mermaid, she had consigned her body to the sea, where she had metamorphosed into foam upon the waves. The heart of the Fairytale Girl was, like that of most romantic heroines, full of love: but the love she safeguarded, the love she treasured above all things, was for her baby daughter.

The name of the Fairytale Girl was Perdita.

The next day, Raoul came upon Lisa writing a letter on airmail paper.

'Who are you writing to?' he asked.

'I'm writing to Sheilah Graham, in Hollywood.'

'Who's she? Your agent?'

'No. She's a gossip columnist.'

'I thought you despised gossip columnists?'

'This one is special.'

It was true. Sheilah Graham had been the last person to see Scott Fitzgerald alive. She had been his lover and constant companion from his arrival in Hollywood until the day he died. She had interviewed Lisa once for her column 'Hollywood Today', and Lisa had been exceptionally charming to her. She hoped that her sucky-up behaviour would pay dividends now.

Dear Miss Graham, (she wrote)

I do hope all is well with you in sunny California! I am taking a break from movie-making, spending some time in the South of France, where I understand Mr Fitzgerald used to vacation.

I was hoping that you might be able to help me garner some information about my mother, who resided near Antibes back in the 1920s. She knew Scott and his wife Zelda, and I believe that Zelda might be able to answer some questions I have. I should love to have an address, if you have one, so that I may write to her myself.

I look forward to hearing from you, and send my thanks and very best wishes.

Yours sincerely,

Lisa La Touche

She posted the letter knowing that there was little more she could do to unravel the mystery that was

Perdita. And then she waited for Sheilah to respond.

When she wasn't playing muse to Gervaise, Lisa filled the days taking life easy. She swam and sunbathed and walked and read and cooked: sometimes she and Raoul ate in the villa, where they would join Gervaise on the terrace, but most of their meals were taken *à deux* in Raoul's house, which was still known locally as the Boat House. Raoul had bought the original building from Gervaise before the war; they shared part of the garden and the right of way to the beach, which was otherwise inaccessible by land. This meant it was possible to swim and sunbathe nude, an activity that Lisa embraced with a pleasure akin to euphoria. She felt so liberated, so comfortable, so *right* in her skin that she took to wearing nothing most days, other than a length of batiked cotton tied as a sarong. It was a revelation, the luxury of rolling out of bed in the morning without having to bother about make-up or hairdos or matching shoes to handbags, or the calorie count in the meal she'd had the night before, or the empty wine bottles she put out with the trash.

She tried to compose a letter to Phil Gersh, but could not find the right words. What was there to say? 'I'm having a ball here on the Riviera, putting on weight, skinny-dipping, and screwing the local talent?'

Instead she wrote endless letters to Cat, in which she told her daughter stories of the magical place in which she was living: a house on a beach with walls of glass, and a purple dog to throw sticks for. What child would not want to live in a boathouse, like a castaway! She told Cat how the sea here was bluer than sapphires and greener than emeralds and more dazzling than diamonds, and how a nightingale sang her to sleep every night, and how a calico cat strolled down from the farm on the hill every morning looking for a saucer of milk with its tail in the air, just like the one in the story about the Cat That Walked by Himself. And she promised Cat that as soon as she could find a copy of Rudyard Kipling's *Just So Stories*, which had been one of her favourite books when she was her age, she would send it to her so that Mammy could read it to her.

One morning she went into Antibes to post yet another letter to her daughter, and, deciding finally to give up on finding the right words for Phil, she sent a telegram instead. It read: AM STAYING ON HERE INDEFINITELY STOP URGENT CONTACT ONLY TO VILLA PERDITA SALAMANDER COVE ANTIBES STOP LISA

The next day she finally received Sheilah Graham's response to her letter and a hastily composed telegram from Phil that read:

WHAT ARE YOU PLAYING AT STOP ZIGGY MAD AS HELL STOP SUSPENSION IMMINENT STOP PHIL.

Sheilah's letter came on deckle-edged paper in a scented envelope.

Dear Lisa,

This is written in haste, I'm afraid.

I'm glad you are enjoying your vacation. When you return, perhaps you would consider doing an exclusive interview for "Hollywood Today"? You may know that Judy Kinnear is suing Lochlan for divorce, and I'm keen to get a little insider info.

Concerning your inquiry, Zelda Fitzgerald died in a fire in

a sanatorium in North Carolina a year ago.

Yours,

Sheilah.

PS: Zelda's body was identified by a charred slipper found beneath it.

So that was it. The original baby vamp, the darling of the Jazz Age, the American beauty who had inspired millions of others to bob their hair and raise their hems and dance till they dropped, had burned to death in a sanatorium. Whatever had happened to Jessie could not be worse than perishing there, locked up and loco among the jazz-mad nuts. Lisa's mother would remain forever Perdita, the muse with the Mona Lisa smile, the Fairytale Girl. Lisa trashed the letter.

The telegram she showed to Raoul later that evening, when he'd got back from repairing someone's roof. They were on the terrace, drinking Campari and soda from cheap Duralex tumblers that Lisa had found in the *quincaillerie* in Antibes. She had hit on the idea of adding borage to the aperitif, for flavour. The plant grew wild on the hill behind the Boat House, along with countless other edible herbs that Lisa had taken to gathering. She had decided that if she were ever to write a cookbook, she could give Countess Morphy a run for her money.

'So, Ziggy's mad at you,' said Raoul. 'So what? Stay here. Live with me.'

'What?'

'Live with me, here in Salamander Cove. You hate Hollywood, and you've told me your career is as good as finished.'

Lisa hesitated. Looking down at the antique ring she

wore on the fourth finger of her right hand, she twisted it, thinking of Scotch, thinking of Jessie, *thinking of* . . .

'If you're concerned about what the scandal sheets might say, why not make it official and marry me?'

'Ha ha, Raoul. You break me up.'

'I'm not joking.'

She looked at him sideways.

'I'm not,' he repeated. 'I'm divorced, you're single. We're both of an eminently marriageable age, and we seem to get along harmoniously, to say the least. Marry me.'

'I can't, Raoul,' she said. 'I'd love to, but I really can't.'

'Is there some kind of impediment?' he asked. 'You're not married already, are you?'

'No. No, I'm not.'

'But . . . ?' he prompted.

'But what?'

'There has to be a "but", doesn't there? There always is.'

'Yes, there's a "but".'

'Out with it.'

She took a deep breath. 'Raoul, I have to tell you that there is somebody much more important than you in my life.'

'That sounds portentous, but I thought as much. You have a child.'

'How did you know?'

'My mother guessed. Like all good grandmothers, she has a knack of seeing such things.'

Lisa nodded.

'And you talk sometimes, in your sleep.'

'I do? I guess it's because I have a recurring dream.'

'A nightmare?'

'No. It's rather a lovely dream. But sometimes I can't

get to her – to my little girl.' Lisa took a hit of Campari.

'Where is she?'

'Her name is Cat, and she lives with my cousin, Róisín, in Connemara, in Ireland. She's seven years old now, and she calls me her Aunt. She calls my cousin Mammy.'

Raoul took a Gitane from a pack, and lit up. 'Are you ever likely to tell her the truth?'

'No. Never. Only, that is, if Róisín decides to say anything.'

'I see.' He looked at her from under his eyebrows. 'Tell, me, Lisa. Do you want more babies?'

'Yes.'

'Then marry me. Don't go back to that vile place you hate so much. Stay here. Salamander Cove was your first home, after all. *Où se trouve le coeur, là est la maison.* You have a phrase for it, in English, don't you?'

'Yes. "Home is where the heart is".'

'Is your heart here, Lisa?'

Gazing down at the beach, she remembered running through the shallows on plump, unsteady legs, giggling, with her mama in pursuit. She remembered the garden of the Villa Perdita lit up by lanterns, and the smell of coconut oil mingled with mimosa blossom, which had always been for her the smell of summer. She remembered the day that a lanky, dark-haired boy with laughing eyes had let go of her hand as she'd stood waist deep in water, and allowed her to swim on her own.

'Yes,' she told him. 'My heart is here.'

Raoul held up the telegram and struck his lighter, holding the flame a fraction away from the edge of the paper. Then he quirked an eyebrow at Lisa. She nodded. The corner of the telegram caught alight. As the flame took it,

Raoul let it drop to the ground, and together they watched it burn.

ZIGGY MAD AS HELL were the last words Lisa saw.

In Hollywood, poor old Ziggy was about to get madder still, and so were the accountants and the agents and the attorneys and the actuaries – and she knew now that she didn't give two figs.

Because this was how things should be, how they were meant to be.

Later that day, Hélène brought Lisa the journals she had spoken of on the night of the Reverdys' party, the ones that had belonged to Jessie. There were six of them.

Lisa had been sitting on the terrace of the Villa Perdita-after a sitting with Gervaise, smoking a cigarette and contemplating sea and sky, feeling content and carefree, the way she had promised herself she would feel some day. When Hélène set the journals on the swing-seat beside her, she tensed, uncertain what secrets might spring out at her from between the red cardboard covers.

'Where did you find them?' she asked.

'They were in your mother's closet. I unearthed them when I first came here to work for Gervaise. They've been in there for around thirty years, I guess. All her stuff's there still – perhaps Gervaise thought she'd come back for it. Would you like to see it?'

Lisa hesitated. Then: 'Yes. Yes, I would,' she said. She extinguished her cigarette, then, on an impulse, grabbed one of the exercise books.

'Has Gervaise read these?' she asked, following Hélène out of the room and up the stairs.

'I don't know. I never mentioned that I'd found them.'

'I wonder should I say anything to him?'

'That's up to you. They're yours now, to do what you like with.'

Hélène stopped in front of a door at the end of the corridor.

'Is this her bedroom?' asked Lisa.

'I guess it's more of a boudoir than a bedroom.'

'What's the difference?'

'The word "boudoir" comes from *bouder*.'

'To sulk?'

'Yes. A boudoir is "a place for sulking", if you translate it literally.'

The room beyond the closed door did not look like a place for sulking. Bright kilims covered the floor. A length of silk had been furled and looped above a divan fit for an odalisque. Two Lloyd Loom chairs flanked the French windows, and on a low table several copies of *Vogue* magazine still lay, the covers depicting powder-pale women sporting sleek bobs and jazzy bangles. In a niche, a dinky beaded cloche was perched atop a stern-looking marble bust.

On the wall, faint lines showed that a painting had hung there. Hélène followed the direction of Lisa's gaze. 'That's where your mother's portrait usually hangs. Gervaise took it down so that he could study it before painting you.' Moving to a pair of louvred panels that ran the length of the room, she pulled at them. The panels concertinaed back to reveal a walk-in closet.

Jessie's brimming wardrobe was a magician's cabinet of drawers, cubbyholes and compartments. There were tall spaces for hanging garments and wide spaces for folding them. There were trays for costume jewellery and racks for scarves and shawls; there were sandalwood clothes hangers, and hangers padded in silk and velvet; there was a vanity table with an array of silver-backed brushes and Lalique flacons; there was a damask-upholstered slipper chair in which to lounge and contemplate the sartorial profusion, and an elegant cheval glass to reflect it.

'Are these her clothes?' asked an astonished Lisa.

'I told you Gervaise kept everything. That's how he has the dress you've been posing in. There's some really gorgeous stuff. I don't know much about couture, but it's clearly top quality – although *démodé* is putting it kindly.' Hélène glanced at her watch. 'I'll leave you to it – I'd better head up to the farmhouse. Bruno'll be wanting his dinner. *Bonsoir*, Lisa.'

'*Bonsoir!*'

Lisa set the red journal on the vanity table. With reverent hands, she took garment after garment from its allocated place and scrutinized the workmanship. She had never seen such exquisite tailoring, such meticulous construction. The cut, the finish, the attention to detail was breathtaking. Not one of the couturiers in Hollywood whose gowns Lisa had begged or borrowed could match this genius. She knew, of course, that one designer only could be responsible for such works of art, and that was Coco Chanel.

As Lisa examined a pocket cunningly concealed in the folds of an embroidered silk tunic, she realized there was something tucked inside. Inserting a careful hand, she withdrew a fine silk ribbon, to which was attached a curious jade-green charm. Suddenly a line from one of her mother's letters came back to her:

Scotch found, tucked away in a dusty corner of an antique shop, a little Egyptian charm – most fascinating – a little figure of a devil or something . . .

So this had been a gift to her mother from her father! As she wound the ribbon between her fingers, her eyes fell on the red book that lay upon the vanity table. She reached for it, then curled herself up in the slipper chair and opened the book at random.

The lined pages were covered in the dense, hasty handwriting that she recognized as her mother's, although it was far less legible than the letters written by the younger Jessie.

I should hate you, Scotch; yes, and despise you too & maybe I do a little sometimes, but only, sadly, when I am loving you & longing for you too much. Oh, darling, so many things I want to know; so many ordinary, everyday things . . .

I am skimming well, I think, but oh God, beneath the surface is a deadly world of my own. How can I go on? Somehow I will. Gervaise needs me, & at present there is so little of me to give, just an automatically moving, speaking, planning shell . . .

I am very low tonight, S., very low indeed and I must write these words to you; words you will never read. I am filled with a frighteningly strange foreboding . . .

The barking of a dog made Lisa look down. Rising to her feet, she moved to the window. Below, Gervaise and Raoul were on the terrace, sharing a smoke. Buster was chasing something between the rows of runner beans – a rabbit, maybe. It was difficult to see. The low sun cast rays of such intense gold upon the garden that all was a burnished blur.

Lisa felt claustrophobic suddenly. She craved air. Looping the ribbon over a doorknob, she shut Jessie's journal, set it on the vanity table and ran downstairs to join the men.

'Sabu?'

'Lisa! Where are you?'

'I'm phoning from the South of France – from Antibes. I can't stay on the line for long – it's so expensive.'

'What are you doing in Antibes?'

'I just got married!'

'What fun! So did I. Who did you get married to?'

'He's – um—' How to describe Raoul? 'He's French. He's an architect. He's very clever and he's very handsome. I knew him from when I was a child here, and we're living in a boathouse.'

'Is he going to make you happy?'

'Yes.'

'Good. That's all I need to know.'

'Who did you marry?'

'She's called Marilyn. She's American. She's an actress. She's very clever and very beautiful.'

'I'm so glad.'

The pips started.

'I'm sorry I can't talk properly, Sabu – the pips are going. Listen. I need to ask you a big favour.'

'Fire ahead.'

'Can you close up my apartment for me, and send on my things – my dresses and all that jazz? I'm care of the Villa Perdita, Salamander Cove.'

'Sure.'

'It's just that I have some really good stuff and it would be a pity if it ended up in a thrift store or something. I'll reimburse you for the shipping.'

'My pleasure. Consider it a wedding gift.'

'Thank you Sabutage! I do love you.'

'I love you too, Lisa. Have a good life.'

'Have a good life yourself. Be sure to make it full of fun . . .'

'. . . and adventure . . .'

'. . . at last!' she finished for him.

The pips went.

Several weeks later, a dozen or so boxes were delivered to the Villa Perdita. Sabu had had her frocks professionally packed between layers of tissue paper.

'When on earth are you going to wear them?' asked Raoul, who had come across Lisa sitting on the floor of Gervaise's hallway, surrounded by yards of tulle and taffeta.

'Probably never,' Lisa told him. 'But I couldn't bear to think of them rotting away somewhere. Aren't they beautiful? Look at this!'

She held up a frothy magenta creation.

'Very nice,' said Raoul. 'But frankly, I prefer you in a sarong. Easier to take off.'

Lisa fluffed out the skirts, and laid the gown carefully to one side before reaching for a spangled chiffon number.

'Dear God,' said Raoul, with a pained look. 'Where's all that stuff going to live? There's no room for ball gowns in the Boat House.'

'I never thought of that. Oh! I'd forgotten about this! Isn't it adorable!'

She placed a little velvet side beret on her head, adjusted the ornamental feather and gave Raoul a winsome look.

'Very becoming. Perfect for a trip to the fish market.'

'And here's my alpaca coat! That'll be very welcome, come winter. How thoughtful of Sabu!'

'Why don't you ask Gervaise if you can use your mother's closet?' suggested Raoul.

'Good idea.' Lisa started to pull pink faille from between layers of tissue. 'It's a lovely notion, when you think of it, that our clothes are hanging together in the same space. Imagine the conversations they could have!'

'Maybe you should install a bugging device,' said Raoul, hefting one of the boxes and moving towards the stairs. 'I'll leave you to it.'

When she'd finished unpacking, Lisa was delighted to find that Sabu had included little gifts at the bottom of one of the boxes: items that would not be readily available in Europe. They included several pairs of Charnos nylons, a box of Elizabeth Arden products, a pair of Ray-Bans and half a dozen magazines.

SCREENLAND
MAGAZINE EDITORIAL
WATCH YOUR STEP, LISA LA TOUCHE!
WARNING to HOLLYWOOD GIRLS!

This editorial is dedicated to all sulky Hollywood girls, and to Lisa La Touche in particular.

Lisa, you're a smart cookie – pretty, popular, talented. You made a stunning debut in *Crimson Lake*. You became increasingly versatile in several pictures. Suddenly life opened up to you. People pointed you out. Your future looked as rosy as an extra's cheeks after a bawling-out by a third assistant director. And then – something happened. You flounced away to Europe, shaking off the 'sordid dust' of that commercial Hollywood. You were cited as co-respondent (among others) by poor little Judy Kinnear in her divorce proceedings from Lochlan – but you didn't have the guts to show up in the courtroom.

The motion picture industry is bigger than you, Lisa. It can get along without you, but you can't, excuse me, get along without it. Because no other profession in the world can give you so much. And don't think that Hollywood will welcome you back with open arms when you get tired of sun worshipping on the French Riviera. (Be warned! We've seen the pictures!) Because, Miss Lisa La Touche, we think you just may have burned those inter-Continental bridges . . .

Recumbent under a peerless sky on a turquoise beach mat, Lisa smiled, tossed the magazine aside, slid on her Ray-Bans and reached for a peach.

CHAPTER THIRTY-NINE

CAT

EUROPE

July 1950

Dear Auntie Lisa,

Thank you for the book of fairy tales. I like the one about Gretel pushing the witch in the oven best. I think the Little Mermaid was an awful eejit to get her tongue cut out just so she could dance with the prince.

I go to school in a place called Kylemore Abbey. There is a farm, and there are goats. We push the girls in the lake on their birthdays and sometimes climb up the cliff to where there are caves to explore. Lessons are boring but I like the art room. Sister Carol is a good art teacher. It's the holidays now.

Love,
Cat

She had included a self-portrait, in crayon. It showed a smiling girl with rosy cheeks and scribbly yellow hair, surrounded by pink hearts. She had put five of them. One for Mammy, one for Daddy. One for Cat's kitten, one for her fat hen. And one for Auntie Lisa, because Mammy had told her to, even though Cat had never met Aunt Lisa.

July, 1952

Dear Auntie Lisa,

Thank you for Alice in Wonderland and Through the Looking Glass. I liked the baby who turned into a pig. I wonder could you do that in real life? My friend Sally has a brother who she would turn into a pig but I told her he is one already. I have no brother yet thanks be to heaven and Mam says I will not get one because I am an only child and Sally says I am a lucky duck.

Thank you for the photographs you sent me of your house in France and your dog. Mam says you were a film star once in America. Sally is from America, but she has never seen any of your films. She says her Mom might have. My favourite film is Peter Pan by Walt Disney. I like Tinkerbell best – she likes to break rules. Mam and Dad took me to see it in the picture house in Galway last week for my birthday.

I hope you are well.

Love,

Cat

This time she enclosed a class photograph. All the Kylemore Abbey students were smiling politely to camera – bar two. Bang in the centre of the middle row, a couple of bold-looking girls were in fits of laughter, sharing a joke. One of them was Cat, the other her friend, Sally. They'd been reprimanded after the photograph was taken and sent to detention, even though, as Cat had pointed out to the Mother Abbess, laughing wasn't a sin.

Dear Cat,

I'm glad you like the books. It is difficult to get books in France that are written in English, so I have had the bright idea of setting up what is called 'an account' with a bookshop in Galway called Kennys. That means that you can have any books you like without having to pay for them, and they will post them to you. I have already asked them to send you two books that I love – the Just So stories and The Secret Garden. (Mary in the book is an only child like you. I was an only child when I was little, and Sally is right – we are lucky ducks.) My favourite of the Just So stories is the one about the cat – you will love it too because it tells everyone how the cat is the most SUPERIOR of all the animals. SUPERIOR is a big word that means THE BEST – I hope you have a dictionary? I will order one specially for you from the lovely people in Kennys.

Maybe you will write back and tell me how you get on with the books? I know how boring it is to write thank you letters because I was made to do it when I was a little girl at boarding school (did you know that I went to Kylemore too? It was a long, long time ago). So don't write unless you really feel like it, although of course I would love to hear from you.

Your loving aunt,

Lisa XXX

But Cat *did* feel like writing. She loved the books so much that she wanted to tell somebody about them, and Aunt Lisa was great at writing back, and it was such a warm, fuzzy feeling when you had a letter waiting for you in the dining room at breakfast time. So when the next batch of books came from Kennys' bookshop, of course she wanted to tell somebody about those, too, and since writing to Lisa was nearly as good as talking to a friend (and Lisa never, ever gave out about her spelling or the untidiness of her writing), Cat decided she would make Lisa a kind of pen pal. She was the best kind of letter-writer; she was much better than the boring so-called 'pal' in Switzerland to whom she was made to write to improve her French (and she had to use words like 'whom' and 'thereof' because the teachers always checked the letters). Pen pals organized by the school were rubbish at writing, but Aunt Lisa was brilliant because she always wrote back at once.

July 1954

Dear Aunt Lisa,

Thank you for the camera you sent me for my birthday. My mam gave me roller skates. My new best friend here in Kylemore Abbey is a girl from Japan called Satomi. She is staying with us this summer, and some day I am going to travel to Japan to stay with her. We swam yesterday, and rode ponies bareback. There was a hawk above the mountain, and a huge great big goat chased us through the woods. I wish I had been able to take a photograph. It would make you laugh, the antics of him.

The new books came from Kennys. I loved the pictures in The Little Prince. I would like to have my hair cut like that but Mam says no. Satomi and me have started a pirate gang like in Swallows and Amazons. When Aslan died in The Lion, the Witch and the

Wardrobe I cried so much that Satomi thought I was going to be sick.

Love,

Cat

This time the enclosed photograph showed Cat standing on a sea wall, nonchalantly defying the drop beyond. She was looking unsmilingly at the lens, Box Brownie in her left hand. She looked like she meant business. She looked as if she knew where she was going, all rigged out with a life plan, a map and a compass. She looked like an adventuress. She was the personification of The Cat That Walked By Herself.

<u>Kylemore – Monday the something-or-other of April '59</u>
Hi, Lisa – I'm writing this in my study when I should be concentrating on the dramatic unities in Racine's Iphigénie. Why do they make us read such BORING stuff? I agree that Lord of the Flies would make a FAB film! V v scary, and v plausible. Did David Niven really introduce you to Scott Fitzgerald when you were in Hollywood? I enjoyed The Great Gatsby, thought Jordan was pretty cool, but Daisy a bit of a drag. I'm starting on The Valleys of the Assassins next (how gutsy is Freya Stark! Someday I'm going to be a trailblazer like her!) and I have a load of Raymond Chandlers lined up. I'm a sucker for his hardboiled heroes!

Exams coming up soon, future coming up soon, que sera sera. Yikes – here comes the supervisor – aaagghh – back to the Greek encampment in Aulis . . . ZZZZZZZZ

Cat.

Quick PS: I have loads of pictures of Kylemore – all

taken at different seasons of the year with the camera you gave me. Sister Carol says that I should get extra prints made and sell them to American tourists. Sister Carol is what you Americans call far-out, even though she is a nun.

July 1963

Dear Cat,

How wonderful that a London agency is interested in your photographs! I am <u>very</u> impressed! Might you send me some samples of your work? Róisín tells me that you have a real artist's eye.

Perhaps you'd like to come and stay with me and your uncle Raoul some time? As I'm sure you know, there is a festival of film in Cannes every year, and you could visit St Tropez, which was a small fishing village when I first came here, but is now very fashionable on account of Brigitte Bardot et al. I'm sure you could get some smashing photographs of this part of the world, it is about time that somebody dreamed up a new idea for photographic postcards: really, the ones of Picasso's house and the Croisette in Cannes are too dull for words – I'm sure you could come up with something much more interesting.

I've enclosed a cheque for you to treat yourself to something for your birthday. I saw a gorgeous dress in my favourite boutique in Antibes, but then I thought that you probably don't want an old 'aunt' choosing your clothes.

Remember, you are always welcome to visit here, but I understand that you are a very busy young woman. Róisín tells me that you have big plans to travel the world. Your grandmother was an adventuress, too.

Your loving aunt,

Lisa

July 1963
London

Dearest Lisa,

Thanks so much for yet <u>another</u> birthday cheque – you really are too kind. I'm far too old now to be getting hand-outs from my aunt! But you'll be glad to know that I put it to good use – I got myself a bike – very handy for getting around London.

Life here is good, although I miss Mam and Dad, of course. I've had a great response to my latest portfolio, and it means I get to meet some really interesting people!

I'm so sorry to have to turn down your invitation yet again – every time I think I'm going to be able to make it over to France something else comes up. Thank you for the offer, anyway. My last boyfriend kept trying to persuade me to visit a town called Cordes, that he said was very pretty – a real artists' town – but things didn't work out.

I hope all's well with you and Raoul. I saw a picture in a magazine of the art gallery he designed in Cannes. Very cool! Maybe I'll have an exhibition there some day. Then I'll definitely come and stay!

Lots of love,

Cat.

PS: I've enclosed a photograph – a self-portrait. I'm afraid my hair looks a bit all-over-the-place in it. I took it on a windy day at Dun Aengus in the Aran Islands

The portrait showed her on a cliff, looking out to sea. The light of the sun setting over the Atlantic. It lent her complexion a preternatural glow, as if her skin, her brows and eyelashes had been dipped in gold. Her hair was a tawny flag, her mouth determined, her expression hawk-like. Her gait was that of the queen she'd been named for.

Summer '64

Dear Aunt Lisa,

I'm in the Mediterranean, in Rhodes! I thought this postcard of a beach called Anthony Quinn Bay might amuse you – apparently he bought it when he was filming The Guns of Navarone, and intends making it into a retreat for artists and film-makers.

I came here with some people on an assignment for NME*. So far, so boring. Sun, sea and sand just don't do it for me!

Love, Cat.

*New Musical Express.

She'd put the asterisk in because she realized that her aunt probably wouldn't know what NME stood for. She certainly wouldn't know that it was the hippest journal on the scene, the barometer of what was with it and what was not in swinging sixties London.

Finding herself in the right place at the right time, Cat had graduated from St Martin's school of art with a BA in photography, and done well. She'd missed the opportunity to take the first famous head shots of Jane Asher (David Bailey had got there first), but she had snapped an up-and-coming Susannah York. Michael Cooper had nabbed

Rolling Stones frontman Mick Jagger, but Cat had stolen an intimate portrait of guitarist Keith Richards. Terence Donovan had got Mary Quant, but Cat found a textile designer called Zandra Rhodes, like herself barely out of art college, and with outrageous hair. Cat was creeping up quietly, stalking the alpha males; but while the men enjoyed leading a posse that *Private Eye* described as Britain's new aristocracy, Cat hated to think she might be part of some snooty elite. Which was why, when she had been invited along to a sunny Mediterranean haven by a group of musicians who were being groomed as the new Fab Four, she had been glad to escape 'swinging' London.

Rhodes was beautiful – a compact world of ruins to be explored and mountains to be climbed and islands to be hopped – but Cat's companions had no sense of adventure. They just wanted to hang out in their villa, writing songs and strumming guitars and drinking Jack Daniels all day, desperately willing themselves to be icons of cool. Cat had read their new lyrics and tried not to smirk. She'd been subjected to their attempts at seduction and tried not to laugh. She had taken their photographs and tried not to despair. She felt sorry for them. They were just boys, after all, and boys were so very jejune. And when they decided to head westward to try their luck in the USA, Cat had decided that there was more action to be had to the east, in Cyprus.

Reports had been rife of political unease on the island reputed to be the birthplace of Aphrodite. Cat had always been fiercely opposed to any regime that smacked of injustice: she guessed it was part of her Irish heritage. Her father had regaled her with tales of insurrection, of Michael Collins and the fight for an Irish Republic, and instilled in her the nationalist politics of Charles Stewart Parnell; while still at school she had wholeheartedly embraced the American civil rights movement, sticking pin-ups of Sidney Poitier and Harry Belafonte on the dormitory wall and quoting chunks verbatim of Martin Luther King's 'I Have a Dream' speech; she was a supporter of the Anti-Apartheid Movement, resolutely boycotting South African imports, and had signed a petition to have the country banned from participation in the Olympics. On a more mundane level, her nursery rhymes had been rebel songs, she was the proud owner of an LP by the Wolfe Tones (autographed by all three band members), and she was inordinately chuffed by the fact that Che Guevara claimed to have Irish roots.

This passionate crusade against injustice in an unfair world had led Cat to a bar in the centre of Nicosia heaving with international press corps. In every city in every theatre of war worldwide, an old guard of hard-bitten reporters, photojournalists and veteran broadcasters sniff out a congenial place to congregate, and in Cyprus they'd hit upon the cocktail lounge of the Ledra Palace Hotel. It was this elite clubroom into which Cat had wandered wide-eyed, unwitting and ingenuous, sporting a Ban the Bomb T-shirt and pigtails.

Sitting on the bar stool next to her was a man with a deeply tanned face, unruly hair, tired eyes and a five o'clock shadow. He was nursing a large whisky. Cat was longing for a Fanta or a Pepsi-Cola; instead she ordered neat Jameson.

'You here on your own?' asked the man, proffering a pack of Camel unfiltered.

Cat was just about to improvise a spiel about being here

with friends, but something about his open, streetwise demeanour made her decide not to mess with him.

'Yes,' she said, accepting a cigarette. 'Thanks.'

'Brave girl.'

'Why brave?'

'Ledra Street is known as the Murder Mile.' He gave her a crooked smile before striking his Zippo and lighting her cigarette.

'I didn't know that.' Cat inhaled and tried not to cough. The Camel was ferociously strong.

'Welcome to the war zone. The name's McCullin, by the way. Don.'

'Good to meet you,' said Cat, taking his outstretched hand. 'I'm Cat.'

'You're a photographer?' He nodded at the camera bag strapped across her chest.

'Yes.' Cat hoped he wouldn't ask for her credentials. She didn't think her degree from St Martin's would cut much ice with a man who exuded machismo, and she certainly didn't want to mention that her last assignment had been with a bunch of velvet-clad musicians.

'So what brings you here?'

'I – I don't really know.'

'If you're that clueless, my advice to you is to get out now.'

'But I've only just arrived!' protested Cat.

'Then go on the guided tour tomorrow; there's one laid on by the RAF. They'll hold your hand, show you what they want you to see, then wave you goodbye. You got a press pass?'

'No.'

Don shook his head in disbelief. 'You show up out of the blue and expect to be treated like a pro?'

'No. I just – I felt that by coming here I might be doing something. Something positive.' She took a hit of her drink and, trying not to wince, made an apologetic face. 'Complacency scares me, you see. I'm sorry. I'm not explaining myself very well: I must sound like a witless dilettante.'

'Go on digging.'

Cat smiled. 'You've heard of Lee Miller?'

'Our paths have crossed.'

'She used to say she was spurred to action by a fear of boredom.'

Don took a deep drag on his cigarette, then shook his head thoughtfully. 'A fear of boredom,' he said, 'is no bad thing. As long as it's accompanied by a sense of outrage.'

'That's it! That's just how she described it.'

'So. Tell me what outrages you.' Don nodded to the barman, who came over to refill their glasses.

'The unfairness of life,' said Cat, stubbing out her cigarette. 'That's what outrages me.'

Cat had written an essay on the subject of 'Injustice' while at school. She had received a lower than usual mark because she had – according to the lay English teacher – not been objective enough.

'How can I be objective about something I care so passionately about?' she'd retaliated. 'Haven't you seen photographs of the Nazi death camps?'

'I've read the statistics,' said the teacher. 'They're what matters.'

'No! You're wrong! A picture paints a thousand words – a million! In the photos, there were piles and piles of bodies, all starved and emaciated. The crematoriums had run out of fuel, so the ones who weren't lucky enough to be gassed died in their own excrement and puke. It doesn't matter how many *statistics* you read. Until you've seen the images you know nothing about injustice!'

'I hardly consider such images appropriate for—'

'Appropriate!' Cat had spat. 'What's *appropriate* about atrocity?'

There was a fierce light in her eyes now as she turned back to Don. 'If the world doesn't know what's going on in the hellish places, no-one will feel the need to help. I want to make a difference.'

'And just how do you think you're going to do that, a girl of what – twenty? Twenty-one . . . ?'

'Twenty-five,' lied Cat.

'. . . Here, on your own without a press pass?'

Cat shrugged to indicate an insouciance she was far from feeling. 'I don't know. I don't know what I'm going to do. Yet.'

Don glanced at the camera bag again. 'What have you got in there?'

'A Rolleiflex 3.5 F and a five-year-old Leica.'

This met with a brief nod of approval. 'Rolleiflex happens to be my own weapon of choice. Lenses?'

'Telephoto; wide-angle.'

'Are you quick on your feet?'

'Very.'

'Fearless?'

'I like to think so.'

'In that case, I know what you're going to do,' said Don, draining his glass. 'You're going to come with me.'

And the next day, while the rest of the press corps were

escorted around the island by the Royal Air Force PR people, Cat and Don set off on their own.

No photographer ever forgets his first foray into a war zone. But even if something radical had happened to erase Cat's memory, if some damage had been done to her brain, or some blessed oblivion or fugue state had descended upon her, or if some sorcery had been worked to make her un-see what she had seen, her photographs would remain as testimony to the carnage that had been visited that day upon the tiny village of Agios Sozomenos.

The hamlet was located about fifteen miles south of the capital. She and Don drove there under a burning sun. The cluster of stone and mud houses were peopled by Turkish Cypriots, but most of the young male inhabitants were dead. They had been killed not long before Don and Cat happened upon them.

Cat had seen dead people before. In Connemara it was common practice to hold a party or 'wake' the night before burial. The corpse would be laid out on a bed; family and neighbours would gather around, and *poitín* or whiskey would be offered while songs were sung and jokes shared and stories told of the deceased. When she was small, Cat had delighted in the task of carrying news of the passing to the livestock and the bees, as was the tradition. Death in Connemara had a homey feel to it, and the dead slept peacefully, hands folded upon their chests. In Connemara there had been no blood.

Here, there was blood. In Agios Sozomenos the eyes of the dead men stared vacantly skyward. They lay where they had fallen on the packed earth, their limbs jutting and splayed at awkward angles as if a puppetmaster had just severed the strings, waiting for the ministrations of their womenfolk; waiting for their wounds to be cleansed, their heads to be cradled, their eyes to be closed, their bodies to be covered; waiting for prayers to be said for their souls.

The women came, and the children, and the old men. Cat wanted to leave; she wished she had not come. What had made her think that she could make a difference? What arrogance had persuaded her to believe that some specious sense of moral responsibility could change *anything*? How naïve had she been?

As the villagers congregated, Cat remained frozen in an attitude of abject deference with her head bowed, face expressionless, eyes fixed on the ground. She felt that a single glance in the direction of the bereaved would constitute an intrusion. Her camera bag weighed heavy against her hip, the strap was chafing the flesh of her neck, her throat was constricted by a hard knot of choked-back tears.

Don stepped forward and said something in a low voice to one of the women. She nodded as another woman, barely more than a girl, took off her headscarf and first kissed, then covered the face of one of the men lying on the ground. Her husband. Then Don turned to Cat and said, 'They want us to do it. They want us to record their grief.'

He raised his camera and started to take pictures in a solemn, dignified fashion, as befitted the cataloguing of an event of such magnitude. Cat followed suit, apprentice to Don's master. And as she framed each image through the lens of the viewfinder, she felt as though she were following in a tradition that went back centuries to the paintings of Delacroix and Goya and beyond, to those artists who had recorded their wars and the anguish they generated in mosaics and tapestries and in bas-relief sculpture, and even on the walls of caves. She felt less observer than participant, as if she too were involved in this age-old universal tragedy.

Take your pictures the womenfolk seemed to be saying. *Take your pictures and tell the world that evil is commonplace, and atrocity just around the next corner.*

That night Cat got very, very sick. It started with a headache. Initially she put it down to emotional stress combined with too much sun. But then her limbs began to ache as they had used to when she was a little girl, a condition her mammy had described as 'growing pains'. Back then the cure had been to go to bed with a hot-water bottle and a mug of cocoa and sleep tight; here in her hotel room there was no chance of sleep. On Ledra Street the night was ablaze with Sten gun fire. Bullets were ricocheting off the walls of the building – one hit the air-conditioning unit attached to her window with a clang that made her yelp; sirens screamed, and from below came shouts, the sound of running footsteps and the anguished wails of women.

All was confusion – both outside and inside her room. People were sprinting along corridors, but Cat scarcely had the energy to drag herself out of bed. She remembered crawling into the bathroom to puke, slipping and knocking her head hard against the tiles; she remembered crouching on the lavatory and shitting until there was nothing left to shit. She tried to drink tap water, knowing how important it was not to dehydrate, but she couldn't keep it down. She just retched it all back up, then dry-heaved over and over again, feeling as though a sinewy creature was twisting and flexing in her gut.

393

Somehow she got through to reception on the phone, and then Don was in the room, telling her he'd organized transport, asking who he could contact, going through her bag. There was a hospital next – but it was overcrowded, there was no room, they would have to go to the community centre. But that was crowded too, crowded with dying people covered in blood. Was he OK, the boy on the ground, the one with the headscarf over his face? No, he was dead, she'd forgotten: his young wife had kissed his dead face. Cat wasn't dying, was she? She just needed a mug of cocoa and all would be well, and her kitten could come and snuggle up with her all cosy under the blankets. She was sleepy now. She wanted to go to sleep.

Don't worry. The jeep will take you to the airport, there's no need to need to worry.

Why should I worry?

There's a line coming. Hurry!

Murray Mints Murray Mints the Too Good to Hurry Mints.

Are you OK?

I'm fine. – no it's.

Medevac will get you to a hospital.

Medevac? Funny name, Medevac. What was that snack? It Bridged That Gap.

You're strong, you're fine. Hook her up to the line.

Yes, I'm Tough and Strong – I'm the Milky Bar Kid. Just Can't Go Wrong.

You'll be safe in Athens, someone is going to meet you there.

Mammy?

Just a sting, another little one in your arm. There. Good girl.

Will Mammy be there?
Yes. Somebody will be there in Athens for you.
Yay! The Milky Bars are on Me!

She woke in a white bed. Her mouth was dry, her eyes felt rusty. Her head upon the pillow was too heavy to move. She felt someone touch her hand.

'Mammy?' she said.

'Yes,' came the answer.

Cat smiled, then sank back into a deep sleep.

CHAPTER FORTY

LISA

CAP D'ANTIBES – 1964

When Lisa got the call it was one of those strange middle-of-the-night moments. Raoul answered, then covered the mouthpiece with his hand and said, 'It's some guy – I didn't catch his name. He got the number from directory enquiries. He needs to talk to you about Cat.'

'What?' Lisa sat up in bed, shaking off a dream of Sabu laughing at her because she was wearing the wrong costume.

'He's calling from Nicosia.'

'Nicosia?' The dream was vestigial already. 'What's Cat doing in Nicosia?'

'Ask him,' said Raoul, handing her the receiver.

'Hello?'

'Is that Lisa Reverdy?' The line wasn't great, but Lisa could make out that the man had an English accent.

'Yes. Who is this?'

'My name is Don McCullin. I'm a colleague of Cat's.'

'Oh, God. There's something wrong, isn't there?'

'Yeah. She's in a pretty bad way.' He sounded brusque, matter-of-fact. He clearly had neither the time nor

396

the inclination for pussyfooting. 'It's probably dysentery.'

'Dysentery!'

'The symptoms correspond. We're trying to get her on a plane to Athens.'

'Oh, God – oh, God.' Lisa reached for Raoul's hand, and clutched it.

'Can you get there?' asked Don McCullin.

'To Athens? Of course. Where is she now?'

'She's at the airport in Nicosia. She's in good hands.'

'Is she going to be—'

'She's a little druggy, but with a bit of luck she'll be OK.'

'Thank you. Oh, thank you.'

'She's asking for her mother.'

'How did you know to contact me?'

'I found your address on a postcard. You're her aunt, yeah?'

'No, I'm . . . I mean yes. Yes, I'm her aunt.'

'I'll tell them you're on your way. When you get to Ellinikon—'

'Ellinikon?'

'– the airport – put in a call to Medevac and they'll tell you where she is.' In the background came the sound of a siren. 'I gotta go. She's some chick, your niece. Tell her to get in touch with me once she's better and I'll buy her lunch.'

'I'll do that. Thank you again, Mr McCullin.'

'Don.'

Lisa put the phone down and shut her eyes, trying to process what had just happened. Then she leaned over and brushed Raoul's lips with hers.

'Is everything OK?' he asked.

'Yes. Yes! It's got to be. Everything's going to be fine.'

Throwing back the sheets, she grabbed her bathrobe. 'Can you get some coffee on? And then drive me to the airport?'

'You're not going to Nicosia, are you?'

'No. Athens.'

'Why Athens?'

Lisa gave him her bravest smile. 'I'm going to get my daughter,' she said. And then she burst into tears.

Cat was beautiful. Her skin was milky and translucent, her hair thick and red gold. Her lashes – look at them! – were impossibly long; her ears were whorled like perfect shells – the kind you'd want to pick up on a beach as keepsakes. She had a little mole – how cute! – just above the left corner of her lip, and a dusting of freckles on her kissable nose. Her mouth curved upward a little at the corners, she had elegant fingers and – Lisa hadn't had the chance to check yet, but she was reasonably certain – she had elegant toes.

The nurses had told her that Cat was stable. She'd had three bags of saline solution administered intravenously since she'd been admitted, and once she was fully rehydrated they would take her off the drip. Then she would be allowed to go home.

Home! There was no question of Cat going back to London, where she would have no responsible person to take care of her, and it was unthinkable that she should try to get to Connemara: the journey would exhaust her.

No. The nursing staff agreed with Lisa that the best thing for Cat would be to fly back to Cannes with her aunt, and spend some time recuperating by the sea in marvellous Cap d'Antibes. So Lisa telephoned Róisín with the news, and assured her cousin that she, Lisa, would take care of everything. And then she sat by Cat's bedside and waited for her to wake up.

She sat there for hours, scarcely stirring. The nurse asked if she could fetch her something to eat, but Lisa declined the offer. She could sit there for ever, feasting her eyes on this wondrous sleeping beauty. At one point the girl opened her eyes, blinked twice and said, 'Mammy?'

Lisa couldn't help herself. She laid her hand over Cat's and said, 'Yes.' Then, as she watched her daughter slide back into the embrace of Morpheus, she added, 'Mama's here. You're going to come to a boathouse by the sea for a rest. Mama's going to look after you for a little while, just until you're better. There, there, my little Cat. Mama's here and everything's going to be all right.'

Raoul popped the champagne cork. It came away with a sigh, and a plume of vapour escaped.

'You're like a phoenix risen from the ashes!' said Lisa, gazing fondly at Cat as Raoul poured Moët into champagne flutes. 'Just think, when I arrived at the hospital, you'd had three bags full!'

'Three bags full of what?' Raoul asked.

'Saline solution. She was like Ba Ba Black Sheep.'

Cat laughed. How Lisa loved to hear her laugh! The joke was of course lost on Raoul, who had been brought up on French nursery rhymes.

They were on the terrace of the Boat House, drinking champagne: they'd popped a bottle a day since Cat had arrived. Lisa had to smile at the notion that Cat might think this was standard practice in Salamander Cove. If she only knew that, while her daughter was here, every day was an occasion to celebrate!

Cat was stretched out on a sun lounger in a bikini. She was a little too skinny for Lisa's liking, but the dysentery was most likely responsible for that, and Lisa would see to it that her daughter would eat nothing but the finest home-cooked fare while she was under her roof. Right now she was scoffing pretzels, of which Lisa heartily approved since they were high both in calories and in salt. She had recently acquired a copy of Elizabeth David's *French Provincial Cooking*, and was determined to prepare as many of the dishes contained within its pages as was humanly possible in the days before her daughter flitted off again like the sprite she was, to London or Cyprus or Connemara, or wherever in the world she was bound.

Lisa had spent three days in Athens, visiting Cat's hospital room at every opportunity, glorying in her daughter's recovery; marvelling as the bloom returned to her face and the lustre to her hair. She'd urged Cat to tell her all about her time at art college and about her love life and her career, and when Cat grew tired, Lisa read to her. She'd have loved to read fairy stories to her daughter, but she knew if she did that Cat would think she was stark raving mad, and the last thing she wanted to do was frighten her off. So instead she read from any English newspapers or magazines that were available at the newsstand in her hotel. The gossipy ones didn't interest Cat; her preference was for international publications like the *Illustrated London News*, the *Spectator* and the *New York Times*; she wanted updates from Cyprus and the Congo and Vietnam. She didn't care about the look that was trending in the colour supplements, the 'floating chiffons coloured with a painter's palette', or that the Beatles had won a Variety Club showbiz award. But when Lisa pointed out a picture in the *Observer* magazine by Don McCullin and mentioned that he had referred to Cat in their phone conversation as a 'colleague', Cat's peach bloom complexion became suffused with a becoming pink.

On her arrival in Salamander Cove, Cat had retrieved an unsent postcard from her backpack – the one addressed to Lisa that had been responsible for Don contacting her – and delivered it personally. Lisa was using the postcard as a bookmark in *French Provincial Cooking*. She reread it now, before sliding it between the pages where a recipe for *Daube de boeuf* had caught her eye.

'"*Sun, sea and sand just don't do it for me?*"' she scoffed. 'Ha! Just look at you now!'

To watch Cat soak up the rays and dive through the waves that washed the shore below, you would think that sun, sea and sand were as much part of her constitution as they had been Aphrodite's. After less than a week of taking things easy in Cap d'Antibes, she had the appearance of a golden goddess. They'd driven into town a couple of times, and Lisa had persuaded Cat to venture into two or three boutiques on the Boulevard Albert. She'd insisted on paying for anything in which Cat expressed interest, until Cat had finally refused point-blank to try anything else on, lest Lisa produce her wallet again.

Today, as well as her bikini, she was sporting a batiked sarong and pretty coral earrings that Lisa had bought for her. 'You look great,' observed Lisa with a smile, then wished she hadn't said anything, because Cat replied, 'I *feel* great. I guess it's time for me to move on and stop abusing your hospitality.'

'You're doing no such thing!' said Lisa. 'You're welcome to stay as long as you like – isn't she, Raoul?'

'Of course,' said Raoul. 'It's lovely for Lisa to have her . . . to have a surrogate daughter around.'

Something had clogged the atmosphere, because Cat said, in an artificially jokey voice, 'Oh, you're better off without daughters, surrogate or otherwise! Mam says I bring her nothing but grief!' A silence ensued, and then Cat said, 'I'm sorry. That was insensitive of me. For all I know, you would have loved to have a daughter, or a son.'

'We did want a family,' said Lisa. 'But unfortunately it didn't happen.'

'I'm sorry.'

'We have our dogs,' said Raoul, ruffling the ears of their most recent acquisition, a sleek Lab called Orlando. He glanced at Lisa with a smile, then stood up to refill their glasses. 'We're very happy.'

'I can tell.' Cat looked around at the house and the view and the dogs stretched out on the terrace. 'There's a real sense of peace here. I'd love to take photographs.'

'Do,' urged Lisa. 'Stay a little longer and take as many as you like.'

'I don't really do landscapes,' said Cat. 'I'm more into portraiture. Or rather, I was until I visited Cyprus.'

'What happened in Cyprus?'

Cat shook a veil of hair across her face the way Lisa had used to, to mask her expression. Clearly things happened there that she did not want to talk about. Lisa guessed she had seen horrors.

'A sea change, I guess,' Cat said lightly, rubbing a finger around the rim of her glass. 'I got to take some extraordinary pictures. At least, I think I did. I can't wait to get back to my darkroom in London to see how they turned out.'

Lisa saw her chance. 'You don't have to wait! Develop them here.'

'There's no darkroom.'

'We can rig one up, no problem. I know it won't be possible here, in the Boat House, but Gervaise has lots of spare rooms you could use as a darkroom.'

'I need a supply of water, and—'

'He has lots of spare bathrooms, too!'

'And chemicals.'

'I can nip into town for those. Just write me a list.'

Cat smiled as Orlando ambled over to her and put his head on her lap. 'The thing is,' she observed, popping a pretzel into his mouth, 'Gervaise scares me a little.'

'But you've only met him once!'

Gervaise had joined them for dinner the previous night, and had spent most of the evening looking quizzically at Cat. Lisa had had to take him aside and tell him to stop being so rude.

'She's the very spit of you,' Gervaise had remarked.

'So what's to write home about?' Lisa had retorted. 'She's my niece. Good looks run in the family.'

Nobody in Lisa's circle in Salamander Cove, apart from Raoul, knew that she had had a daughter before becoming Madame Lantier. Nana Reverdy had suspected, Lisa knew, but had never been indiscreet enough to pry. Lisa was sorry that, unlike Nana's daughters and her *belle-fille*, lovely Hélène, she alone had been unable to give Nana a grandchild.

Now she turned to Cat and said, 'Don't be scared of Gervaise, darling. He's a big softie, really.' She knew that

Gervaise was no such thing, but she would have said anything to make Cat stay. 'And the Villa Perdita is like a second home to us. Please don't go back to London just yet. You're not well enough. You may think you are, but you could relapse. We'll find a space for you to work in the villa. I'm longing to see your photographs!'

'I may not want to show them to anyone. They may not be good enough.'

'Then you can take others! Look around at the loveliness, at the light! It's what brings artists here.'

Orlando was gazing up at Cat, imploring her to give him another pretzel.

'Do stay,' said Raoul. 'You're the first cat the dogs haven't tried to take a bite out of.'

Cat looked at Orlando, then at Raoul, and finally her eyes met Lisa's.

Lisa suspected that the expression on her face was as abjectly beseeching as the Labrador's. Between the three of them they must have swung it, because Cat smiled.

'All right,' she said with a laugh. 'Let's give it a go.'

CHAPTER FORTY-ONE

CAT

CAP D'ANTIBES – 1964

Cat fished with her tongs for the photograph that floated in the dish of developing fluid, and turned it over. This was what she loved the most about the process: from the moment the image began to shimmer into perspective, until the moment when the spectral outline finally took on recognizable human characteristics and – most importantly – a human expression. One more second . . . two . . . There. She rinsed the photograph, dipped it in fixer, rinsed it again, then pegged it up on the line to dry with the rest of the series.

Cyprus had affected Cat to her core. It had expanded her vision, sharpened her focus, and made her realize how narrow and narcissistic was the lifestyle she had embraced in London with its veneer of intellectual sophistication and liberalism. She had laughed at herself, along with the groovier-than-thou students at St Martin's who had called her an Irish potato head, not understanding that to grow up surrounded by the wild beauty of Connemara was the rarest of privileges. She had dismissed her education at the hands of Benedictine nuns as archaic and irrelevant, unaware that they had cultivated in her the seeds of self-knowledge and the basics of what they called Christianity, and she called empathy. Cyprus had made her see that through the lens of her camera she could share other people's emotional experiences and convey them to a world which was ignorant of suffering and unwilling to admit that evil flourished in dark places. She could transmit the essence of experience in black and white – both literally and metaphorically – through the medium of her photographs. She had a powerful message to communicate.

When they'd emerged from the tray, the photographs she had taken of the Turkish Cypriots had made her press her hands to her mouth in stupefaction. They had made her weep. In her mind's eye she revisited Agios Sozomenos, saw the girl draw her scarf over her dead husband's face, saw again the weathered features of the womenfolk stretched in agony, the grotesque pastiches of pietàs, the dark countenance of inhumanity unmasked. Her photographs were affecting, disturbing, arresting; they were different, and Cat almost loathed herself when she understood how very, very good they were.

Taking a last look at the row of grainy black-and-white ten-by-eights drying on the line above the sink, Cat slid out from behind the heavy blackout curtain that Gervaise had unearthed for her makeshift darkroom and closed the door behind her. She needed a drink.

There was one waiting. On the terrace, the master of the Villa Perdita was sitting in the gloaming, a dog at his feet, a *pichet* and two wine glasses in front of him.

At her approach, he set aside the book he was reading, and took off his spectacles. 'I thought you could do with an apertif,' he said, sloshing red into a glass and handing it to her. 'I always used to need one after a long day in the studio. Now that I don't spend as much time there, I don't bother with the excuse.'

'Why don't you spend as much time there?' asked Cat, taking a seat opposite him.

'I spend more time doing work *en plein air*. I find it liberating, and the landscape's become as dear and eloquent to me as the faces of loved ones. Besides, my eyesight is beginning to go, and my muse abandoned me years ago.'

'They say that the worse Monet's eyesight became, the more his landscapes improved.'

'His waterlilies got bluer, that's for sure,' he said, raising his glass. '*Santé*.'

'*Santé*,' she echoed, mirroring the gesture.

'How did your session go?'

'I don't know. I don't know whether to say it went very well, or that it was bloody awful.'

'May I be the judge of that?'

'The prints won't be dry until tomorrow.'

'I can wait. You're in a hurry, aren't you?'

'In what way?'

'To get on with the things that matter.' He took a hit of wine, then regarded her with interest. 'What makes you think your photographs might be bloody awful?'

'I don't really. Distressing is a better word.'

'You took them in Cyprus?'

'Yes.'

'That's all you need to say. Let me look at them when they're ready and I'll give you an honest assessment. If I think they're any good, I'll get in touch with a friend of mine – an editor on a picture desk. You don't have any scruples about influence, do you?'

'You mean nepotism?'

'That's a big word that means the same thing.'

'I guess if I have any talent, it'll be recognized at some stage.'

Gervaise shook his head. 'It's not axiomatic—'

'That's a big word!'

'Shut up and listen. What age are you?'

'Twenty-five.'

'That's a lie.'

There was no point in denying it. 'Yeah. It is.'

'See? You think you can dupe me with a little swagger. That's akin to stepping into boots that are too big for you.'

Ouch! He'd succeeded in making her feel small and stupid, and even younger than she really was.

'Most people your age are egocentric enough to believe that they can get by without help,' he resumed. 'It's an attitude that's scuppered countless promising careers, and it's a bad one. To allow someone to help you is a sign of humility. Is that too big a word for you?'

'No.'

'Show me your work tomorrow. And if I tell you to work harder, work harder.'

From a stand of pine trees over by the path that led down to the Boat House came a sudden magical, complex trill. Cat's jaw literally dropped.

'A nightingale,' remarked Gervaise, sounding blasé. 'I can tell by your expression that you've never heard one before.'

'I haven't. I used to complain about the noise the cuckoo made outside the study room in the boarding school I went to, in Connemara.'

'Tch tch. Noise pollution is the coming bane of our

times. Is that where you learned to take photographs?'

'Yes. There, and at St Martin's in London.'

'Exciting place, London.'

'I used to think so. It seems vapid now, after Cyprus.'

'War does that to you. I went through two.'

'That must have been hard.'

Gervaise shrugged. 'I partied through the first one and its aftermath. I sobered up sufficiently to take the next one a little more seriously.'

'You fought in the last war?'

'I worked for the Resistance.'

In the pinewood, the nightingale began its aria again. Cat listened, rapt, unaware that Gervaise was studying her expression. When she turned to him again, she was smiling.

He returned the smile. 'Once I would have asked your permission to make a portrait of you.'

'I have a better idea,' she said. 'I'll make one of you.'

'That makes a lot more sense.'

Spitting on her hand, Cat extended it to him to shake. His grip was muscular, his fingers firm. It was an honour, she thought, to clasp the hand of such a venerable artist in her own small paw.

The next day Gervaise looked at her work and pronounced it better than good.

'These photographs can't have been easy to take,' he said.

Cat shook her head. She couldn't speak when she looked at the pictures; her throat constricted and her face went scarlet with emotion.

'They're dignified,' Gervaise said, holding a print at

arm's length. 'There's nothing remotely intrusive about them.'

'We asked permission.'

'But you didn't stage-manage them.'

'Oh, no. No. That would have been unspeakably unethical.'

'They wouldn't have worked if you'd tried. You can't stage-manage calamity.' He gave the photographs another once-over. 'The most eloquent artist allows his subject to do the talking for them. Remember that, Cat. These are eloquent pictures. But there's more to be said, and if you're set on taking pictures like this, it's never going to get easier.'

She managed a smile. 'So I have to work harder?' she asked.

'You do. Complacency is a killer. Now, go get your camera.'

'Does that mean you're ready for your close-up, Monsieur Lantier?'

'I'm ready.'

Cat slid the photographs into a manila folder. 'Where will I shoot you?' she asked.

'You're doing a portrait of the artist. Can you think of any famous ones you'd like to emulate?'

'Vermeer. *The Painter in his Studio.*'

'Top marks.'

'You mean, you're inviting me into your studio? But you never allow anyone in there!'

'Who told you that?'

'All the newspaper reports I've ever read have described you as "famously reclusive".'

'I am famously reclusive. I haven't allowed anyone apart from your . . . aunt into my studio for nearly four decades.

410

Just think – you can sell the picture to some rag for a small fortune.'

'I wouldn't dream of doing that!' protested Cat.

'Why not?' returned an insouciant Gervaise. 'I would.'

Cat made portraits of her new mentor and of Lisa and Raoul and Orlando. She was invited to lunch in the farm where Lisa had spent the first years of her childhood, and there she took photographs of the entire Reverdy family; babies and adults and – as they were called in Connemara – auld wans. She visited the *marché provençale* in Antibes and photographed the buyers and sellers, and the produce piled high on stalls. Further along the coast she photographed the trendy, the jaded, the beauties and the beasts in St-Tropez and the sad hopeful girls on the Croisette in Cannes.

She had just started experimenting with landscape when she got word from a picture editor in *National Geographic* magazine to say that they were interested in buying some of her photographs, and were thinking about commissioning more.

CHAPTER FORTY-TWO

LISA

CAP D'ANTIBES – 1964

When word came that Cat was to have her photo-graphs published – in *National Geographic*, no less! – Lisa felt a mixture of emotions. She felt buoyant with pride and giddy with excitement for her daughter, and yet she was heartsick at the prospect of her departure. Her heart grew sicker still when Cat told her where she was heading next.

'The Congo!' she said. 'You can't possibly *think* of going there! Haven't you heard the news stories?'

But nothing Lisa said could dissuade her. She sat in the living room of the Boat House listening with her head in her hands while Cat discussed her itinerary over the telephone in the hall; she watched as Cat and Raoul pored over an atlas murmuring a litany of place names – Owando, Komono, Impfondo; her stomach lurched when she sneaked a look at the checklist Cat was compiling – Swiss Army knife, whistle, hand-crank radio – and she could do nothing to stop the tears coming when Cat asked her for a pair of sewing shears so that she could cut off all her hair.

'It'll be hot where I'm going – I don't want that great

unruly mess sitting on top of my head like a tea cosy, ramping up my body temperature and getting in my face,' she said with breathtaking pragmatism as she hacked off a thick pigtail.

Lisa escaped to the Villa Perdita to seek solace from all the travel plans in the company of Gervaise, but he wasn't there. She went instead to the library, to try to find refuge in a book. She and Raoul treated the place like their very own public lending library: if they'd had to pay overdue fines they would have owed Gervaise a fortune by now. She had spent many hours of her spare time over the years contentedly cataloguing volume upon volume for him, with a diligence born of the respect that David Niven had instilled in her for books.

Gervaise's collection was a bibliophile's utopia, part of the very fabric of the Villa Perdita. Lisa remembered the libraries in some of the Hollywood mansions she'd visited, where books had been bought by the yard; shelf upon shelf of tooled Morocco leather tomes dusted religiously every week by some hapless maid, but never opened, let alone read.

If Cat was hellbent on travelling to Africa, Lisa supposed that she ought to bone up a little on the continent. She helped herself to a copy of Joy Adamson's uplifting *Born Free*, and Karen Blixen's elegiac *Out of Africa*. Running her hand along the aligned titles on a row further down, she also selected a slim hardback. The cover was patterned with a design of copra half-shells, beautiful concentric circles of ochre, black and grey. *A Tahitian Journal by Patrick Lawless*, she read, *With Wood-Engravings by an Artist*. On the flyleaf was written – in a fine, copperplate hand – 'Memories of Raguenez'.

How Lisa wished that Cat was heading for this island paradise in the South Seas instead of the war-torn Congo! There were vivid descriptions in the book of market stalls heaped with all kinds of exotic fruits and vegetables, of beautiful, smiling girls in jewel-coloured pareus, of scarlet-blossomed hibiscus, of white tiare and red pandanus flowers, of purple mountains and endless ribbons of silvery sand edging emerald bays. The illustrations were wood engravings of exotic fish, and palm trees snaked around with vines, and of bare-breasted beauties lazing by lagoons; all in simple black and white, all exquisite. No wonder Tahiti had become a Mecca for painters; no wonder Gauguin had settled there.

A sound came from upstairs; Gervaise must have returned. Lisa slipped the books into her shoulder bag and left the library to go and say hello.

On the landing, Cat was folding the heavy blackout curtain that had been used to convert the spare bathroom into a darkroom.

'Hi,' she said. 'I'm just finishing up here. I was hoping I might run into Gervaise; I have a present for him.' Cat laid the curtain on a carved blanket chest, then looked back at Lisa. 'What's up?' she asked.

'Your hair,' said Lisa.

'You mean my lack of hair,' joked Cat. 'What do you think?'

'It makes you look . . . like an elfin creature,' said Lisa.

'A pooka?'

'That's Irish, isn't it?'

'Yes.'

'A pooka, then. Or a sprite. Something from a fairy tale.'

It was true. Cat's cropped hair gave her the appearance

of an illustration from a book that Lisa remembered from her childhood, of Rapunzel whose marvellous hair had been shorn by a witch. But the loss of her hair had ultimately given Rapunzel her freedom, and she saw now that freedom suited Cat. She looked just the way she did in Lisa's recurring dream, when they found each other on the mountainside.

'You're beautiful. Beautiful and strong. What a joy it's been, to watch you get better.' Lisa stepped forward and embraced Cat, then took her hand. 'Come with me,' she said, leading the way down the corridor. Outside the door to Jessie's boudoir, she paused. 'Oh, God,' she said. 'I'm going to cry.'

'Why?'

'You'll see.' Turning the handle, she opened the door, gesturing for Cat to precede her into the room.

The portraits that hung over the baroque divan were mirror images of each other: Jessie and Lisa, barefoot and clad in floral patterned silk. Luxuriant hair cascaded over their shoulders, and their generous mouths were curved in smiles.

'It's you!' exclaimed Cat. 'You and . . . ?'

'My mother,' said Lisa.

'Gervaise knew your mother?'

'They were lovers.'

'So you're Gervaise's daughter?'

Lisa smiled. 'If only it were as simple as that. No, I'm not. His daughter Ghislaine lives in Paris. My mother was pregnant with me when she met Gervaise. But he loved her, and was very good to her. She lived here once-upon-a-time; her clothes are still here, in that closet.' Lisa indicated the double doors behind which her Balenciagas and her

Molyneux languished in the arms of Coco Chanel's price-less creations.

'How amazing!' Cat's eyes went back to the portraits on the wall. 'You're wearing the same dress.'

'Yes. The Liberty silk. It's in there somewhere still.'

'What happened to your mother?'

Lisa shrugged. 'Nobody knows. She went missing.'

'And your father?'

'Oh, he was a vagabond artist. The kind, I imagine, who kissed the girls and made them cry.'

'They're beautiful paintings. Companion pieces.'

'Yes. I'd like to think that wherever they end up, they'll always hang side by side.' Lisa gave Cat's hand a squeeze, and was just thinking how tender a moment this was, when a voice came from behind them.

'A sentiment worthy of a Mother's Day card.'

Gervaise was standing in the doorway.

'You horrible old cynic,' said Lisa, giving him a cross look.

'Gervaise! I'm so glad to see you!'

The smile Cat sent him was one of ingenuous delight, like that of a schoolgirl seeking approbation from her favourite teacher. How funny to think that just a week ago she'd been scared of him!

'I have a present for you, to say thank you.' Cat moved to him, and linked his arm.

'Thank you for what?'

'For sorting out a darkroom for me. I've cleared every-thing out now, and your bathroom's back to normal.'

'So you're off?'

'First thing in the morning.'

Gervaise looked at her fondly. 'I'll miss you, little Cat.

How sweet of you to think of getting me a present. What is it?'

'It's the portrait I made of you. I had it framed, and left it on the table in the kitchen with a bottle of Margaux. I know that's your favourite.'

'In that case, we shall uncork it at once, and toast your next adventure. Will you join us on the terrace, Lisa?'

'In a minute.'

Together Gervaise and Cat left the room. Lisa could hear their voices receding as they made their way along the corridor to the back stairs, Cat's light and animated in *contrappunto* to Gervaise's dark baritone.

Lisa wished that Cat could stay a while: just a week or two longer, a month – or more; a year, a lifetime. She wished she could make up for all the time that she had never spent with her daughter, and now never would. She wished she could imprison her in a tower, just like Rapunzel, and keep her safe from harm for evermore.

What scared her more than anything was that, by going to the Congo, Cat was effectively playing Knocky Door Ginger with Death. If only there were some talisman that could protect her, an invisible sword or shield that would keep her safe.

Moving to the closet, she pulled open the double doors. She knew that none of the costume jewellery laid out in the leather-lined trays would interest Cat, but there was one item there that Lisa sensed might have totemic powers. It was the little charm she had found that had belonged to Jessie.

She had questioned Gervaise about it shortly after she had happened upon it, and he had told her that it was fashioned in the image of Anubis, the Egyptian funerary god. On seeing Lisa recoil, Gervaise had smiled and said: 'He's actually one of the good guys – the god you wouldn't mind having on your side if you were in danger. He was a pal of Isis, the mother-goddess.'

'So he's benevolent?'

'Yes. He takes care of the most precious souls,' said Gervaise, 'and makes sure that they get safely into the next world.'

Lisa opened the drawer where the charm lay in a tiny velvet casket. If Cat was heading off on her own into a theatre of war as bloody as the Congo, she would need somebody to watch over her.

CHAPTER FORTY-THREE

CAT

LONDON – 1968

Cat was strolling through Piccadilly, having just seen the Beatles cavorting in a mildly enjoyable *Yellow Submarine* at the Odeon. Although it was bitterly cold it was a dazzlingly sunny December day, and a wino sitting on a bench was holding his face up to the sky. The geezer behind the counter of a nearby hotdog stand was frying onions, and Cat's mouth started to water as it always did when she was assailed by delicious smells. The food she'd been offered while travelling a year ago had smelt disgusting. But she'd overcome her disgust and accepted it with good grace because the alternative was – well, there *was* no alternative. The bottom line was you just didn't get to eat.

When it came to the 'eat or be eaten' credo, jungles were the worst, especially after sundown. Even by day in the city, Cat instinctively watched shop windows for reflections, because that way you could see what was going on behind you. She always walked towards oncoming traffic, and listened out for what might be heading from the opposite direction. In a restaurant, she would sit with her back to a wall, near a service door or window. She kept her wits about her at all times.

At night her jangled nerves would not allow her to sleep without copious amounts of local brew to dull her senses to a tolerable level, and every morning she relied on hits of strong black coffee to blast herself into activity. The energy that was left over from keeping herself alive, she spilled into taking photographs.

Cat had covered the Congo in '64, Vietnam in '66 and famine-stricken Biafra in '67, and her vision of hell came back to her every night in the form of a recurring dream. In this dream she wandered the wards of a children's hospital. None of the children spoke – they just gazed at her with wide, unseeing eyes – but she could hear their unvoiced thoughts whispering to her, pleading for help, and the sound was like dead leaves rustling in the wind.

Cat saw them as through the lens of her Leica. There were children with missing limbs, children with shattered faces and children with gaping shrapnel wounds. There were palsied children tied to their beds, lying in their own vomit and excrement, there were children with bellies distended by hunger. And there was no-one to feed them, no-one to look after them.

Clutching her camera, Cat drifted between the beds like a revenant, weeping, crying out for someone to come and clean the wounds, administer morphine, hold cups of water up to parched lips, but no-one came. No-one. Cat was the only grown-up, the only undamaged person in that hellish place, and she could do nothing to help.

Every night the dream ended the same way. She rounded a corner and found herself in a corridor. At the end of the corridor a child stood on legs that looked too fragile to bear his weight, clasping to his chest an empty tin bowl. His eyes were the saddest and wisest Cat had ever seen – wise with awful knowledge, and sad with the horror of experience. *Take my picture*, he commanded her mutely as she approached. *Take my picture and tell the world that evil is commonplace, and atrocity just around the next corner* . . .

And Cat took his picture again and again, wanting to vomit with self-loathing each time she clicked the shutter, struggling to focus through increasingly blurred vision. She would wake with a great howl of anguish and raise her head from a pillow saturated with sweat and tears, then reach for the vodka bottle on her bedside table, hoping that its contents might help her escape for a while.

But Cat knew that, however far she ran, she couldn't hide. Liberty lay some place else entirely, and so far, she didn't know where.

'I hope you don't mind me saying so, but you've some appetite for a skinny chick.' Stuart Seow – her editor – and Cat were having lunch in a restaurant not far from his offices in Kensington High Street. He had been outlining how his publishing house proposed to market Cat's forthcoming book of photographs.

'I've learned to eat my fill when I can get it,' she said, scooping up a last mouthful of pavlova and setting her spoon down. 'You have no idea the kind of food I was expected to eat in Biafra. Congo meat has no blood and no bones.'

'I'm sorry – what do you mean?'

'Have you ever eaten giant snail?'

'Jesus! I'm glad you told me that *after* I'd finished lunch.' Stuart leaned towards her with his elbows on the damask-covered table; steepling his fingers, he regarded her with an expression of intense interest. 'Tell me about Biafra,' he said.

Cat shook her head. 'No. I don't talk about it. The photographs speak for me.'

'I guess that's fair enough. Nobody could argue that your pictures aren't extraordinarily eloquent.' He reached for the heavily embossed menu. 'I'm not sure I've room for cheese,' he said. 'How about you?'

Cat shook her head as the waiter set a cafetière on the table and plunged it. 'Perhaps you'd care for a brandy with your coffee, madam?' he asked.

Stuart gave Cat a look of enquiry.

'A brandy would be good,' she said.

'You can bring us two Rémy Martins VSOP,' instructed Stuart.

'Certainly, Mr Seow,' said the waiter, removing the dessert dishes. The smooth response was accompanied by a nod that was borderline obsequious. Mr Seow was clearly a regular in this very exclusive joint.

Because of the exclusivity, Cat had made an effort with her appearance today. She knew that if any of her colleagues happened to stroll into the restaurant, they'd walk right by her. They'd never seen her in anything except fatigues or camera jackets or dripping wet oilskins.

'It's difficult to imagine you on the battlefield,' Stuart remarked. 'You're so very feminine.'

'That's an illusion,' Cat told him, with a smile. 'I'm tough as old boots, really.' *I'm also a terrific liar*, she could have added.

'Well, if that's what old boots look like, I think they look great.' Stuart winked at her, then held out a pack of Marlboro.

Cat accepted the cigarette. She had no truck with remarks like that, but she'd let it pass. This man was publishing her book, after all, and she wanted it to sell. The more people who sat up and took notice of the horror contained within its pages, the more likely it was that something would be done to put an end to said horror. She was determinedly lighting candle after candle in benighted places.

'It can be useful to be a woman in a war zone,' she said. 'People don't perceive you as much of a threat. I've gained access to areas that my male colleagues would never be allowed to penetrate.'

'I have to say that I don't know how you could have taken some of those pictures without breaking down.'

Cat couldn't tell him the truth: that visiting these places had become more and more difficult for her. She had spent every night of every assignment lying on the ground in a foetal position, wrapped around her Leica, crying the tears she wasn't allowed to cry by day.

Instead she said, 'It can be tough. I'm thinking of taking some time out.'

'I'd say you've earned it. Where will you go?'

'I'd like to go home to Connemara. A friend of mine – an artist – once said that landscapes had become as dear to him as the faces of his loved ones. I'd like to familiarize myself with those faces.'

'Take some photographs?'

'Yes.'

'There's a market there, you know, that's ripe for exploitation.'

'What do you mean?'

'Postcards.'

'Postcards!' Cat almost laughed.

'Sure. Have you ever seen a postcard that would make you want to frame it?'

'No. Well actually, yes. I had an idea of making a collage of the tackiest postcards ever.'

'The kind you get in souvenir shops?'

'Yeah. Someone once sent me a postcard of Preston bus station for a joke.'

'You should give it some thought, seriously. If you're taking time off from war zones, I can't think of anything more relaxing than landscape photography. My wife swears by it.'

'Your wife is nifty with a camera?'

'No. She's a weekend painter. She does little water-colours.' Stuart folded his napkin, and got to his feet. 'Will you excuse me for a moment? I have to pay a visit to the Gents.'

'Sure.'

Cat smiled as she imagined Stuart's little wife in front of her little easel with her little paintbrush working on her little watercolours. And then she thought of what Gervaise had said, about how landscapes could be as eloquent as portraits and how liberating he found spending time *en plein air* . . . Cat was looking for a new kind of freedom. Maybe Stuart had a point.

She took a long, luxurious draw on her cigarette, helped herself to more coffee and leaned back in her chair. She'd consumed a glass of champagne before lunch and half a bottle of very good Bordeaux during the main course, so a hit of coffee was no bad idea – especially since there was brandy on the way. But Cat prided herself on her ability to hold her liquor: she drank with the boys, after all, and when she drank with the boys she didn't drink vintage champagne or château-bottled wine or VSOP brandy. She drank hooch and rotgut and jungle juice when they were dossing in fleapit hotels or bivouacking round feeble campfires, or holing up in officers' messes. All the war correspondents drank, and most of them drank to excess because liquor guaranteed emotional anaesthesia.

The brandy arrived. Cat swirled the topaz-coloured liquid around the glass and raised it to her lips. As she did, she caught sight of a man leaning against a pillar, watching her. The hem of her dress had ridden up high on her thigh, and he was looking at her legs with evident enjoyment. Pointedly, Cat drew her skirt down and looked away – but not before she'd seen a smile curve his lips. She tried to keep her gaze fixed on the street beyond the plate-glass window, but it wasn't easy in view of the reflected distractions that were going on behind her. She could see that the stranger had been joined by a woman, and that the woman was wearing one of those neat little suits with the boxy jackets.

'Geraldine! I didn't know you were lunching here today.' It was Stuart Seow's voice.

'Oh, hello, Stuart. Yes. Nick and I were discussing his next book. You two know each other, of course.'

'Sure we do,' Stuart told the woman. 'Are you rushing off, Geraldine, or would you care to join me and my companion in a post-prandial brandy?' Cat saw Stuart motion towards the table where she sat.

'Not for me, thank you,' said the woman. 'I have a meeting to get to. But perhaps you would, Nick?'

'I'd be glad to. I haven't shot the breeze with you in a while, Stuart. Thanks for lunch, Geraldine.' The man dropped a kiss on the woman's cheek, and she prinked a little before leaving the restaurant with a self-important clacking of heels.

Stuart and the man he'd called Nick approached Cat's table.

'Cat? I'd like to introduce you to Nick Ryder. Nick, this is Cat de Courcy.'

'Pleased to meet you,' said Nick, extending a hand.

'Likewise,' said Cat laconically, mirroring the gesture.

Stuart signalled to the waiter to bring another brandy, and the two men sat down.

'Nick is one of my writers,' explained Stuart. 'He specializes in travel books.'

Of course! She'd heard the name before. Nick Ryder was an author who wrote backpacker guides to countries all over the world, compiling and combining practical information with historical and cultural details. She'd found his guide to Jamaica particularly helpful, but she was damned if she was going to tell him that after the lecherous way he'd eyed her up.

'Where are you off to next?' she asked him politely, stubbing out her cigarette.

'Ireland.'

'Really? Have you been there before?'

'Yes. I have grandparents there.'

'Are you covering the entire island?' Stuart asked him. 'Or just the Republic?'

'I'll be taking in all thirty-two counties.'

'The North is a real hot spot at the moment.'

'Yeah. But you know me. I like to do all my own stunts.'

Stuart laughed.

'Excuse me, Mr Seow.' The waiter had materialized at

Stuart's elbow. 'There's a telephone call for you at reception.'

'Dammit,' said Stuart, getting to his feet. 'D'you mind if I take this? My secretary never disturbs me unless it's urgent.'

'Fire ahead,' said Nick Ryder.

'Sure. Fire ahead!' Cat watched her editor go, then returned her attention to Nick. 'So. You say you have Irish grandparents? Ryder's hardly an Irish name, is it?'

'My mother's side was Irish. My father is from Boston. I was born and reared there.'

'I see.' She slid a cigarette from her pack, and Nick leaned forward to light it. She saw his gaze go to her braless breasts, and she narrowed her eyes and smiled sweetly at him as she exhaled. 'Ireland's a trendy place to visit, then?'

'What makes you say that?'

'Stuart mentioned a "hot spot".'

'He was talking about political unrest.'

'Politics?' Cat held her napkin to her mouth to disguise a tiny yawn. 'What's going on?'

'Well, in the North there's a city called Londonderry where civil rights marches have been banned—'

'Civil rights? I didn't know there were blacks in Ireland.'

'Well . . . there aren't that many—'

'I've heard they're very small, the Irish.'

'Small?'

'Aren't they known as "The Little People"?'

'No, no. That's just the leprechauns.'

Cat giggled. 'You don't mean to tell me you believe in leprechauns?'

'Er – no. Of course I don't.'

'Well, that's a relief! Go on explaining about the blacks and the unrest.'

'There really aren't very many blacks,' he said, with a heroic attempt at a smile.

'So how come there's fighting over civil rights?'

Nick adopted a manner not unlike that of a teacher with a first-grader. 'Well, there's a great schism – a *divide* – between Catholics and Protestants in Ireland. Catholics are discriminated against in all walks of life – jobs, and housing and voting rights.'

'Why's that?'

'It goes way back – to Cromwell's time and beyond.'

'Cromwell? Who was he?'

'You must have heard of Cromwell! Didn't you study history at school?'

'The past doesn't interest me.'

Nick looked stoical. 'Well, Cromwell was responsible for perpetrating . . .' But the expression Cat adopted was so blank that Nick clearly decided to skip the history lesson. 'You see, to vote in local government elections over there, you have to have a house,' he resumed, bringing her up to date. 'And in order to prevent Catholics from getting on the electoral register, the powers that be in Londonderry won't build houses for Catholics.'

'Why not?'

'Because the Housing Commission is comprised of Protestants.'

'How mean!'

'It's more than mean. It has the potential to be incendiary. Um. *Explosive*. There's been rioting recently.'

'Why can't the Catholics build their own houses?'

'Because they have no jobs and no money,' explained Nick, gently.

'You don't need money to buy a house in Ireland!' said

Cat, scornfully. 'I learned a poem in school by a famous Irish poet who said that he was going to build a house of clay and wattles – whatever they are.'

'"I will arise and go now."'

'Oh? You go right ahead and do that. It was very nice to have met you. Goodbye, Mr Ryder.' Cat disguised the smile she felt creeping onto her lips by taking a sip of brandy.

'No – I mean "I will arise and go now, and go to Innisfree." It's the first line of the poem you mentioned – "The Lake Isle of Innisfree", by Yeats.'

'Oh, yeah.' Cat made a dismissive sound. 'He must have been a *complete* weirdo.'

'What makes you say that?'

'Well, didn't he want to go and live on an island all by himself and eat nothing except beans and honey? What person in their right mind would want to do that? Beans and honey – yeuch! Worse than giant snail.' She took another dainty sip of brandy and looked pensive. 'Although – perhaps it's *not* such a bad idea after all. I know of another poem that was written along similar lines.'

'Oh? Which one's that?'

'I eat my peas with honey,' pronounced Cat. 'I've done it all my life. It makes the peas taste funny, but it keeps them on the knife.'

'Cat?' Stuart was back. 'I'm really sorry, but I have to get back to the office. Something urgent's come up.'

'Oh, that's all right, Stuart. Nick and I are enjoying a lovely chat.'

'Of course. You've got a lot in common.'

'We have?' Nick looked slightly aghast.

'For sure. You both have jobs that allow you to travel the world.'

Cat kept schtum, her catlike smile still in place.

Stuart looked from Nick to Cat and back again. 'You didn't know that Cat's a photographer? She's had pictures published in all the important periodicals.'

'Fashion pictures?'

'No,' said Stuart, looking bemused. 'Cat doesn't shoot fashion. She shoots war zones.'

'Excuse me,' said Cat sweetly, getting to her feet and reaching for her purse. 'I just *have* to visit the little girls' room – I need to powder my nose and repair my lipstick. Please don't allow me to keep you. And thanks so much for lunch, Stuart.' Cat picked up her duffel bag and dropped a kiss on her editor's cheek. 'It sure beat feasting on giant snail.'

In the Ladies, Cat divested herself of her frock and heels and slid into motorbike leathers and boots. On her way out of the restaurant she blew a kiss at Nick Ryder, who was still sitting over his brandy, and laughed at his astonished expression. Outside, parked on the footpath next to the window, was a Kawasaki 250. Slinging her leg over the machine, Cat gunned the engine and took off down Kensington High Street, still laughing.

CHAPTER FORTY-FOUR

LISA

CAP D'ANTIBES – 1969

Dearest Cat,

I think of you often. I'm posting this letter to Connemara rather than London because Róisín tells me that you are planning a visit there, but goodness knows when you will receive it. You have always reminded me of a will-o'-the-wisp: what's the Irish word for it? – you said it once. A pooka?

A will-o'-the-wisp sounds so fey, doesn't it, when I know your life is anything but. How many years now have you been covering war zones? It's not the most suitable job for a woman, but then, what is? A housewife? A mother? That was, once upon a time, all that women had to look forward to in life. I was very lucky to have squeezed in a career before I settled down with Raoul – even though life in Hollywood was tough in its own way, and very different to the life you have chosen. In those days everybody thought that Hollywood was the epitome of glamour: what a joke! I have often wondered if I should pen an autobiography, tell the truth and shame the devil.

I rarely go near Antibes now, or Cannes – they really have become such preposterous places. I never dreamed when I escaped here from LA that its culture would come creeping all the way across the Atlantic like a poisonous miasma. Maybe there are no good places left in the world to live. Although Róisín tells me that 'peace comes dropping slow' in Connemara still, like in the Yeats poem.

Anyway, I just wanted you to know that I am thinking of you, and would love to see you any time you feel like it. There are riots in Paris – perhaps you'll be covering those? How strange a thing, to be luring a young woman to Paris with promises of riots rather than romance and fashion! But if you come, you could always head down here to the Cap afterwards for a breather.

Raoul sends his love, as do Orlando and Gervaise.

Your loving aunt, Lisa

That night Lisa had the dream again, of Connemara and the lake shore and the laughing sprite who was Cat. She was wearing around her neck the little jade talisman Lisa had given her, and she was moving in slow motion down a purple hillside towards Lisa, seeming to take for ever. And then all of a sudden Cat was in her arms, and her voice was in her ear, and she was saying, 'Anubis will help you, Mum. You mustn't be afraid.'

'I'm not afraid,' Lisa told her, kissing Cat's face; her forehead and her eyes and her nose and her chin. 'Thanks to you, I'm not afraid. You've passed your fearlessness on, from daughter to mother.'

And then Lisa woke with the kisses still on her lips, and the scent of her daughter on her skin.

She sat up in bed; beside her, Raoul was still asleep. The clock told her that it was four in the morning; she knew she would not go back to sleep. She'd go for a walk on the beach, and think about the day ahead. It would be one of what Lisa called her 'real life' days. Every so often she picked a date in her diary to do the maintenance stuff she most hated – dentist, hairdresser, banking, marketing, whatever – fitting in as many appointments as possible before treating herself to a leisurely lunch.

She threw a coat over her nightdress and went out onto the terrace. The sun had not yet risen, but there was enough residual moonlight for her to see her way down to the water's edge and walk the patterns traced by the tide. At the end of the beach she stopped and looked back. Her footprints were the only ones glimmering on the wet sand, and she knew the sea would come in again later that day and wash them clean away. How many thousands of foot-prints had come and gone in the ebb and flow? Who would walk there next? Lisa gave a shiver as a goose trod on her grave.

Turning, she placed a bare foot on to the last print she had last made, and followed her tracks back home.

Along with the handful of appointments she had lined up, shopping for a new outfit was on Lisa's agenda: Gervaise was to be honoured soon with a retrospective at a chic gallery on the Croisette. As she strolled along the boulevards and in and out of the exclusive boutiques, she could not resist the fripperies that clamoured for her atten-tion. How she would love to be young again! To wear flirty skirts and fringed silk gilets and sheer chiffon blouses and tiny bandeau bikinis and feathers in her hair! As she handed over a silly amount of money for a velvet purse, the vendeuse enquired, 'Is it for a present, Madame?' and Lisa said, 'Yes. It's for my daughter.'

'Would you like me to show you something else? We've just taken delivery this morning of a brand new range of

Missoni stripes!' The vendeuse spoke with barely disguised glee, and Lisa – feeling excited as a teenager herself – said, 'Yes, I would. Thank you.'

The Missoni stripes were just the beginning. Lisa emerged from the shop with three glossy bags full of packages wrapped in tissue and tied with ribbons and sprinkled with dried lavender.

After her spree she had lunch in one of the waterfront cafés, and treated herself to crab mayonnaise, a chilled glass of Sancerre and a copy of British *Vogue*, scanning the pages with anxious eyes to make sure she'd bought the right things. She was amused to see that the retro look was in fashion, that tiered silk dresses were featured in the forefront of Liberty's new season's trend, and that their prints were now collectors' items. She wondered what design archivists would make of the fabulous gowns stashed away in the boudoir in the Villa Perdita.

She was pleased with her own look today, and guessed it had something to do with the fact that Raoul had made love to her this morning after breakfast. She had found herself running late as a result, and had flung on faded blue jeans and a kaftan top before quitting the house, leaving her hair loose and managing only a desultory make-up job. But she must have done something right, because on her way past the Villa Perdita with the soft-top down, Gervaise, out for a morning stroll had hailed her to tell her she looked *magnifique*, more desirable even than Brigitte Bardot.

Draining her espresso, Lisa gathered up her shopping bags and set off for her last 'real life' appointment of the day. On her way, she stopped by the fish market. She'd treat Raoul to sardines tonight, grilled with olive oil and lemon juice, and parsley fresh from the garden. Perhaps they could share a bottle of champagne? It wasn't a special occasion, but it was good sometimes to celebrate the fact that life was so very sweet.

CHAPTER FORTY-FIVE

CAT

CONNEMARA – 1969

The click and whirr of Cat's camera was the only sound in the hushed wilderness that was Connemara. She had made the long journey by ferry and road from London a week ago, having won a commission to photograph a series of landscapes for an Irish postcard publishing company.

The distributors had finally come round to Cat's proposal of a more tasteful take on the traditional image of seaside towns and nondescript piers and kids posing with donkeys, that had been peddled to tourists in Ireland for years. Amongst the mountains on the doorstep of the little town of Clifden there were no red-haired children or smiling colleens or windburnt old men brandishing shillelaghs to distract you from the beauty of the landscape. Here you could walk for miles without coming across another living soul. In Connemara, you might startle a hare or a pine marten or a pheasant, but human beings were rarely seen.

So that was why Cat was more than a little surprised to see a woman sitting by the edge of one of the myriad lakes that dotted the landscape, skimming stones across the black water. The sudden call of a kestrel made her look up and push her hair back from her face, and as she did, her eyes met Cat's. It was Lisa.

'Hi,' she called. 'Róisín told me I'd find you here.'

'Lisa! Hi!' called back Cat. 'What an amazing surprise!' Laughing, she made her way down through the dense heather, until she drew level with her aunt and pulled her into a tight embrace. 'What are you doing here?'

'I thought it was about time I revisited Connemara,' said Lisa. 'And Róisín told me where exactly I'd find you.'

And suddenly her aunt did an extraordinary thing. Her hands flew to her mouth, and then she hunkered down on the ground and started to cry.

'What is it?' asked Cat, alarmed.

But Lisa didn't answer; she simply continued to sob. At a loss how to respond, Cat got to her knees and began to stroke Lisa's hair. It seemed to be the right thing to do, because gradually the sobbing subsided.

'Has something happened? Something awful?' Cat asked.

'No,' said Lisa, pulling a handkerchief from a pocket in her shoulder bag. 'No. I'm just being utterly silly and sentimental. I used to holiday here, and they were such happy, happy times. How lucky you were, to grow up surrounded by all this beauty.'

Lisa blew her nose and wiped her cheeks, and then she slid a pair of sunglasses over her eyes, masking her expression.

'Let me look at you!' she said. 'Oh, how lovely you are, my little Cat!'

Cat didn't think she was looking particularly lovely today. Up since dawn, anxious to get the early morning sunlight slanting across the mountain slopes and the rising mist on the lakes, she hadn't bothered even to take a shower. As for her clothes: stout walking boots teamed with shorts, T-shirt, camera jacket and a bandana were hardly the last word in style.

'When did you arrive?' she asked Lisa.

'I got to Clifden around midday.'

'And how did you get out here to the back of beyond?'

'I have a little hire car.'

'Is Raoul with you?' asked Cat.

'No. I came alone. He couldn't take time off.'

'Shame!'

'Don't worry – I have lots of photographs and home movies to bore you with.'

'Home movies I would love to see! Have you had lunch?'

'Yes. You?'

'I made myself a sandwich before I came out. But I'm always starving after a day spent taking photographs. It's the fresh air.'

'Maybe I could buy you dinner tonight? I'm staying at Ballynahinch Castle.'

Cat looked dubious. Ballynahinch Castle was quite posh, and she had absolutely nothing to wear. 'Aren't you staying in Clifden with us?'

'No. I didn't want to intrude – I know you're a little strapped for space. But I thought it might be nice if you could join me in the hotel for a couple of nights, as a treat. I booked two rooms.'

'That's really kind of you, Aunt Lisa—'

'Oh, please stop calling me "aunt"! You know I hate it! It makes me feel like such an old frump.'

Cat smiled. 'The thing is, Lisa, I don't have anything to

wear to a swanky hotel; I don't think they'd allow me into the dining room. It's the kind of joint where men have to wear a tie, isn't it?'

'I guess – I guess it is.'

For a horrible moment, Cat thought that Lisa was going to cry again, and she knew she really wouldn't be able to handle it.

'But, wait! I have an idea,' she said. 'I have a friend who has a cottage to rent. Would you fancy that? It's a really nice little one, with half-doors and an inglenook and all that jazz. He lets it out to holidaymakers, and since the season's hardly started, we might be in luck. I'll call in to him on the way home, shall I?'

Not even the dark lenses of her sunglasses could conceal the look of relief on Lisa's face.

'Oh!' she said. 'I should love that!'

The cottage was as picture postcard perfect as Cat had remembered. While Lisa drove back to her hotel in her hire car to fetch her luggage, Cat did some grocery shopping, lit a fire and made up the beds, putting hot-water bottles in for good measure. Then she opened a bottle of wine to let it breathe, picked some sea pinks and put them in a jug beside Lisa's bed, and set about making supper. She wasn't much of a cook, but she could manage a spaghetti bolognese, and she sensed that Lisa needed comfort food.

When she'd told her mam that she was going to spend three days with 'Aunt' Lisa, Róisín had evinced no surprise. 'I think that's a lovely idea,' she said. 'After all she has done for you.'

Lisa's luggage, when she arrived, consisted of a portmanteau, a rather elderly Vuitton make-up case, and a glossy tote bag full of beautifully gift-wrapped packages.

'These are for you,' she told Cat, holding out the bag tentatively. 'I hope you like them. I asked the salesgirl's advice.'

Cat took from the tote bag pretty package after pretty package containing items of adornment. There were delicate filigree earrings, a set of three slender bangles in different shades of gold, a pair of Grecian-style sandals and a tasselled belt in soft blue suede. There was a pair of aviator glasses, a candy-striped waistcoat, hosiery in dozens of colours, and yards and yards of floaty silk scarves, all wrapped in tissue paper. The *pièce de résistance* was a pretty floral-patterned dress in pale chiffon. A row of tiny buttons ran from the demurely high neck to around four inches above the hem, which was modishly short. The sleeves were fluted, with scalloped edges.

'Well, wow!' exclaimed Cat. 'It'll mean my flatmate'll want to borrow from me, for a change! I'm always borrowing from her.' The dress she had worn to lunch with Stuart, the one that had garnered a tacit thumbs-up from Nick Ryder, had belonged to her flatmate.

'I'm glad you like them,' said Lisa. 'I know you don't take much interest in fashion, but I've always been a complete sucker for clothes.'

'This stuff is perfect to wear to posh joints. It's what I'd choose for myself if I ever bothered to set foot in a boutique. Maybe we should go to Ballynahinch after all? Now that I've something appropriate to wear.'

'No, no! This place is much more special,' Lisa protested. 'How clever of you to suggest it.'

Actually, Cat thought, nowhere was more special than Ballynahinch Castle, but then she guessed that Lisa had never stayed in a quaint Irish cottage before. She smoothed the skirt of the chiffon dress, and a cuticle snagged on the fabric. Maybe she should think about having a manicure? She'd never had one: her nails were always ruined from scrambling up rock faces and through sand dunes and jungly thickets.

Lisa moved to the rear window of the cottage. It afforded a glorious view of the coast: rugged rocks tumbling down to a small, deserted pink coral beach, washed by aquamarine waves. Coarse tufty grass grew between the rocks, kept short and springy by the sheep that roamed wherever they liked, and by the wild Connemara ponies that grazed there.

'Uh-oh. Bad weather's coming,' Cat told Lisa. 'Look over there, to the west.'

The sky on the horizon was pewter, with fierce diagonal stripes indicating rain on the wind.

'The forecast isn't great for the next few days,' continued Cat. 'They say about Ireland that you can experience all four seasons in one day, but it looks like we're in for a really nasty spell.'

'I don't mind,' said Lisa with a smile. 'I love the sound of rain on the roof.'

And that's exactly what they got. For three days and nights the rain drummed down on the corrugated iron roof of the cottage. There wasn't a hope of an excursion or a walk or a swim, and there were certainly no photo opportunities for Cat. But Lisa didn't seem to mind. Every morning she made breakfast – coffee and toast and porridge – while Cat cleaned and reset the fire; and then they'd read or play Scrabble or talk: and while Cat was fascinated to hear all about Lisa's former career in

Hollywood, Lisa seemed much more interested in hearing all about Cat's childhood in Connemara and her new career in London.

'Have you a boyfriend?' Lisa asked her.

'No-one special, right now. I did have a rather tempestuous fling with someone whose name I'd rather not mention.'

'Why?'

'He has a bad boy reputation.'

'I'm intrigued. Go on! Who?'

Cat took some Scrabble tiles from the board and spelled out a name.

'Oh, my!' said Lisa, all aflutter. 'He *is* a bad boy!'

'But so must be a lot of the people you met in those golden days of Hollywood. Did you ever meet Clark Gable?'

'I saw him at a party once. But at those kinds of parties you never really talked to anyone. It was all about show, and making contacts. My only real friend there was the actor, Sabu.'

'I've never heard of him.'

'He died, suddenly, of a heart attack, about five years ago.'

'I'm sorry.'

'Lots of people I knew then are dead now.'

A silence fell.

'I know!' exclaimed Cat, anxious that no melancholy mood take hold. 'Let's make hot chocolate and watch those home movies you told me about.'

'But we've no screen.'

'We can improvise with a sheet. I'll organize it. You make the chocolate.'

Cat set up the home cinema with a starched linen sheet, a clothes line and some pegs. Lisa lobbed more turf on the fire, heated the milk and served hot chocolate. And then 'Ta-dah!' carolled Cat, setting the projector rolling. 'It's movie time!'

They sat through nearly an hour of grainy footage, most of which had been filmed in the garden of the Boat House, and on the adjacent beach. Cat watched Lisa swimming with Raoul, picnicking on the beach, and lounging in a hammock. She watched a birthday party with friends around a long trestle table on the terrace: it featured a cake with candles, and Raoul, with an arm around Lisa's shoulders, curling a strand of her hair around a finger and urging her to blow them out and make a wish. The expression on Lisa's face when she raised it to Raoul's for a kiss told Cat exactly what she was wishing for: complete happiness.

And yet, she already seemed to have it. Every inch of footage of the film showed a couple no longer young, but still quite rapturously in love. The final shot showed Raoul at his drawing board, looking saturnine and handsome and sunburnt, sublimely unaware that he was being filmed. Then, realizing that the camera was on him, he turned, laughing, and mouthed into the lens, over and over: 'I love you! I love you!'

Cat felt her eyes blur with tears. She looked over at Lisa, who was curled up on the couch; but she was fast asleep. The sound of the reel rotating came to an abrupt end. Cat fetched a blanket from the bedroom and laid it around Lisa's sleeping form. Then she pushed the older woman's hair back from her face, and tucked her in. 'Night, night; sleep tight,' she whispered, kissing her on the forehead.

She removed the reel from the projector, set the fireguard on the hearth, and turned the lamps off.

As she crept from the room, she missed Lisa's dreamy smile, and her murmured response: 'Sleep tight, my beautiful, beautiful girl . . .'

The next day, Lisa departed for France. Cat took a picture of her standing on the steps up to the aeroplane, laughing, flamboyantly blowing a goodbye kiss. Cat wore her chiffon frock, the filigree earrings, and – because she'd been chasing rainbows to photograph for her publishers earlier – her walking boots. The camera she used to snap Lisa was – for old times' sake – the Box Brownie that her aunt had sent her for her fourteenth birthday.

CHAPTER FORTY-SIX

CAT

IRELAND 1969

Any time she visited her parents in Connemara, Cat made a point of touring the rest of the country randomly on her motorbike, seeking out material for photographs. Since she had never been north of the border, she decided to follow the coastline around the wild beauty of the Inishowen peninsula, and then along the Foyle estuary to the troubled city of Londonderry.

There her camera granted her access to the brave new world of the Bogside, a neighbourhood not much bigger than a football pitch, which had just proclaimed itself a free state and a no-go area for the police.

'Are you from the paper, love?' A middle-aged woman dandling a baby on her hip was standing outside one of the mean little terraced houses, eyeing her camera.

'I've had a few pictures published, yeah.'

'You're very young-looking to be such a big gun.'

'I'm twenty-six.'

'Twenty-six? No way! Sure, that's the age I am.'

Cat tried not to look shocked. The woman looked at least twenty years older; worn out. She was wearing a miniskirt and plastic sandals, and her legs were bare and mottled with cold. She took a deep suck on the butt she was smoking, then tossed it into the gutter.

'Would ye ever take a photograph? Of me and the new babby? He's never had his picture taken before.'

'I'd be glad to. Is it your first baby?'

The woman gave a bark of laughter that turned into a paroxysm of coughing. 'I've a clatter of them. Five, and another on the way. Will this picture get in the paper?'

'If it's any good.' Cat removed the lens cap from her Leica. 'Would you mind if it did?'

'Why would I mind? Sure everyone wants to get their picture in the paper. Put my name in, too. It's Valerie McDevitt.'

Cat felt like kicking herself. For this woman, having her picture published would constitute an honour, even though her she was malnourished and ragged and missing some teeth. It would be her fifteen minutes of fame.

She checked the light reading on her meter while Valerie readied herself for her portrait.

'Here, babby,' she said, tickling the baby under its arms. 'Don't be afraid of the camera. Give it a big smile.'

The child laughed – its grubby face gleeful suddenly – and Cat laughed too, because the only alternative was to cry, and she had learned that you couldn't focus through tears.

She took a couple of dozen shots, and had just rehoused her camera when an almighty banging and clattering arose. Further along the street, a group of women had come out of their houses and were pounding bin-lids on the pavements and shouting slogans in what was clearly a rallying cry.

'Take the wean, Jacinta!' shouted Valerie, thrusting the baby into the arms of a passing child. 'The fuckin' peelers are tryin' it on again!'

A photo opportunity! As Valerie hurtled down the street, Cat segued directly into Mohammed Ali mode – dancing sideways on the balls of her feet, floating like a butterfly, stinging like a bee, moving to the rhythm of the clicking of her camera and the atavistic tattoo of metal on concrete – until she ran out of film.

Reluctantly she stowed the camera back in its bag and retreated across the border of the tiny new Republic of Bogside without saying goodbye. She'd almost be afraid to say goodbye, for Valerie now had the appearance of a woman possessed by some tribal buzz as she yelled abuse at the police and beat a bin-lid with the heel of her hand. Cat had just started off in the direction of her Kawasaki when she became aware that she was being observed by somebody on the other side of the street.

It was a man – a damn handsome man – and he was photographing her. Pissed, Cat gave him the V-sign. He put the lens cap back on his camera, and, smiling, gave her one right back.

It was Nick Ryder.

In the fuggy bar of the City Hotel, where the international press corps was billeted, Cat chain-smoked her way through half a dozen Marlboros. She'd been badly shaken by the rage that had erupted in the Bogside. For an hour or so she fulminated about the Brits and their bullying tactics, and when she calmed down, Nick said: 'You're way more complex than I imagined from our first inauspicious meeting. I took you for a bimbo.'

'And I took you for a lech.'

'It was hard not to ogle you. You were wearing a rather fetching little number, as I recall.'

'I borrowed it from my flatmate.'

'She has excellent taste. It suited you.'

'I don't enjoy dressing up. I was a tomboy when I was at school.'

'Where were you at school?'

'Kylemore Abbey, in Connemara.'

'I've heard of that place. It's on my list of locations to cover: it's spectacularly beautiful, isn't it?'

'Yes. I was very lucky to be educated there: it's where I took my first photographs.'

Nick hooked his elbow over the back of the banquette. 'Tell me more,' he said.

Cat shook her head. 'No. People only want to know about the pillow fights and the best friends in gymslips and the sadistic nuns.'

'*Were* there pillow fights?'

Cat returned his smile. 'Of course there were.'

'Have you any photographs?'

'You're some chancer.' She went to take a sip of her drink, then paused and looked at him over the rim of her glass. 'If you're heading west, come with me and I'll show you around. I know all of Connemara's secret places.' She spoke the words in an exaggerated, lilting brogue.

'I can still hardly believe you're Irish.'

'Kylemore is an international school; I have friends from all over the world from there, and all of them speak posh.'

'So you're well travelled?'

'Yep. I've read some of your guidebooks, by the way. They're not bad.'

'Thanks. After I met you, I got hold of some of your photographs. They're not bad, either.'

'Maybe we should collaborate?'

'That's not unthinkable.'

'How long will you stay in Connemara?'

'As long as it takes.'

Cat gave him a level look. Then her lips curved in a smile as she saw Nick's eyes go to her mouth.

'Do you mind if I ask you a personal question?' he said.

'Fire ahead.'

'You went to a convent school?'

'What of it?'

'You know what they say about good Catholic girls.'

Cat gave him a look of pure disdain. 'I'm not a Catholic. And as for "good", I'm with Mae West on that one.'

'What did Mae West say?'

'She said "When I'm good, I'm very, very good. But . . ."'

'But?'

'"When I'm bad, I'm better",' said Cat.

They headed west, Cat on her motorbike, Nick in his Citroën DS – by which Cat could not but be more than a little impressed.

'How could you afford such a classy car?' she asked him.

'I could never afford it,' he told her. 'I won it in a game of poker.'

Having arranged to meet up for something to eat, they stopped off in a hotel just off the Clifden road, a beautiful place which overlooked the Atlantic and was surrounded by acres of woodland.

'What time are your parents expecting you?' Nick asked.

'They aren't. I guess I'd better phone them and ask them to make up a spare room.'

'Don't.'

'You mean you don't want a bed to sleep in tonight?'

'Sure. But not in your parents' house.'

'Why not?'

'Because I want to sleep with you, and it would be a very disrespectful thing to do under their roof. I've booked us a room here.'

'What makes you think I want to sleep with you?'

'Because something tells me you're dying to find out if, like you, I'm better when I'm bad.'

He was.

Cat and Nick spent a magical week travelling through Connemara with the roof of his convertible down. Basing themselves in the Capital of Connemara (population five hundred and something) they visited Kylemore, where Cat introduced him to the nuns and the goats and showed him the rec room, where a crowd of giggling school girls blushed and fluttered. They motored by the coast along the Sky Road – one of the most beautiful drives in Ireland, and so-called because the road rises to meet the sky. They walked along deserted beaches and boreens, and listened to fiddle music over pints of Guinness in quirky little pubs. They took a curragh out to an island in Bertraghboy Bay and skinny-dipped. And by the end of the week, Nick and Cat had, to her infinite surprise, fallen in love.

*   *   *

Nick had made an appointment to meet a bodhrán maker in the sleepy village of Roundstone, about fifteen miles from Clifden.

'Drive carefully in that car of yours, Nick,' Róisín told him. 'The bog road is riddled with potholes.'

'Maybe you should take the Kawasaki, instead,' suggested Cat.

'No,' he said, turning on the ignition and making the engine purr. 'I like the way the women eye me when the soft top's down.'

'Get away with you now!' Róisín scolded him.

When he had gone, Róisín closed the front door, turned to Cat, and said, 'It's time we had a chat. Come into the kitchen and I'll pour us some tea.'

In the kitchen, Cat sat down at the table, feeling jittery. Róisín's 'chats' were usually anything but chatty.

'Is it about Nick?' she asked. 'Don't you like him? I'm sorry – maybe he's outstayed his welcome. I didn't think we'd be here for more than a few days.'

'It's not about Nick,' said Róisín. 'He's a fine fellow – not a bother on him. It's about your aunt Lisa. I kept the headline from you – I didn't want to spoil your lovely holiday with your boyfriend.'

'What headline?'

Róisín went to the dresser and took a newspaper from a drawer. On the front page, Cat read the following words: 'FORMER FILM STAR DIES.'

She looked at her mother in disbelief. 'Not Aunt Lisa?' she said.

'Yes.'

'What happened?'

'She had cancer: it was terminal.'

'She told you this? When?'

'In a letter. She wrote it in advance and asked her sister-in-law to post it before the news hit the headlines.'

Cat's hand went automatically to the charm Lisa had given her, which she wore on a chain around her neck. 'May I see it?' she asked.

'Yes. But if you read this letter, Cat, you're going to learn something about yourself – something that both Lisa and I decided you shouldn't know until after her death.'

'What?'

'Do you want me to show you the letter?'

There was a pause. Then: 'Yes, I do,' said Cat.

'I'd better forewarn you of its contents, so.'

'Go ahead.'

Róisín set the teapot and the milk jug on the table, and poured. Then she took a deep breath and told Cat the story of how things had transpired from the moment that Lisa had arrived on the doorstep of the house in Clifden, clad in Hollywood casuals and bearing extravagant wartime gifts, to the arrangement that had been set up between the two cousins after Cat's birth. And all the while Cat kept casting her mind back to the time she'd spent in the cottage overlooking the beach, the three days when she and Lisa had played Scrabble and talked and talked and drunk wine and hot chocolate and watched home movies together, and how any time she'd looked round, Lisa's eyes had been on her, transfixed. She was silent for many moments. Then: 'May I see the letter now?' she asked.

Róisín took it from the envelope and handed it to her, and Cat steeled herself for the tears she knew would come.

Dear Róisín,

This letter is difficult to write because it will be the last you will ever receive from me. I have asked my sister-in-law Hélène to post it as soon as what is going to happen, happens, because I do not want you to get a shock when the news hits the headlines, as it is sure to. These words will be upsetting for you to read, so be brave.

Some time ago I was diagnosed with breast cancer. It is of an invasive kind, and has, unfortunately metastasized. It is, therefore, terminal. I may have less than six months left to live. That is why I visited Connemara last spring – I'm sorry for arriving unannounced. It was so good to see you again!

As for my beautiful Cat, I will leave it up to you to tell her of her true parentage, or not. I have sent a package to you for her, containing letters that belonged to her grandmother. If you do not wish her to know that I was her birth mother, you may of course destroy them. But please allow her to keep the enclosed ring: it is a very pretty one that Scotch gave my mother on their engagement.

Also enclosed is a book that Gervaise told me had been sent to the Villa Perdita, addressed to my mother, Jessie. I found it in the library there, and going by the inscription, I thought that it might be a gift to her from my father. Pure speculation, of course, based on little more than the fact that Raguenez in Finistère – which they visited on honeymoon – is known as 'Little Tahiti'. Still, I love it for the illustrations, which I think may be by him.

Most importantly of all, I have enclosed a certificate of authentication and provenance that pertains to a painting Jessie left me. It is an extremely valuable Picasso that currently hangs on the stairwell in Gervaise Lantier's house. This document certifies that I am the legal owner of the work, and

I want Cat to have it. I have not had the painting shipped over because that could lead to unseemly wrangles between Cat and Ghislaine – Gervaise's legitimate daughter from a previous marriage. French bureaucracy is always so tangled in red tape. But once Cat has all the relevant papers, it will make things easier.

When she comes to pick it up, she can help herself to anything from my wardrobe that she fancies: there are original pieces by Chanel that belonged to my mother as well as some fantastic couture gowns from my Hollywood years that she could sell. They are all stored in my mother's room in the Villa Perdita above the Boat House.

Unfortunately, I have little in the way of valuable jewellery to bequeath – the little sapphire is not worth a great deal – but the Picasso will leave Cat very comfortably off. I have also made provision for you in my will.

I hope I have said everything I needed to say. I could have said so much more – I could have written pages and pages and pages! But now, of course, I've run out of time. It's been a funny old life.

Tell Cat I love her. I met her in my dreams before I met her in reality, you know, and loved her then. I've loved her since the day she was born, and carried her in my heart everywhere in the world I went; but I couldn't have entrusted her to parents more wonderful than you and Dónal. Thank you for rearing a beautiful daughter.

Lisa

CHAPTER FORTY-SEVEN

IRELAND 1969

When Nick came back from Roundstone, he brought with him a heap of prawns for supper, still in their shells. 'Prawns for dinner tonight – fresh off the boat!' he announced, with satisfaction.

'You're a thoughtful creature,' Róisín told him, 'but once those are peeled you'll be lucky if there's enough for two.'

'You and Daddy go off down to Foyle's Hotel,' said Cat with alacrity. 'My treat. Nick and I'll stay in and have the prawns.'

Róisín took the hint. After she'd given Nick instructions on how to shell and devein the shellfish – 'And don't over-cook them!' – she and Dónal got into their Sunday best and left Nick and Cat together in the kitchen.

'I have some news,' Cat said, as Nick threw the prawns into a colander.

'Oh? What's up?'

'You know the aunt I told you about? The one who used to be a film star?'

'Lisa somebody?'

'Yeah. Well, it turns out that she was actually my mother.'

Nick smiled. 'Nothing much surprises me about you,' he said.

'She's dead.'

Nick crossed the kitchen floor and, hunkering down, took Cat's hand in his. 'Oh, Christ, sweetheart! I'm so sorry.'

'Yeah. It was all a bit shocking earlier, when Mam told me. She – Lisa – wrote a letter, saying how much she loved me.' She gave him an apologetic smile. 'That's why my face is so blubbery – I'm all cried out.'

'I didn't notice anything blubbery about your face. You look ravishing,' said Nick, loyally.

'Stop stalling and get on with my dinner,' commanded Cat, scared that she might cry again.

Nick jumped to it. 'How did you find out?' he asked.

She told him the story while he peeled the prawns.

'A *Picasso*?' he said, when she'd finished. 'What are you going to do about staking your claim to it?'

Cat shrugged. 'I don't know. It's there in Antibes waiting for me.'

'If it belonged to your grandmother there might be something about it in her letters.'

'We'll read them after dinner, shall we?' ·

'Sure.'

While Nick decapitated the prawns, Cat had a look at the book by Patrick Lawless that had arrived in the package from Lisa.

'Maybe you should think about getting a gig in Tahiti,' she said, leafing through the pages.

'Could do,' said Nick. 'I've covered nearly all of Europe now.'

'Listen – here's a description: "in the morning all the beauty and youth of the island forgather in the marketplace to purchase their daily needs: mangoes, avocados, limes, guavas, melons, and passion fruit in profusion, pyramids of bread-fruit, baskets of crayfish and all the gossip of the day"'.

'Their *daily* needs?' remarked Nick. 'Imagine having to shell basketfuls of these buggers every day.'

There were stories in the book of picnics by lagoons with whole roast suckling pigs and wine fermented from oranges, and hula dancers in grass skirts, of spear-fishing expeditions and encounters with sharks and love affairs with native girls. There were descriptions, too, of the other refugees from real life who'd wound up on the island, blow-ins from all over the world. One Frenchman had devised rudimentary scuba from a clothes peg and a length of hosepipe; a Chinaman was full of stories about Gauguin that had been passed on to him by the local barber; an Englishman had made a fortune dealing in pearls. They'd all been given nicknames by the native Tahitians: Mr Lawless was 'Big Fella' on account of his great stature; a man living by a signpost became 'Six Kilometre Brown'; a white man with a bad case of sunburn became known as 'Blackie White'; and one individual, a Scottish painter, was named 'Sandyman' from the French *sans main*, on account of his missing hand.

'You've *got* to get to Tahiti,' Cat said, as Nick set plates piled with prawns in front of them. 'It sounds like heaven on earth.'

'If I go I might never come back,' said Nick. 'Why don't you come with me?'

She closed the book with a smile. 'Thanks kindly for the invitation, mister. I just might take you up on that.'

After supper, Cat and Nick took themselves off to the front

parlour to read through Jessie's letters. Cat was wearing the cabochon sapphire that Lisa had said was 'not worth a great deal', but which was to Cat's mind invaluable.

When they finished, Cat looked at Nick with perplexed eyes. 'They sound like such a lovely couple, Scotch and Jessie.' She picked up the last of the letters, the one that Jessie had written in pencil on the beach at Finistère. 'Listen to this. "We are as fit as fiddles, and Scotch is so brimming over with energy and good health that he can't leave me in peace for two seconds."'

'They must have had one hell of a honeymoon.'

'I guess they were the original backpackers. That was a tough itinerary – especially post-war. Imagine ending up in Finistère! You know what it means, in French?'

'I do. It means the end of the earth.'

As their eyes met, Cat knew that they were each thinking the same thought.

'Well . . . ?' said Nick.

'We'll do it, shall we?' said Cat, her eyes shining. 'Follow in their footsteps?'

'Except we'll take the Citroën.'

Sliding down from the sofa, Cat joined Nick on the floor. She reached for her satchel, and produced pen and notebook. 'Let's start on an itinerary. Tell me where they stayed.'

Nick picked up a letter at random. 'In Florence they stayed at the Pensione Balestri. I know that guesthouse! It's still there – it overlooks the Ponte Vecchio.'

'We'll stay in that very same place then, shall we? We'll trace their journey as faithfully as we can. Tell me more places.'

'Um. Paris, rue du Sommerard, number 15; Florence,

458

Albergo Romaqua; Chambéry, Hôtel Central; Pont-Aven, Hôtel Simonet; Siena, The Bandini Palace – Posh! This is going to be some road trip. Don't forget to put Antibes on there.'

'They didn't go to Antibes.'

'No. But you're going to want to visit your mother's grave.'

'Oh, God. Yes, I am.'

'And you're going to want to lay claim to that Picasso.'

'I'd forgotten about the Picasso.'

Nick laughed. 'You are some blasé broad!'

'I'm not so blasé, really. I can't wait to get started. When'll we go?'

'When I'm done covering Ireland, I guess.' Nick raised an eyebrow at her. 'I hope you travel light. The chick who came on my last trip practically needed a sherpa to carry all her luggage.'

Cat didn't want to hear about the last chick. She was about to retaliate with a random story of her own about her bad boy, but something told her Nick wouldn't be impressed.

He was distracted, anyway, perusing one of the letters. 'He had exquisite copperplate handwriting, your grandfather,' he observed.

'How do you know?'

'This PS was written by him,' he said. 'Listen:

"Dear Pawpey,
Have just made Jessie bubble with laughter by asking her how I should address my father-in-law! It was sporting—"

Sporting! Cool word!

459

"—it was sporting of you to help us with the wherewithall to get to Venice, especially as I think myself to be the most hopeless person at money matters. The past fortnight in the hill villages could not be beaten, and on the whole life seems to be impossibly good. We were befriended by a Greek aristocrat who has adopted one of the sweetest kids I've seen in my life. He has great plans of proposing me to carry out some work in Corfu under the Greek government."

Then there's stuff about his new niece, blah blah blah. The writing is meticulous – look. It's amazing to think that he was an amputee.'

Cat took the proffered letter and stared at it.

'And an artist, to boot,' continued Nick. 'Hey! Maybe that's where he ended up – working for the Greek government. Cat? Do you think he might have ended up in Corfu? Are you even listening, Cat?'

'Yes, I'm listening,' said Cat. 'And I don't think he ended up in Corfu. I think he ended up in Tahiti.'

Dear Mr Lawless,

I recently came across a memoir written during one of your sojourns in the South Seas. I am writing to ask you for some information about one of the characters you describe. You mention a Scottish artist, with just one hand. I have reason to believe that this man, whom you call 'Sandyman', is my grandfather. He was born in 1898, and his real name was Albert Charles McLeod. I wonder if you can tell me if he is still alive? I should be most grateful for any news of him.

Yours sincerely,
Caitlín de Courcy

Dear Miss de Courcy,

Thank you for your letter. It was forwarded to me from London by my father's publishing house.

I regret to have to tell you that my father Patrick Lawless passed away ten years ago after a full and adventurous life.

How interesting to think that your grandfather may be the famous Sandyman, of whom there is frequent mention in my father's diaries, recalling many pleasant evenings spent over a dram or two of Scotch whisky! He had been living in Tahiti for several years when my father first arrived there, inspired to come – like numerous other artists – by the work of Gauguin. My father records that Sandyman was a demon at snooker and had volunteered during the Great War in France, helping to rehabilitate soldiers who had, like him, lost limbs.

While his nickname was bestowed on account of his missing hand, my father wrote that it seemed to him that Sandyman was directionless, without any great hope for what the future might bring. He described him as 'a lost soul'. Sans demain, as I'm sure you know – literally translates from the French as 'no tomorrow'. I have one of his watercolours – a beauty of the old school.

You might try writing to your grandfather at the village of Papeari, where he lived not far from my father. I wish you the very best of luck.

Yours sincerely,
James Lawless

CHAPTER FORTY-EIGHT

TAHITI

At the bustling airport in Papeete, the capital of Tahiti, Cat and Nick chartered a motor to take them southeast to Papeari, along bumpy, potholed roads. Away from the town, the countryside was wild and luxuriant. They drove through a landscape dense with trees dripping moss and looped with vines, and past vertiginous hills with peaks lost in mist, and slopes awash with waterfalls. They passed palatial millionaires' pleasure houses and shacks so wretched it was difficult to imagine how people could live in them. These were patchwork houses of haphazard construction, with roofs of corrugated iron. Goats capered and chickens scratched in the mud by the side of the road. Most of the dwellings were painted in vibrant colours – cerulean blue or hibiscus blossom orange – and decorated with jewel-like patterns, but much of the paintwork was faded and peeling, and Cat was appalled to find herself contemplating how picturesque poverty could be.

The house was not hard to find: a man cutting bananas with a machete pointed it out to them, and gave a smile at the mention of Sandyman. It was a bungalow constructed from bamboo panels and supported by palm stumps. The roof was thatched with pandanus; the door and windows protected by mosquito lattice. It stood on the edge of a lagoon with a small pier and a ladder that descended into a bathing pool.

They climbed the steps of the veranda, and as Cat raised a hand to jangle the silvery chimes that hung by the door she felt beads of sweat trickle down her ribcage. There was no response to the ringing. She knocked: still nothing. Turning the handle and pushing the door open, she called a cautious 'Hello?', then stepped across the threshold, followed by Nick.

The main room was furnished simply, with a table and chairs, an armchair and a rattan sofa draped with a bright pareu. There was a nook for cooking, with utensils and crockery lined up neatly on a shelf. On other shelves, books and periodicals were stacked: bundles of the *London Mercury* in their yellow covers, a batch of *The Times Literary Supplement*. There was a scattering of carved curios, a portfolio was propped up against a low divan, and paintings – displayed in unassuming frames – covered one wall. They were watercolours; some landscapes, some townscapes, all bearing the signature A.C. McLeod.

'Oh, God,' said Cat. 'I feel as if I'm a detective in my own story.'

'The pieces are all falling into place,' said Nick. 'That's Rouen Cathedral. And there's the Ponte Vecchio in Florence near where they stayed . . . the Piazzale Michelangelo . . . the Boboli Gardens . . .'

Cat moved to a windowsill, where a leather-bound book lay next to a woven straw hat. The book was embossed with three simple fleurs-de-lis and secured with leather strips. She untied the thongs holding the book shut, and opened it. On the first page, she read in her grandmother's handwriting, the following:

This book is the record of an impromptu birthday. It came as a ray of sun and illuminated with its glow a whole day. It is a festive book, and is the child of a happy Love whose face is always smiling and contented, but who has moments of thoughtfulness and moments of wild unrestrained joy. It first saw the light opposite the Strozzi Palace amid an aroma of delicious tea and delectable cakes.

A present to my true-love!

'My true-love hath my heart, & I have his,
By just exchange one for the other given:
I hold his dear, & mine he cannot miss;
There never was a better bargain driven.
My true-love hath my heart, & I have his.'

It was the sketchbook given to Scotch by her grandmother all those years ago, the one described in the letter she had written in May 1919.

Cat leafed slowly through the pages covered with drawings and marginalia and commentary: she had in her hands a unique record of her grandparents' magical honeymoon, she was seeing for the first time the deft penmanship of her grandfather's left-handed sketches.

The sound of a conch shell blown by a fisherman on the reef made her look up. A woman clad in a floral-patterned pareu was making her way along the path that led to the house, a basket on her arm. She had the graceful carriage of a Polynesian dancer; her lustrous hair was so dark as to appear purple, with one lambent stripe sweeping back from her bronze forehead. She wore a necklace of shells and a white tiare flower behind her right ear, which, Lisa had learned from Patrick Lawless's book, was to indicate that she belonged to one man alone. She stopped short as she caught sight of the automobile parked outside the house.

Cat moved to the door, and called a greeting. The woman gave her a wary look.

'*Parlez-vous anglais?*' Cat asked.

'Yes.'

'I'm Cat,' she volunteered, stepping down from the veranda. 'I wrote to say I was coming.'

'My name is Tèha.' The woman's voice was musical. 'I am the housekeeper of Sandyman. You say you wrote to him?'

'Yes. I'm his granddaughter.'

'The letter came, but he could not read it. His eyesight is waning. He is sick.'

'Sick? How?'

'Coral poisoning. I dressed the wound as best I could, and treated it with lime juice. I nursed him here for several days, but the wound festered and he had to go to the hospital in Papeete.'

'Is he there still?'

'Yes.'

'How is he?'

'Sometimes good, sometimes bad. But last night I heard the flute of the tupaupau in the dark.'

'What's that?'

'The vivo – the ghost flute. And the banana leaves were shivering even though there was no breeze. I am fearful that death is near. If you want to see your grandfather, you must come quickly.' Tèha looked at the sketchbook, which Cat still held in her hands. 'I came by motor coach to fetch some items he requested. That is one of them.'

'We can drive you back to Papeete,' Cat said.

'Thank you. It will be quicker that way.'

Inside the house, Tèha moved around with swift, restrained grace, selecting various items: three or four books; a tiny oil on bark that could have been a Gauguin; a wood engraving. This depicted a voluptuous Tèha – naked but for a grass skirt – dancing in a trance-like state, eyes closed in rapture, arms sinuously entwined over her head. As well as the sketchbook, Tèha consigned to the basket a photograph she fetched from the bedroom.

'May I see?' asked Cat.

Tèha handed it to her. It was a copy of the studio portrait that had been enclosed among Jessie's letters.

'Your grandmama,' Tèha said.

Cat nodded.

'You are alike,' the other woman remarked as Cat returned the portrait to her. 'You have her eyes.'

Scotch – or 'ce *méchant* Sandyman!' as the nurses affectionately called him – was in a morphine haze. He had periods of lucidity but, the staff advised her, they were coming less frequently. Cat passed through corridor after corridor and past row upon row of hospital beds, and as she walked, she found herself thinking: *Why am I here? Why have I travelled halfway across the world to visit a man who neither knows nor cares that I exist? A man who abandoned my grandmother and my mother with such callousness?* And even as she thought these wretched thoughts, she knew the answer.

Because he is my grandfather and his blood flows through my veins.

A *lei* of frangipani hung above the door of the ward where Sandyman lay. Allowing Tèha to precede her, Cat watched as the older woman took his hand, and murmured into his ear. She caressed his face, and straightened the coverlet on his bed. This woman was more than a housekeeper to Scotch, Cat thought. The tenderness of her demeanour told her that Tèha had been her grandfather's mistress; the white tiare flower bore testament to that. Then Tèha stood aside, and gestured to Cat to take her place on the rickety chair by the bed.

Cat looked down at her grandfather. His face was cadaverous, but handsome still. She saw at once that his eyes, though bluish and cloudy with age, had the percipience of a painter.

'Jessie,' he said. Then he smiled. 'I'm sorry, Mademoiselle. I mistook you for a moment for someone I knew many years ago.' His voice was low: it had that burr that Jessie had described as *Scotch, but not too Scotch . . .* 'Tèha tells me you have travelled all the way from Europe to visit me.'

Cat nodded.

'Why have you come so far to visit a dying man?'

'Because you are my kin,' Cat said.

'I have no kin,' said Scotch.

Cat's throat constricted. How could she tell this man that the daughter he never knew was dead; that she, Cat, was his granddaughter? It was preposterous: she should never have come here. She should leave this old man to die in peace. She rose to leave, and as she did, her chair made a loud scraping noise against the linoleum floor, and Scotch winced.

A passing nurse gave Cat a look of mild admonition. 'Shh! Don't tire him, please,' she said. 'Five minutes, no more.'

'I'm sorry – I'm going now.'

'Wait,' said Nick, laying a hand on Cat's arm. 'We've come all this way. You've got to do this for his sake, as well as for your own. Come on, Cat. Be brave.'

Cat looked at him helplessly. 'How can I tell him? I don't have the words. You're the writer – can't you help me?'

'That's some call.'

'You know the right questions to ask. Please,' said Cat. 'I don't feel brave any more.'

Nick gave her a look of capitulation, then sat awkwardly down by the bed. 'How do you do, sir? My name is Nick Ryder.'

'Are you a doctor?'

'No. I'm a journalist. May I ask you some questions?'

'Ask away,' said Scotch. 'They'll help pass whatever time is left to me.' It was impossible to tell if his grimace was one of pain, or if it was a wry smile.

'I understand you were married once?' said Nick.

'I married a long time ago,' said Scotch. 'I married a beauty with Pre-Raphaelite hair.'

'Was her name Jessie? Jessie Beaufoy?'

'Yes.'

'You married in 1919, after the Great War, didn't you? And honeymooned in France and Italy.' Nick's tone was encouraging, coaxing. 'You went to Rouen, Paris, Florence . . .'

'Yes! Siena, Venice, Padua . . .'

'Chambéry, Pont-Aven . . .' prompted Nick.

'I would have gone to the ends of the earth for her, I loved her so much. I loved her so much, I had to let her go.'

'But you left her with a legacy. You left her with a beautiful daughter.'

Scotch shook his head. 'I have no children. Jessie had a child, I know. I saw her.'

'When did you see her?' Cat found her voice.

'In Paris. In the springtime of 1920. It was outside the Galerie Pierre on the rue La Boétie. By then she had found a protector. A rich fellow; an artist. She was at a *vernissage* of his paintings, big with his child. And then . . .'

The nurse passed again, and looked pointedly at her watch.

'And then?' urged Nick.

'And then she went off to live in the South of France and I never saw her again.' Scotch's eyes closed. 'She went to a place called the Villa Perdita. That's the name she was known by, then. Perdita. Demetrios told me.'

'You sent her a book, didn't you?' asked Nick.

'I sent her a book, yes, I don't know why. To remind her that I was in the world still, maybe. I had illustrated it. I thought . . . I thought perhaps she might have come to me.'

Cat remembered the inscription on the title page of the book – 'Memories of Raguenez' – in her grandfather's copperplate hand, and underneath, the date of publication: 1932. Scotch had sent the book to Jessie six years too late.

'Your time is up.' It was the nurse, cordial, but emphatic.

'The baby she was carrying wasn't his, sir,' said Nick.

Scotch's eyes opened, then closed again.

'She was your child, sir. Jessie's child was yours.' He reached for Cat's hand and drew her forward. 'This is your granddaughter.'

The nurse cleared her throat pointedly.

Turning to her, Nick sent her a smile that was at once charming and beseeching. 'One more minute, please. Just one.'

She gave a brusque nod, then withdrew.

'It's up to you now, sweetheart,' said Nick. He stood up to allow Cat to sit by her grandfather's side. 'Good luck,' he added, in an undertone. 'This may just be the bravest thing you've ever done.'

Cat blinked and fidgeted and cast around for something to say, then caught herself. She needed no preliminaries, no concerned enquiries about the state of Scotch's health, no labyrinthine explanations as to why she was there. 'My name is Caitlín,' she said.

'I don't know you.'

Scotch's voice was feeble. Cat had to lean in close to hear him.

'I'm Cat,' she said. 'My mother was called Lisa: she was as lovely as Jessie, lovely as a film star. She inherited Jessie's beauty: people loved to make pictures of her. I'm Lisa's daughter, your granddaughter. I didn't inherit her beauty, but I inherited your talent. I'm an artist, like you.'

'An artist? What do you paint?'

Cat didn't want to tell Scotch that she was a photo journalist who covered atrocities. Instead she said, 'I paint landscapes.'

'I painted landscapes once.'

'I know,' said Cat. 'I've seen them. They're beautiful.'

'I have a granddaughter,' said Scotch, in wonderment. Opening his eyes, he gazed at her, a smile tilting his mouth. 'How grand a thing, to have a granddaughter!'

*

Fireflies flit in the hedge, and suddenly the whole rose garden is lit up. The dancing lanterns of the gondoliers play all manner of tricks with the water, the cafés fill, music is every-where – in the piazzas, canals, and the lagoons, drifting through the hours into sleep. Venezia.

Cat had headed outside for some air in the hospital garden while her grandfather slept, and was sitting with his sketchbook in her lap. His description of Venice, where he and Jessie had longed so to go, had been penned on the page opposite a pencil drawing of a bridge spanning a canal. It was tinted with the palest pastel, like a sketch by a ghost, and underneath was printed in minuscule letters, 'View from our hotel window.'

This was where they had sat together, watching the dusk descend upon the place known as the Floating City, listen-ing to music wafting up to them from the narrow streets, and the dip and plash of the gondoliers' oars. This was where they had haggled with porters and feasted on apricots and peaches and cherries and oranges and figs and felt like Americans when they swanked to the railway station in a gondola. Remembered snatches came to Cat, from one of Jessie's letters:

We're here at last, after all the dreams of years . . . Venice is blazing with clear light and radiance at every corner . . . night is just dreamland . . . lights on the water and gondolas filled with men singing and decorated with Chinese lanterns . . . you feel at any minute the whole thing might be wafted away! Oh, it's great to be alive in a place like this . . .

'Mademoiselle?' It was Tèha's voice. 'Come now.'

'Is he dying?'

'Yes. I have said my farewell.'

The flower in Tèha's hair was wilting now. Cat followed her back into the building. The corridors were striped with sunlight. Somewhere in the hospital girls were laughing, and then one of them started to sing:

> *Te reva nei hai aue*
> *Na te patu aue.*

'What does it mean?' Cat asked Tèha.

'She is singing of her lover, who is going away on a ship,' Tèha told her. 'But his image will always be in her heart.'

Scotch's eyes were open, but they were dreamy, morphine-glazed. Sitting on the edge of the bed, Cat took his hand. He raised it to his lips.

'Jessie,' he said, focusing on the cabochon sapphire. 'You're wearing my ring.'

'Yes,' Cat replied.

'Did you write to your parents, to tell them we were engaged?'

'Yes. I did.'

'We'll be married as soon as we get back from this monstrous war. Won't we?'

'Yes.'

'And then we'll travel. Paris, Florence, Siena. Venice! Damn the expense! We have to get to Venice.'

'We will. I'll – I'll ask Pawpey for money to cover the cost.'

'I won't take money from your father.'

'Let's not talk about that now. Where do you think we shall we end up?'

'Finistère, of course! The end of the earth! We'll picnic on the sands of Raguenez, and swim in the sea.' A look of confusion crossed her grandfather's face. 'I'm not in Chambéry, am I? I'm not dying?'

'No. No.'

'It hurts to breathe.'

'Shall I fetch a doctor?'

'No, don't. I can't bear to let go of you. Let's take a stroll through the woods beyond Rouen – d'you remember Canteleu? Where we walked the first time, and then again before Christmas, when I asked you to marry me.'

'I remember,' said Cat. She tried to conjure up what it must have been like, to walk through woodland in winter. 'It's cold, isn't it?' she ventured.

'Yes. But the frost feels good – crunchy under the soles of our boots.'

'Look! Our breath is mist.'

'There was a little burst of cloud when our lips first met, here in this very wood, remember?'

'Yes. I felt so happy. Look up!'

'There's snow on the branches.'

'And there's Venus, the evening star.'

'Listen. A robin.'

'He's calling for his mate.'

'Imagine, in the springtime. There'll be nests with blue speckled eggs.'

'Will we have a baby, Jessie?'

'Yes.'

'A girl or a boy?'

'I'd like a girl first.'

'A girl. It's a tough world to bring a little girl into. But she'll be all right. We'll look out for her.'

There was a long silence. Then Cat said: 'Oh! Some snow just fell down the back of my collar.'

'Come here. Let me hold you. I'll keep you warm, and safe.'

Leaning down, Cat embraced her grandfather.

'I love you,' he said. 'I will always love you. I will love you to the ends of the earth and beyond.' He smiled again. '*E mauriru a vau, te tiare vareau.*'

Cat turned to Tèha, a question in her eyes.

'It means, "I am utterly happy and content"'.

Scotch's eyelids closed. His breath faltered.

Cat dropped a kiss on her grandfather's sunken cheek. 'I love you too,' she said. 'I love you to the ends of the earth. I love you to Finistère and beyond.'

She hoped he had heard.

CHAPTER FORTY-NINE

CAP D'ANTIBES

The headstone in the graveyard translated from the French simply as:

Lisa Reverdy: 1920–1969
Beloved wife of Raoul

Not far from where Lisa lay, another tombstone read:

Gervaise Lantier: 1896–1969

There was no mention of his muse and companion Jessie, no mention of his former wife or of his daughter, Ghislaine. Cat and Nick had seen the headlines in the papers, but they hadn't made it in time for Gervaise's funeral. The earth was still fresh on the grave.

According to reports, he had died at his easel, so suddenly that his paintbrush was still gripped between his fingers. A good way to go, Cat decided. Once upon a time she had rather fancied the notion of dying in action, her Leica in her hand, but now she was looking forward to a less dramatic demise.

There had been debate in the media about having Gervaise interred in Père Lachaise in Paris, alongside other luminaries of the French art world, but it was discovered that there was a plot here in the local cemetery designated and paid for by him. Of course he would want to be laid to rest in the landscape that had become so dear to him, with the sea at his feet.

The graveyard was a miniature labyrinth, a city of the dead, peopled by marble angels and mourning damsels. There were ornately sculpted tombs and mausoleums; an ossuary and a small Gothic chapel adjacent to a cypress grove, with benches where one could sit and contemplate mortality.

'I'm going to say a prayer,' announced Cat.

'But you don't believe in God.'

'I'm going to say a prayer to *her*. To Lisa. It's got nothing to do with any god.'

Nick smiled. 'Good idea.'

So Nick took himself off to explore the serpentine avenues and examine the carved tributes to the people who lay beneath the headstones, while Cat took a seat on one of the benches.

'Lisa,' she began. 'It doesn't feel right to call you "aunt" now that I know you're my mother, and because you said it made you feel like a frump. But Róisín has always been Mam, so you have to be Lisa. And here I am – Cat. I'm here now, talking to you for the first time, as your daughter.

'I wonder what you made of me? All those letters you wrote! I threw them away – what else does a teenager do with letters, unless they're from boyfriends? Now I understand why you felt compelled to write. I wish now we had talked about *you* more in the time we had had together. I know so little really about your life, and about Jessie. I guess that daughters always leave it too late, don't they? I don't know much about Mam or Daddy because they're just always *there*, like a familiar reassuring voice in the background that you never listen to but you know you'll miss when it's gone. I should listen to them more. I should write to them when I'm off on my travels. Just think – if Jessie hadn't written those letters from France and Italy, we would know nothing about her.

'Still, look what we got in the end! Three days in Connemara, with rain on the roof. I wish we'd had loads more days. I wish there had been some days when there was no rain, when we could have gone walking and fed apples to Connemara ponies, and maybe gone swimming. You know there are seals that swim off Gurteen Strand, and I once swam with a pod of wild dolphins in Killary? I so wish we could have done that together. And climbed Errisbeg, if you'd been fit enough. But the cancer was well in there, by then, wasn't it? Maybe three days with rain on the roof was enough.

'What else? What else can I say? This sounds really silly, but because you had such style I wish I could pick up the phone to you and dial your number and say, "Lisa – help me! What should I wear to this stupid photographic award ceremony tonight?" And you would say, "Darling, nip into Biba and help yourself to one of their black and yellow striped jersey numbers." And because you and Raoul were so happy together I'd love to ask – and I'm sorry, so sorry that I could never ask this of Mammy because I'm not sure she'd understand – I'm in love! So, so in love, and how do I know if it's the real thing? You see, Lisa, I've always been known as the cool girl – the savviest girl in school, the one with the camera, the one with the famous aunt. I'm not cool. I just get by with a little – what's the word? Chutzpah. Maybe I got the genes from Jessie. Or you, my beautiful, beautiful Lisa.

'I'll never forget the look on your face when I ran down the mountain to you. I'll never forget your expression when I tucked you in the night you fell asleep on the sofa. I'll never forget the comforting sound of rain on the roof. I'd like to think of you at peace now, listening to that sound, in deep blue sky heaven or wherever. How blissful. I hope that Nick and I will do that some time. Rain on the roof, hot chocolate and – oh! We forgot to do toasted marshmallows! We should have done that, Lisa! Maybe we will, when we all meet up. Jessie and Scotch and you and Raoul and Róisín and Dónal and me and Nick. Goodbye, goodbye, and love.'

'Cat? Come here.' Nick was calling to her from a far corner of the graveyard.

'No. I'm crying.'

'Then you've definitely got to come here.'

'Why?'

'Because I've never seen you cry, and when you get a load of this, you're going to cry a whole lot more.'

'You're an unfeeling bastard, Nick Ryder.' Wiping her face on the sleeve of her jacket, Cat got to her feet and joined him by a memorial stone overgrown with ivy. He had pushed aside the tendrils to reveal the inscription beneath.

Perdita.
Wherever you may be, be at peace.

'Perdita. The Lost One,' said Nick.

'They were both lost, she and Scotch,' said Cat. 'I hope they've found each other now.'

And then Scotch's words came back to her, the last ones he'd uttered before he went to join his muse.

I am utterly happy and content.

It was all beginning to make sense.

The graveyard was a short drive from the Villa Perdita. The gates to the villa stood open; a powder blue Mercedes was parked on the gravel sweep. The garden was more over-grown than the last time Cat had been here. The walls of the house dripped thickly with unpruned wisteria, the hammock strung between palm trees looked no sturdier than a cobweb, and the art nouveau angel that stood guard over the lily pond had lost a wing. On the terrace, a game of chess sat half finished on a marble pedestal table. All the shutters on the windows of the villa were closed.

But some things remained unchanged. The unceasing susurration of waves rose as before from the seashore, wind soughed in the branches of the pine trees, cicadas fidgeted, and a cockerel crowed from the Reverdys' farmstead.

Cat and Nick entered the house by the main door. Cat was impressed by the symmetry of the hallway: while she'd recuperated there, after Cyprus, she had only ever accessed the villa through the kitchen. Ghislaine Lantier was wait-ing for them. She was in her fifties, very thin, with carefully coiffed hair. She wore an autocratic look and a Chanel suit. Her shoes were Gucci; her handbag, Louis Vuitton. From it she took a pack of Dunhill. She offered neither Cat nor Nick a cigarette.

'I think we should get down to business without preamble,' she said, in faultless English. 'You're here for the Picasso, and I am here to tell you that you will not get it. Everything in this house belongs to me. My father died intestate, which makes me the sole beneficiary of his estate.'

'I told you in my letter, Madame,' said Cat with schoolgirl politeness, 'that I have the documentation to prove that the Picasso belonged to my mother.'

'And I have one of the most powerful lawyers in the country to prove that it doesn't,' snapped Ghislaine. 'If you want to challenge me for it, I must warn you that it will be a long battle, and a very costly one. Procedure in these cases is notoriously tortuous. I will drag you through courtroom after courtroom, and I am a tenacious opponent.'

Cat took a manila envelope from her satchel. 'The proof's in here,' she said.

'Show me,' challenged Ghislaine.

Cat held it at arm's length, obliging Ghislaine to take two steps forward. The older woman took the envelope, and slid on a pair of spectacles that hung from a tortoise-shell chain around her neck. But the light was clearly not sufficient for her to read by, so she moved across the hall to one of the floor-to-ceiling windows, and pulled open the shutters.

The sunlight streamed in, highlighting a floor patterned in jewel-like mosaic, a filigreed chandelier and an elegant, cantilevred staircase. At the top of the staircase hung a painting of a ghostly blue pierrot with a baby in his arms: the Picasso. Cat climbed the stairs and gazed at the painting, and at the signature in the bottom left-hand corner.

How insane that oil on canvas should be worth so much money, and so much angst!

The grandfather clock on the landing struck two o'clock; Raoul was expecting her and Nick for lunch in the Boat House at half past. But first, Cat wanted to pay respects to her mother and her grandmother. She continued up the stairs and along the corridor, passing open doors that led to rooms where furniture languished shrouded in dust-sheets, until she came to the room that had been Jessie's boudoir.

From below came the clatter of furious footsteps, as Ghislaine's kitten heels negotiated the staircase.

Cat steeled herself for confrontation.

'What do you think you're doing?' Ghislaine barked as she stormed across the threshold. 'I could have you arrested for trespassing.' She crossed the parquet floor and thrust the envelope at Cat. 'Don't think I won't dispute this. You may think you're being very clever, but this kind of documentation is easily forged.'

Nick sauntered into the room, and dropped onto the divan. 'Oh, lighten up, lady,' he said, with a laugh. 'It's only a painting.'

And suddenly Cat was laughing, too. 'It *is* only a painting. And what's more, it's a painting of a *clown*. Clowns give me the creeps.'

'It's a *Picasso* clown!' The outraged look on Ghislaine's face made Cat want to laugh even harder, but it was time to get down to business.

'Listen up, Madame Lantier,' she said. 'I'm prepared to cut a deal with you. You can keep the clown. I'm not going to argue over its provenance. But there's a condition. In return for the Picasso, I want these.' She gestured towards the two portraits that had brought her here: her mother and her grandmother, both clad in Liberty silk.

'You can't be serious?'

'I'm perfectly serious.'

'But they're worth nothing in comparison to the Picasso!'

'They are to me. These ladies are my kin.'

Ghislaine opened her mouth, then shut it again. She clearly didn't want to jeopardize her unexpected advantage by further unnecessary argument. 'They're yours,' she said, abruptly.

Cat spat robustly on her the palm of her hand, and extended it to Ghislaine. 'Shake on it,' she said.

A distasteful expression crossed Ghislaine's face.

'It's a tradition of ours in Connemara to spit when we shake on a deal,' Cat told her.

Ghislaine paused for only a fraction of a second before taking Cat's hand. Her grasp was surprisingly strong for such birdlike fingers, and Cat was in no doubt that if she hadn't resolved this dispute so adroitly, Ghislaine Lantier would have pursued her through the French courts for year after year with dispiritingly dogged determination. Life really was far too short.

The deal done, Ghislaine looked as if she were barely resisting the temptation to wipe her hand on the skirt of her beautifully tailored suit. 'Give me the envelope, please,' she said, coldly.

'Not yet,' said Cat. 'You said that everything in this house belonged to you. That's not quite accurate.'

She moved to the double doors that led to the walk-in wardrobe Lisa had told her of. Here was a treasure trove of tulle and taffeta, silks and satins, lace-trimmed velvet and gossamer chiffon. There were shelves with shoes, hand-bags, neatly folded scarves; gloves and hats – one of which, a simple straw cloche, rather battered – held a peculiar appeal.

'These are my mother's clothes,' said Cat. 'Before I let you have this -' she waggled the envelope '- I want you to have every single item in this room carefully wrapped and boxed and sent to me in Ireland. You will likewise crate the Lantier paintings, and deliver them to the same address. Upon receipt, I will visit you at your Paris residence and personally put this document into your hands.'

A guarded look crept over Ghislaine's face. 'How do I know you're not bluffing?' she said.

'I don't double-cross people,' said Cat. 'I was educated by Benedictine nuns who told me that it was a sin to lie. They also told me it was a sin to covet my neighbour's ox, his ass, or any Picasso clown he might happen to have hanging on his wall.'

Cat reached for the straw hat and set it on her head at a jaunty angle, and as she turned to appraise the effect in the cheval glass, something reflected therein caught her eye. A pennant of silk hung apart from the other elegant occupants of the wardrobe. It was an evening dress, patterned like a field of flowers in cornflower blues and primrose yellows and faded poppy reds. It was a dress made for dancing. It was the Liberty silk which Jessie had worn to the party on Boxing Day 1918, when Scotch had given her the ring which now belonged to Cat.

Ghislaine followed Cat's eyeline. 'You can have *that* now,' she said, pulling the gown off its hanger and bundling it into Cat's arms. 'I'm sure you'll be quite the belle of the ball at your little provincial "hops".'

'Thanks, Ghislaine,' said Cat. 'Top of the morning, and *póg mo thóin*.'

'I beg your pardon?' said Ghislaine.

'It's Irish for "'Twas a pleasure doing business with you."'

And with that, Cat turned on her heel and strode out through the door.

Behind her, she heard Nick's low laugh.

They made for the beach below, and by the time they reached the bottom of the steps that led there, Nick was still laughing.

'*Póg mo thóin!*' he crowed, slinging an arm over Cat's shoulders. 'It means "kiss my ass" in Irish, doesn't it?'

'Yep,' said Cat. 'Ha! I trust Ghislaine doesn't suffer from coulrophobia if she's going to live with that Picasso on her wall.'

'What's "coulrophobia"?'

'It's the technical term for an irrational fear of clowns,' Cat told him. 'I've always suffered from it. My best friend used to sellotape pictures of them on the wall above my bed in the dorm in Kylemore, just to freak me out.'

'What if it hadn't been a clown? What if it had been one of Picasso's blue ballerinas instead? Would there have been a problem then?'

'I'd still have done the deal. Those two Lantier portraits mean more to me than any masterwork.'

'It could have fetched you a cool million or so.'

Cat shrugged. 'I'd prefer to make my own money, in my own way. Both my mother and my grandmother lived off men. I live on my wits.'

'I'd say they had plenty of wits about them too, those

old gals. It was a man's world in those days. If they hadn't had men to support them, they'd have had a tough time of it.'

Cat took in a deep breath of sea air. How she'd love to strip off and swim! But there was lunch waiting and a journey to be made and she didn't want to delay the final stage of their quest.

'Let's have a paddle, to cool down,' she suggested instead.

She kicked off her sandals and walked towards the sea, loving the feel of the sand between her toes.

'I bet Madame Lantier will never paddle here,' she said, as Nick joined her. 'She'll probably sell the villa Perdita.'

They walked through the water in silence for several moments, and then Nick said: 'You know the way you wouldn't call yourself a girly girl?'

'I do.'

'Then why insist on having all those dresses and stuff sent over to you? There's hardly room for them in the house in Connemara, and you told me that whenever you moved flats in London all you took with you was a duvet and a backpack. You're not the type to accumulate gear like that. What'll you do when wanderlust sets in?'

'That wardrobe belonged to my mother, *ergo* the clothes belong to me. I want to visualize her in them, and imagine how she felt when she wore them. I want to photograph them. I might even want to make a book of them. And when I'm done, I'll invite Mam to take whatever she wants, and I'll donate the rest to the V&A. I think Lisa would be pleased by that.'

As she strolled through the scalloped shallows, hand in hand with Nick, Cat felt as though she were walking in her mother's footsteps; her grandmother's too. She smiled as she pictured Lisa and Jessie before her doing the very same thing – perhaps even wearing the very same hat, gazing out towards the horizon to where sea met sky in an infinite, matchless blue haze.

'Besides,' she added with a laugh, 'I couldn't bear the idea of Ghislaine Lantier strutting her stuff in my mother's vintage Balenciaga.'

Later, while Nick and Raoul pored over a map to work out details of their itinerary, Cat made her way to the graveyard again. There was one final thing to be done. Hunkering down by the side of Lisa's grave, she unclasped a fine silver chain from around her neck. Then she scraped a hole in the earth with her fingers, and, sliding the little Egyptian charm from the chain, buried it as a gardener might plant a seed or the bulb of a flower.

'Anubis will help you, Lisa. You mustn't be afraid,' she said. 'Sleep tight.'

They travelled south in the Citroën to Italy, retracing the route travelled half a century ago by Jessie and Scotch. In Florence, they booked into the Pensione Balestri where the honeymooners had stayed, and where Scotch had drawn the view from their window in his sketchbook of the River Arno and the Ponte Vecchio.

They had lunch at the 'swagger' restaurant on the Piazza Repubblica where birthday tea and cakes had been taken (Cat and Nick had a couple of beers instead), they visited a Franciscan monastery high in the hills of Certosa and sampled the liquor, as their predecessors had. In the shop where Jessie had undoubtedly bought the book she'd given Scotch, the one she'd inscribed with a love poem, Cat bought Nick a leather-bound sketchbook to write in, copying into it a poem by Yeats.

They travelled to Siena, where they visited the palace that had been owned by the old countess Bandini, and where the newly-weds had met the mysterious Greek count and his pretty charge, and then on to San Gimignano, Venice, Padua, Verona, Chambéry, Paris; Nick all the time writing in his beautiful book, Cat with her Leica permanently loaded, making – as her grandparents had done – a record of their own love story.

EPILOGUE

FINISTÈRE

Towards the end of the summer, on a grey and windy day in September, Cat de Courcy and Nick Ryder arrived at the final destination on their itinerary: Pont-Aven – the *cité des peintres* in Finistère, north Brittany.

They pulled up outside the Hôtel Simonet, on the rue Gauguin. The *auberge* where her grandparents had spent the final night of their honeymoon was now derelict. Cat had been told, when she'd made her enquiries, to call on the daughter of the ex-proprietress, Mme Simonet, who lived opposite, and who still held a key. When Cat had mentioned she was on a sentimental journey, Madame had declared that she would be delighted to grant her access to the old hotel.

'Do you fancy a swim, once we're through here?' Cat asked, turning to Nick and lighting up a Gitane.

'At Raguenez?'

'At Raguenez.' She smiled at him.

'Full circle.'

'Full circle. Funny, isn't it, to think that my grandmother was pregnant when she swam that day, just like me.'

'What?'

'Oh, it's too hilarious! The look on your face!'

'Hang on. What are you saying? Are you telling me you're pregnant?'

Cat gave him the benefit of her most catlike smile.

'*Are* you pregnant, Cat? Jesus – this is – wow!'

'Calm down, Nick! Stop having kittens. Yes, I am pregnant.'

'You!' Nick crowed. 'You're the one who's having kittens! My little Cat's going to have a baby! Oh – I love it already! I love you two!'

'Two? Just one kitten. I hope. One kitten's portable. Two means we might have to start behaving like grown-ups with a house and a garden and everything, like the parents in *Janet and John*.'

Nick snatched the cigarette from her, chucked it onto the side of the road, then took her in his arms and kissed her again – a prolonged one, this time. When he broke the kiss, he laid his hands on her belly and said: 'I will be the best daddy you could ever wish for. I will write stories for our baby. Adventure stories. I will climb mountains with our baby and dive the depths of the seas and cross deserts and sail through skies in a rainbow-coloured balloon and journey to the centre of the earth to slay dragons.'

'Ah,' said Cat. 'But will you forsake all others, and love and honour me, the baby's mother?'

'I already love and honour you,' he said, 'and I forsook all others the day I saw you dancing through a war zone.'

'*Bonjour*.'

'Oh! *Bonjour*.' Cat turned to see an elderly lady, birdlike and brown as a berry, approaching.

Swinging her legs out of the passenger seat, she went to introduce herself. 'Madame Simonet?'

'*Oui.*'

'I'm pleased to meet you. I'm Cat de Courcy.'

'You are most welcome. This is your husband?'

'No, he's my—'

'I plan on being her husband some day, Madame,' said Nick, with a smile, 'if she'll have me. In the meantime, I'm just her chauffeur.'

'You're dismissed, for now, Ryder,' said Cat. 'Pick me up in an hour.'

'Sure thing, ma'am.' Nick saluted the mother of his child, then put the Citroën in gear and took off down the street.

'Are you artists?' asked Madame Simonet, pulling a bunch of keys from her pocket, and selecting one.

'I'm a photographer.'

'Many famous artists stayed here in Pont-Aven, in this very hotel,' said Madame. 'They still come, for they say that the light reflected by the sea is incomparable. It was the favourite place of Gauguin, before he went to Polynesia. He called it "Little Tahiti".'

Cat smiled, and followed Madame to the steps of the old hotel.

'It is to be pulled down soon,' Madame told her. 'They are going to build a new, smart hotel here, with a swimming pool. A swimming pool – imagine! Who would want to swim in a pool when we have the sea on our doorstep, and miles of beautiful golden beaches?'

She inserted a key in the lock with clumsy fingers and twisted, but nothing happened.

'Let me try,' said Cat, taking the key from Madame. It was of heavy wrought iron, and when Cat tried the mechanism, it was clear that it had not been oiled for some time. When she finally succeeded in turning the handle, the door wouldn't budge.

'The timber has swollen,' observed Madame. 'Use your shoulder.'

'I don't like to force it,' said Cat. 'It feels disrespectful, somehow.'

Madame shrugged. 'The developers will have no qualms about forcing it.'

'I suppose you're right.'

Cat shoved, twice. The door gave way on to a dilapidated hallway that smelt of must and damp.

'Do you mind if I explore?' asked Cat.

'Not at all. Be my guest. I shall wait for you here on the bench and take my ease. You take your time, Mademoiselle.'

Cat stepped across the threshold.

It took some time for her eyes to become accustomed to the dim interior. The hallway had a pleasing shape, with an odd crooked staircase that led to the upper floors. Cat wandered from room to abandoned room. There was something slightly unsettling about the atmosphere of the place – something expectant, as if the ghosts of her grand-parents had been waiting all this time for her to turn up. In the dining room there were tables still, with bentwood chairs upturned upon them. In the sitting room an old upright mahogany piano stood, with yellowed ivory keys, the once rich patina mapped with scars and cobwebs. In one bedroom she found an old leather hatbox; in another, a shaving brush; in yet another, a tea dress of faded artificial silk hung limply on a peg in a wardrobe.

People had *lived* here once, in these rooms! They had eaten and slept and laughed and cried; they had danced and sung and painted pictures and told stories. They had argued and celebrated and got drunk. They had conceived babies, and given birth to babies, and they had got old and sick and died. Because that was the rowdy way of the world.

In a room on the top floor Cat paused to admire the vista beyond the window – and felt an electrifying frisson when she recognized it as a view that her grandfather had once sketched. This room – with its peeling paintwork and creaky floorboards and rusty fireplace surmounted by a mantelpiece of curlicued wood – the mirror of which was flyblown and cracked – this room was where her grandparents had lived! This was where a young, newly-wed Jessie would have washed, dressed and arranged her hair; inspected her face, regarded herself curiously in the glass: striking poses, maybe – smiling, frowning, wondering what her future might be, expecting it to be happy. Cat stood in front of the looking glass and pictured her grandmother there, gazing back at her through time and space, wishing her well.

She turned to where light flooded into the room above the window seat. Brushing dust from the sun-bleached wood, she sat down upon it, took her grandfather's sketchbook from her camera bag, and started to leaf through its pages. There it was – the very same view – the last sketch in the book! There was the vista of terracotta rooftops, with pigeons perched on chimneypots and a cloudless sky above. It felt a little spooky to realize that this was exactly where Scotch had worked with his sketchbook on his lap, sitting just as she was sitting now.

Below her on the street a gaggle of women was gossiping. They fell silent as a much younger woman sauntered past them wearing a miniskirt and a halter-necked top, and sent poisonous looks in her direction before resuming their tittle-tattle.

Cat opened the casement. A gust of wind burst through. She pushed her hair back from her face, then she took her Leica out of its case, selected a lens, knelt up on the window seat and adjusted the focus. The camera made its familiar purring, clicking sounds – four, five, six times. As she readied herself for the seventh shot, something happened that told her it was The One. The clouds shifted momentarily, and the sky to the north – where the sea was, and the sands of Raguenez – was afire suddenly, strafed with sunburst. Purr, click!

Cat remained kneeling there with the sketchbook between her hands for several minutes until a sudden fierce blast of wind swept through the window, and sent the pages turning in a flurry.

> *My true-love hath my heart, & I have his,*
> *By just exchange one for the other given:*
> *I hold his dear, & mine he cannot miss.*
> *There never was a better bargain driven*
> *My true-love hath my heart, & I have his.*

Cat put her camera back in its case, and as she passed the open bedroom doors on her way down the stairs, she bade each of the former tenants *adieu*. It felt comforting to say goodbye to ghosts.

Downstairs, by the front door step, Madame Simonet was waiting for her.

'You have finished your quest?' the old woman asked.

'Yes, thank you. It was quite strange – I found the very

view from the third-floor window that my grandfather once painted. See? Here.'

Cat passed the sketchbook to Madame, and the old lady frowned.

'Your grandfather?' she said. 'But I know this book! I'm certain of it. This is the book that belonged to the painter known as Scotch.'

'How on earth would you know that?'

'I would recognize it anywhere! He drew a picture of me once and tore it out for me to keep. I was only a small child then, but I remember him well. Who could forget an artist who could paint as he did with just one hand!'

Cat smiled, full of a sudden pride for the man whose genes had been passed down to her. 'What was he like, my grandfather?'

'Scotch? He was a man who was full of *joie de vivre*. I remember he was such fun! He had time for everybody – even an annoying little girl such as I was. And he was a truly accomplished snooker player – no-one could best him. I loved Scotch. Everybody loved him.' Madame shook her head in wonderment. 'I have just remembered something. Wait here a moment, please.'

Madame Gloaunec scuttled across the street, disappeared into her house, and returned some minutes later with an envelope in her hand.

'You should have this,' she said. 'I have been waiting for years to pass it on.'

Cat gave her a look of incomprehension. 'What do you mean?'

'This was left by Scotch, the day he went away. It was intended for your grandmother. He must have left it on the mantelshelf of their room, but she never received it.'

Madame handed Cat the sealed envelope. It was yellow with age, and the name 'Jessie' was printed on it in faded, brownish ink.

'Maman found it behind a skirting board where it had fallen out of sight,' continued Madame. 'She would have posted it on, but when your grandmother left for Paris she left no forwarding address. It has been in a drawer ever since, waiting for one or other of them to return. Read it. Read it!'

Cat opened the envelope with careful fingers, and drew out a thick wad of old French francs. So, he had provided for her! How much was here, she wondered, in old money? Enough for Jessie to have forged a new life for herself? Or just enough to cover her fare back to her parents in London? However much was there, it told Cat that Scotch had not left her grandmother destitute.

Setting the money aside, she slid a sheet of paper from the envelope, and read in her grandfather's distinctive script the following words:

August 1919

Beloved,

Believe this. I love you so consummately that nothing would make me happier than to travel with you to the end of the earth and beyond. But I can't do it. I can no longer subject you to this life. I have no money and no prospects of ever having any, and I shall never be able to keep you in the manner you deserve.

It breaks my heart to see you mend your own clothes – you who once had a maid to do that for you. It breaks my heart to see you window shop, knowing that you can't afford the fashions on display. And I think the most heart-breaking thing of all was when you had to nurse me through my illness that time in Chambéry, when you missed your mother and father so.

I want you to return home to England, to your parents who love you despite everything, and to that swagger house in London. I know you will be devastated, to begin with, but you are young, and before long you will forget me and find some chap who will fall desperately in love with you as I did, and who will be able to provide for you, as I cannot.

Please do this, beloved. And please do not try to find me, for I must be strong if I am to start a new life. A life – without you? That is not a life.

I shall never stop loving you.

Scotch

Cat looked up. The window of the room where her grandparents had lived and slept and made love was lambent now with reflected evening light. Jessie had rested there in the embrace of the man who would never stop loving her, gazing towards Finistère, contemplating the future, harbouring within her the child who would be born Baba, become Lisa, and beget Caitlín.

Madame Simonet gave Cat a look of concern.

'I did the right thing, to give it to you?' she asked.

'You did the right thing. Thank you, Madame. Thank you from the bottom of my heart.'

Cat laid a hand over her belly, and smiled.

THE END

KATE & JESSIE BEAUFOY: A CONVERSATION PIECE

Liberty Silk is a tribute to my grandmother, Winifred Jessie Beaufoy: artist's muse, adventuress, and one of the first women to receive a degree from Cambridge. It was inspired by some two dozen letters she wrote from France and Italy nearly a century ago. All the extracts from Jessie's letters in the novel are reproduced exactly as they were written. Key plot devices – the ring, the charm, the sketchbook and, of course, the Liberty silk evening dress – all belonged to her, and are now in my possession, along with the letters.

Jessie Beaufoy died in 1985. The following is the conversation I wish I could have with her today.

KATE BEAUFOY: Grandma, I've written a book.
JESSIE BEAUFOY: What kind of book, darling?
KB: A novel. I've put you in it; I hope you don't mind.
JB: What do you mean, you've put me in it?
KB: Well, I've included bits from your letters – the ones you wrote from France during the Great War. Do you remember?
JB: I was doing library work there, darling. I didn't see any warfare.
KB: That's because the Armistice happened the week after you arrived.
JB: Armistice Day! I remember it so well! There were

carnivals and victory parades and all kinds of festivities in the streets.

KB: That's when you met Grandpa. He protected you from the drunks and the fireworks, and you got engaged just five weeks later. That was fast work, Grandma!

JB: I was lucky: he was a very handsome, dashing man. You'd describe him, nowadays, as being 'hot', I think.

KB: You were pretty stunning yourself. I have a studio portrait of you taken around then. I have your engagement ring, too.

JB: The cabochon sapphire?

KB: Yes. And a charm – a little carving of jade or agate, that Grandpa gave you for your birthday that year.

JB: A little Egyptian devil, or something, wasn't it? He found it tucked away in a corner of an antique shop in Rouen. I'm surprised you still have it.

KB: Do you remember the birthday present you got for him?

JB: His birthday was in May – we were on honeymoon then.

KB: You gave him a sketchbook.

JB: It was the most beautiful book! Leather bound, with handmade paper. I inscribed a love poem in it, and we had a birthday tea that day, in a swagger tea-shop with an orchestra.

KB: It was the Caffè Giubbe Rosse, in Florence. I've been there. I sat on the terrace where you and Grandpa sat, and that's when I decided to write my novel. I was inspired by your letters.

JB: Inspired? We didn't do anything so very inspiring.

KB: Oh, you did! You were jazz-age adventurers – the original backpackers! I feel privileged to have had such glamorous grandparents!

JB: There was nothing very glamorous about our

adventures, darling. We travelled third-class everywhere, and slept on station platforms. Padua was particularly ghastly. We were eaten by mosquitoes there.

KB: You went to Siena after Florence, didn't you?

JB: Yes, by a bumpy old motor-bus, through the mountains.

KB: But you stayed in the Bandini Palace. That must have been glamorous!

JB: The old countess Bandini was taking in paying guests; she lived on the ground floor. Our room had views as fine as any, I believe, in Italy. Scotch did a lot of painting while we were there. His portfolio was crammed full of watercolours by the end of our holiday.

KB: Siena was where you ran up against the Greek count and his little girl.

JB: She was the most charming creature – so dainty and ethereal it made you wonder if she'd ever grow up. He told us her parents had gone missing during the war, and he had brought her up from babyhood. But there was something . . . malign about him. I remember she called him 'her naughty boy', for some reason.

KB: He was very well connected, wasn't he?

JB: Yes. He had been presented at courts all over Europe. He followed us to San Gimignano, but we gave him the slip there, and went on to Venice. I'd dreamed about going to Venice for years, and Pawpey was a complete brick and treated us to it. Then it was back to Paris via Chambéry – we stayed in a hotel there for nearly three weeks, because poor Scotch fell terribly ill.

KB: That's where you met the Italian girl, wasn't it?

JB: Yes. She was a friend of the Italian attaché. She was very good looking, if you care for that kind of sallow beauty.

She sat for Scotch wearing black velvet, holding a fan of white ostrich feathers . . .

KB: I put her in my book.

JB: Take her out! We met people far more deserving than her to be put in a book: painters and poets and musicians – such cosmopolitan, charming people, too, of all nationalities.

KB: I put the count in, too.

JB: Another shady character! Didn't you put anyone of merit in your story?

KB: I put some famous people in. Picasso. The Fitzgeralds. Coco Chanel.

JB: I so adored her style. But I couldn't afford Chanel.

KB: I'll give you one of her embroidered tunics to wear, in the book.

JB: Thank you, darling! I felt such a frump sometimes, especially in Paris.

KB: You had your Liberty silk evening dress, Grandma!

JB: I suppose that was rather a ripping dress.

KB: I have it now: it's a design classic. I'm passing it on to your great-granddaughter.

JB: How lovely! What are you calling this book, by the way?

KB: *Liberty Silk*.

JB: Hmm. I suppose that has a certain *je ne sais quoi*. Will anyone want to read it?

KB: If it gets published, they might.

JB: Why shouldn't it be published? Isn't it any good?

KB: My editors think it is. But I don't want to go ahead without your blessing.

JB: I wonder if it's possible to confer a blessing from beyond the grave.

KB: You could give it a go.

JB: Oh, very well, then. 'I bless this novel, and all who sail in her.'

KB: Thank you, Grandma Beaufoy. That's perfect!

JB: You're welcome, darling. I'm awfully glad you kept those letters, you know.

KB: So am I, Grandma. I'm awfully glad you wrote them.

If you would like to see images of the Liberty Silk dress, the ring, the charm, the sketchbook and letters – along with places and characters who appear in the novel – please have a look at the Liberty Silk Pinterest page:

www.pinterest.com/libertysilk/

LIBERTY SILK QUIZ –
WHICH CHARACTER ARE YOU?

1: **On a shopping trip to Liberty of London, which
    department do you visit first:**
a: Accessories, for a travel wallet and passport holder.
b: Designer womenswear.
c: Stationery, for a selection of Liberty patterned
    notebooks.
d: The beauty rooms.
e: The gift department, to buy presents.

2: **Your dream date would buy you tickets to:**
a: Glastonbury.
b: Ascot.
c: Glyndebourne.
d: The Cannes Film Festival.
e: A West End Musical.

3: **Your perfect Sunday morning is spent how?**
a: Settling down with the papers after an early morning
    hill walk.
b: A little al fresco yoga followed by Bellinis and fresh fruit.
c: In bed with your lover, breakfasting on smoked salmon
    & scrambled eggs.
d: By a pool with champagne on ice.
e: Brunch with friends before the game.

4: **You've reached your holiday luggage limit. What can you simply not leave behind?**

a: Your camera

b: A silk sheath that doubles as day/evening wear.

c: Your journal.

d: Sunhat and sunglasses.

e: Mask and snorkel.

5: **Each year, you buy a themed calendar that features:**

a: Destinations to visit before you die.

b: Classic fashion photographs.

c: Reproductions of Pre-Raphaelite paintings.

d: Iconic movie stars.

e: Gary Larson cartoons.

6: **You've been asked to appear on** *Strictly Come Dancing*. **Your dance of choice would be:**

a: A fiery Paso Doble.

b: A stylish Quickstep.

c A dreamy Viennese Waltz.

d: A polished American Smooth.

e: A lively Lindy Hop.

7: **You accept delivery of flowers. What would you like them to be?**

a: Something in a pot that's easy to look after.

b: A streamlined sheaf of Arum lilies.

c: A dozen red roses.

d: An extravagant bouquet of hothouse orchids.

e: You don't mind. It's the thought that counts.

8: You're perfectly happy with your mutt or moggy, but your fantasy pet would be:

a: A Pueblan milk snake.

b: A white cockatoo.

c: A Balinese cat.

d: A Bichon Frisé puppy.

e: A pygmy goat

9: Your fictional heroine is:

a: Katniss Everdeen of *The Hunger Games*.

b: Truman Capote's Holly Golightly.

c: *Twilight*'s Bella.

d: Sayuri from *Memoirs of a Geisha*.

e: Jane Austen's Elizabeth Bennet.

10: Your birthday party would be:

a: A beach barbecue.

b: A tasting menu in the newest Michelin-starred restaurant.

c: *A deux in* a café in the Latin quarter of Paris.

d: Cocktails, canapés and cupcakes in the Hotel Bel-Air, LA.

e: In front of a flatscreen with pizza and popcorn.

11: Your dream honeymoon destination is:

a: Adventure safari in Africa.

b: A suite in a Venetian palazzo.

c: A villa on Cyprus, birthplace of Aphrodite.

d: Celebrity haunt Sandy Lane, Barbados.

e: Disneyland.

12: Before leaving the house you:

a: Check that you have your charger.

b: Mist yourself with your signature scent.

c: Slip a book or Kindle into your bag.

d: Retouch your lipstick.

e: Make sure the cat/dog/goldfish has been fed.

13: Your underwear is:

a: What underwear? You prefer to go commando.

b: What underwear? There's nothing worse than VPL.

c: Pretty sprigged cotton from Liberty.

d: Victoria's Secret.

e: Calvin Klein.

Mostly a: You are a beguiling mass of contradictions: you have the cunning and inner strength of a Ninja, but *Bambi* can make you cry. You are independent, yet aware of the strength of solidarity; happy-go-lucky, but fiercely opposed to injustice; solitary, but a good companion. Avarice is alien to you, and you are horrified by complacency. This disdain for the material world lends you a vagabond glamour, which in turn inspires others to examine their consciences; thus, you lead by example. When you choose to, you can be playful, sensuous and light-hearted, but you are neither sex goddess nor sex kitten.
You are Cat.

Mostly b: You are the ultimate swan: at ease on the surface, hard-working beneath. You combine ambition and intelligence to devastating effect, and know how essential it is to add a sprinkling of charm to the mix. Creativity is important to you: you are painstaking in your efforts to make ideas become reality, for it is your firm belief that you make your own luck in life. Your femininity veils considerable business acumen: you have learned the value of a meticulously groomed exterior. You appreciate the good things in life, but are always mindful of the calorific content. **You are Coco Chanel.**

Mostly c: You are a true Romantic, creative and artistic. You escape whenever you can into the realm of the imagination, and crave beauty, freedom and passion. Your expectations may occasionally be unrealistic, but you know that seemingly insurmountable obstacles can be overcome by turning them to your advantage. You are a quick study, and pass most tests with apparent ease. You are equally at home in town or country, but are not at your best when deprived of creature comforts. You would be lost without pen and paper, or the modern day electronic equivalent with which to express yourself.
You are Jessie.

Mostly d: You radiate star quality, but are smart enough to lean on the dimmer switch when appropriate. Your unshakable conviction that this is the best of all possible worlds makes you a delightful companion. You are enviably self-assured and commendably candid, but your benign world view makes you rather too susceptible to sweet-talking opportunists. When it comes to self-promotion, however, you are not averse to bringing some perfectly permissible ruses of your own into play. You are impetuous, fun-loving and passionate, and your weakness for glitter and glamour means that you would rather go barefoot than wear sensible shoes.

You are Lisa.

Mostly e: You are a people person: others are drawn to your warmth and unforced charm. Your loyalty and generosity make you a trusted confidant but, you are choosy about the company you keep and set extremely high standards. Those closest to you know how to tap into your silly side, and love to hear you laugh. You have no truck with affectation or bombast, and a frown or a smile from you is more eloquent than a thousand words. Even though you have an abundance of energy, you never waste it in futile argument: sometimes life's sweeter when you go with the flow.

You are Sabu.